The Inspector's Opinion

The Inspector's Opinion

The Chappaquiddick Incident

Malcolm Reybold

Saturday Review Press | E. P. Dutton & Co., Inc.
NEW YORK

FIRST EDITION

10 9 8 7 6 5 4 3 2 1

Published simultaneously in Canada by
Clarke, Irwin & Company Limited, Toronto and Vancouver
ISBN: 0-8415-0399-0

Library of Congress Cataloging in Publication Data

Reybold, Malcolm.
    The inspector's opinion.

    1. Kennedy, Edward Moore, 1932–   —Fiction.
2. Kopechne, Mary Jo, 1941–1969—Fiction. I. Title.
PZ4.R4566In [PS3568.E86]   813'.5'4   75-15731

To the memory of

SHERMAN MILLS FAIRCHILD
1896–1971
and
CHARLES STEWART PARNELL
1846–1891

The Inspector's Opinion

One: Anatole France Also Said

There are so many ifs in this temporal sojourn we call life, one cannot but ponder Jaques's lines: "All the world's a stage, and all the men and women merely players," and then wonder who really writes the script and plots the plot?

If I, Faulkner Trulimann, had not insisted that Pierre, the chef, be relieved of dinner preparations for the night of July 25, 1969, in view of the copious amount of entertainment planned for Pidg Paley's boat, *Réjouir;* if the docking area of Lewis Bay had not been too crowded for proper handling of *Réjouir's* 126-foot length; if I had not hosted Pidg and her guests for dinner at the Hyannis Yacht Club; we would not have anchored just off the neighboring Kennedy compound. We would not have assembled *in toto,* guests and crew, in the main salon to see and hear Edward Kennedy make his Chappaquiddick statement on television. We would have been outward bound for Nantucket on a rolling sea.

And if this group of fifteen people, varying in age from nineteen to sixty-three, in vocation from steward to bank president, in outlook from student to priest, had not en masse voiced their skepticism, their uneasy suspicions, their outright disbelief, this tale would not be. And two, perhaps more, lives would not have changed direction so completely.

Moreover, I would not be seated here many moons later, on the stern deck of my boat, *Vitellus,* anchored in almost the same spot, beginning the writing of this tale. I would not be being ably assisted by a lovely, blue-eyed blonde, known to her very close friends as Prissy.

But somebody—somewhere, up there, out there—writes a script, I believe; and we mortals are often cast in parts from which there is no escape, like it or not, if we want to continue as members in good standing in the Rector's Equity. Else, how do I explain my sudden preoccupation with the Chappaquiddick incident beginning that night in the Hyannis harbor? Until that night I was just one of millions—interested, yes, and sorrowful about Mary Jo Kopechne; skeptical, yet not wholly without commiseration for Edward Kennedy.

For a full week after the incident, rumor and surmise grew like mushrooms named Topsy. While the first statement to the police was, euphemistically speaking, inadequate, the veil of mystery seemed tightly woven into the shroud of tragedies past. Forbearance of judgment was not too difficult. Then came Kennedy's nationwide broadcast, the second statement—murky but decorative coquetry. Something like draping tinsel on a leafless scrub oak to make a Christmas tree.

Shortly after dawn the morning following the TV broadcast, captain and crew gently upped anchor and tiptoed *Réjouir* from wave to wave out of Hyannis harbor. Our party awoke surprised to find the beautified waterfront docking area of Nantucket replacing the Kennedy compound. A day of varied pastimes (Pidg always arranged a choice for her guests), then dinner aboard, followed by the usual Nantucket-visitor pilgrimage to hear the Silent Man play and sing. If that sounds like contrariety, it is, to call an excellent guitarist and vocalist the Silent Man. A better description is the Silent People. You can hear a pin drop in a packed night-club room when this Australian chap speaks musically of life and love.

By Sunday night we were anchored off Edgartown, Martha's Vineyard, amidst a veritable circus swarm of pennant-flying sailing yachts arriving for New York Yacht Club's annual cruise to the Vineyard. *Réjouir*'s cocktail flag drew the attention due a candy bar dropped near an anthill.

> Old Friends, New Friends, all around the bar;
> Bold Friends, Dew Friends, tell me how you are.

Because of *Réjouir*'s size, our overnight stay would be in the outer harbor; but now, for the cocktail hour, we were positioned in the wide area of the pass between the harbor and Katama Bay. To our starboard lay the slightly rolling terrain of Chappaquiddick Island. We might better have gathered on the Cape in Buzzard's Bay, such was the predacious interest and carrion attitude of successive boarding parties. At least 75 percent of all conversation concerned itself with the Kennedy affair. And I use the word *affair* advisedly, a deliberate double entendre, since 98 percent of the 75 percent was salacious in character. Stephen Harvey, in the seventeenth century, said it well:

> And there's a lust in man no charm can tame
> Of loudly publishing our neighbor's shame;
> On eagle's wings immortal scandals fly,
> While virtuous actions but born and die.

At one point I found myself understanding for the first time the festive jollity and detachment of Coliseum spectators watching Christians and lions. Everyone seemed to have their own personal one-line joke, their own bit of inside information, their own sanctimonious hypocrisy for turning thumbs down. It was rather sickening, and several times I found myself staring at the silent, unprepossessing landscape of Chappaquiddick Island. What was the truth?

The restless Pidg Paley was never one for long stays, includ-

3

ing the marital status. In the past twenty years she has moved on from four consecutive wealthy husbands. She has also moved on to the board of five major corporations and ownership of a bank account that *is* a bank. But the charitable, charming, and very wise Mrs. Paley is herself a depositary of that most priceless of all assets—many devoted friends, from every walk and every level. It is my privilege to be among them.

When Mrs. Paley suddenly announced a noontime departure for Chatham on the Cape during breakfast on Wednesday, I made excuses for returning to New York, giving way to what I thought of then as plain curiosity and a desire to play detective, a desire nurtured by years of avid interest in mystery novels. Looking back now, I realize that something more than idle curiosity got the better of me—a strange inner compulsion to know the truth about Chappaquiddick. It is my conviction that such compulsions often play important parts in human life, and that we should listen more often to what the mechanisms of intuitive senses try to tell us. Though sometimes well disguised, the "message" conveyed may become a turning point in the path of our lives. If I did not so believe, there would seem to be little reason to write this story, which is, in effect, a record of the rather astonishing results of the compulsion mentioned above.

After a "bon voyage" to my fellow passengers on *Réjouir,* I checked in at Edgartown's Shiretown Inn, bought camera and film, rented a car, and joined the now sizable trek of the morbidly curious to the bridge area on Chappaquiddick. Later, I combed through the back-issue files of the local *Martha's Vineyard Gazette,* spoke with staff members who had covered various aspects of the tragic event, and just "visited" with summer-resident friends, townspeople, et cetera. Listening became, for two days and nights, a way of life. Making notations was already a personal habit.

The local interest was intense, the skepticism more so. Theory upon theory, rumor upon rumor, but nowhere was there belief and acceptance. Here again, in a maelstrom of Chappaquiddick chatter, I found only roots of doubts, suspicion, and speculation reaching out in all directions—crabgrass encroaching on the lawns of Camelot. Where, indeed, lay truth?

The following week, my pictures now developed, I arranged them, along with the accumulated data from my visit in Edgartown and items from the world press assembled for me by my secretarial assistant, Pat Johnson. Seldom has an automobile accident, apparently simple in substance, been given such intense and exhaustive coverage. And the essential facts as then presented by the press were little altered or expanded by later testimony in a court hearing on a petition for exhumation of Mary Jo Kopechne's body in Pennsylvania, or in an inquest proceeding held in Massachusetts.

Summarily, the situation concerned the death of a young woman attending a reunion of aides and secretarial workers in the 1968 presidential campaign of Robert F. Kennedy. In the early part of July 1969, Edward Kennedy's cousin, Joseph F. Gargan, son of a sister of Mrs. Rose Kennedy, rented a small cottage on Chappaquiddick Island, close by the larger island of Martha's Vineyard, to be used as a center of reunion activities, which included beach-bathing, a cookout dinner, regatta attendance, et cetera. Gathered at the cottage for a cookout party on the night of July 18–19 were Senator Edward Kennedy; Mr. Gargan; Paul F. Markham, a close friend of the Kennedys and a former U.S. attorney for Massachusetts; Charles C. Tretter, a lawyer on Robert Kennedy's staff; Raymond S. LaRosa, a political aide; and John Crimmins, a Suffolk County attorney's-office investigator often used by Edward Kennedy as a chauffeur.

Also attending were six female former Kennedy-campaign workers: Mary Jo Kopechne, Susan Tannebaum, Maryellen Lyons, Ann Lyons, Rosemary Keough, and Esther Newburgh. All of the young women were registered at the Dunes Motel in Edgartown and were conveyed to the Chappaquiddick cottage

5

by auto. Most of the men were also registered in Edgartown hotels.

According to Senator Kennedy's statements given to the chief of police in Edgartown and to the general public on television, the senator left the party accompanied by Mary Jo Kopechne about 11:15 P.M., intending to drive back to Edgartown. Because of his unfamiliarity with the roads on Chappaquiddick, he made a wrong turn and came suddenly upon a bridge without railings angling away from the approach road. An error in Senator Kennedy's steering judgment then caused the car to leave the bridge and sink upside down in the waters of Poucha Pond.

The car completely submerged, Senator Kennedy escaped entrapment and came to the surface and to safety; but Miss Kopechne remained in the car and drowned. According to the Kennedy version of events, after making several unsuccessful attempts to save Miss Kopechne, he walked back to the party cottage and returned to the bridge with Mr. Gargan and Mr. Markham. They, too, failed in rescue efforts and later drove the senator to the ferry landing on Chappaquiddick, only 250 yards across from Edgartown. Because of the late hour, the ferry had ceased operating, so Kennedy swam across the intervening waters with the intention of going directly to the local police and obtaining their assistance. Mr. Gargan and Mr. Markham returned to the party cottage, but made no mention of the accident to the other party participants.

Delayed, Senator Kennedy stated, by a terrible mental confusion brought on by his traumatic experience, he did not arrive at the police station until 10 A.M. Saturday morning, accompanied by Mr. Markham. This was after the submerged car was discovered by two young fishermen and the body of Mary Jo had been removed. Kennedy gave an unsigned statement to Chief of Police Arena, admitting that he had been the driver of the car in which Miss Kopechne died. By four o'clock in the afternoon, all members of the reunion party had departed from

Martha's Vineyard and the jurisdiction of the local authorities. There were no witnesses to question. There was also no accident-victim's body; it had been claimed by an aide of Senator Kennedy and flown out by plane to Pennsylvania by 12:30 P.M. Sunday. To go into further detail at this point would only lead to a repetition of the information that follows in the telling of this story.

Reviewing all of the material assembled at the time, it was apparent that the chain of events as reported in the statements was clouded by numerous inconsistencies. Application of my mystery-novel, pseudo-private-eye instincts produced nothing more than sleuthing trivia, and there was nothing I could do about it but retreat to a position of laissez-faire.

And then one night in late August, a possible truth source suggested itself to me. Not truth as it could be told from actual experience, but truth as it might be deduced by one of the great detective minds of our time.

A memory flash took me back to the late forties, to special case assignments I had had as a government investigator seeking recovery of art treasures stolen by the Nazis during the German occupation of Western Europe. One case in particular seemed relevant to the Chappaquiddick incident—a situation where there were no immediately concerned witnesses to question and therefore none who could offer substantial, tangible evidence in solving one of the most fantastic mysteries of World War II. The witnesses were either dead or had vanished.

Briefly, this is the story. In 1942, the French underground began reporting to Allied intelligence the day-by-day arrival of heavily guarded vans at a Château Fernand near Segre, France. The château was described as a veritable fortress, with 40-foot battlements surrounded by a wide and deep moat. It was famous for its vast main hall some 70 feet wide, 120 feet long, and 50 feet high.

Throughout 1942 and 1943, guarded vans arrived at the

7

château from all points of the compass. Intelligence reports sifting back to Allied headquarters in London indicated that the flow of vans bore carefully disguised loads of priceless paintings, sculpture, rare books and manuscripts, officially appropriated or unofficially stolen from public and private owners in France and Belgium.

Suddenly, late in 1944, the flow reversed. Heavily guarded van convoys began leaving the château. Intelligence reported that the Nazis were removing the art treasure; and in 1945, following the German surrender, a thorough inspection of the château produced not a single piece of the missing artifacts. Many priceless pieces suspected of having been stored there had vanished without palpable trace. A network of clue-seeking investigators spread out over Europe and the world without producing cogent evidence. And no witnesses could be found to offer even a tenuous lead in solving the mystery.

Then one man, Scotland Yard Inspector Charles Darby, presented the authorities with an astounding unravelment. Reviewing a synthesis of the enormous file of accumulated reports, this world-renowned detective, never departing his office, told them, through extraordinarily perceptive reasoning, where to look, and why. The treasure was found intact in the Château Fernand in the huge main hall. It had never been removed; the exodus of heavily guarded convoys had been camouflage.

To hide the art objects, the Nazis brought in skilled craftsmen who removed the wall paneling in the great hall and rebuilt it four feet out on both sides of the room. Before replacing the original walls, the artifacts were stored on towering racks behind the new wall positions. The craftsmen then rejoined the new walls to the end walls so skillfully that it was impossible to detect the change by inspecting the walls. The hall had no windows, and the new walls had no secret doors. The treasure was completely sealed off.

As an officer in American intelligence assigned to recovery

8

of the stolen artifacts, I was the liaison between Inspector Darby and the Allied authorities, and we became very good friends. Last year, when the Inspector retired, he came to this country for an extended stay with American relatives living near my home. He is a great storyteller and, through my efforts, received a publisher's offer for publication of his memoirs.

On this particular August night, following our second after-dinner snifter, I said:

"Charles, are you familiar with the Kennedy car accident that stirred up so much public interest this summer?"

" 'Familiar with'?" he replied, "meaning 'a thorough knowledge of'? No, I am not familiar with it. You suggested I write memoirs. Memoirs are memories, and my memories treat of criminal activity, not auto accidents. Why should I familiarize myself with such things?"

"I was hoping for your opinion."

"Opinion of what?"

"Of Kennedy's statements relating to the accident and his refusal to give more details."

The Inspector glared at me for a moment, then spoke rather brusquely: "But has he refused?"

I was somewhat taken aback and replied a bit sheepishly: "Not flatly and finally."

Charles continued, not quite so brusquely: "Then of what possible interest is my opinion? Senator Kennedy knows what happened, and he has told the authorities and the public, to the best of his ability, as I understand it."

"It isn't what he has told but what he hasn't told that piques my curiosity and arouses my interest in your opinion," I answered.

I went on at some length about the notes made and pictures taken during my recent stay in Edgartown. When I finished, he spoke again: "Your curiosity—your curiosity," he repeated, more to himself than to me. "Haven't you something better to do with your time than indulge your curiosity about another man's adversity?''

"Just *any* man, yes. But dammit, Charles, this is not just any man, this is a Kennedy—THE Kennedy—and a possible candidate for the presidency. I feel I have a right to be curious about him. Maybe not about his personal affairs, but sure as hell about his response and actions as a man in a jam. And what's wrong with a little curiosity? In discussing professional detection in general and Scotland Yard methods in particular, you once quoted Anatole France to me in London: 'The greatest virtue of man is perhaps curiosity.' ''

"Mr. Trulimann! Anatole France also said: 'The unknowable envelopes and throttles us.' There is only one living witness to the Chappaquiddick accident as far as we know, and he has publicly claimed, or at least indicated, a state of non compos mentis from the time of the accident to the middle of the following morning because of injury. Isn't it likely we are speaking of the unknowable to a large extent?''

"Inspector Darby,'' I replied, trying to match his precise formality and feeling a little stupid in doing so, "may I remind you that Mr. Kennedy pleaded guilty to the charge of leaving the scene of an accident, that he was so found by the presiding judge, that he was given a two-month suspended sentence and one-year probation?''

"So—?''

"So, this is legal acknowledgment of compos menti, 'OF SOUND MIND,' '' I poured emphasis on the three words by tone and manner, "from the moment of the accident until it was reported TEN HOURS LATER!'' I poured it on again, and when I saw his immediate reaction, I felt a little less stupid.

I seldom see sudden, apparently uncontrolled, changes of expression on the countenance of Charles Darby. The original mold for a poker face could have been stamped with the signet

C D. But now, his eyebrows shot up, and he stared at me in silence for several seconds.

He crossed the room to a small table and began pouring brandy with his left hand while executing a pipe refill from a tobacco jar with his right. I sat quietly.

"Where is this nosy little compendium of yours?"

"In an old briefcase in the trunk of my car."

"Fetch it, leave it on my desk, and we will discuss it later. I may or may not have an opinion for you. But just now, Truly, I have work to do!"

He remained standing until I returned with the briefcase, and I knew the wise-departure time had come. It is a work habit of the Inspector to write when "the pen grows wings," as he expresses it; and, invariably, after one of our sessions of reminiscence, the wings spread and the memoirs expand.

I could not help wondering if those memoirs would someday include just one episode of successful detection on American soil. Perhaps the first by a Scotland Yard detective—intriguing thought.

It may have been this thought that served as the nucleator of the book you are now reading, a running account of the events that preceded and followed the deposit of my nosy little compendium upon the desk of Charles Darby, Inspector–Scotland Yard, retired—events that led to an opinion that I personally accept as something very close to the truth about what happened on Chappaquiddick Island the night of July 18–19, 1969.

P. Faulkner Trulimann

Two: The Noble Nature of Man

Obviously stung to action by adverse public opinion, Massachusetts authorities pressed for permission to exhume the body of Mary Jo Kopechne in order to perform an autopsy. Her parents refused to grant the necessary permission. A legal petition for exhumation was then presented in the court of the Pennsylvania jurisdiction where her body was buried. Months later, the court ruled against exhumation. In Edgartown, Judge Boyle, the presiding judge at Senator Kennedy's trial, announced that an investigatory inquest would begin on September 3 and would be open to the press.

A mammoth and long drawn-out effort on the part of Kennedy attorneys postponed the inquest until January 1970, failing in an attempt to prevent it, but succeeding, by a ruling of the Massachusetts Supreme Court, in having the proceedings held behind closed doors, thus barring both press and public. The ruling contained a proviso that Judge Boyle's report and the transcript of the testimony would remain impounded and made available to the public only, in essence, if no criminal proceedings followed. Because of this proviso, the testimony was not published openly until May 1970. The press was saturated with both fact and fancy during the many months of legal proceedings in Pennsylvania and Massachusetts.

Late in November I received an invitation to dine with Inspector Darby and a suggestion that he was willing to reopen our earlier discussion of the Chappaquiddick incident. His niece Betsy and her husband were away when I arrived at their home (this was to my regret, for without the niece as hostess, before-dinner cocktails were not made available, and I had had a most trying day at my office). Among other accomplishments, Charles Darby is an excellent chef; but a most restrictive attitude toward alcoholic libations prevails when *he* presides in the kitchen—wine with dinner and brandy after—period. I had never summoned the courage to even hint at a lifting of the restriction since the night I received a stern lecture on the dulling of the taste buds with predinner alcohol, thus rendering myself incapable of full appreciation of whatever gustatory delight he prepared.

I was pleasantly surprised when we had completed the usual amenities (including a progress report on his memoirs) to hear that we had a reservation at the OoLaLa, a small, intimate French restaurant nearby. There were no cocktail restrictions when we dined out, and it was the tenth anniversary of the breakup of my only betrothal. I wanted to feel unrestricted. When we were seated at the restaurant in an old-fashioned parlor to await the preparation of our dinner selection, I ordered a dry martini. Inspector Darby had requested a quiet conversational spot when Madame Thibeault, the proprietress, greeted us.

My drink was served by a petite blonde in a French maid's costume straight out of a Noel Coward play, brought up to date by several inches. I am positive Coward would have named her Yvette, Yvonne, or Fifi. For no more logical reason than the impishly daring look I received when our eyes first met, I decided upon Fifi. Charles and I vied with each other in casting admiring glances at the young lady; then my illustrious companion broke the spell by coming immediately to the point:

"Where would you like to start, Truly?" he said, as he lighted his meerschaum pipe.

I tried to match his directness: "Assuming there is to be an inquest, Kennedy will take an oath to tell the truth, the whole truth, and nothing but the truth. Do you believe his two earlier statements abide by such an oath?"

The Inspector paused. "You cover a broad field with that question, but I'll answer it in this manner: I believe the statements contain some truth, but not the whole truth, and there is something more than truth—fabrications, perhaps—born of panic in a desperate situation."

"Then Kennedy was lying about Mary Jo!"

For a moment I thought he was going to be angry with me; there was a sudden glitter in his eyes, and I noticed the grip tightening around his pipe. He pointed the pipestem at the tip of my nose and said curtly: "Stick a pin right there! I can see now I should not have asked you where to begin this discussion!"

I shrugged my shoulders and waited.

"To borrow an oft-spoken American phrase," he said, "the 'credibility gap' is wide and deep if for no other reason than Deputy Sheriff Look's encounter with a black sedan turning into Dyke Road at the juncture with School Road. If there had been no such encounter, the Kennedy story would have been more self-supporting and credible. With it, however, the story falls apart of its own weight if you accept as fact that it was the Kennedy car Deputy Look saw making the Dyke Road turn at 12:45 A.M. approximately."

"And you think it was the Kennedy car?"

"I think it possible, and probable."

"Is that an answer or a hedge?"

"It will have to serve for the time being," he was amusing himself at my expense, and I knew it, "else we will spoil the effect of my simply smashing conclusions." It was spoken with a smile; I shrugged again and waited again.

"If you please, Truly, perhaps it is best that I lead our discussion in the beginning." He hesitated, and I decided to relax and enjoy the mental rape of one P. Faulkner Trulimann. After all, doesn't the Scotland Yard Inspector always lead the discussion? I nodded my acquiescence and sipped my drink as he continued:

"So much attention has been directed to marginal subject matter. Did Kennedy leave the cottage *intending* to catch the last ferry? Did he really make the wrong turn by mistake? Was he having an affair with the girl? Did he actually make that swim to Edgartown? Why did he not telephone for help? Why did he ask for the correct time at the Shiretown Inn?

"Emotionally and mentally titillating questions, these and many others, but mostly irrelevant and immaterial to the central question: Why did the car go off the bridge and how did Mary Jo die?"

"She died of drowning," I said firmly. "That's medically settled. She was found under water in the car and pronounced dead of drowning by a proper legal official."

"Granted," the Inspector said, "but the examiner spent less than fifteen minutes inspecting the body, did not remove all her clothing, and made only one laboratory test to determine blood content of alcohol, barbiturates, and so forth. An autopsy might establish an entirely different cause of death, and also contribute to knowledge of the time of death more accurately. She could have died from skull fracture, a broken neck, internal injuries, strangulation, and other causes. I agree, of course, that if there is to be no exhumation and autopsy, the pronounced medical cause of death will continue to be 'death by drowning.' "

"And don't you have to draw your professional conclusions based upon this pronouncement?"

"Certainly not. You haven't asked me to solve a crime, you wanted a professional opinion about an incident."

Emboldened by the martini, I said: "That is a very fine line

15

you are drawing, Charles. However, I am willing to give you an absolutely free hand so a-sleuthing we may go.''

He laughed, and I signaled Fifi for another martini. I really didn't need it, but I knew Charles would appreciate having Fifi in close proximity again. I will do anything for a friend.

''All 'sleuthing,' Truly, begins with infinite patience.'' He pointed to a game table at the far end of the room, a table covered by a huge, unfinished jigsaw puzzle. ''It is much like solving a jigsaw puzzle. You start with a myriad of unrelated pieces, find a pattern of relationship, and build upon it. If you have all the pieces available from the beginning, the ultimate solution is mostly a matter of patience. In detection work, you seldom start with all the pieces; so there is a dual need for patience: first, in finding the pieces, and second, in fitting them to a pattern.

''An autopsy report following exhumation could provide a single puzzle part, namely, cause of death, with very clear-cut outlines. Without this particular piece, I must make various assumptions of the cause of death, including, of course, drowning. As a result, I will have several extra parts for my puzzle, all extraneous except for the one that fits the entire pattern. The end result will be the same when the puzzle is completed, but it does require a bit more patience. Do you agree?''

''Yes, and I recall from my vast jigsaw-puzzle experience that one always starts by fitting two obviously matching pieces together. Do you have two such pieces as a starter?'' I tried not to sound impatient, but my infernal curiosity was at work. Furthermore, I am the warm, loving, emotional type, and intellectual exercises frighten me when carried to the extreme on a single martini.

''I believe I do, but we need more and better defined pieces before we start fitting them together. Would you bear with me a few moments longer?'' He had sensed my impatience.

There was a bit of silence before I realized my good friend

was politely awaiting my answer. Fifi had arrived with my drink, then daintily lifted a small log and dropped it on the red coals in a fireplace close by. The snow season brings its chill, but a mini-skirted, properly proportioned blonde bending over to stoke a fire has a doubly warming effect. The Inspector, having extracted a sheaf of papers from his pocket, was pretending to glance through them; but I knew he was looking at what I was looking at, and I didn't want to hurry him. Finally, feeling quite warm and content, I said: "Of course, of course!" and Charles continued.

"I find evidential peculiarities in this cause célèbre just too inconsistent with human nature to warrant acceptance without question."

"For instance . . . ?"

"Put aside Mr. Kennedy's postincident actions and consider the attitudes and actions of Mr. Gargan and Mr. Markham concerning their television-announced joint rescue effort. In Mr. Kennedy's first statement to the police chief, no mention was made of this effort to extricate her from the car. With Markham beside him at the time the statement was presented to Chief Arena, such an omission could not be a mere oversight. We must wonder if it was a rational ploy, or due simply to the fact that no such effort was ever made.

"In Kennedy's later broadcast statement he somewhat dramatically describes the strenuous, life-risking effort by these six-foot-tall men in water only slightly over their stand-up breathing level. Admitting extraordinary difficulties because of fast-moving tide water, let's look at some facts.

"There were two retracted windows on the driver's side and two blown-out windows on the passenger's side. The wrecked car had an inside width of say fifty-five to sixty inches at floor level. The arm of a six-foot man, fully extended from the outside of the car, could reach all but eighteen or twenty inches of the inside area in any direction.

17

"Isn't it reasonable to assume that a would-be rescuer could hold to the car frame, submerge momentarily, reach into the car interior, and at least touch the form of Mary Jo? If he could touch, he could grasp; if he could grasp, he could feel response or the lack of response. Now, would this not be the objective thought in a man's mind—to locate, to touch, to communicate and reassure, above all else? Particularly, if the person making the attempt was not a professionally trained rescuer? And under such extremely difficult conditions would he not realize the absolute need for expert assistance?"

The answer, of course, was obvious, unless we were speaking of morons. And we were not speaking of morons. The Inspector continued:

"Assuming the passenger may have been swept against the opposite side, it does seem strange that they were unable to even touch the form of Miss Kopechne, affirming that she was still in the auto."

"Are you questioning the statement that a rescue effort was made?"

"Not at all." He paused, obviously for emphasis. "I am questioning the grounds on which we are asked to accept that Miss Kopechne was beyond rescue, that she was drowned, that further effort would be futile, when it is never stated by any one of the three gentlemen that she was known to be in the car. Whatever the rescue attempt may have been, it produced no concrete evidence that Mary Jo was alive or dead."

"But Charles, in a situation like that, why didn't Kennedy call on the help of his friend LaRosa? Reportedly, he had been a professional fireman for almost nine years, highly trained in rescue work. He was the most logical person to assist Kennedy, and the least likely to fail under the circumstances."

"I believe I have an answer for that, Truly," he hesitated, and I noticed a slight sharpening in the tone of his voice as he continued, "and it is one of the key pieces for our jigsaw puzzle. This apparent oversight, planned or unplanned, going against reason, provided a substantial clue to what I now believe is a reasonable solution to our mystery.''

I hitched myself forward in my chair with the expectant air of a puppy waiting for the toss of a rubber bone, but Charles wagged his forefinger from side to side in a quite obvious gesture. I recognize a no-no when I see one. I sank back, trying not to show my disappointment, then decided to carry on with another obiter dictum that had been gnawing away at my sensitivities: ''There is a dreadful alternative to Miss Kopechne escaping from the car. John Farrar, the diver who removed her body from the automobile, said that he was positive air had been trapped in the rear seat well, the highest point of the interior in the upside-down position, and this was where he found Mary Jo's head when he entered the car. Large bubbles of air burst from the vehicle when it was removed from the water, and the trunk area adjacent to the rear seat well was almost completely dry. Farrar's reported statements indicate a strong conviction that he could have saved the passenger if he had been called upon immediately following the accident. He was less than a half hour away.''

My esteemed friend arose, poked at the fire for a moment, and began refilling his pipe. I drained my martini glass for the second time.

''Yes,'' he replied, ''there is some confirmation of a struggle for life in an air pocket suggested by the position of her hands in front of her chest when she was removed in a state of rigor mortis. Persons have lived for hours on air trapped underwater in capsized boats, sunken autos, and the like. But the most disturbing thing in this line of thought was something reported in the press from the testimony at the exhumation hearing. The undertaker said he found very, very little water in the lungs and indicated that there should have been much more if the true cause of death had been drowning. In my professional career I have seen death in many, many forms, and in this case I have my doubts."

I could not help it. I leaned forward expectantly. The rapt puppy dog again. This time the finger waggle was just beginning when I gave up with a shrug and sat back. I started to speak, but he anticipated me:

"For the moment, let us stay with the thought we have been pursuing, the personal response of Gargan and Markham after their failure to rescue Miss Kopechne. These men are not hardened, inhumane criminals. We would expect them to react humanely to a situation in which the life of another human being is endangered. We might expect, even condone, irrational and unjust actions from an injured man such as Kennedy claimed to be, but certainly not from two uninjured men acting in concert with him."

He paused for a few seconds, referring to a stack of notes taken from his pocket; then tapping the folded notes on his knee, he demanded: "Think on this from the TV statement. Kennedy said: '. . . all kinds of scrambled thoughts went through my mind during this period . . . including such questions as whether the girl might still be alive somewhere out of that immediate area . . .' " Again the pipestem was pointed at my nose for emphasis, and he said, rather harshly: ". . . and it is reported that, early the morning after the accident, Gargan told several of the cottage party people that Mary Jo was missing, saying that 'we can't find her,' indicating a fruitless search had been and was taking place."

"Meaning what?"

"Meaning this!" He was annoyed by my weak, opaque mind. "If they thought she had escaped from the car, then they must have concluded she was swept out and away by the tidal currents. Is this what Kennedy and Gargan meant by their statements?" He waited again, then with a lowered voice just short of anger, he went on. "Were they even partially convinced that

20

Mary Jo had escaped? If this is the implication, the spectre of a frightfully inhumane action arises, for we have three men leaving the scene of the accident under circumstances where Miss Kopechne is totally abandoned, left lying somewhere in the marshland of the pond unquestionably in a desperate and perilous condition."

The Inspector had run out of talking breath and seemed to be lost in a swirl of indignation at even the thought of such unjust treatment. He returned to his chair, and I waited patiently, silently. He was disturbed, and I was afraid I would say the wrong thing.

"Truly, we won't jump to conclusions; and we should not pursue conjecture too far at this time. I am hoping you will agree with me on this reflection: that there is something inconsistent with the noble nature of man when three men profess to risking their lives over a two-hour period trying to rescue a friend, a fellow human being, from a most perilous situation, and then, when faced with failure, they further profess to walking away in defeat as though they had lost a game of—"

He was grasping. I felt impelled to fill in for him.

"—touch football?"

"Yes! Whatever that is!"

Three: A Collection of Thoughts

Our dinner was announced, and we were seated in an alcove off the main dining room. Charles Darby had made known his menu and wine choices when our reservation was arranged. We began with a Moet et Chandon 1954, a pure delight of sunshine and laughter, made more scintillating by caviar and pâté de foie gras. Chappaquiddick and serious conversation was shelved while we reminisced about London and Paris, French and English cooking.

Meanwhile, now that we were ensconced in the dining area, Fifi was in constant attendance, and I noticed something in the brighter lighting that had not been evident in the softer light of the parlor—the entire black part of Fifi's French-maid uniform was see-through. And there were four other maids scurrying about, all pert, pretty, and seen-through.

Madame Thibeault, I thought to myself, how could you and your husband, Leon, spend years serving the finest of French food and wine and then come to this? Seminude feminine enticement. I resolved to patronize their establishment repeatedly in the coming months until I could summon the courage to ask for the whole story.

My introspective attitude was noticed by my dinner companion and evidently misinterpreted to indicate impatience with chitchat. The Inspector motioned to Fifi for our service to continue, then picked up our earlier conversation in this direct manner:

"As I was saying, Truly, it is the emotional and to some degree the rational, response of Kennedy, Gargan, and Markham that I find both baffling and illuminating. Every detective has his own modus operandi for solving criminal cases, just as every criminal eventually settles upon a pattern of lawless behavior and repeats it over and over."

"You are calling *them* criminals?" I was astonished!

"Oh! Heavens no! Forgive my unfortunate parallel. I was trying to explain what I regard as my own peculiar forte in detection. I call it 'pivotal thinking,' a viewpoint that assumes that basic human nature evokes a predictable response to a given situation, the pivotal point. And when the response is not compatible with my own prediction of what it should be, I become suspicious, I bring out my Sherlock Holmes magnifying glass, and I scrutinize."

I nodded knowingly, and Charles continued: "The response of the three men under discussion does not relate properly to the major pivotal points in their story."

"What do you do when responses don't relate properly? Where do you go from there?"

"Well . . . when I am convinced that the response can be read in depth, I move my pivotal points around until I find acceptable relationships. Then, and only then, do I begin to fit my pieces into the larger jigsaw patterns. Does this make sense to you?"

"Of course, Charles, but how do you allow for the exhaustion and confusion factors with which this Chappaquiddick incident seems to abound?"

"I allow for them with Kennedy to some degree. His rather impressive list, if I recall it correctly: 'jumble of emotions:

23

grief, fear, doubt, exhaustion, panic, confusion and shock,' is enough to short-circuit any natural human response."

"How about Gargan and Markham? How could Kennedy's confusion transfer to them? Why didn't they call the police for help?"

"Perhaps they were so instructed by Kennedy, and, acting as his attorneys, made certain decisions with him for defense against charges far more serious than failure to report an accident. There are a number of possibilities."

"Such as—" I waited.

"Such as murder, premeditated or unpremeditated; manslaughter, voluntary or involuntary; aggravated assault; driving while intoxicated and having an accident involving a fatality; driving in a reckless manner and causing a fatality, to name a few."

I was startled. Hearing these things spoken out loud was shocking, to put it mildly. I decided to pin him down.

"Charles, are you saying it could have been murder?"

"Now, Truly, you've read enough English mysteries and seen enough English movies to know that the Yard Inspector always suspects the foulest play possible under the circumstances. And under the circumstances, of course it could have been murder!"

I am not above admitting that, on occasion, I have momentarily lost my insouciant aplomb and my native wit; but never before had a single remark left me speechless, dumbfounded, and reduced to mutter. Where in the hell is this leading, I thought, while Charles sat quietly enjoying my discomfiture.

"Truly, you look as though you need a drink."

There was the typical English fetish for understatement. My wine glass was full, and I swallowed the contents whole, like any normal, healthy python enjoying a morsel. With the concerned look of a lifeguard watching a struggling swimmer, he continued:

"Perhaps we should permit the young lady to serve our dinner."

"Perhaps we should." I can understate with the best of them.

Fifi was waiting patiently beside me with my dinner plate. I looked up, apologized, and motioned for her to place it before me. As our eyes met, I sensed something out of the ordinary in her expression. Little did I know at the time how extraordinary were the thoughts that gave flame to the light in her eyes. But I would know, and before the evening was over. To borrow Hamlet's Danish for it:

> My fate cries out,
> And makes each petty artery in this body
> As hardy as the Nemean Lion's nerve.

The sequential effect on my life has been undeniable.

I must say, the dinner interruption was not unwelcome. The objective thinking of a professional criminologist is best taken in small doses. Also, I began to appreciate how vitally important true objectivity could be in any discussion of the Chappaquiddick incident. Like so many others, I found difficulty in trying to refrain from subjective thinking when faced with all the puzzling aspects of the story as it had been told to the world. After all, we were discussing an event involving a public figure whose aura of public interest was worldwide, and a personality that generated subjective responses.

Our dinner was served. As usual, Charles Darby's choice was superb:

> Les Champaignons en Grillade
> Le Pigeonneau au Vermouth
> Le Celeri à la Eschoscholtzia
>   Le Rôti de Boeuf
>   Les Asperges Polonaise
>   Une Salade Verte Gauloise
> Les Crêpes Suzette
> Le Café Diable

25

The wines were rare vintage Romanée Conti.

After appreciative comments on the culinary art of Alphonse, the chef, our dinner conversation ranged from the historical background of various European eating habits to Greek philosophy and Zoroastrianism, a rather wide range. Strange how human thought sprouts and runs with such ease in multitudinous directions when the stomach is pampered and pleased.

Fifi served our after-dinner brandy with a delicacy comparable to an explosives expert handling nitroglycerine. The see-through effect on a de Milo figure was assuming devastating proportions. And the net effect—if you will excuse the pun—was admittedly disturbing to a mellowing forty-six-year-old bachelor.

I looked up to find the Inspector studying me with a somewhat jaundiced eye. The words "dirty old man" seemed to float in the air between us. Inwardly, I bristled. In the first place, I don't like the word *dirty*. Tarnished, perhaps, but not dirty. It may have been Ben Franklin who put the whole thing in proper perspective, in *Poor Richard's Almanac:* "Wouldst be no tarnished old men 'twere not there tarnished young women, and far more of the latter than the former." I assume this was based upon actuarial tables for males and his reputedly prodigious interest in the opposite sex.

Somewhat miffed, and with an air of injured innocence, I turned to give Fifi only casual attention as she said: "Do you wish anything more?"

"No thank you," Charles responded, before I could speak. "Mr. Trulimann and I have to leave now."

"We do?" I hoped Fifi would catch the disappointment in my voice and understand the consoling message implied.

"We do if you feel ready for my opinion."

"Why not here?" I loudened my voice as Fifi continued to

listen unobtrusively but with frank interest.

"I think it would be more suitable in my niece's home, where I can be assured of your undivided attention." There was an unmistakable twinkle in his eyes, and I felt a little foolish. There was also the fetal beginning of a taunting smile on his face, and I felt somewhat more than a little foolish. And "old fool" foolish at that—the worst kind.

The Inspector arose, crossed the dining area, and began a lively conversation with the delightfully animated Madame Thibeault. Now came the ritualistic process of paying the bill. One did not simply confront Madame with "how much" by word or gesture; one commented upon each course with judgment and appreciation, then added tinsel to the tree of compliments by genteelly raving about the wines selected. Then, and only then, was a small ragtag slip of paper proffered stating the total amount due.

My absorption in this fascinating procedure was abruptly ended by a soft feminine voice near my right ear:

"Sir—?"

I turned to find Fifi standing within a few inches of my shoulder.

"Yes?" I replied, keeping my thoughts in the abstract and my demeanor calm and unruffled. No doubt about it, though, the chemistry of this beautiful girl shook me up.

"Sir, I hope you will forgive my intruding like this, but I could not help overhearing your conversation with Inspector Darby, and I think I—" she hesitated, and I rushed to cover her obvious embarrassment—to hell with the abstract:

"Perfectly all right, perfectly all right—" then I hesitated. What part of our cosmopolitan conversation had appealed to her? My adventures in Paris? My comments on Zoroastrianism? I rose and started to offer her Charles's chair. She must have sensed this, and to cover any possible embarrassment on my

27

part, she retreated to the opposite side of the table, after sticking something under my crumpled napkin. In a low but very distinct voice she said:

"May I see you later this evening? I will be at home by twelve o'clock. I know where the Inspector lives, and I am only a short distance away. Could you call me later? The number is there." Her eyes focused on the napkin.

"Of course I will . . . delighted . . . perfectly all right . . . don't mention . . . why not . . . only a short distance away . . . Miss er—" I was as cool as a cucumber, and the very essence of helpful urbanity.

"Rogers, Priscilla Rogers. Thank you." She moved, or rather, glided away toward the kitchen. What grace! And I could have sworn her lips were puckered in the tiny impulse of a blown kiss. My now very concrete thoughts began popping and hopping about like popcorn in boiling oil.

Calming myself, I went about collecting my thoughts in the following manner: I reached for the folded slip under the napkin. The cigar in my hand struck the side of the table, and the entire lighted end fell to the floor. I bent quickly to extinguish it, and my head hit the table. Swinging my left hand across the table to console my head, I upset a tumbler of water and a vase of flowers. Striving to prevent the torrent of water from reaching my lap, I rose abruptly, and my chair overturned. Grasping for the napkin to stem the tide of water dripping from the table, I upset my partially filled brandy glass. It rolled off the table and smashed at my feet.

During this entire process of thought collection, I had managed to hang on to the paper slip. I examined it carefully to be certain all the necessary numbers were there—they were—seven very clearly defined figures.

Only then did I become aware of my audience, a room full of people. Then and only then did I become aware of the simply fantastic performance I had put on. My audience, though somewhat stunned and transfixed, seemed appreciative, so I bowed. The applause was deafening!

"Truly," it was the Inspector, "are you all right?" He took me by the arm and, with a gentle but firm shove, cleared me from the area of disaster. Madame Thibeault and a band of good fairies began restoring order. Everyone was solicitous, kind, and loaded with understanding. Then came the stern voice of the Inspector in my left ear:

"Can you make it to the car, old boy?"

I was too indignant to answer.

During the ride back to the Inspector's home, I tried to fend off his disapproving and insidious silence by slow-feeding my indignation. But it was like taking shelter from a spring shower under a weeping willow tree.

Charles was so ingrained and encrusted with the official Scotland Yard demeanor toward wrongdoers that a mere glance from him could have you standing at attention before the assembled regiment, buttons and rank insignia ripped away, broken sword at your feet, drums rolling out the ultimate disgrace. If you saw John Mills play the Yard Inspector in *Dial M for Murder,* you know what I mean. (Incidentally, to picture Charles Darby, think of John Mills—they could be twin brothers. I am more the Cary Grant type, in a suave, more dashing way, or so I have been told—by my mother.)

In the Inspector's eyes I had punctuated an epicurean sonnet with a huge question mark. But I felt no guilt whatever. A man born with strong animal magnetism, attracting and affecting women as Fifi was obviously affected, must learn to rise above the errant censure of others not so gifted.

I knew I would forgive him if the end result of the evening was what I wanted in the first place—a detailed explanation of the Chappaquiddick incident that I could believe was the truth. Fortunately for our friendship, that is exactly what I got.

As we left the car in front of his home, I broke the long

silence with what must be considered a pleasant and conciliatory statement:

"Thank you, Charles, for an excellent dinner."

He was equally pleasant and conciliatory:

"It was my pleasure, Truly."

Two adult-minded, well-intentioned men, casting aside pettiness—rare and rather inspiring.

I followed his suggestion of poking up the long-neglected fire and adding logs while he took care of the inevitable brandy routine. Warming to the new mood, I said:

"Charles, I want you to know how much I appreciate your taking the time and trouble to give me your opinion of this Kennedy thing."

"Your gratitude is gratefully accepted but wholly unnecessary. I must admit to a considerable amount of self-gratification in pursuing the conclusions I have reached. Old war-horse-back-in-the-saddle, you might say. I will even tell you that I could not refrain from making a few discreet inquiries on my own."

This was a surprise, and I wondered if I would be told more, but he switched tracks and said:

"I hope to give you a credible explanation of the incident in all its ramifications, but," he paused and gave me the old pipe-stem thrust, "in so doing, I trust you to understand my desire to refrain from moral judgment of any and all persons concerned. Before expressing what I believe to be the truth, I give you two quotes that seem apropos, the first from the *Meditations* of Marcus Aurelius: 'I search after truth, by which never yet was man harmed'; and the second from Democritus: 'But we know nothing really, for truth lies deep down.' "

Secretly bursting with pride at the erudition of my own mind, I responded:

"In the same vein, Voltaire put it this way: 'Love truth but pardon error.' "

"Exactly!" He seemed impressed.

30

With this challenging bit of preamble out of the way, Inspector Charles Darby of Scotland Yard, retired, gave me his opinion of what actually happened that July night and in the days that followed. I asked for permission to record his words, and a conference mike was properly placed to pick up our conversation.

Four: Triggers to a Tragedy

"I will begin," said the Inspector, "with a summary conclusion that may come as a bit of a shock: The statement given to the authorities and later embellished on television verges on pure fabrication.

"In my opinion Kennedy—

Did not leave the cottage with intent to catch a ferry;

Did not make a mistaken wrong turn onto Dyke Road;

Was not misled by the hazardous angle of the bridge and road;

Did not, consequently, drive his car off the bridge;

Did not submerge with the car and escape therefrom;

Did not walk back to the cottage party;

Did not ask LaRosa to summon Gargan and Markham from the cottage for the purpose of rescuing Miss Kopechne;

Did not drive back to the bridge with Gargan and Markham.

There was no *second* attempt to save Mary Jo; and Kennedy was not too mentally incapacitated by shock or injury to report the car in the water. Quite the opposite—he participated fully in the concoction of a cover story designed to absolve him of any knowledge of the sunken car, a knowledge that he shared with Gargan and Markham almost from the moment the car entered the water.''

As the Inspector proceeded item by item, plain old-fashioned astonishment was my bosom companion. I had expected some sort of switch in facts and details, but not this! The Inspector continued:

"For a few moments, Truly, try to wipe the Kennedy story from your mind. I am going to reconstruct events bit by bit, and I would prefer that you postpone commingling or comparing the two stories until you have thoroughly assimilated my version. Then you will better understand why the true story, as I see it, was altered, why the fabricated story took the final form that it did, and why such a story was basically incredible.''

The telephone rang, and he excused himself from the room. I was caught up in a strange mood of anticipation, respectful awe, and more than a small amount of apprehension. What was the Inspector telling me? would his ''truth'' be stranger than Kennedy fiction? and even more incredible? Ay, there's the rub, Darby! Incredibility I've had, give me something I can believe!

"It was Betsy,'' he said, on reentering the room. ''She and Thomas are returning tomorrow.'' He began pacing up and down before the fireplace; the phone call had interrupted the rhythm of his thoughts.

"As I was saying, I want you to hear my version of the Chappaquiddick incident without your mind being cluttered with the Kennedy statements, if that is possible.''

"I will do my best, Charles. Proceed.''

"One other consideration—I said there was no objection to

your recording what I have to say at this time. However, the recording is for your ears only. Is this understood?''

''May I ask why?''

''Of course—my detective renown is at stake,'' he faked a harsh frown and a threatening tone, then added, with a smile of whimsy, ''and I may be *forcing* my jigsaw pieces to fit.''

''Not cricket?''

''Definitely—not cricket!'' We both laughed, and he continued: ''I would prefer that further exposure await an opportunity for me to study the inquest testimony.''

''But the inquest is to be conducted behind closed doors.''

''Yes, in January. At some future date, however, the testimony will probably be made public,'' he replied, ''and I can compare sworn testimony with what we have now, which is best described, perhaps, as hearsay evidence.''

I decided not to push the point further. It was somewhat apparent that Charles thought he might be walking on thin ice. Still, his opening summation was so completely contradictory to the Kennedy statements, it was equally apparent he had formulated a plausible solution to our mystery. The question was: could pivotal thinking prove mightier than the sworn.

If the Inspector was right, some person, perhaps several persons, would have to lie, and lie under oath, to substantiate a fabricated story. On the other hand, it would be impossible for all testimony to be false; most, if not all, would be given honestly. Some of it could be honestly mistaken, too, considering the lapse of time and the circumstances surrounding the incident. More importantly, some crucially pertinent evidence might never come to light if the right questions were not asked of the witnesses. An inquest is not a trial; it does not allow prosecutor cross-examination nor does it permit participant defense counseling.

Swinging the stem of his pipe in cadence with his voice, much as a baton in the hands of a Stokowski, Inspector Darby proceeded to give, at length and in detail, his version of the events leading to the death of Mary Jo Kopechne. Also, the subsequent events leading to the police and television statements made by Edward Kennedy.

I had never before seen Charles in this particular mood and manner. His whole personality seemed to change, smoke became fire and justice became a flying banner. The air of a retired English country gentleman was blown away by the lowering skies of a northeaster. No wonder 'tis said British criminals literally quaked with fright when this particular top-dog official of Scotland Yard barked at their heels.

At the point in his narrative where the Kennedy car crashed into the water, he suddenly stopped talking and walked out of the room toward the kitchen. I knew it was deliberate. Charles was indulging in his natural flair for the dramatic, leaving me alone with my thoughts. And dear God, what thoughts! I felt as though someone had kicked me in the stomach. The circumstantial progress of incidents and events to this climactic moment was so senseless, if not downright stupid. And so goddamn unnecessary! But I could believe it. The entire sequence was so in keeping with human nature, I could not deny the rationality.

Triggers to a tragedy. Each little incident so mundane, so trivial, when isolated. In toto, they shook the emotions of a nation, perhaps shaped the course of human history. And, if this was truth, why wasn't it told as truth? What human foible would grasp the mind and conscience of man so firmly that verity could be torn, shredded, and discarded for some crazy patchwork quilt that no one could wholly accept?

Camelot? the Camelot complex? the Kennedy name and image at stake? what else?

I opened and walked through a door leading onto a small patio and stood for several moments in the crisp night air and darkness. Okay, world, I thought, would you believe this? Is

35

what I have just heard an acceptable alternative to the disbelief, the doubt, the suspicion that so many seem to hold to?

There was a rattle of pans in the kitchen; I glanced at my watch; it was 10:45. Charles would be preparing our nightcap: hot chocolate and fresh-baked wafer biscuits. Shades and shadows of Sherlock Holmes. I felt more and more like Dr. Watson.

The watch face reminded me of Fifi—scratch that—Priscilla. But I knew there was much more to come from the Inspector, so I hastily covered my watch with my sleeve. Down, boy, down!

Charles returned bearing a tray with our chocolate cups and a platter of biscuits. There are only three recipes he guards zealously, and one is the biscuit mix that he makes and refrigerates until baking time. My bachelor cooking is neat and adequate, but never superb, never in the Darby class. However, I am not above theft of a recipe on occasion. Just recently I had slipped two of his biscuits into my pocket and later asked a friend, the current president of a famous gourmet society, for a hypothetical analysis of the flavoring.

This esteemed gentleman consumed both biscuits, asked for more, hinted at an early introduction to Inspector Darby, mumbled something about dill and chives, then pleaded a headache, like any woman using evasive tactics. A revolting performance.

Charles passed the biscuit platter and said: "I have a few extra biscuits wrapped up in the kitchen for you, Truly. I wouldn't want to be found guilty of staining the lining of your pockets."

My God! He knew!

I thanked him, and quickly changed the subject. Flattery might get me somewhere—somewhere else.

"Charles, I want to congratulate you, if congratulate is the proper word, on the succinct and perceptive analysis you have given me. I can find no flaw in your reasoning."

36

I knew this was stupid. I wouldn't be expected to find a flaw in *his* reasoning. But I had to say something. And the biscuit thing flustered me.

He overlooked my audacity, ever the English gentleman: "Thank you, Truly, but we have much further to go." He offered chocolate, but I refused. Hot chocolate after brandy is his thing, not mine. A second and third biscuit, however, seemed a polite thing to do. I did it.

The Inspector picked up his account where he had left me floundering. Every step in the progress of events from the moment the car left the bridge to the arrival of Kennedy and Markham at the police station Saturday morning was covered.

They tell me a storyteller must never stray too far afield from his central plot lest new plots develop to the detriment of his story. I pray thee, therefore, to sustain your patience and indulge me in a return to the Inspector's fireside without further disclosure now of the Darby deductions. In so doing, you will allow the author to continue in the sequential form he feels is best suited to the vitality and validity of his narrative. Let this suffice: The opinion expressed on the night herein described, prior to the January 1970 inquest, was substantially the same as the final expression given to a group of my friends in the summer of 1970. The latter is presented in full detail in a later chapter. This procedure is in keeping with the Inspector's prohibitive request relating to his original opinion. A request that was abided by, with one exception.

A single chime from the mantel clock reminded me of the time: 11:30. Priscilla! I had promised to telephone just after midnight . . . must not disappoint her. I thought for a moment of the hesitancy she must have felt in doing what she did. Obviously a very nice girl, not accustomed to being forward with a strange man. But who can deny the sometimes irresistible attraction of man for woman, and woman for man, under the most unlikely circumstances. It was chemical; both had felt it; I could

37

not fail her. And under such conditions it was important that I place the call when it would be expected. Otherwise—a blow to her psyche—never! Most ungentlemanly.

Charles thoughtfully suggested I join him in the refreshing enjoyment of a tall glass of ice water. A splendid, sobering idea. There is a certain attitude of responsibility necessary on the part of the sophisticate rendezvousing with the innocent in the wee hours of the morn. These are the hours of witchery and the ascendancy of human frailty. Sweeping a damsel off her feet at such times with the charm born of long and varied experience can lead to serious guilt complexes. I was determined to be in full control of myself.

As my mother would say, if a man remains in full control of himself, eventually he will marry *the right girl*. As my analyst has said, a number of times, he will also remain a bachelor. For mental exercise when I have nothing else to do, I sometimes try to reconcile these two viewpoints.

"Truly, you seem a bit preoccupied. Do you wish to continue?"

"Oh yes! Yes indeed!"

He rose, crossed to his desk, and brought back two large manila envelopes. I was informed that one of them contained a timetable map showing minute-by-minute movements of all the principal actors in the denouement of the Chappaquiddick incident. I was free to study and question it, but the hour was late, and I sensed that he had other matters in mind. The envelope remained unopened on my lap.

We did discuss, briefly, the contents of the second envelope: the chapter of his memoirs covering experiences at Dunkirk in the year 1940. It is my impression that nothing in his illustrious career gave him as much personal gratification and sense of achievement as the small role he played at Dunkirk as a participant in the Mosquito Armada rescues. Without this intrepid fleet, described by Churchill as unsinkable as a whole, almost one hundred thousand men would have bowed to surrender on the beaches of France. It was these little boats, fishing craft, pleasure yachts, lifeboats from liners, tugboats, et cetera, that plied back and forth from the beaches to the larger ships lying offshore in deep water, ignored constant air bombardment and strafing, and delivered so resolutely their human cargo.

The highly trained specialists of Scotland Yard are not called to combat duty in time of war. In reminiscence, Charles has told me of the sense of fulfillment he enjoyed during four days and nights as second-in-command to a close friend, owner of a pleasure yacht that crossed the Channel and joined the Mosquito Armada. I had insisted that this experience should be a part of his memoirs. The pattern of our earlier conversation was broken momentarily while we discussed the relationship of his Dunkirk chapter to a following chapter on other wartime experiences.

As the word *evacuation* was often on our tongues while we talked of Dunkirk, it seemed only natural for me to use it in returning our conversation to Chappaquiddick. Charles had removed my nosy little compendium from his desk and deposited it with the manila envelopes. I asked if he had any quarrel with my comments on the Saturday "evacuation" of the reunion-party participants from Martha's Vineyard. He laughed at my descriptive terminology, denied any quarrel, then made his own comment, stressing the urgency of the situation.

All three of the principals were lawyers, Kennedy, Gargan, and Markham, and they would quickly recognize that it was crucial, he said, to remove the witnesses from the possibility of questioning, because of the frailty of the fabric, the veil they had woven to cover the true facts of the incident at the bridge and the events following.

Just past midnight I again expressed my gratitude for the Inspector's time and thought devoted to subject matter of my choosing. The response led to my conclusion that for the present, to Charles, the Kennedy matter was *in nubibus,* "up in the clouds," and his interest would lie solely with the completion of his memoirs.

His last remark before we parted was in answer to my mention that I was toying with the idea of writing about Chappaquiddick and of quoting his theory. I expected some sort of an Englishman's understated explosion of horror at the mere suggestion. I was wrong. Charles paid me a compliment and extracted a promise all in one breath.

"As you wish, Truly," he said, "providing your good taste is equal to your confounded curiosity. And I believe it is."

Five: Sister of a Female Pirate

I called from a phone booth in the neighboring village. There was an immediate answer and rather businesslike directions given by the calm voice of Miss Rogers. I had expected more of a breathless quality of impatience. After all, I wasn't delivering groceries or laundry. She sounded pleased, however, and I was thanked for my punctuality. It was 12:15.

Follow Treebrook Road out of the village one mile and watch for a large, round, multicolored lollipop sign on the right. Turn into Lollipop Lane—only one house on the lane.

The lollipop thing was so in keeping with the youth, the naiveté. I reminded myself: control, gentlemanly conduct. Another thing—we had not been formally introduced; we really should shake hands.

The lane was short. I parked and walked up a long path to a doorway covered with a trellis. Before I could knock, the door began to open; then I heard: "Welcome! Truly Trulimann!" The door swung wide, and Miss Rogers came toward me with both arms outstretched. I raised my hands, and she grasped them, pulling me into the dimly lighted room. Under the circumstances, it was very difficult, no—impossible—to shake hands in the normal manner.

"Miss Rogers!" I said, pumping both hands up and down. I tried to conclude with a customary one-on-one handshake, but she swung around beside me, joined her left arm with my right, and guided me toward a large sofa near a brightly burning fire.

"I am honored," she said, "Faulkner Trulimann, the bon vivant, the Beau Brummel, the world traveler, patron, philanthropist, financier, Casanova, clubman, et cetera, in my humble abode!" I was rather stunned. True, every word of it, but how——? "One of the world's most eligible bachelors," she continued, "heir to a fortune, successful in his own right. Tall, dark, handsome, and debonair——"

"Miss Rogers!" She was holding both of my hands again, gazing deeply into my blue eyes.

" 'Priscilla,' please, Mr. Trulimann . . . member of Piping Rock, Racquet, Everglades, Seawanaka, boards of Standard Petroleum, Metropolitan Art—" she had turned loose of my hands and started counting on her fingers. Such a child. Such a lovely, sexy child. Should be more of them.

"How do you know all this?" I spoke sternly.

"Madame Thibeault. She has a cerebral dossier on all her regular customers, especially the Old Long Island Family customers. Your father was the highest ranking Prussian officer captured in combat during World War I; your mother was Dallas Faulkner, madcap debutante and heiress to oil millions. They met when she Red-Crossed a prison camp, and after the war, your father, Baron Heinrich Otto von Trulimann, pursued, wooed, and won her. You were born in 1923, their only child."

"But why would Madame Thibeault tell you all this?"

"Because fifteen years ago you took my sister to her restaurant many, many times."

"Your sister?"

"Dolly."

"Dolly? Dolly Rogers?" Now I am really stunned.

"Yes, the girl you persisted in calling the Female Pirate. My mother thought it was very unfunny."

"And you are—"

"The youngest of the four daughters. The towhead, the tomboy——"

"The tree climber," I finished for her.

"Yep!"

"They couldn't keep you out of the trees."

"Nope! Trees are great vantage points for eight-year-olds. I was right above you one day when you were waiting for Dolly, and you sneakily emptied your car ashtrays under one of Mother's favorite rosebushes, then scuffed over the debris with your foot. Mother never did understand why that bush died. Too much nicotine."

This was embarrassing. I thought nicotine kept bugs away. I gave them credit for having more sense than human beings.

"There was another tree, down around the curve in the driveway, a nice spot, hidden from the house, where you always seemed to run out of gas——"

"Priscilla! You didn't!"

"Yep! Many times."

Now I knew how George Washington must have felt. There are some trees that *should be* chopped down!

"So that's why you lured me here," I pretended to be very angry, "a threat to expose my lurid past. What is it, blackmail?"

"No, Truly. As I told you earlier, I could not help overhearing some of your discussion with Inspector Darby about the Kennedy accident. I heard him tell you that he would give you his conclusions when you returned to his home tonight. I'm terribly curious about the whole thing."

Aha! Now I understood. But I must admit to considerable disappointment—no chemistry and all that. "Priscilla, I am not at liberty to tell you at this time what conclusions the Inspector has drawn. Perhaps later——''

"Oh, I don't expect that. There's something else. But first, would you care for a demitasse or brandy?" Ah! Chemistry, sweet chemistry!

"A coffee would be perfect, my dear, and thank you." I rose and gave her my most gallant bow. Back on the beam again. She retreated behind a serving bar at the far end of the room. It was quite a long room, about forty feet, and probably twenty feet wide. At one time a four-car garage, obviously, and each car port doorway was now floor-to-ceiling glass. The outside driveway was ringed with huge flower pots to form a patio effect.

Behind the serving bar I could see a modern kitchen and, rising from one side, a staircase passing over it to the floor above. An old back service door had been converted into a front-door opening on a new driveway approach, Lollipop Lane. Two multipaned bay windows with seating flanked the entrance door. Heavy supporting beams ran across the ceiling and down the walls. The concrete floor was stained and highly polished.

The decor was superb. Genuine antiques mixed with stylized junk, chintz with linen, velvet with brocade, color, color, color. The total effect was delightful, but the pièce de résistance was a beautifully carved wooden-framed telephone booth in a corner near the stone fireplace. Inside was a modern pay telephone.

Priscilla returned with a tray and found me examining the carving.

"One of my roommates' ancestors was a founder of the telephone company," she said. "She inherited that, one of the first public phone booths. I have five roommates, and we find a pay phone ideal for cost accounting of outgoing calls. Took a bit of doing to get the phone put in, but Gayle's father had the necessary pull."

As she filled our demitasse cups, I took my first long look at her. She was beautiful, from every angle. Clean, clear-cut beauty in every detail, but best of all, her eyes—unpolluted is a way of expressing it in this day and age. Rolling-surf, mountain-stream, fresh-snow immaculacy, if the poets gave it a try. No one could ever tire of looking at or into eyes like that.

Passing the cup and saucer, she looked up and caught me staring. I had to say something. I'm always having to say something. Is it a defense mechanism?

"Priscilla, why did you climb trees?" Now there's a great opening line!

"Because my father, when I was four years old, began calling me Prissy. When I became old enough to know what it meant, not to him, but to most people, climbing trees seemed the best way to fight back."

Pivotal thinking would have told me that. I hadn't caught the knack of it yet. I was reminded of Charles:

"You were going to explain your interest in the Inspector's comments, or something else—" I let the *something else* dangle with an inflection I hoped would sound as delightfully romantic as Tibetan temple bells.

"Truly, I work five nights a week at Madame Thibeault's. Four of my five roommates work there. We have three bedrooms and two baths upstairs, and we are very comfortable here. We earn enough to pay our expenses and to take postgraduate courses at the state university near here. I want a masters degree in psychology. Recently I had to write a term paper different from anything I had ever done before: the stream-of-consciousness thoughts, all the terrifying mental twists and turns, of a woman's mind coping with a critical situation leading to her death. Classic examples: Marie Antoinette and Joan of Arc. I chose for my subject: Mary Jo Kopechne." Stunned again. What was this leading to? "May I ask why Mary Jo?" I asked hesitantly.

"Two years ago I was driving an enclosed Jaguar XKE on a

country road in the south of France. There was a blowout, and I lost control. The car left the road and plunged into a canal; it completely submerged. Because the road was terribly dusty I had all vents and windows shut tight and, very much to my surprise, I found enough air trapped in the car for me to breathe fairly comfortably. The car had remained upright. There were slow leaks of water, but I wasn't badly injured, and I just sat there. I had no idea how deep the canal was, but opening a window or door and escaping meant giving up my precious air. I just could not do it.

"I prayed, I cried, I gave myself pep talks, but most of all, I waited—for something, for anything that did not call for an initiating act on my part.

"There was a farmer plowing a field a few hundred yards from the spot where I drove off the road. He saw me go into the canal. God bless him, he unhitched his plowhorse and rode to a neighboring farm with a telephone. He called for help. About an hour later several horses were hitched to my car, and it was pulled out of the canal. Water inside was just reaching my shoulders. I still had trapped air to breathe. When I opened the door and stepped out with a huge gush of water, one of my rescuers fainted. No one expected me to be alive."

She started to refill my demitasse cup, and I motioned to her to wait. I filled the cup half full of brandy from a carafe and then asked for the coffee fill. Something told me to start bracing myself for another something, I didn't know exactly what. My mother never told me there would be nights like this.

Priscilla joined me in the coffee-with-brandy, but I noticed that she poured her brandy high and her coffee sparse. With a quick lift, she drained the cup. There were tears in her eyes as she turned away suddenly and stared at the blazing fire. It was the brandy, or was it?

They say Mother Nature will not allow recall of the sensation of physical pain. You can't remember and relive even a pinprick. But how about recall of unrelieved terror, of gut-bursting fright, of abysmal despair? I could not answer that. No experience in my life could equal Priscilla's hour in the canal. Plainly, she was caught in a spell of choking emotion, and I desperately wanted to reach out and pull her head to my shoulder. Instead, being the goddamn repressed fool that I am, I made a dead-pan try for a funny.

In a very concerned voice I said: "The man who fainted, I hope he is all right now."

Her eyes swung back to mine, and there was a startled little gasp before the laughter burst out like a fireworks rocket at its zenith. There were tears now, lots of them, but they seemed to be dancing. She caught the mood and replied: "Oh, yes, he's improving every day. I've paid all of his hospital bills, and we correspond regularly."

Now we were both laughing. To keep the roll-out play moving, I inquired about Dolly. She replied: "Married, divorced, one child; married again, divorced, one child; married again, two more children. She has been very busy, Truly, trying to forget you."

I knew it. I knew it. I felt most humble and almost ashamed of myself. Sometimes I feel there has just been too much of this sort of thing in my life. May the saints forgive me.

Priscilla, trying to be helpful, said: "I knew you would be concerned; I brought these down from my room for you."

She picked up a small accordion-fold album from the coffee table and spread it before me. Husbands, children, pets, home in Palm Beach, home in Dallas, home in St. Louis. I had to say something and said it. But what, I can't remember. It was time to stop the roll-out before somebody fumbled. Back to the old-fashioned straight-ahead ground game.

"Priscilla," I said gently, "you were telling me why the subject you chose was Mary Jo Kopechne. You had a somewhat similar experience. Was this your reason?"

47

"No, not entirely, there were others, now that I think of it."

"Can you recall them?"

She paused for a moment, studying a ruby and pearl ring while twisting away carefully at selected strands of her hair. I was reminded of Charles Darby. There was the same detached air of thought marshaling, and since my mother was very fond of the Inspector, it occurred to me that if Priscilla was astrologically endowed with some or all of his good traits and qualities, my mother would be very fond of her, leaving the rest of Priscilla for me. And I could get along on that—very nicely, thank you.

Holding several golden strands straight out from her head, she looked directly at me with those marvelous eyes and said:

"I don't believe the Kennedy explanation of Mary Jo's death. After I submitted my term paper, our class instructor held a general discussion of the incident, and I found that disbelief was quite prevalent. Yet there seems to be no animosity toward Kennedy, nor do the students condemn him. They just don't believe he has been completely honest, and neither do I.

"Jack and Bobby Kennedy were respected in their public lives by so many younger people because they did project an honesty and a humaneness that was inspirational to us. No one expected them to be perfection itself in their private or public lives. Every student knows he can read biographies of great leaders of history and find human vices and weaknesses in all of them. In one of my philosophy classes, I remember being impressed by the words of some obscure writer who said: 'A vice that is a personal blemish is regretful, but a vice that harms another is a sin.' "

"Are you suggesting then, that Ted Kennedy, by not being completely honest, is harming Mary Jo?"

"And himself. I'm not sure, Truly. After the accident, all the loyal knights assembled to save Camelot, and whatever he

48

did must be thought of in the light of the Camelot charisma; but charismatic imagery bestows no divine right to place self before righteousness. I listened to Ted Kennedy's TV speech, but I never really heard a word of it. All I could hear was trickling water, and all I could feel was horror and sympathy for Mary Jo. If she did not die almost instantly, I know what terror went through her mind, and how she would try to fight it.

"She would think of her parents, her friends, her work, music, sunlight and sunsets, common everyday talk, inspiring words and thoughts, love and fun and thousands of little fleeting memories. She would hope for understanding and help and believe she would get both and be saved from death. She would not want to say good-bye forever to the good things God and life had given her, and would give her in the future. If she lived as long as I did underwater, Truly, she knew terrible fear and doubt and confusion.

"The rear seat she collapsed in was not taking her back to a warm bed and dry clothes, to a swarm of lawyers and political prop men. It was a place to hang on to—to keep her head up in a tiny, pitch-dark doll's room of air, while her body slowly froze in cold water. She couldn't make any phone calls, but she would do as I did—try to open up a line to God and ask why, and beg for help, and make promises.

"There would be no one to advise her, no one to admire her courage, no cheering throngs to herald her future, and no speech writer to tell the world what a dreadful spot she was in and why.

"To put it plainly and frankly, I thought Mary Jo deserved such a speech writer, and I nominated myself."

During most of this torrent of thought pouring from Priscilla, she had remained seated but bent forward, with her body in an attitude of pleading for understanding of her own emotions. When she paused, I arose, then bent down, tilted her head upward, and kissed her gently but firmly for a moment. It was the only way I could think of to express the way I felt. As I straightened up and moved toward the coffee tray, her eyes followed me, and she said quietly:

"Forgive my soapboxing?"

"First woman president! Why not?" And I meant it! And then a funny thought struck me. Would the husband of a woman president, protocol-wise, outrank the vice-president? I hoped so.

She saw me reaching for the coffee and, with a wink and a smile, outreached me and prepared two brandy coffees for us. We clinked cups, and she toasted. Then:

"Truly, there was one more big reason why I had to write about Mary Jo."

"And that was?"

"I suppose you could call it introspective selfishness on my part, but I wanted so desperately to release by some kind of action, any kind really, some of the emotional hangover from my own experience. I'll give you one or two examples, if you want to listen."

"I'm listening—to every word you're saying, believe me."

"I want to tell you about the farmer who went for help when he saw my car go into the canal. When he reached a telephone and called the nearest village, the local gendarme came to the canal, saw my car completely submerged, and announced that he would return to the village, call a garage in a nearby town, and obtain the services of a wrecker truck. It was his decision that no one in the car could possibly be alive, so he departed.

"The farmer who saw me go in the canal had returned with a number of his neighbors. To these simple people, the authorities had spoken; no one could remain alive under water for almost an hour. The problem was out of their hands. But my farmer angel insisted that the four farm horses standing nearby could pull the car out of the water, and he argued his friends into making the effort.

50

"You know what happened when I stepped out of the car: One man fainted. But the others were overwhelmingly excited, happy, and kind. I was taken to a farmhouse and given dry clothes, hot soup, and wine. Everybody had the wine. You would think Joan of Arc had materialized before them. But the real hero of the moment was my farmer angel. He had saved my life, and they knew it. When they couldn't get wine down his throat, they poured it on his head.

"I speak French quite well, and after giving him my tearful appreciation and after hearing the whole story, I asked one question: Why did he insist on pulling the car out, instead of waiting for the wrecker, if he too agreed there was no hope of rescue? His reply absolutely shattered me, and still does. It was because my body, in the canal water, would be so wet, so cold, so lonely.

"His peasantlike simplicity in concern for a fellow human being only began when he left his plow and rode for help. Even the finality of death didn't end it."

Human magnificence in peasant costume.

Her eyes were brimming again, but this time I was the one who turned away, walked over to the fireplace, and stared at the coals, through quivering little pools of my own.

I turned when Priscilla arose and stood beside me. She was smiling, and I joined in, silently. Finally she said:

"Do you want to hear more?" as if she couldn't believe I would. Her head tilted down and rested on my shoulder. We both took deep breaths and let out big sighs. I moved back, tilted her head up, and kissed her lightly on the top of her nose.

"Priscilla, I suspect you have wanted to talk about these things for a long, long time. Am I right?"

"Yes, the things I have said to you I have said to no one else—but they have needed saying; I've felt them so strongly."

"I'm sure there's more."

51

"Just one more, Truly, at least for tonight. It has to do with existentialism. Are you familiar with the writings of Jean-Paul Sartre?"

"No, not in depth," I replied, with a touch of apprehension. Existentialism close on the heels of pivotal thinking was worrisome. I have always felt, too, that complex cerebral gymnastics are dangerous practice when conducted in Platonic dialogue with femininity such as Priscilla's. In such circumstances, a man must form a tortoise shell around his true self, for it is one thing to willingly and hopefully expose oneself to shafts sent flying from Cupid's heart-shaped bow and quite another to stand unarmored before shafts let go at you from an intellectualizing female brain.

"In his book *Being and Nothingness*," she went on, "Sartre defines consciousness in this manner: Consciousness is a being such that in its being, its being is in question insofar as this being implies a being other than itself."

You see what I mean!

"Please don't shudder, Truly, it is not becoming."

"I apologize."

"Don't, please." (Was she taunting me?) "I made a poor start by quoting Sartre direct; he takes explaining."

And explaining, and explaining, and explaining, I thought.

"Can't we leave Sartre in France, and you tell me in your own words? I can rapp with you, but Jean-Paul is just too far-out!"

Her eyes widened in astonishment.

"You dig *rapp*," she said.

"I dig. Just don't get too heavy and we'll pulse."

"Pulse?" She walked straight into my trap, a trap baited with my vast two-word modern vocabulary—*rapp* ("rapport") and *heavy* ("deep, sincere interest"). Puzzled she was, yet I knew her respect for me had grown. I turned my last card face up:

52

"Pulse, meaning 'communicate' . . . electronics . . . it's *the* new word. I'm sorry, I thought you had it. Now you were saying something about consciousness."

"Truly," she was pondering, "I'm beginning to understand why Mother called you Devious Dapper Dan—"

I was hurt.

"—the Prussian Leprechaun."

I was mortified. A leprechaun is a tricky old man.

"Mother did say something very nice about you, though," she continued, "when Dolly counted up fourteen different malfunction reasons you gave for your car stopping dead beneath that big tree down the driveway."

"She did?"

"Mother said that took brains! She called you a mechanical genius." The coffee and the brandy were having an effect. Priscilla raised her cup high over her head, as if toasting my genius, then spoke more seriously: "If you don't want me to talk of Sartre, I won't!"

"Priscilla, what does Sartre have to do with you and Mary Jo?"

"And Ted Kennedy, don't leave him out."

She poured brandy into both cups, saying:

"Truly, do you have early-morning appointments?"

"A ten thirty director's meeting."

"Do you have to be bright and sharp as a tack?"

"Yes, but I brighten and sharpen beautifully on standard hangover remedies."

"Good! Then . . . cheers!" She raised her cup again, and took a large sip. I toasted back and said the obvious: "Why?"

"Because I'm about to climb back onto my soapbox, and I don't want my audience of fellow countrymen walking out on me!"

"Your audience is breathless with anticipation, Lady President."

53

"Thank you! When my car went into that damned canal, I was running away—from everything and everybody—in particular, from a bastard named Auguste."

There was a very large, very soft pillow at either end of the sofa. Priscilla suddenly swung the pillow next to her over her head and onto my lap. Then she curled into a tight ball of torso and legs and placed her head on the pillow, with the back of her head toward my chest.

"Truly," (there was a slight tremor in her voice) "when I say some of the things I am going to say, I don't want to look at you and I don't want you to see my face. There's a part of my life I'm just a wee bit ashamed of. Do you mind?"

"Of course not."

"Are you comfortable?" she asked.

"Yes, but I can't find my hands. I think they are somewhere beneath the pillow, but I can't swear to it."

"Fool!" She raised herself on one elbow. "Pull your arms out and up. There should be one hand at the end of each arm!"

She was right.

"Now, when I put my head down, you can rub my scalp, ever so gently, with your fingers. But no nails! Understand?"

"Yes, but this kind of soapboxing won't win many votes. People like to have a politician look them straight in the eye when she lies to them."

"Well, this speech is going to be different. I'm going to say some things I've never said out loud before. Will you please shut up and let me say them?"

"My lips are zipped."

She reached back with her left hand, ran her fingers across my closed-tight lips, then patted me on the cheek before she began:

"When mother and father died in that plane crash five years ago, I was the only daughter unmarried and still living at home with them. Overnight, I became an orphan, an heiress, and a

54

little bitch, but not exactly in that order. The bitchiness was well along, because I was spoiled something awful. What Priscilla wanted, Priscilla got!

"Three boarding schools and three dismissals later," she continued, "brought me to the Sorbonne in Paris. I had my own apartment, a circle of self-proclaimed intellectuals as friends, and I was rather happy. Then came love and sex—by name, Auguste; by reputation, notorious. But Priscilla wanted him for her very own, so she gave him food, shelter, and spending money—and thought she had found life and happiness.

"On my twenty-first birthday I had to appear in court in New York. One third of my inheritance—two million dollars— became mine, all mine. No more executor's allowances.

"When I left Paris, I gave Auguste a thousand dollars and told him to get some proper clothes for a honeymoon. I couldn't stand being away from him; so, in New York, I changed my plans and returned to Paris three days ahead of the time Auguste expected me. I walked into the apartment from the airport at two A.M. My dear, beloved Auguste was in bed with a red-headed Eurasian. My clothes were scattered all over the place— the lady would wear what she liked and throw what she didn't like on the floor!

"Father and I both loved trapshooting, and I had my double-barreled skeet gun on a wall rack. I took it down, plunked in two shells, walked back into the bedroom, and fired once at the wall just over their grinning faces.

"In twenty seconds flat, I had the apartment all to myself."

Priscilla sat up, thanked me for the scalp massage, and said: "That was the end of Monsieur Auguste's personal appearance; but it wasn't the end of my attraction to him. After three days and nights of misery, talking to him on the phone and through the door, I bought the XKE and headed south for Italy. Purely on a whim, I took a back-road shortcut. And there was the canal . . . waiting . . . patiently."

55

She walked the length of the room, opened the refrigerator door, and returned with a bottle of champagne and two glasses. There was a challenging look in her eyes. I thought to myself, This is turning into quite an evening. My standard remedies would not be adequate. I made a mental note to include an early-morning session in my new sauna.

"Toasting with brandy is like kissing through a veil. Im————proper! And I want to drink to the new Priscilla, who emerged Aphrodite-ish from the waters of the canal."

"The *new* Priscilla?"

"Yes! I've been a changed woman since that little one-hour episode. There's nothing like terminal underwater confinement for contemplation and self-appraisal. I started to tell you how Jean-Paul Sartre got into the act, but you rudely sent him back to France."

"Try me again," I popped the cork and filled our glasses almost to the brim. A glance at the label was reassuring, a sip test seemed unnecessary, so I toasted: "But first—to the Priscilla I see tonight, new or old!"

"Thank you. Now to the changed woman!" We both toasted, then she tapped me on each shoulder and said: "And now to you, Sir Cornball!"

"SIR? CORNBALL?"

"Yep! Champion of right, seeker of truth, and deserving of knighthood, complete with shield bearing a gilt-edged stock certificate emblazoned with a beautiful fluffy white cornball!"

My ego-central was disturbed. I am always fearful of the frank and open speech of a beautiful woman somewhat inebriated. Her lowered eyelids can lower your guard, then her sozzled wit strikes you with all the subtlety of a heavy medieval mace.

"Sartre," she went on, "believes we make ourselves what we are by the choices we make, day after day, year after year.

Man's most important possession is this freedom of choice. Without it, we are animal or inanimate.

"When the water closed around my little cubicle in the canal, it wasn't long before I understood with perfect clarity how precious this freedom of choice really is, and how it does make us as we are. For then my choices were very simple and in a very narrow vein. Do I pray and have faith, or scream and revile fate? Do I try to escape, or sit and wait for death? Do I collapse and weep silently, or lower a window and die quickly—and bravely? The choices I made would determine what kind of a human being I actually was, to myself, if to no other.

"Suddenly I knew, with great sadness, how many times in the past I had made the wrong choices—always the easy, never the difficult; often the selfish, seldom the selfless. I believed it was more blessed to give than to receive, but I gave trouble and expected to receive understanding.

"The Priscilla with cold water creeping over her was not a very nice Priscilla. A take-it-all, give-the-least spoiled brat of a young woman. The only gift of myself had been, in the end, a sickening experience. The recipient had mocked the donor, as the donor had so often mocked the gifts bestowed on her.

"Truly, this is a terrible way to die—having time to reflect and using it the way I did. I was destroying my self-respect, my ego, as the water rose to destroy the life in my body. I could think of only one thing I really wanted more than life itself: another chance, to have freedom of choice again, and in choosing, find a Priscilla I could respect."

"Well, you have certainly found one *I* can respect!"

"Thank you," she paused for a moment, then continued. "I know you are wondering what all this has to do with Chappaquiddick."

"Yes, I am."

"Simply this: I would like to believe that Edward Kennedy is just as humane, just as compassionate, just as selfless as my farmer savior in France.

"However, in writing Mary Jo's stream-of-consciousness thoughts, I could not simultaneously project his thoughts, only his spoken words as I imagined she heard them. As a consequence, it is possible you will receive the impression that I judge and condemn Kennedy. But this is not my intention. Nothing could be more unfair. I think he was mistaken in his choice of actions, yes; but I simply cannot bring myself to the conclusion that there was true evil involved. I have tried to give you a personal parallel. I want you to realize that I myself feel no less guilty of perhaps placing self before righteousness if I have nevertheless portrayed this in Kennedy."

She offered her empty glass to me and concluded: "With that bit of lofty sermonizing, Mr. Trulimann, I descend from my pulpit. You may refill my glass."

I responded by refilling both glasses, then raised mine and said:

"Priscilla, it is always inspiring and comforting to find that great beauty is not skin-deep."

She leaned over, tweaked my nose, patted my cheek, arose from the sofa and walked around behind it. She leaned over again, tilted my head back with the tip of a finger placed lightly under my chin, brushed my forehead with her lips, then proceeded to mess up the nice, straight part in my hair with dancing fingers. I remembered my mother's advice to a young man: "Keep their hands out of your hair," she said.

I too arose, straightened my hair as best I could, then took a firmly planted stance before the fireplace. Mother's advice again—beware a woman who has just indulged herself in highly emotional thoughts. "It stirs them up," she said. She might have added: "and makes them much more interesting."

Priscilla crossed the room to an old rolltop desk, opened a

drawer, withdrew a large manilla envelope, and joined me at the fireside.

"There it is," she placed the envelope on the mantel, "if you want to know what really happened, read it. Then you may call me Prissy Rogers, the Female Sleuth."

"Prissy——"

"Whup! It's Priscilla until you admit I'm a darn good detective too, Sir Cornball. I'll match a woman's intuition with Scotland Yard any day!" She drank her champagne, and I asked a question.

"Shall I read it now?"

"If you wish, or you may take it home and read it. If you read it now, a tipsy blonde may be a disturbing influence. Will you forgive me if I say good-night? Make yourself at home, but close the door tightly when you leave; it has a tricky latch."

"Of course. And thank you, Priscilla, for your hospitality."

"Gratitude accepted; but, instead of flowers tomorrow, I'd much rather know what the Inspector told you tonight."

Now how in the world did she know I planned to send flowers in appreciation? A woman's intuition? or is that the thing a cornball would do? At times, I feel I am not keeping pace with the approach of the new world we will soon live in. Perhaps a world without florists?

"I have a tape of the Inspector's opinion. If I can get his permission, would you like to hear it?"

"Oh! Yes! Yes! When?" She gave me a very tight hug and a very loud, smacking kind of a kiss on my chin. I find sudden misdirected physical attacks of this type very disturbing.

"At your convenience," I said, rubbing my chin.

For some reason she laughed, then: "I have next Tuesday off, and two tickets for a campus play that should prove to be interesting. It is Sartre's *No Exit*. How about dinner, the play, and back here for a brandy and the tape?"

"Pick you up at what time?"

"Six thirty."

"Six thirty. And I'm punctual."

"I'll bet you are. Good-night, dear Truly." She leaned forward on tiptoe, and her lips brushed mine twice before she started for the stairs. Yes, Mother, control! I sat down and opened the large envelope.

"Truly?" I looked up to find an upside-down face staring at me through the highest bannister opening; her blonde hair fell around and away from her head. A natural-born tree climber grown older.

"Yes?"

"I have decided to elevate you."

"How very thoughtful."

"You are now *Lord* Cornball!"

For a rather foolish reason I felt highly pleased. My mother has often said I should have been a girl so she could have arranged a proper marriage and brought an English title into the family. She would be very happy now. We had our title.

I sat down when Priscilla disappeared without another word, drank the last of the champagne in silent meditation, started to open the envelope, then paused. Was I ready for this, Priscilla's stream-of-consciousness thoughts of Mary Jo Kopechne? Well, maybe; then again, maybe not. I placed a large mesh screen before the dying fire, turned off four of six lamps, tucked the envelope under my arm, walked out the door. Priscilla was right about the latch. It *was* tricky. As quietly as possible, I pulled the door closed three times before the latch caught. What these girls needed was an available man who could fix things like that. Perhaps a man of mechanical genius . . . ?

I stood beside my car for a moment, searching my pockets for keys. A glance upward caught the blink-out of the only lighted upstairs window. Then a phrase Priscilla had spoken cut sharply into my own stream of consciousness: ". . . in a tiny, pitch-dark doll's room of air."

A shivering streak of cold horror crept slowly up my spine, across my shoulders, and down my arms. Behind those darkened windows were whole rooms of air, and in them slept six girls of Mary Jo's generation who would awake in the morning with their lives still before them. But no one lives very long in a tiny doll's room of air. And knowledge, even pretended knowledge, of last thoughts under such conditions, was not my idea of a way to top off an evening.

Two nights later I read Priscilla's term paper. Two nights earlier I had made a wise decision. It was not pleasant reading, and I can see no purpose being served in its inclusion with this story. Let this suffice: Priscilla's "womanly intuition" was remarkably close to the Inspector's opinion on the series of events leading to the tragic accident. But "events" is one thing, while "thoughts" motivating events is quite another. I think it best to leave the expression of such things to the Scotland Yard temperament coupled with deductive reasoning or "pivotal thinking."

Six: Chaumière Canot

Sartre's one-act *No Exit* is not my cup of tea. Watching the antic desperation of a nympho baby killer, a patient lesbian, and a cowardly, brutish man locked in the same hotel room throughout eternity, just doesn't grab me. If the room clerk at the Hades Hilton has a foul-up registration like this waiting for me, I'm taking along a sleeping bag and a pup tent when I cross the River Styx.

Priscilla, however, seemed entranced with the play, loving every minute of it. So, for conversation after the curtain, I chose my smile of interested intellectualism and good intent when we were joined by several of her friends and classmates. One of the exchange students, an able-bodied, sloe-eyed, sultry young woman from Turkey, singled me out for an in-depth brain-to-brain discussion of the true meaning of the play. A few minutes of this was enough; to engage in ratiocination with a ratiocinator such as Miss Karounin on a subject involving such a trio could only lead to complete dismantlement of intellectual purpose. I felt my aforementioned smile slowly dissolving into a wishful leer exhibiting no intellectualism and good intent whatever.

"Truly, I want you to meet our dramatics instructor,

Tommy Highsmith. He directed the play." It was Priscilla, walking in where angels should never tread.

"It is a pleasure, Mr. Highsmith. You know Miss Karounin, of course?"

"I certainly dooo—" I found the amount of *oooo* on the end of his *do* disturbing. Quickly, I cut in: "The play was most enjoyable. You and your students are to be congratulated."

"Thank you. Too bad you didn't see our performance three weeks ago. Priscilla played the part of Estelle, and she was simply sensational!"

I must present a comic appearance when I gulp, judging by the tittering of a certain Thespian nymphomaniacal baby killer.

"Sorry I missed it," I replied. "Sounds like excellent casting." This was a defensive move against the titterer, and it worked. Suddenly quite serious, she said: "Just what does that mean, Mr. Trulimann?"

"It means I am hungry, and I told Pim to expect us for supper no later than eleven o'clock." I had bunted safely, but I did not want another "at bat." There was the scary chance of a high inside fast ball aimed directly at my left ear. Business engagements had made it impossible for me to meet Priscilla for dinner before the play. She had agreed to a late supper, prepared and served by Pim, my Filipino genius of a houseman. And after supper, the Inspector's-opinion tape. He had had no objections to my playing the recording for her after reading her term paper. In fact, he was as intrigued as I was by the coincidental qualities of the paper and his opinion.

The mention of available food had a relaxing effect, as it so often does with the hungry female. She pulled me out of the chatty little group and whispered: "What do you think of asking Tommy to join us? He helped me in writing the term paper."

"Splendid idea," I responded, "and I'll invite Miss Karounin. We should have some indication of the international reaction."

63

This polite and friendly suggestion led to our arrival, just the two of us, at my home, Chaumière Canot.

Madame Thibeault's dossier was a bit outdated. She had told Priscilla I lived with my widowed mother at Avondale, built in 1928 as a modernized replica of the von Trulimann castle in Bavaria. When my father died in 1960, Avondale's forty-two rooms were remodeled and refurbished to provide a new headquarters for the Faulkner Foundation. A suite of six rooms was set aside for my mother, chairman of the foundation. The "Garden Suite," as it was called, became her American residence, but in her heart, the Bavarian estate, where my father was buried, was "home." Shortly after his death, she expressed a desire to live for the remainder of her life in Bavaria, and this, coupled with her age and declining health, resulted in my becoming chairman of the board.

Priscilla was "all eyes" for Chaumière Canot, a separate residence on the grounds of Avondale, built on a steep slope descending to the waters of Long Island Sound. Originally the location of a small guest cottage and boat house for canoes, Canoe Cottage had acquired a much more pretentious name at the insistence of my mother when I had designed and constructed a six-level home and center of personal business activities. At the water level, the new boat housing is spacious enough to enclose my power cruiser, *Vitellus,* and above that is suspended a swimming pool surrounded by a large deck area adjacent to dressing rooms and a game room. Above, on the next level, is my bedroom, a guest room, and a personal office area. The top level consists of the main living area.

Priscilla's natural enthusiasm and exuberance, though more contained by the restricting processes of maturity, still sparkled with the excitement and delight of the eight-year-old tree climber discovering a highly desirable new tree to conquer. Our early supper conversation centered on the play, her classmates, and other friends, with the exception of Miss Karounin and

Tommy Highsmith, whose names seemed omitted by mutual accord. Priscilla's matter-of-fact attitude slowly gave way before squirming curiosity, and finally the squirm won out completely.

"Truly, this room is magnificent. Who designed it?"

"In essence, I did."

"But the amphitheatre effect—it's so unusual. There must be a reason."

"There is. It is an amphitheatre."

She paused, a big California strawberry impaled on a fork midway from dish to mouth, and waited, the eyes like two dots below two question marks.

"Finish your strawberries, Prissy, and I will give you my out-of-season Cook's tour. You will like it better in the summertime."

"Can I still see everything, every room?"

"Within reason, young lady, within reason."

In a small room just off the kitchen I said: "Press this button, and presto! we have a bar opening into the outer room." In an adjoining room, I pressed another button, and part of the wall opened to expose a round aperture. "Now watch through the opening—" I began pressing buttons, and opaque screens in decorative patterns descended from the perimeter beams, completely shutting off all window space. Simultaneously a large movie screen descended from the window wall facing the center of the tier seats, "—and you are now in Faulkner's Neighborhood Movie House."

"Do you really show real movies?"

"The very latest, the very oldest, anything your little heart desires."

"My little brain desires a drink. This is a bit overwhelming."

"Suppose we share a split of champagne, take our glasses along, and get a refill at a later stop in our tour?"

"Wonderful!"

I told Priscilla how the tiered room was used for many things besides movies: business meetings, lectures, community and foundation group meetings, presentations, musical auditions and intimate performances of musical groups and individuals, et cetera, et cetera.

We hit the road and wandered through my private offices, my bedroom, the sauna, the wine cellar, garage, utility rooms, and finally, on the way back to the stairs, the guest bedroom. It was a cold night, but she wanted to walk out on the balcony deck. From there Prissy spotted the swimming pool one floor below. It was empty and tarpaulin covered. "Oooh! When do you fill it?"

"In May."

"In May, may I come back and have a swim?" She turned to face me, and I noted a change in her expression. There was an earnestness I had not seen since our Kennedy and Mary Jo Kopechne discussion that first night on Lollipop Lane.

"Of course, and bring Tommy and Miss Karounin." The earnest look was disconcerting; I wanted to tease her out of it for some unknown reason.

"Leave them out of this!" She turned away and walked inside, her arms crossed and her hands rubbing cold shoulders. I came up behind her as she stood quietly studying the guest bedroom. I put both arms around her and hugged. I am an enthusiastic practitioner of hugging weather-chilled beautiful women. "This coat is vicuña," I said lightly. "When applied with pressure, it has a warming effect."

Without a word, she turned within the cylinder of my arms, placed two hands behind my head, pulled downward, and kissed me with what F. Scott Fitzgerald would probably call "reckless abandon."

Added years have slowed my reflexive reactions, and lack of practice has definitely dulled my technique. But nothing has affected my willingness to cooperate; it is as great as ever. Unfortunately, the quail had flushed itself and was halfway out of the room before the startled gunner could aim and fire. At the threshold of the door it looked back and burst out laughing. "Wipe the stun off your face, Lord Cornball, and let's go get that champagne refill you promised."

Docilely and dazedly I obeyed, picking up the two champagne glasses from the dressing-table top. Down the stairs, through a connecting hall, I led the way. We came to the game room, and I headed straight for the bar, then pulled a full-size Taittinger from the cooling rack below. A split after that kiss would be like covering a manhole with a thin dime—totally inadequate. We played a game of averting eyes while I uncorked and poured.

There had been hunger in Priscilla's kiss. My psychic antennae had picked up spiritual-need signals as bold and powerfully motivated as anything physical. Prissy was suffering what we all suffer from time to time: the "solitaire" feeling of life, the excruciating awareness of being "alone." Philosophy suggests turning inward to seek adjustment and acceptance through mental process. Religion, a more regimental philosophy, suggests seeking the God within or the God without through the spiritual process. But the need to avert and alleviate the hunger of the all alone begins and ends, in its most compelling and urgent form, with the human hope to find human response.

Priscilla, an adored and spoiled child growing to maturity, suddenly orphaned, had begun the process of personal philosophy, that I knew. And religious conviction was a part of her upbringing. Still, I sensed the hunger to receive, and give, the fulfillment that might well be called the process of love.

"Truly, is that a pool table under the cover?"

"Yes. Is expert handling of the cue another of your surprising accomplishments?"

"I've never learned, but it's very popular on campus. Do you give lessons?"

"Only to advanced players. My friend Timothy Batchelor teaches beginners. He's the champion in these parts and is very good at explaining the fundamentals. I only give pointers in the gamesmanship aspects."

"Such as—?"

"How to sneeze or cough or burp just as your opponent is making a crucial shot."

"That sounds as though you are returning to normal, milord. You had been showing signs of being 'shook up.' "

We were both sparring and we both knew it. The most difficult thing to recover is a spontaneous, volatile emotional situation that has come and gone. Compare it to solving a Chinese trick puzzle. Out of a thousand possibilities only one is correct, and the more you try, the more of a fool you can make of yourself. I decided to set aside the puzzle.

"Are you ready for the Inspector's taped opinion?"

"Would you forgive me if I said I am not in the mood?"

"Yes. Neither am I. Some other time. Is Tuesday your only 'night off'?"

"Tuesday and Sunday."

"I seldom fix door latches on Sunday—against union rules; but I could make an exception."

"If you will guarantee to fix that old latch, I'll cook your dinner, and you can meet all my roommates. They are anxious to meet you, and when they hear about Chaumière Canot, they'll be even more so."

"That's encouraging. Why don't we come back here for dessert, coffee, and the tape?"

"I'd rather spend my calories on more of this champagne."

"Sold!"

Seven: Visions and Voices

I am not certain of the proper word: presentiment, premonition, or precognition; but one of them must surely apply to the next chapter of this tale. We Pisceans are supposedly endowed with a very strong psychic sense. Well, maybe so and maybe not; my betting record at the tracks is just plain lousy. Then again, it may be the lack of psychic ability on the part of the horses, a failure to get through to me with straight information—just as my mechanical genius failed to repair Priscilla's door latch without a kibitzer. The offer of a Sunday dinner in return for the latch repair was accepted, and I arrived with a hastily assembled batch of tools sneakily borrowed from Chaumière Canot's several tool racks in the garage, the house workshop, and the laboratory. At least 90 percent of the curiously formed things were completely foreign to my experience as well as to my nature. Once past a screwdriver, a saw, a hammer, and a pair of pliers, modern tools begin to take on strange shapes that I find completely baffling.

On this particular rainy Sunday afternoon I arrived on Lollipop Lane with my tool assemblage and a large bouquet of mixed garden flowers from our greenhouse.

Priscilla met me at the door, and I was introduced to three of her five housemates: Lucy Mae Cantrell from the deep South, Peggy Marckstein from Chicago's North Shore, and Natalie O'Connor from St. Louis. Attractive, winsome young women, also bright and brainy, as I would come to realize. I was charmed and delighted and tried my best to make them feel the same. When the customary opening remarks and small talk shrank too far, I turned to an apron-adorned Priscilla: "What's cooking? The aroma is tantalizing!"

"A surprise! Do you like Mexican food?"

"One of my favorites. Am I allowed to peek into the kitchen?"

"Not now. This is a joint venture, with all four of us contributing, and we want you to relax and make yourself at home. If that means female companionship, we can rotate our chores so you won't be alone. Lucy and Peggy have dates coming later. Natalie and I are your dates; can you manage two at a time?"

"Indubitably!"

"I forgot to thank you for the flowers; they are lovely. And what is in the big bag, may I ask?"

"My tools. I promised to fix the door latch, remember?"

"Oh, that's not necessary, Truly. Do you really feel up to it?"

"A promise is a promise. Why don't I get started while the cooks tend to the dinner?"

"Okay, Mechanical Genius! There's the monster, and I'll give you an outside key." She pointed to the front door, and I had to agree, it was a monster—about fifteen inches wide, eight inches high, and almost two inches deep. It was black iron, with a huge wrought-iron key for the inside and a smaller key for outside use. I deposited my bag alongside the door and studied the thing with what I tried to project as confident, professional awareness. The girls were all watching.

"Need any help?" asked Peggy. "I'm the handyman around

70

here, but I've never been able to summon the courage to tackle that thing.''

"No thanks, Peggy. I'll just remove it from the door first, then take a look inside." I began spreading my tools out on the floor, and I think the array was a little overwhelming; they left me alone, and I was most thankful—already I was frightened of the consequences of a possibly rash promise, and I hadn't even touched the thing. However, it came off the door rather easily. It was held on by only four large screws sunk into the thick oak; they responded willingly to my screwdriver.

I carried the heavy iron box to a nearby table, pulled up a chair, and removed seven smaller screws holding what appeared to be a cover plate. Finally, I removed the cover plate. The damned thing absolutely disintegrated! Springs, gears, rods, and other indescribable metal pieces went in all directions. I was horrified! I sat in stunned silence hoping for the instant arrival of some natural catastrophe, such as a tornado or dam-break flood, to divert the attention of my hostesses.

"Trouble?" It was Peggy, suddenly materializing over my right shoulder. "We forgot to tell you it's not only a latch lock, it's a music box with chimes that play 'Yankee Doodle.' "

Now, I am not a deeply religious person, although I do have a firm belief in the Almighty. But I've always figured He's got so many supplicants coming to Him at all hours of the day and night that in a crisis like this, where I am desperately in need, it is only fair to first petition, say, a good Irish saint. So I petitioned, and a most peculiar inspirational form of advisory assistance came through. I heard myself saying: "No, Peggy, not really. Nothing serious, but this thing will have to be soaked in Casper oil, or it will never work properly after I repair it."

"Casper oil?"

"Yes. This is a very old lock made in Dusseldorf. See, it's stamped on the plate—*Dusseldorf Metalworken*. Locks of this kind have a tendency to go to pieces unless they are soaked in

Casper oil every few years, especially if they have chimes.''

''Oh!'' She was too baffled to say more, or too kind. Very few people know that Johnny Balken, our top engineer at Chaumière Canot, has the middle name Casper. He is a bit touchy about it. ''I'll need a small box,'' I said matter-of-factly, ''and may I use your phone?''

It was an unhappy situation. Not only had I been tried and found wanting in Mrs. Rogers's past appraisal of my talents, there was also the matter of a delightful Mexican feast obtained under false pretenses. I called Johnny and entered a plaintive plea for help. He came by, carried away the pieces in the box, and returned the lock in perfect working order two hours later. We replaced it on the door, and then I spent several strained moments, after Johnny left, explaining to Peggy the special effect of Casper oil on old iron.

To appease my doubly disturbed conscience, I took the whole group back to Chaumière Canot after dinner to see a new movie a producer friend had sent out for my enjoyment. During the movie I suddenly remembered the avowed purpose of the evening—a playback of the Inspector's opinion for Priscilla—so after the film ended, an apology was in order: ''I forgot about the Inspector's tape with champagne, Priscilla.''

''I didn't. But the movie was terrific, and everyone enjoyed it. We are surrounded by officially unapproved listeners for the tape. What do we do?''

''Tuesday night?''

''Tuesday night is fine.''

I still recall most vividly Priscilla's enthralled fascination with Inspector Darby's recorded accounting of the events surrounding the death of Mary Jo Kopechne. The strange parallel between his theory and her stream-of-thought composition might well be termed a marvel of intuitive coincidence. And when I told her of my own inner compulsion to seek out the truth, beginning with the moment when I felt compelled to leave

72

Pidg Paley's yachting group in Edgartown, there seemed to be a welding of our spiritual selves, an undeniable bond of something I am unable to explain. It was this, at least in part, that led to a pattern of Tuesday and Sunday "dating" that continued into the spring of 1970. Then one of our Tuesdays had to be canceled when I received an urgent call from my mother in London. She had decided to dispose of her Paris abode, there was an offer by a prospective purchaser, and she wanted my advice and assistance as soon as possible. Intending to return on an early-morning 747 flight from Heathrow airport near London on the following Sunday, I made a date with Priscilla for dinner. On the flight to London I found my mind applying itself to a form of speculation reminiscent of my more youthful days. Where is she now? what is she doing? is she thinking of me?—that sort of thing.

Mother and I have always been very close, and she reads me as a third-grader's book—quick and easy. She never cared much for Dolly, Priscilla's sister, why I never knew. Mothers appraising other females in a relationship with their sons may not give one a succession of correlated facts in expressing their opinion in such matters; the word is passed by shades of difference in attitude, delicate gradations of voice tone, and subtle variations in facial expression. But you get the point! Slowly but surely, the baroness drew me out about Priscilla, and, somewhat to my surprise, all attitudes, voice tones, and facial expressions were "affirmative" and "go." This is probably one reason why I didn't hesitate to do what I did on the following Saturday at the home of her very dear friend Sir Arthur Bosewater, near London.

It happened during an early-morning stroll through the formal garden for which the Bosewater estate is justly famous. I had stopped to stare at a cloud bank on the horizon and to wonder whether a spring shower was on the way. Suddenly, a strange vision came into my consciousness: I saw Priscilla's

73

face, chalk white, eyes closed, surrounded by a boiling dark gray cloud. Poking out of the cloud on one side was what appeared to be the face of the Parliament-tower clock, Big Ben, and under it a pendulum swung back and forth. The sensory feeling of PRISCILLA–DANGER–TIME was overwhelming. Within minutes I made brief apologies to my fellow guests, expressed sincere regrets to my host and hostess, asked Mother to forgive me, packed my bag, and left Sir Arthur's estate for Heathrow and the first plane out for New York. Call it, as I said, presentiment, premonition, or precognition, I knew I had to get to New York and to Priscilla. Something was wrong, and it concerned her in a deadly serious way.

My plane was late in landing, and I didn't reach a phone until after nine o'clock. I called the OoLaLa restaurant. Madame objects to phone calls for the girls during the serving hours, so I asked for Madame and gave my late arrival from London as the excuse for calling.

"Faulkner, she leave here not ten minutes ago feeling very bad. You call her at home and you take good care of her. She have Natalie with her but you get her doctor. Comprennez-vous?"

"Je comprends et vous remercie, Madame."

I hung up and immediately called Priscilla's home number. There was no answer. I grabbed a cab and headed for Chaumière Canot. Twice we stopped, and I called—still no answer on Lollipop Lane. That dark-cloud thing I had experienced in London now had me frantically worried. This was not the first time I had received premonitory warnings in my life.

As the taxi driver began unloading bags at my front door, Pim came running down the path from his cottage.

"Miss Priscilla very sick. Miss Natalie call from school nurse's room. Miss Priscilla say she want see you quick now right away! This is number!"

"Thanks, Pim, take care of the driver and the bags." I gave

him a twenty-dollar bill and rushed into the house. When Natalie got on the phone, it was obvious she was scared; her voice was trembling. Priscilla was on a cot in the college nurse's quarters, in great pain and almost unconscious, temperature 103 degrees. The pain was in the lower abdomen. They had been trying for half an hour to get in touch with the college doctor without success. The nurse was just going to call the village police. I told her to go ahead, but that I would have a doctor and ambulance there in twenty minutes or less. When I hung up, Pim was standing alongside me with his hands clasped tightly. He is very fond of Priscilla.

"Pim, get on the kitchen phone. Get Captain Berky and the emergency wagon. Have the crew meet us at the main gate in five minutes. I'll meet you in the garage."

Captain Berky is head of the Security and Emergency force for Avondale. I called Pat Johnson, my secretary, and told her to reach Dr. Wickstrum, our family doctor and surgeon, give him the college main-entrance address, then get an ambulance, any ambulance, to come to the same address and meet us. And be standing, Pat, in front of Avondale House in five minutes. Now that sounds like one helluva group of instructions to give and expect execution of, but Pat Johnson can do it, and did it. The emergency wagon was waiting when Pim, Pat, and I arrived. I gave the wagon driver the college address and let them lead us with their siren. Natalie had not been explicit in how to find the nurse's quarters on the campus, so I left one of the emergency crew at the entrance gate with a walkie-talkie taken from the wagon. When we found the nurse, I took another walkie-talkie and radioed back the campus street directions for the doctor and the ambulance.

Captain Berky and his other man had entered the nurse's quarters, taken one look at Priscilla, and come back for the wagon's stretcher. She was totally unconscious. Then we heard the ambulance warbler, and my talk box came alive: The doctor and the ambulance had arrived at the gate at the same time and were on their way through the campus. I motioned to Captain Berky to put the stretcher back as Natalie came running out of the building teary eyed. Before she could say anything, Dr. Wickstrum arrived, and I asked her to guide him inside to Priscilla. The ambulance men followed and in seconds were back and removing their wheeled stretcher. I couldn't go in. I knew I would see a chalk-white face with closed eyes instead of the peach-blossom cheeks, grinning lips, and devil-take-the-hindmost blue eyes. And at that moment I knew I couldn't take it. Pisceans can be awful softies, real breaker-uppers, in an emotional situation. I felt sick deep down in the pit of my stomach. Had I come too late?

"Truly—" It was the doctor. "It's the appendix, I believe, and it's probably ruptured. We have very little time. I called Harbor Shore General and alerted the staff. We will very likely operate as soon as possible. I want to go with the girl in the ambulance. Can someone drive my car to the hospital?"

"Of course, Ben. Will she be all right?"

"Time, Truly, time. I think we are in time, but I can't say anything for sure at this point. God willing, she'll be all right."

A county police car arrived, offered an escort to the hospital, and it was accepted at once. Just before they pulled away, remembering Pim's message from Priscilla and hoping she might just be conscious and recognize me, I stuck my head in through the side door of the ambulance. There it was—the dark cloud, the white face with closed eyes, the clock, and the pendulum. Only, it was a dark gray blanket tucked all around Priscilla's head to keep out the cold night air, a white face, an oxygen-tank pressure dial, and an oxygen mask swinging from an overhead hook. I drew back in shocked recognition of the symbolism.

Pat arranged for one of the emergency-crew men to drive the doctor's car, then Pim drove us to the hospital: me, Pat, and

Natalie. Natalie tried to give us a description of earlier events, but she was slightly incoherent with anxiety. For me, it was in one ear and out the other. I was too busy bypassing the Irish saints and going straight to the Head Man. I felt sure He was listening. Who else could have arranged that dark-cloud thing in England?

We sat in a small waiting room for nearly two hours; then Ben Wickstrum came in.

"Ruptured appendix, badly infected, but we were in time, Truly. She'll be okay. And you look like a Chinese opium eater. Pat told me you came in from London tonight. Go home and take these. Come back at two o'clock in the afternoon. I'll be here. And I'll be in touch if it is necessary. Good-night."

"Thanks, Ben!" I was so relieved, there was just nothing more to be said. I took the small box. He was right, I needed sleep. Almost twenty-four hours had passed since I awakened on a Saturday morning in the quiet, peaceful countryside of Merrie Olde England.

Because of the hour, I invited Natalie to stay in the guest room and return with me later to see Priscilla. When we arrived at Chaumière Canot, Pat made Natalie comfortable with the necessities, then returned to her apartment in Avondale House. I swallowed my two pills and prepared for bed. Then a thought struck me. Had I saved Priscilla's life? What would have happened if there had been no vision? if I had not acted so positively in every step taken after it appeared to me? And what internal or external force made me so damned positive in the first place? I had accepted so much for so little reason.

Priscilla's recovery was slow but steady after a touch-and-go situation for the first four days. Dr. Wickstrum's confident attitude never faltered, at least not in my presence, but human instinct can sometimes sniff out more peril than human speech and demeanor can hide. I was sure there were some very bad moments never reported to me before the antibiotics conquered

77

the spread of the abdominal infection. She was fortunate in a way; not too many years ago a ruptured appendix meant almost certain peritonitis and a very small chance of survival.

When Priscilla was ready for discharge from the hospital, Ben Wickstrum indicated that a long recovery period should be expected, with absolute rest a requisite. I moved her into the guest bedroom at Chaumière Canot and arranged for the care and attention of a nurse-companion during her convalescence.

The incident of the premonitory warning deepened my interest in a subject moving more and more into the public consciousness of today: ESP, extrasensory perception. With Priscilla off the critical list, I spoke at length over the phone with my mother in England, giving her the entire story of the strange vision and the subsequent happenings. She must have repeated my story to Sir Arthur, because I received a letter from him asking that the complete details be put in writing and forwarded to a venerable institution with which he was involved, the British Society for Psychical Research, at Number One Adam and Eve Mews in London. The address alone was enough to stimulate my interest. I found myself wishing that Chaumière Canot could be listed at Number One Adam and Eve Mews rather than the dull, prosaic 220 Roosevelt Drive. The incident of the vision has been set forth here almost verbatim as it was described in my reply to Sir Arthur's request.

As for my interest in ESP, I am still wondering about the forces that seem to have ordained that this story itself be written, forces that seem to have brought about a procession of events leading step by step to Inspector Charles Darby's highly detailed explication of the Chappaquiddick incident. An interesting interpretation came to light during the latter part of Priscilla's convalescence, in April. Still physically weak but suffering the mental restlessness of the convalescent, she suggested a dinner guest, Charles Darby. The Inspector had provided a typewritten copy of his memoirs for her amusement, and she was loaded with questions and comment.

"Charles," Priscilla remarked after dinner, "your memoirs must have at least a dozen marvelous mystery plots. Your book reads like an Ellery Queen anthology. My father was a nut on Ellery, and I used to sneak-read his stories—much more fun than Louisa May Alcott. May I ask a very personal question?"

"How do I compare myself with Ellery Queen?" The Inspector pretended shock.

"Oh, no. Quite different. Was there ever a time when you just wanted to throw up your hands and walk away, when there seemed to be no answer to a who-done-it?"

"Naturally, and more often than I care to recall."

"Then what does a great detective do in a situation like that?"

Charles chuckled. Still, I knew he was most pleased to be the *great* detective in Priscilla's eyes.

"I am not sure I should give away professional secrets to a competitor sleuth such as you, Priscilla. After all, you never told me how you evolved the Chappaquiddick solution presented in your term paper, and that was something not too easy to come by, a highly professional job of deduction expressed in a most remarkable way!"

Prissy tried desperately to find the handle for a proper show of humility, but failed: "That *was* pretty good, wasn't it? And I really do hate to admit it wasn't deduction but plain old so-called woman's intuition."

"Never underestimate intuition, young lady. It is the *great* detective's greatest ally! And sometimes, when you are at your wit's end, it is your *only* ally!"

"Then what do you do?"

"Bring your psychic abilities into play and give them absolutely free reign. The conscious mind has failed; let the subcon-

79

scious prevail. I have my own peculiar way of going about this, but I won't bore you with details. Do you remember the chapter in my memoirs about the missing artifacts hidden in the French château during wartime?''

"Of course. You solved that one by measuring the great hall inside and out and finding the walls to be too thick. I guessed that from what you wrote, even though you didn't explain it in detail."

"No. It was probably implied by my statement that the solution was a matter of measurement, leaving you to believe I had done as you said and found something wrong. Not so. I must admit I skirted the whole truth on that one as a matter of pride. The facts may come as more of a surprise to Truly than to you, Priscilla. Remember, I was never at the actual scene, and to be perfectly honest, it simply did not occur to me in the beginning that the walls had been tampered with. In prewar and postwar photographs of the château provided by the investigators, the exterior and interior walls looked exactly the same, and the Nazis took care to restore all the furnishings to the original arrangement. Every possible hiding place in and around the château was painstakingly examined. So, like many others, I came to the conclusion that the artifacts had been removed and shipped elsewhere. I concentrated on the various probabilities and got no further than my colleagues.

"Very, very much discouraged, the case having been brought to me as a last resort by the Allied authorities, I decided to 'play hooky,' as you Americans say, and just go sailing—to ease my worries.

"On my second day out from port, right in the middle of a very nasty squall, I began to have mental flashes of the great-hall photos, with strange lines drawn across them. Even at the height of the squall winds, when I was completely occupied with preventing a swamping or capsizing, interior scenes of the hall continued to stir in my mind. To keep on course, I was doing a bit of mental triangulation with two dimly seen but familiar landmarks off my starboard.

"Suddenly, I knew exactly what to do in the château case. My home port was a full day's sailing away, much too far for my impatience. I began a downwind beat for a nearby port. Putting in there, I acquired motor transportation and arrived at the Yard about ten o'clock that night. Within minutes I had drawn perspective lines on the prewar and postwar interior photos from an exact same spot in the foreground to the far corners of the long hall. If the angles of the lines were not identical, it meant the corners of the room had been moved. The angles were not identical; the postwar hall was narrower. Because of its original great size, the difference had not been noticed. Angular measurements indicated that the wall paneling had been moved toward the center of the hall from both sides. I suggested that an opening be made in one wall to check my theory, and the artifacts were found.

"What I experienced during the squall, Truly, was a form of clairvoyance similar to your experience at Sir Arthur's estate. And it solved the château case. Under great stress and strain or under the most commonplace conditions, the mind can perform marvelous deeds, given its freedom to act subconsciously. Intuition acts in a similar manner."

"Well, I'll be damned!" It was my very own spontaneous little outburst, and Priscilla seconded me.

"That makes two of us! Charles, that's a fantastic story. Why didn't you explain all that in your memoirs?"

"What? And have my devotion to duty shamed by every member of dear old Scotland Yard, past, present, and future? No thank you! Yard Inspectors are not supposed to play hooky and go sailing off into the sunset when assigned to a case. I am swearing you both to secrecy right now!"

"Agreed, you ol' cheat," I said. "And may I ask a question now?"

"Of course, after you have Pim replace the old cheat's brandy."

"Agreed again." I motioned to Pim and continued: "Your concept of the Chappaquiddick incident seems to me to be amazingly complete even without the details in the secret inquest testimony that will eventually be released. Was there ever a time when those psychic forces of yours piped into the Kennedy situation?"

Charles did not hesitate: "Yes, more than once. I confess my deductive reasoning powers may be getting a bit rusty with old age. However, there seems to be a compensation factor in increased psychic impressions. Truly is fairly familiar with my normal modus operandi, Priscilla, a little something I call pivotal thinking."

He swung a smiling face in my direction for a moment, and I was perfectly content to let sleeping hippopotamuses lie. I had accomplished very little with my own brand of pivotal thinking, even with his patient coaching. Charles glanced at Priscilla as if to ask if this was too much serious conversation at the late hour for a convalescent young lady. The glowing, rapt expression on her face while he was talking should have been enough, but she read the look and hastened to reassure the inspector.

"Please go on, Charles. I am quite all right."

He nodded and went on: "Now, in relation to Chappaquiddick, when you first brought up the subject, Truly, and left me with your collection of photos and data, I did feel a bit put upon because of my endeavor to please your publisher friend in meeting his deadlines. Oh, I admit I was intrigued by the circumstances surrounding the bridge incident. No doubt about that. But it *was* an intrusion on my memoir effort."

I started to offer a belated apology. He anticipated me and held up the traffic cop's flat-palm stop signal.

"Not important," he emphasized. "I could have said no, and well might have, except for a white mouse that began scampering around in the farther recesses of my mind, squeaking away to be noticed, urging me to give every possible attention to your request for an opinion." He was showing amusement with his smile; still, there was a depth of seriousness not to be overlooked. I nodded my understanding.

"I studied your compendium and tried to dismiss it temporarily from my thoughts. Then, through no conscious wish or effort on my part, a series of thought visions began occurring at odd moments. Scenes descriptive of Senator Kennedy's story were followed almost immediately by scenes somehow related but completely different. As is my longtime custom, I made written notes of all this and began applying my own reasoning to certain situations as we then knew them, Faulkner. Gradually, piece by piece, a wholly new concept of the sequence of events began taking shape. Finally, the pattern was complete, and obvious—to me at least. I could see no other answer. All that remained for my own absolute conviction was the tie to what sworn witnesses would say in the inquest testimony.

"As you know, I am into that now. I conclude from all this that perhaps I *can* contribute something of value about Chappaquiddick; generally speaking, any form of genuine clairvoyance does have good purpose. And it may well be you have been right all along, Truly, in suggesting that strange forces have been at work—upon all three of us."

A fortnight later, returning to Chaumière Canot after a full day in Manhattan, I stopped by the greenhouse to pick up the daily bouquet for Prissy. Moments later I knocked and walked into her room with my usual be-bright-cheer-up-the-patient smile, the flowers, and a watch from Cartier's. The flowers were received with feminine gratitude. I will not go into the reception given the watch. Women can go a little overboard about things like that, and I find it difficult choosing an adequate group of descriptive terms.

When she finally climbed back into the boat and we were once more resting on an even keel, I inquired:

"How's the schoolgirl?"

"Fine. All homework completed, and the student is ravenous with hunger for Madame Thibeault's specialties!"

This was a big night for Priscilla, her first time out for dinner since the emergency operation seven weeks past. Mrs. Gahagan, the nurse-companion, had been gone for two weeks, and Priscilla had resumed her studies by special arrangement with the college for off-campus tutoring. The wasted, pale look of the early convalescent days had disappeared, replaced by that special suffusion of coloring that makes Priscilla and *prismatic* almost synonymous.

Madame Thibeault had offered to deliver dinner every night for the past week, but Dr. Wickstrum had been adamant about diet: no deviations from the hospital nutritionist's selections—until tonight.

Our arrival at the OoLaLa was the signal for a complete cessation of all normal activity by the restaurant staff while Priscilla was welcomed. Madame's clientele was fairly constant, and the diners were, for the most part, aware of Priscilla's serious illness. They, too, joined in the welcome. Natalie, in whom I had confided the story of the premonition, evidently passed it along, for Madame Thibeault, in an aside to me, said I had been blessed as an angel of mercy, or something to that effect. Angels of mercy must have a very special place in Madame's scheme of things: For the first and only time in my more than twenty years of patronage, no ragtag slip of paper awaited my departure. On the morrow I sent flowers and a note of appreciation.

Priscilla was allowed, by doctor's orders, three glasses of champagne in celebration. With the OoLaLa back to normal, we were seated and soon reached the second refill.

"There seems to be a general feeling that you saved my life, Truly. I now propose a toast to my favorite lifeguard!"

"Thank you, my dear! And will you please stay in the wading pool hereafter? Crossing the Atlantic to affect a rescue is not in the line of ordinary duty and leaves me a little short of breath."

"Nut! Since when are you complaining about a gorgeous, sexy young woman taking up residence under the same roof with you?"

"I'm not complaining. I just think she was overpaid for the work she did."

"Overpaid? Who?"

"Mrs. Gahagan."

"The middle-aged, gray-haired Mrs. Gahagan is not the gorgeous, sexy woman I'm referring to. I mean the one who is returning to Lollipop Lane this weekend, leaving a scented note of deepest appreciation for her benefactor."

"When did you make this decision?"

"The moment I realized I wanted never to leave. Excuse me, I want to tell Natalie to expect me Saturday."

She walked away hurriedly. I reached down with both arms, picked up two thumbs, and began to twiddle. I was conspicuous by her absence. The bar at OoLaLa is not really a bar; it is a large round table in a rear alcove, with all the ingredients made available. If one feels so inclined, one mixes one's own drink, and one wanders, perchance one wants to wander, through a small door to a small garden, and one sits perchance on a wide old-fashioned swing and swings. I mixed, I wandered, I sat, I swung.

Never to leave . . . never to leave . . . never to leave . . . the squeak of the old swing sang a song. I swung through a dry martini on the rocks, got up, got a refill, glanced toward our empty table, went back to the singing swing, requested my favorite song, and pushed off again. Priscilla appeared in the door frame, a picture that needed no framing.

"Drink up. Dinner's ready in five minutes," she ordered.

Madame and Priscilla had conspired over the telephone for days, and I had no choices to make, except how to get out of

85

my chair without use of a derrick when the meal was finished. During dinner Priscilla remarked:

"I was so disappointed not to join you and Charles here the other night, Truly, but there was all that classwork to catch up, and Dr. Wickstrum had set tonight as my back-to-normal debut."

"We realized that. It was our loss, but we bore up manfully."

"After how many drinks?"

"I can't speak for Charles, but I stopped crying in my beer about my second martini."

"What did he say about the testimony? Did he discuss it at all?"

It was now May of 1970, and the Kopechne inquest testimony had been publicly released. I had obtained a copy for Inspector Darby's study.

"Priscilla, Charles appears to me to be more deeply concerned with the truth about Chappaquiddick than I ever imagined he would be, but there is a certain closemouthed attitude about it on his part now, something I have heard him refer to in the past as the 'official investigation' status, meaning he will not discuss details until there is a whole-ball-of-wax of some kind."

"When do you think that will be?"

"I honestly don't know—a month, two months, six months. In the meantime, I doubt if he will give out 'here and there' details for our edification. We know the general outline of his thinking and quite a few details, but relating all that to the inquest testimony and the judge's report is something entirely different in his eyes. During an official investigation the Scotland Yard Inspector does not answer random personal questions nor offer explanatory comments to such as you and me. That's how serious he has become about this thing. Which leads me to a question for you, Miss Psychology Master."

"Yes?"

"Just how do you feel about the Inspector's 'visions,' or whatever you call them, about Chappaquiddick?"

"The proper word would be 'clairvoyance,' as Charles said. He told us his reasoning powers were growing rusty with old age; he might better say his psychic powers are improving with use. Psychologists do admit that psychic powers exist, you know, at least this neophyte does. Charles's entire adult life has been spent in development toward unusual, paranormal mental powers, whether he realizes it or not. The gathering of facts, impressions, both concrete and abstract, and the sorting of emotions, sentiments, and other motivating factors are as natural to him as breathing. Observation, correlation, and concentration are tightly woven into his psyche. The result *can be* psychic powers and phenomena you and I could never analyze or define, just accept."

"How does my Big Ben–clock thing get into an act of *that* kind?"

"That was clairvoyance of the premonition type. Could happen to anyone. Also impossible to clearly define and explain. As so often happens, it came to you not as pictured reality, but as 'allegorical vision.' And you acted on it—for which I am most grateful!"

"For which I am most grateful, too! One more question, teacher—"

"Go ahead—"

"—where did you get all those stream-of-consciousness thoughts of Mary Jo's in your term paper?"

She hesitated. I think the question caught her completely by surprise, and for several moments I thought she would not answer.

Then: "Truly, I have sworn to myself I would never answer a question like that." There was another long pause. "However, since you and Charles and I seem to be in the same boat, I might as well tell you. I *heard* most of it—word for word—spoken in a female voice that was at times gay and lively, and at others, trembling and pleading. The word this time is 'clairaudience,' not something you visualize but something you hear."

I felt a shivery little streak traveling up, down, and around my back like a badly frightened spider bent on escape from a murderous pursuer.

"The song lyrics, the Kennedy-speech excerpts, the quotations, were you already familiar with them, Priscilla?"

"With none of them, except possibly one or two of the quotations."

"And the Catholic prayers?"

"I am a born and bred Presbyterian, you know that."

"You didn't just dream up that line about 'Camelot, where are you now'?"

"I *heard* it!"

"Oh, dear Lord!"

"Truly, can we change the subject? This is depressing."

"Of course." I signaled Natalie for more coffee, then turned back to Priscilla with my damned-glad-to-change-the-subject-let's-talk-about-how-beautiful-you-are smile, while my mind raced madly with tactics and stratagems to keep her at Canoe Cottage. On Saturday she returned to Lollipop Lane, but my efforts were not entirely without result.

While sipping carefully from a steaming-hot cup of coffee, I managed a few remarks concerning the dangers of a sudden change of living conditions during a convalescence, each of which was flicked aside by Priscilla as though they were solitary ants invading a picnic tablecloth. Then some degree of inspired genius struck me, and I remarked:

"Priscilla, what are you going to do after you get your psychology masters degree in June?"

"Go forth into the world job-hunting with high hopes, like everyone else in my class."

"Would you be interested in coming to work with me?"

"But what would I do?"

"You know the kind of things I become interested in and develop in the lab at Chaumière Canot. I need someone to organize and execute certain details in some of these involvements. We call it project managing."

"Do I work for you or for the foundation?"

"For me. Money for development of Chaumière Canot projects comes out of my pocket, not the foundation funds. There will be a desk for you in the office space where Pat Johnson works, and you will receive all the fringe benefits that Pat and the foundation employees receive. Your starting salary will be two hundred and fifty dollars a week, if that is satisfactory."

"Doesn't Pat Johnson do what you are talking about me doing?" There was the vague hint of a note of suspicion in her tone and manner, as though Devious Dapper Dan might now be invading with a whole army of ants. Choosing my words carefully, I replied:

"She's swamped handling foundation matters and personal things for me; she never gets involved in what I'm talking about now."

"Is there something specific you have in mind for me to do?"

"Yes. In the research lab we have developed a new system for encouraging and teaching youngsters in school to speak out confidently in group discussions. A small TV screen is placed before each pupil in a group discussion about history, art, current events, and so forth, and in turn each lights up with questions, answers, or comments that the child reads. Each series of messages is preprogramed to tie in properly with the general discussion, and the children gain a sense of participation in give-and-take conversation. School authorities who have tested the system with shy and reticent pupils—and there are many of them in every class—are quite enthusiastic about the results and the potential.

"Now that we have passed beyond the technical-detail development, I need someone to manage an applications program, and it seems to me your training in psychology is ideal. The Trulex system, as we call it, is based on developing the human psychological need, adult as well as child, to readily and openly communicate one with another.''

There was a long silence. Impulsively her fingers went to the temple seeking long strands to pull on, but the hairstyle for the evening would not permit her usual method of contemplation and thought marshaling. For some reason, I thought of the Inspector, and inspiration struck again.

"Priscilla," I said, "there is one other thing I would want you to do this summer. When Charles and I had dinner here the other night, he had very little to say about the inquest testimony, but I made a suggestion that he agreed with. I made it half-jokingly, but the great detective picked me up on it quite seriously and rather heartily, much to my surprise.

"I reminded him of the night of Kennedy's TV speech when fifteen people on Pidg Paley's boat unanimously agreed that something was smelly in Denmark, that the full truth had yet to be told. It would be impossible to gather the same fifteen persons again, but I proposed to Charles that he present his final analysis and opinion to another group of fifteen or more just to see what their reaction to *his* explanation would be—would it be more readily believed?"

Still in her meditative mood, she was soft-spoken in remarking: "I think he's hit it right on the nose, barring maybe a few minor details that will show up in the testimony. But what's your idea got to do with me?"

"I need someone to select a method of presenting his opinion to such a group and to execute all details. If you were working for me, that would be part of your job later this summer."

That was the clincher. I had chosen the correct fly to cast into Priscilla's still pond, and the trout struck with exuberance. Suddenly, she was again the daring tree climber, bubbling with suppressed excitement and on venture bent.

"You couldn't possibly do such a thing properly without my help, Mr. T. I will now have my allowable third glass of champagne and drink to my brilliant future as your employee." This time there was no mistaking it—her lips *were* puckered in the impulse of a blown kiss, and it wasn't tiny, far from it! I felt an almost irresistibly insane desire to rear back in my chair and shout Hallelujah!

Eight: Guess Who's Coming to Lunch

"Sir, Miss Pat say champagne cocktails at one o'clock and buffet at one thirty; cocktails in game room at six thirty and dinner on pool deck from seven to seven thirty."

Pim's statement was a question without a question mark. I was not being told; I was being asked. His years of service as houseman for three navy admirals in the Philippines, Hawaii, and Newport have set a pattern that I could never change. Pim will "caucus" with Pat Johnson and others on planning social, business, or foundation activities within Chaumière Canot, and then, in those areas of his responsibility, make no move until he has stated to me precisely what he plans to do. The final okay must come from my spoken approval.

"Very good, Pim. Who do you have to help you?"

"Kotu and Nadia." Kotu serves table in the executive dining room at Avondale; Nadia is his daughter.

"We will serve the champagne cocktails before luncheon only, Pim, and nothing after that. No wine with the buffet. What do we have planned for dinner?"

"Shish kebab on the pool-deck grill, sir."

"Excellent. I will leave the choice of wine to you with this suggestion: It will be a very warm evening; we will serve on the pool-deck tables outside; perhaps a chilled rosé."

"Right on, sir." I successfully stifled a chuckle. Pim is very proud of his use of mod language.

My breakfast tray and the Sunday newspapers had been placed on the deck table outside my bedroom door. I noticed a mischievous, conspiratorial light in Pim's eyes when I bent forward in my chair to begin the grapefruit and read the headlines. As he retreated through the bedroom door, my eyes were covered by soft, cool fingers, and a deep, ominous voice said: "Guess who!"

I paused, thinking hard, then made a stab: "Edward G. Robinson."

"No, guess again!"

"Robinson Crusoe."

"No, but that's close."

"Enrico Caruso's ghost."

"Right! Complete with filmy ectoplasm!"

I turned to look over my shoulder at the apparition. I was surprised and disappointed to find, instead of Enrico, a very lush, softly rounded female body outlined in detail by sunlight sifting through layers and layers of ectoplasm. Caruso was the greatest tenor of all time, and I pride myself on the collection I have made of his old recordings. To be visited by his ghost would be thrilling to say the least. Now you can understand my disappointment.

The erstwhile ghost gave me a pecky kiss on the cheek, and I recognized the touch; it was "the girl next door," my weekend guest.

"Prissy, you should not frighten me like that!"

"I didn't know you were afraid of ghosts."

"Not the ghost, the sunlight through that naked-as-a-jay thing you are wearing."

She turned to glance over her shoulder at the sun, then, with an impish grin, sank quickly into a chair, and said: "I asked Pim to serve my breakfast out here with you. May I stay?"

93

"Very well," I tried not to be condescending, "but stay under the umbrella; sunlight goes through that stuff like radar through clouds. These Polaroid glasses give me the impression I am examining X-rays of a Priscilla Rogers without bones."

"How horrible! But I did not notice you turning your head away."

The impish grin again as I hastened to change the subject: "What time did you arrive from New York?"

"About one thirty. I peeked at your window. You were sound asleep."

"I have a long day ahead, Peeping Prissy. When am I to be honored by the committee with details?"

"Pat will be here in thirty or forty minutes. She will brief you on the battle plan, Herr General. She is my briefing officer." It was my turn to grin—at the title and the staffing. I had approved the "battle plan" in essence, but I was not aware of the details. This day, a sunny Sunday in the late summer of 1970, I would see the results of Priscilla's maiden voyage as a project manager. In July, when the Inspector informed me he was ready to offer his final analysis and opinion on the Chappaquiddick incident, I had formally given Miss Rogers the assignment: organize and execute Veritas. She promptly gained the enthusiastic support and cooperation of Pat Johnson and Tommy Highsmith and appointed them to her ways and means committee, as she called it.

Incidentally, my rather pompous title was eventually spelled backward by the committee to become Satire Cinq. I have never asked for an explanation. Experience with committees has taught me that there simply are no explanations for much that they do.

"Guess who's coming to lunch, Truly!"

"Edward G. Robinson and Sidney Poitier."

"Now don't start that again!"

94

"All right. Who is coming to lunch?"

"Mia Joycelyn, my friend from Iowa. She is driving out from the city with Noland Hammond and Paul Walters."

"That is not what I would call 'failsafe' company. Two lecherous rakes in search of a falling leaf."

Pim placed her tray on the table, and I continued: "Eat your breakfast, then tell me all about what's-her-name. Start at the top of her head and work your way down. When you reach her ankles, I'll tell you how much more I want to know. And don't talk with your mouth full; it is not becoming to a chief of staff!"

"Yes, Daddy," she replied in a child-actor voice. "And may I say you need a shave? And something a little more in adornment than that ten-year-old robe? Please wear the new robe I gave you. I spent a whole day picking it out."

Ten minutes later, shaved and showered, I modeled the new robe. It was not so much of a robe, more of a toga—folds and folds of maroon velour with white and gold trim along the edges. There were instructions on how to stand and walk holding the folds in the best patrician style. Included in the package was a laurel wreath, which rested on my head perfectly after a little adjustment.

I thought the toga thing quite becoming, and when I returned to the deck outside my bedroom, Prissy was dazzled by my Romanesque appearance. And, as so often happens when a person is greatly awed, she laughed hysterically. Then a voice descended upon us from above.

"Hail Nero!" We looked up to find Pat Johnson leaning over the terrace-room deck railing. "May I come down and join the old Roman's orgy?" she asked.

"Of course," I replied lustily. "The more the orgier."

Pat Johnson, London born and bred, is my indispensable necessity, my alter ego in the daily conduct of my work with the foundation and outside interests. She is my executive secretary by title, but far more the Mother Superior by nature. She runs a tight ship in her domain of responsibilities.

Pat came through my bedroom door and stood staring silently. I stared back. Finally she spoke: "Would you mind standing up in that thing?"

Solemnly I rose, draped myself according to the instructions, and waited for the complimentary applause. Instead, I found I had another hysterical woman on my hands. Not until I stalked into my dressing room with great dignity and head held high did I understand why they were laughing. My laurel wreath was missing several leaves, sort of an end-of-the-season effect that somehow they found amusing.

There was fresh coffee waiting when I reappeared in more circumspect and contemporary costume, and reconciliation was in the air, even though for some inexplicable reason Pat and Priscilla seemed to be averting my steadfast gaze. They had papers spread out before them on the table, and I said: "I don't want to read things. Just talk, Pat."

"The luncheon guests will arrive about noon and the Inspector about two fifteen—he telephoned regrets because of an after-church meeting. By two thirty everyone should be in their proper places and you can make the introductory. Here it is in outline and some detail. After that the testimony script will be followed using the Trulex readers."

"Have our guests been properly briefed on the entire proceeding and on the use of the Trulex system?"

"Yes. Each participant has already received a procedure outline and an explanation of the individual parts each is to play, with the suggestion that they speak with me or Priscilla during luncheon if there are any questions."

The plan was simple. Charles Darby had arranged a succession of excerpts from the Kopechne inquest testimony presenting what he thought was the most relevant material; the excerpts had been edited and condensed, the extraneous wording eliminated, without changing the meaning in any respect. Then, in proper order the excerpts were recorded on the Trulex videotape in computer sequence and time-feed control, with manual override under my control. Priscilla had managed to combine two assignments: find applications for the Trulex system and create a method of presenting the Inspector's opinion.

Thirteen of our friends had been selected to assume the characters of and read the testimony of sixteen male and five female witnesses. I would read the testimony questions, acting as district attorney. Paul Walters would preside as Judge James Boyle.

Placed before each individual participant would be his own microphone and Trulex screening tube, on which would appear lines to be read when the script called for his or her particular testimony.

"What about prompting, Priscilla? This is all unrehearsed."

"I have the master script here," she replied, "and prompting is my job. With the Trulex, though, I don't think there will be much need for it." She pushed forward a large loose-leaf binder.

"Okay. How about the Inspector? Is he happy?"

"We had an outline run-through with him last week when you were in Washington. He is pleased and excited about the presentation. And frankly, I think he missed his calling; he should have been a Shakespearean actor, what a voice and delivery!"

"We must go to hear one of his lectures. Since the publication of his book, he does at least one a week. Anything else?"

"Charles wants out from cocktails and dinner. He will return at ten for his summary. Tommy and I will pick him up at nine forty-five.

"Good show! Good show!"

"Thank you, milord."

"Pat, do you have the list of witnesses and their counterpart assignments? I would like to go over that."

"Yes, right here. And there is one other thing. Inspector Darby wants to make off-the-cuff comments at certain points in the testimony. None of this is on the tape, except for a green-light signal on the Trulex indicating you should stop the feed-through and give the Inspector the floor. Is that clear?"

"When the green light shines on my Trulex, I stop the feed to the readers, prompt Charles, then start up again when he is finished."

"Right."

For the second time, a voice from above joined the conversation.

"What a stage set for my next movie: *La Dolce Vitamin*. Everyone looks so robust and healthy!"

"Hi, Tommy," Priscilla answered. "It's the caffeine in Pim's special coffee. Come have some."

"What do I do? Climb the railing and parachute down?"

"No, take the stairs by the pianos, and I will come meet you."

When Prissy had gone, I said to Pat: "How's she doing?"

"Just couldn't be better, Truly. She has worked night and day on every little detail. I insisted she take two days off and go to New York to be with her friend while you were away. You can trust her with anything in the future. What is it you Americans say: just give her the ball and let her play with it?"

"Let her *run* with it, Pat."

"Pardon. Let her run with it."

Half Scotch and half Spanish, Tommy Highsmith is simultaneously an ugly man and a very handsome man. Bright gray blue eyes peer out from a great shock of rust red hair, shaggy eyebrows, and bushy beard covering an unusually large head with rugged facial features. He is well liked and respected at the college, where he teaches dramatics and English literature.

"Well, well, I see you have the star's part in this afternoon's performance," I said, directing my comment to Tommy as he and Prissy arrived on the deck.

"Why not? The committee made me casting director, and the voice for the principal must have range and technique to match the eloquence of his television speech." He grinned, and so did I. It was an apropos remark.

"Tommy, I think you should make a short talk about line reading before we start. Something about speaking clearly, simply, and directly into the mike. And no hamming it up. I don't want this thing to turn into a farce."

"I get the point. Just give me the the floor for a moment, and I'll give them the classroom text."

"Thank you."

I did not know at the time that Tommy could imitate Edward Kennedy's voice so realistically it was startling. In the afternoon proceedings, when he first came on the mike using the imitative voice, it shook everybody. He glanced at me after several lines as if asking for a go-ahead. I could see no harm, I gave it, and a whole new dimension of realism was suddenly added. It seemed to inspire everyone to a serious sense of purpose in the participation. Such is the professional, the truly talented. I felt myself metamorphosed into a questioning district attorney. Paul Walters *was* Judge Boyle. It was amazing. I have since played back the tapes made of the readings for several groups and they have found the realism spellbinding.

We went through the reader list, and it was obvious much thought had been given to the choice of voices for the various witnesses. I had no suggestions to offer. Brief descriptions of the readers and witnesses follow, along with the cast lineup. Members of the reunion party are shown with the letters *PM* (party member).

99

The voice for:	*Played by:*
Christopher F. Look, Jr. County Deputy Sheriff	
Dr. Donald R. Mills Medical Examiner	Raymond Angelo (Ray) Faulkner Foundation executive
Dominick J. Arena Chief of Edgartown Police	
Raymond S. LaRosa (PM) Kennedy political aide	David Dallas (Dave) Motion picture producer-director
Joseph F. Gargan (PM) Kennedy cousin	
Eugene Frieh Undertaker	Timothy Batchelor III (Batchey) Stockbroker
Paul F. Markham (PM) U.S. District Attorney	
John N. Farrar Volunteer Fire Department Rescue Diver	Noland Hammond (Gabby) Public relations executive
Senator Edward M. Kennedy (PM)	
Richard P. Hewitt Ferryman	Thomas Highsmith (Tommy) College instructor
Charles C. Tretter (PM) Kennedy staff lawyer	
Russell E. Peachey Hotel manager	
Jared Grant Ferry owner-operator	Peter Steinway (Pete) Postgrad dramatic-arts student
John B. Crimmins (PM) Kennedy chauffeur	
George W. Kennedy Motor Vehicle Department Inspector	
Ross W. Richards Yachtsman	Syrus Boynten (Sy) Financier

The voice for:	Played by:
Judge James Boyle	Paul Walters (Paul) Lawyer and former appellate judge
Esther Newburgh (PM) RFK campaign worker	Rita Angelo (Angel) Wife of Ray Angelo and former actress
Susan Tannenbaum (PM) RFK campaign worker	Natalie O'Connor Postgraduate student
Rosemary Keough (PM) RFK campaign worker	Jeanette Boynten (Jenny) College student—daughter of Syrus Boynten
Maryellen Lyons (PM) RFK campaign worker	Sue Boynten (Susie) Wife of Syrus Boynten
Ann Lyons (PM) RFK campaign worker	Martha Foster Paley (Pidg) Businesswoman of renown

Our luncheon guests began arriving shortly after noon. Prissy was the official greeter. When I came up from my room, Tommy was working with Johnny Balken checking out the Trulex system, and most of the guests were present, with champagne cocktails in hand. I made my round of welcoming chatter.

Gabby Hammond, Paul Walters, and Mrs. Joycelyn were the last to arrive. I could hear the effusive social greetings from the entranceway while standing near the bar in the terrace room. Gabby and Paul were two keyed-up blabbermouths. The primordial and adolescent urge of the male to show off in front of a newly discovered attractive female was exerting itself. This Mrs. Joycelyn must really be something, I surmised.

She was.

She entered quietly, slowly, seemingly oblivious to the two aging juveniles tossing out greetings from behind her. Priscilla had been remarkably apt in her description of Mia Joycelyn.

Point by point, her comments came floating back as I watched from a distance: ". . . age twenty-nine, divorced, reddish bronze hair, pageboy, shoulder length, squareish but softly rounded face with high cheek bones, sexy mouth, lovely nose, tanned complexion, greenish blue eyes with just a touch of the almond shape, result of a Scotch ship-captain ancestor who married a Polynesian beauty named Miamanami. Statistics? I just spent two days clothes shopping with her: five eight, one hundred and twenty-four pounds, thirty-six, twenty-four, thirty-four, broad shoulders, good posture, gorgeous legs, trim ankles—and now that I have reached the ankles, may I have some more coffee while you sit and drool?"

A nigh perfect physical description, but what Priscilla could not put into words, and with justice neither can I, was the composite substance of the woman herself, the aura of nature's volatile fertility and greatest accomplishment, the ultrafeminine female.

She came toward me, led by Gabby, who was saying: "Truly, I am forever grateful to you and Priscilla. At long last I have met eternal woman, a true goddess who walks in beauty, like the night of cloudless climes and starry skies——"

To stop the gush pouring from an entranced facsimile Lord Byron, I interrupted: "Noland, you might introduce us."

"Oh! Sorry! Mrs. Joycelyn, may I present Mr. Faulkner Trulimann, the proprietor of this fabulous roadside inn."

"How do you do, Mr. Trulimann."

"Charmed and delighted, Madame. A table for two?"

"No, just one of those champagne cocktails I see floating by on a tray, s'il vous plaît."

"Oui, Madame."

In all this folderol our eyes never parted company. To say I was fascinated by the feminine magic and bewitchery of Mrs. Joycelyn would be putting it where it belonged, in the world of the spellbound. We were soon separated, Gabby and Paul saw to that, but during the afternoon's proceedings I could not desist in sneaking glances in her direction. My entire being felt mysteriously drawn to an awareness of her presence and a sense that she was somehow fateful to my life. As things turned out, my psychic qualities were infinitely correct.

Nine: Answers in Search of Questions

Following is a transcript of the proceeding in which Inspector Charles Darby presented his analysis of the Kopechne inquest testimony. I began the presentation with a few introductory remarks.

Faulkner Trulimann:

"Ladies and gentlemen, if there are any questions, please try to ask them now before we start. If at any time this afternoon you feel confused about your part in the readings, just raise your right hand for my attention. I will stop the Trulex readings until your question is answered. May I remind you, however, that we do not wish to stop merely to discuss the testimony. . . . Very well, since there are no questions now, we are going to begin with the reading of Judge Boyle's findings in his report summarizing the inquest proceedings.

"You have all met Inspector Charles Darby, and it is at his request that we start with Judge Boyle's opinion. It is also his desire that I make no introductory remarks about his career as a detective or criminologist. I respect his desire with this reminder only: Inspector Darby spent forty-eight years of his adult life in the service of Scotland Yard of London, England; and the highlights of a most remarkable career are contained in the current best-seller autobiography *Criminals Are Clever . . . and Foolish*. I heartily recommend it.

"From time to time, a green light will appear on all of our Trulex cabinets. This is the signal for me to stop the testimony readings so that the Inspector can make interim comment. Priscilla Rogers will call each witness by name before I, acting as the district attorney, Mr. Dinis or Mr. Fernandes, his assistant, question you. We start now with Mr. Walters, Judge Boyle."

JUDGE BOYLE'S REPORT

As previously stated, there are inconsistencies and contradictions in the testimony, which a comparison of individual testimony will show. It is not feasible to indicate each one.

I list my findings as follows:

I. The decedent is Mary Jo Kopechne, 28 years of age, last resident in Washington, D.C.

II. Death probably occurred between 11:30 P.M. on July 18, 1969, and 1:00 A.M. on July 19, 1969.

III. Death was caused by drowning in Poucha Pond at Dyke Bridge on Chappaquiddick Island in the Town of Edgartown, Massachusetts, when a motor vehicle, in which the decedent was a passenger, went off Dyke Bridge, overturned and was immersed in Poucha Pond. The motor vehicle was owned and operated by Edward M. Kennedy of Boston, Massachusetts.

The statute states that I must report the name of any person whose unlawful act or negligence *appears* to have contributed to Kopechne's death. As I stated at the commencement of the hearing, the Massachusetts Supreme Court said in its decision concerning the conduct of this inquest "the inquest serves as an aid in the achievement of justice by obtaining information as to whether a crime has been committed." In *LaChappelle* vs. *United Shoe Machinery Corporation,* 318 Mass. 166, decided in 1945, the same court said "It (the inquest) is designed merely to ascertain facts for the purpose of subsequent prosecution" and ". . . the investigating judge may himself issue process against a person whose *probable* guilt is disclosed." (Emphasis added)

Therefore, in guiding myself as to proof herein required of the commission of any unlawful act, I reject the cardinal principle of "proof beyond a reasonable doubt" applied in criminal trials but use as a standard the principle of "probable guilt."

I have also used the rule, applicable to trials, which permits me to draw inferences, known as presumption of facts, from the testimony. There are several definitions and I quote from the case of *Commonwealth* vs. *Green,* 294 Pa. 573: "A presumption of fact is an inference which a reasonable man would draw from certain facts which have been proven. The basis is in logic and its source is probability." Volume 29 American Jurisprudence 2nd Evidence Section 161 states in part "A presumption of fact or an inference is nothing more than a probable or natural explanation of facts . . . and arises from the commonly accepted experiences of mankind and the inferences which reasonable men would draw from experiences."

I find these facts:

A. Kennedy was the host and mainly responsible for the assembly of the group at Edgartown.
B. Kennedy was rooming at Shiretown with Gargan, his cousin and close friend of many years.
C. Kennedy had employed Crimmins as chauffeur for nine years and rarely drove himself. Crimmins drove Kennedy on all other occasions herein set forth, and was available at the time of the fatal trip.
D. Kennedy told only Crimmins that he was leaving for Shiretown and requested the car key.
E. The young women were close friends, were on Martha's Vineyard for a common purpose as a cohesive group, and staying together at Katama Shores.
F. Kopechne roomed with Newburgh, the latter having in her possession the key to their room.

G. Kopechne told *no one,* other than Kennedy, that she was leaving for Katama Shores and did not ask Newburgh for the room key.

H. Kopechne left her pocketbook at the Cottage when she drove off with Kennedy.

I. It was known that the ferry ceased operation about midnight and special arrangements must be made for a later trip. No such arrangements were made.

J. Ten of the persons at the cookout did *not* intend to remain at the Cottage overnight.

K. Only the Oldsmobile and the Valiant were available for transportation of those ten, the Valiant being the smaller car.

L. LaRosa's Mercury was parked at Shiretown and was available for use.

I infer a reasonable and probable explanation of the totality of the above facts is that Kennedy and Kopechne did *not* intend to return to Edgartown at that time; that Kennedy did *not* intend to drive to the ferry slip and his turn onto Dyke Road was intentional. Having reached this conclusion, the question then arises as to whether there was anything criminal in his operation of the motor vehicle.

From two personal views, which corroborate the Engineer's statement (Exhibit 29), and other evidence, I am fully convinced that Dyke Bridge constitutes a traffic hazard, particularly so at night, and must be approached with extreme caution. A speed of even twenty miles an hour, as Kennedy testified to, operating a car as large as this Oldsmobile, would at least be negligent and, possibly, reckless. If Kennedy knew of this hazard, his operation of the vehicle constituted criminal conduct.

Earlier on July 18, he had been driven over Chappaquiddick Road three times, and over Dyke Road and Dyke Bridge twice. Kopechne had been driven over Chappaquiddick Road five times and over Dyke Road and Dyke Bridge twice.

I believe it probable that Kennedy knew of the hazard that

lay ahead of him on Dyke Road but that, for some reason not apparent from the testimony, he failed to exercise due care as he approached the bridge.

IV. I, therefore, find there is probable cause to believe that Edward M. Kennedy operated his motor vehicle negligently on a way or in a place to which the public have a right of access and that such operation appears to have contributed to the death of Mary Jo Kopechne.

February 18, 1970

(GREEN LIGHT)

Inspector Darby:

"Ladies and gentlemen, I direct your attention to Judge Boyle's use of the rule, applicable to trials in the American jurisprudence, which permits him to draw inferences, or presumption of facts, from the testimony. He also offers two legally acceptable definitions of a presumption of fact, and a list of twelve proven facts from which he concludes that Mr. Kennedy and Miss Kopechne did *not* intend to return to Edgartown when they left the cottage, that Mr. Kennedy did *not* intend to drive to the ferry slip, and that his turn onto Dyke Road was intentional.

"With all due respect to the Honorable Judge Boyle, I agree with the conclusions drawn from a totality of the facts he has listed; but I intend to take liberties with the limitation he has set upon the facts available from which conclusions may be drawn. In short, I believe that far more facts, proven in the same manner as his list of twelve, are available to be viewed in totality. And, when so viewed in the light of, quote, the commonly accepted experiences of mankind and the inferences which reasonable men would draw from experiences, unquote, that these additional facts will enable us to reach far more indicative conclusions. With your assistance, additional acceptable facts is what we will seek for consideration this afternoon.

"Some time ago, Faulkner asked for my professional opinion on the incident in question, and I am now ready to offer such an opinion. However, I will say to you what I said to him in the past: It is not my desire or intention to render moral judgment of any acts, committed or implied, by any person or persons concerned. I am a detective, not a prosecutor, not a defender, and certainly not a judge and jury. It has been my lot in life for many years to seek truth. And to seek it in the face of falsehood, evasion, fiction, pretense, exaggeration, all the sham clothing with which truth may be costumed and that permits it to walk unrecognized past our gates of doubt and disbelief. I give my assent, however, to the words of Democritus: 'But we know nothing really, for truth lies deep down.'

"Like the visible ten percent of an iceberg, the visible action of man is only the tip of his total experience, heredity, environment, and momentary process of reaction. In my work, the submerged bulk of man is important, if even partially known and recognizable; and it is often the indicator of the true meaning of action. I want you to know as much as possible of the basis for my conclusions. Perhaps, then, you can better understand the rationality of my final opinion, and further, perhaps better understand why I am always reluctant to express an opinion as final judgment.

"In a moment we will attempt to extend Judge Boyle's list of available facts by scrutiny of the inquest testimony. I want to pay tribute now to the remarkably dedicated assistance of Miss Rogers, Miss Johnson, and Mr. Highsmith in preparing a procedure for the exposure of my dialectics. All of you are important to this procedure, so I also wish to pay tribute to your interest and cooperation and express my gratitude. Accept my word for it, no Yard Inspector, active or retired, ever experienced such an unusual opportunity for indulging his sense of showmanship, with the possible exception, of course, of a certain friend of Miss Agatha Christie."

He paused for a moment, studying the outline detail pro-

109

vided by the committee. While he was speaking, I could feel the growing intensity of his audience. Charles has the charisma of the unquestionably authoritative manner, plus the aura of the noble, and all that such an aura implies in superior moral qualities, excellence, and dignity. Would that the politics of democracy could produce more of such men to become our political leaders. Unfortunately, by the very nature of the democratic process, politicians generally are spawned by the mediocrity of political circumstance and nurtured through their growth by self-seeking pragmatists, strategists, and, too often, the ignoble—frightfully high odds against the emergence of dedicated excellence and the noble.

The reference to Agatha Christie drew laughs from everyone before the Inspector continued: "By close observation of testimony this afternoon, I trust we can agree upon a new and larger group of apposite elements, a whole new set of building-block facts; then, tonight, I will attempt to construct, quote, a probable or natural explanation, unquote, of what occurred on Chappaquiddick Island and in Edgartown on July 18–19, 1969.

"We will begin with testimony that I consider the keystone of our structure. First-testimony elements cover the only occasion in which an outside witness comes into contact with witnesses from the party group at the approximate time of the incident at Dyke Bridge. From this encounter we can set a time sequence, both forward and backward, that gives us a hub for our wheel of evidence. Let us proceed now with this testimony, see what facts are turned up, and go on from there.

"Truly—"

CALL
CHRISTOPHER F. LOOK, JR., (Sworn)
Q. Where do you reside and what is your occupation, Mr. Look?
A. In the wintertime I live in Edgartown and in the summer

on Chappaquiddick Island. I am an oil dealer and since 1953 I have been part-time Deputy Sheriff for Dukes County.

Q. Where were you and what were you doing on the evening of July 18?

A. I was at the Edgartown Yacht Club at the foot of Main Street. I go to work at 8 P.M. and continue until 12:30 or 1:00 A.M. I wear my deputy's uniform, a dark shirt with silver buttons down the front and on the lapels, a badge with nameplate, an arm patch, and light tan pants with a dark-brown stripe. I finished work and left the club on the morning of the 19th around 12:25 A.M. I remember Mr. Richards commenting that we had gotten the people out earlier than usual, and I said: "Yes, it is only 12:25."

Q. What did you do on leaving the Yacht Club?

A. I went on the Club launch to the ferry landing at Chappaquiddick, a five minute trip, then got into my automobile and proceeded to my home up a macadamized road known as Chappaquiddick Road then on to a continuation known as Schoolhouse Road after the juncture with Dyke Road.

Q. Would you tell us the approximate time you reached this juncture, and did you see anyone or anything?

A. I would say I was at the juncture at approximately 12:40 or 12:45. As I approached I saw car lights coming from the righthand side up Schoolhouse Road. I practically came to a complete stop because automobiles, when they make that curve, usually cut it very close and I was afraid I might run into him. My headlights were on the car as it passed directly in front of me about 35 feet away and then stopped part way into a little dirt road commonly known as Cemetery Road. I proceeded around the corner, looked into my rearview mirror, and noticed the car starting to back up. Usually on Chappaquiddick, people get lost so I stopped, thinking they might want information on the way to the ferry or someone's house. I got out and started walking towards the backing car. When I was about 25 or 30 feet away it drove off down Dyke Road.

Q. Could you describe the lighting conditions as they were at the time?

A. There is no street light but my car lights and those of the other car were on, including his backup lights.

Q. With these lights could you see reflections and shadows?

A. Yes, on my body and uniform.

Q. And what did you observe about the other car and its occupants?

A. It was a dark car with a Massachusetts license beginning with an L and it had a 7 at the beginning and a 7 at the end. When it passed in front of me and also when I was walking towards it there appeared to be a man driving and a woman in the front righthand side. Also either another person or an object of clothing, a handbag or something sitting on the back shelf. It looked like an object of some kind.

Q. How long and how far did you observe the car after it started to move away from you?

A. Just a matter of ten seconds. The roads were dry, there was a lot of dust and all I could see was just the lights going down the road. I wouldn't know how many feet. I would say it hurried moderately. It didn't spin the wheels when it left the macadam road.

Q. Did you see the people in the automobile looking at you, did you say anything to them . . . cry out?

A. No, sir. I walked back to my car, got in it and proceeded home.

Q. On the way did you encounter any other people?

A. Yes, sir. I came upon a tall girl, a shorter one, and a

fairly short man walking single file down the road going in the same direction I was.

Q. Did you see any other cars, or anyone else other than these people on the road?

A. No, sir.

Q. Did you have a conversation with the people on the road?

A. I stopped my car about 5 or 6 feet away from them and asked if they wanted a lift. To the best of my recollection, the tall girl said "Shove off, buddy" or "Shove off, mister, we are not pickups" or something to that effect, and the man said "No thank you, sir, we are only going to this place over here," and he pointed in the direction of the Lawrence Cottage. The two girls were wearing slacks, and what looked like boat sneakers. They were very jovial, happy.

Q. Did you make any observation as to drink . . . liquor?

A. I couldn't say. I just say they were very happy-go-lucky people.

Q. When you passed by the Lawrence Cottage did you observe any lights at the cottage or any motor vehicles outside it?

A. I could not say. I don't know.

Q. What time would you say you passed the cottage?

A. It would have to be a few minutes after 12:45 and before five minutes of 1:00 because I got to my home a mile away at five minutes of 1:00.

Q. The next morning were you aware there had been an accident on Dyke Road at Dyke Bridge?

A. Yes, the Communication Center called and said there had been an accident and I might be needed to give Chief Arena some assistance, so I went down there. I met Chief Arena walking up towards the Dyke cottage where the Malms lived and he said I could probably help keep traffic away. There was a car overturned in the water and they were trying to find out if anyone was in it.

Q. Was the car removed from the water in your presence?

A. Yes, quite a long while later.

Q. And what if anything did you observe or say at that time?

A. Well, prior to the car coming out of the water, I spoke to the Chief and also to Patrolman Robert Brougier about seeing people walking on the road and observing the car, and I told him I hoped this wasn't the same one. About a half hour elapsed then Chief Arena came back from Edgartown and said to the patrolman and myself, gee, do you know who was driving that car last night. I said I hadn't the slightest idea, only from what I told him it appeared to be a man and a woman and somebody else. He said, it is Senator Kennedy. I said, oh my God.

Q. What time was this that he told you that?

A. It would be just a guess, sometime around 10:15 or 10:30. The car was still in the water. You could just see the four wheels sticking up.

Q. What did you observe when it came out of the water?

A. As soon as they started to pull it out and it became visible I walked over and told Officer Brougier, gee, that is the same car I saw last night. I didn't examine it closely. I just looked quickly at the car and the license plate and decided in my own mind that it was the same one I had seen, and I walked over and mentioned it to Officer Brougier.

THE COURT. You said, I think, that the night before you saw a dark-colored car. Could you be any more definite about its color?

A. No, sir. It was either black or dark blue or dark green, any dark color.

114

THE COURT. Then you couldn't identify it as being the same color as the car you saw taken out of the water?

A. No, sir.

THE COURT. And you saw a letter, a seven, and then another seven at the end on the plate? Do you remember how many numbers, letters and numbers there were on the plate? Whether it was four, five or six numbers?

A. No, sir.

THE COURT. So you can't identify the exact color or the exact number plate?

A. No, sir.

CALL

JOHN B. CRIMMINS (Sworn)

Q. Do you recall what your activities were Friday afternoon, July 18?

A. Yes, I do. About 1:15 I picked up the Senator at Martha's Vineyard Airport and drove him to the house. He changed into swim trunks and went to the beach for a swim.

THE COURT. In what car did you drive him to the beach?

A. The black Oldsmobile 88.

THE COURT. Did you drive over Dyke Bridge?

A. Yes, I did.

THE COURT. Did you have any difficulty negotiating it, any trouble keeping the car on the bridge?

A. Not that I recall, sir.

THE COURT. And you brought the car back over the bridge?

A. Yes, sir.

THE COURT. If you are familiar with the registration of that vehicle, Mr. Crimmins, would you tell the Court what it is?

A. L 78-207.

CALL

RAYMOND S. LaROSA (Sworn)

Q. At some time around a quarter of 1:00 on the night in question do you know whether any members of your party were outside on the street in front of the house?

A. Yes, sir. I believe the two Lyons sisters and myself went for a walk out on the road, towards the ferry.

Q. Did an automobile slow down while you were out on the road?

A. One automobile stopped and I believe there was another one that slowed down.

THE COURT. Tell us about the cars.

A. Well, I recall this car came along heading towards the ferry and I held my hands out in this fashion (indicating) for the two girls to kind of protect them. It slowed down but didn't stop, just kept on its way, and we continued on down the road. I just don't recall how far or how long we walked, but another car came along the other way, from the ferry, and stopped, and a man asked us if we needed help or something, and one of the girls made some kind of a statement, and I think I apologized. I think she said "Shove off" or something of that nature, and I said, "I'm sorry, we are staying very close."

Q. Was this some time around quarter of 1:00?

A. I'm not sure about the time, but it might have been.

CALL

ANN LYONS (Sworn)

Q. At this time did you encounter anyone on the road?

A. Yes, sir, we walked well past the fire station on this particular walk and we were walking down the middle of the road because it was dark and I'm not sure if I recall if a car passed us on the way to the ferry, but as we turned to come back and were walking towards the cottage, we heard a car approaching behind us and I as-

sumed that it was Mr. Gargan and Mr. Markham returning and I said, move along, move along, we are all
right; and at that point the person in the car made a statement that told me it wasn't Mr. Gargan and Mr. LaRosa
spoke to the gentleman in the car and told him that we
were all right and just returning to our cottage.

Q. How far away from the cottage were you?

A. We were past the station towards the ferry.

Q. How long would it take you to walk to the cottage from
where you were?

A. No more than about five minutes, ten.

Q. And after this conversation did you return to the cottage?

A. Yes, sir. There were some people outside sitting on the
fence, I think Miss Tannenbaum and Miss Newburgh.
Mr. Crimmins was inside the cottage. Mr. LaRosa and
Maryellen were with me.

CALL
MARYELLEN LYONS (Sworn)

Q. Now, directing your attention to the walk on the roadway, did an automobile slow down?

A. Yes, it did. A car slowed down as it approached us and
asked if we needed any help. We assumed it was Mr.
Gargan and Mr. Markham who prior to this time left the
cottage. My sister made a comment then we discovered
it was someone we didn't know. I would say this was
some time after midnight but I really don't know the
time.

(GREEN LIGHT)

Inspector Darby:

"FACT I. A large dark-colored sedan bearing a male driver
and a female passenger in the front seat came from
the direction of the Lawrence cottage at approxi-

117

mately 12:45 A.M., July 19, stopped momentarily at the intersection of Chappaquiddick, Schoolhouse, and Dyke Roads, then drove hurriedly off down Dyke Road in the direction of Dyke Bridge.

"FACT 2.   The license plate of the car was partially identified by Deputy Sheriff Look as of Massachusetts registry, beginning with the letter *L* followed by the number 7, followed by an unknown quantity of intervening numbers, ending with number 7.

"FACT 3.   The bridge-accident car was identified by Crimmins as Massachusetts registry number L 78-207, in the name of Edward M. Kennedy. Color of car: black. Type: sedan.

"FACT 4.   Because of various auto lights and reflections, it was possible for the driver of the car at the intersection and/or the passenger to see and recognize the form and dress of Deputy Look as that of an officer of the law.

"FACT 5.   Look arrived at his home one mile past the cottage at 12:55, having spoken with LaRosa and Ann and Maryellen Lyons just after leaving the intersection. He noticed no other cars or persons on the road.

"FACT 6.   Gargan and Markham had left the cottage in the white Valiant before Look's encounter with the black sedan, their whereabouts at 12:45 being unknown to LaRosa and the Lyons sisters."

The Inspector finished reading from his notes, then made the following comment: (This was to be his pattern throughout the testimony—detail the facts, then comment—so I will not intrude upon his thoughts again merely to give you the pattern-PFT.)

"Please do not assume that I begin with the Look testimony simply to cast doubt on Mr. Kennedy's accounting of events.

The purpose is to set a reasonable starting point in time with which there can be little or no argument. A complete study of the testimony offered by the cottage group suggests quite clearly that members of the group were seldom conscious of exact timing and sometimes gave confused testimony because of obviously improper recall of succeeding events. We should bear in mind that testimony was given almost six months after actual occurrences, and about matters of trivial importance at the time. Utterly inconsequential events are particularly susceptible to time inaccuracy with the average memory ability.

"By a most peculiar coincidence, however, a clearly marked point in time is available to us from the Look statements; and this point in time enables us to consider and compare all other pertinent testimony. As you will see from my final opinion tonight, TIME is the real key to our mystery.

"Let us proceed now to build with other time factors at hand. Truly—"

CALL
EDWARD M. KENNEDY (Sworn)

Q. Will you please give us the sequence of events with regards to your activities at the cottage after 8:30 P.M.?

A. Well, during the course of the evening, I engaged in conversation and recollections with those that were attending this group which were old friends of myself and our families. Some alcoholic beverages were served.

Q. How many times did you leave the cottage that evening, Senator?

A. Two different occasions.

Q. Would you tell us about the first time?

A. The first time I left at approximately 11:15 the evening of July 18, and I left a second time, sometime after midnight, by my best judgment it would be approximately 12:15. On the second occasion I never left the cottage itself, I left the immediate vicinity of the cottage which was probably fifteen or twenty feet outside the front door, to return to Edgartown. I did not immediately return to Edgartown.

Q. Now when you left on the first occasion, were you alone?

A. I was not alone, Miss Mary Jo Kopechne was with me.

Q. Anyone else?

A. No.

Q. And were you driving the 88 Oldsmobile that was taken from the river? Was Miss Kopechne seated in the front seat?

A. That is correct.

Q. On leaving the cottage, Senator—Mr. Kennedy, where did you go?

A. Well, I traveled down, I believe it is Main Street, took a right on Dyke Road and drove off the bridge at Dyke Bridge.

Q. Did you at any time drive into Cemetery Road?

A. At no time did I drive into Cemetery Road.

Q. Did you back that car up at any time?

A. At no time did I back that car up.

Q. Did you see anyone on the road between the cottage and the bridge that night?

A. I saw no one on the road between the cottage and the bridge.

THE COURT. Did you stop the car at any time?

A. I did not stop the car at any time.

D.A. Q. Did you pass any other vehicle at that time?

A. I passed no other vehicle and I saw no other person and I did not stop the car at any time between the time I left the cottage and went off the bridge.

Q. Now, would you describe your automobile to the Court?

A. Well, it is a four-door black sedan, Oldsmobile. I do not recall the license plate.

RECALL
JOHN B. CRIMMINS
Q. Now what time did Mr. Kennedy leave the party?
A. About 11:15. I looked at my watch.
Q. Where were you when he asked you for the car keys?
A. I was in the cottage and he called me outside.
Q. Did you see Mr. Kennedy leave?
A. Not actually see him leave, but I saw the car pull away.
Q. He was driving?
A. I assume so.
Q. Where were you standing when you saw the car pull away?
A. Going back to the cottage.

CALL
DOMINICK J. ARENA (Sworn)
Q. Did you speak with Mrs. Malm and did you ask her whether or not she had seen or heard an automobile?
A. Yes, she said she heard a sound of an auto engine close to around midnight. I asked her if she had heard any sound of anything hitting the water or anything like that. She said no.
Q. Where was she staying?
A. At the Dyke House.
Q. I think you said this was approximately 100 feet from the bridge?
A. Right. I have a statement from the mother and her daughter.
Q. How old is this daughter?
A. I think she is a college student, probably 17 or 18.
Q. Could you tell us what they said?

A. This is from Sylvia R. Malm; she is the mother of the family. On Saturday morning, July 19, 1969, two boys knocked on my door and said there is a car upside-down in the water by the bridge. I called the Communications Center, and reported the car and its location. The operator said she would relay the message. Sometime during the evening before I was aware of a car going faster than usual, going toward the Dyke. I have no idea of the time. I think I went to sleep sometime between 11:30 and 12:00 midnight, but I do not know the time. I heard nothing during the night. We have two dogs and a night light was burning all night.

Then I have a statement from Sylvia A. Malm, the daughter. On Friday night, July 18, 1969, I read in bed underneath an open window which faces east (toward the bridge) from 11:00 to 12:00 midnight, looking at the clock just before I turned my light out. Between 11:15 and 11:45 I heard a car going fairly fast on the Dyke Road. I didn't look out the window, so I am uncertain of the direction, but thought at the time it was heading towards the Dyke. I heard nothing further that night.

Q. Is there a house across the street?

A. Yes, there is a house diagonally across the street on the right occupied by a Mrs. Smith.

Q. Did you have a conversation with her?

A. Yes, she stated she had a night light in one of her children's rooms which she left on all night. This was on the road side of the house.

Q. Did she hear anything?

A. She said she did not hear anything.

Q. Did you confer with anyone else concerning the accident?

A. No sir, these are the only people that lived on that street.

Inspector Darby:

"FACT 7. Kennedy and Crimmins testify that Kennedy and Kopechne departed from the cottage at 11:15.

"FACT 8. Kennedy was the driver, and he passed no other vehicle, saw no other person, and did not stop his car from cottage to the bridge. He drove off the bridge at approximately 11:20–11:25.

"FACT 9. A car passed the Malm house near the bridge between 11:15 and 11:45, going toward the bridge.

"FACT 10. Before midnight, when both were awake, neither mother nor daughter Malm heard the sound of a vehicle hitting the curb rail of the bridge or falling into the water, in spite of the close proximity and open window facing the bridge next to the bed where daughter Malm was reading.

"FACT 11. Until 12:00 midnight the light in this room was on, and could easily be seen from the bridge. By actual clock-time notation by the daughter, this light was turned out at midnight. Shortly after, mother and daughter were asleep.

"FACT 12. There were only two occupied homes between the Curve intersection and the bridge. Both had night lights burning, one had dogs, but neither occupant heard sounds or had visitors after midnight.

"FACT 13. A telephone was available in the Malm house.

"We now have a tentative beginning for our time structure: 11:15 when Miss Kopechne and Mr. Kennedy depart from the cottage. Mr. Kennedy's statement that he drove directly to the bridge places the accident time at no earlier than 11:20, no later than 11:25; and a car did pass the Malm house at that time. But isn't it rather remarkable that the daughter Malm failed to hear the car going off the bridge, since I personally heard, quite clearly, a five-pound rock dropped from the bridge into the water by a fellow investigator while I stood just outside the window opening mentioned?''

This was news to me. I did not know that Charles had been to Chappaquiddick. But I should have known better; it would not be characteristic for him to do otherwise. From the quick glance in my direction, I knew he was enjoying my surprise.

"Again," he continued, "an outside witness gives us a pinpoint relative in time. Miss Malm states: 'I read in bed—from 11:00 to 12:00 midnight, looking at the clock just before I turned my light out.' This statement poses a real question for Mr. Kennedy, as you will see shortly.

"In the meantime, our next time point is Mr. Kennedy's reappearance at the cottage. From his own testimony we get an estimate of the time consumed between his departure and arrival there after the accident, then his return to the bridge and the time spent in rescue effort by Mr. Gargan and Mr. Markham. Distances, too, become important now, so we will take another look at Judge Boyle's report."

RECALL
EDWARD M. KENNEDY

Q. Mr. Kennedy, how many times if you recall did you make an effort to submerge and get into the car?

A. I would say seven or eight times. At the last point, the seventh or eighth attempts were barely more than five- or eight-second submersions below the surface, I just couldn't hold my breath any longer. I didn't have the strength to even come down close to the window or door.

Q. And do you know how much time was consumed in these efforts?

A. It would be difficult for me to estimate, but I would think probably 15–20 minutes.

Q. How did you remove yourself from the water?

A. In the last dive I lost contact with the vehicle again and I started to come down here and I let myself float and came over to this shore. I sort of crawled and staggered up some place in here and was very exhausted and spent on the grass.

Q. On the west bank of the river as indicated on that chart?

A. Yes, that's correct.

Q. And how long did you spend resting?

A. Well, I would estimate 15–20 minutes. I was coughing up water and I was exhausted, the best estimate would be 15 or 20 minutes.

Q. Now, following your rest period, Senator, what did you do?

A. After I was able to regain my breath I went back to the road and started down it. It was extremely dark and I could make out no forms or shapes or figures. The only way I could see the path of the road was looking down the silhouettes of the trees on the two sides and I started going down the road walking, trotting, jogging, stumbling, as fast as I possibly could.

Q. Did you pass any houses with lights on?

A. Not to my knowledge; never saw a cottage with a light on it.

Q. How long did it take you to make that return walk to the cottage?

A. I would say approximately fifteen minutes.

Q. And when you arrived at the cottage, what did you do?

A. Well, I came up to the cottage, there was a white car parked there, and as I came up to the back of it, I saw Ray LaRosa at the door and I said, Ray, get me Joe Gargan; and he mentioned something like, right away, and as he was going in to get Joe, I got in the back of the car.

Q. And now did Joe come to you and did you have a conversation with him?

A. Yes, he did, and I said, better get Paul, too. Then Paul came out, got in the car, I said, there has been a terrible accident, we have got to go, and we took off down the Main Road there.

Q. How long had you known Mr. LaRosa prior to this evening?

A. Eight or ten years.

Q. Did you have any knowledge that Mr. LaRosa had some experience in skin diving?

A. No, I never did.

Q. Before you drove down the road, did you make any further explanations to Mr. Gargan or Mr. Markham?

A. No, sir, I said, there has been a terrible accident and we took off. Mr. Gargan drove the vehicle across the bridge to some location here (indicating) and turned it so that its headlights shown over the water and over the submerged vehicle. Mr. Gargan and Mr. Markham took off all their clothes and proceeded to dive repeatedly to try and save Mary Jo.

Q. Now, do you recall what particular time this is now when the three of you were at the——

A. I think it was 12:20, Mr. Dinis, I believed that I looked at the Valiant's clock and believe it was 12:20.

Q. Was Mr. LaRosa or anyone else at the cottage told of the accident?

A. No.

Q. How long did Mr. Gargan and Mr. Markham remain there with you on that particular occasion?

A. I would think about forty-five minutes.

CALL

JOSEPH GARGAN (Sworn)

Q. Do you know how much time was used in trying to get into the car?

A. I would say we were probably there forty-five minutes.

CALL

PAUL F. MARKHAM (Sworn)

Q. How long would you say you and Mr. Gargan were in the water trying to get into the car?

A. I will say forty or forty-five minutes.

JUDGE BOYLE'S REPORT

ITEM (3) Chappaquiddick has few roads. At the ferry slip, begins a macadam paved road called Chappaquiddick Road, the main road of the island, with a white center line which is partly obliterated at the Curve. The road is approximately twenty feet wide, running in a general easterly direction for two and one-half miles, whence it curves south and continues in that direction past the Cottage to the southeast corner of the island. The road is sometimes referred to in the testimony as Main Street and, after it curves, as School Road or Schoolhouse Road.

ITEM (4) At the Curve, and continuing easterly, begins Dyke Road, a dirt and sand road, seventeen to nineteen feet wide, which runs a distance of seven-tenths mile to Dyke Bridge shortly beyond which is the ocean beach.

ITEM (8) Cemetery Road is a single-car width private dirt road, which runs northerly from the junction of Chappaquiddick and Dyke Roads.

ITEM (9) The Lawrence Cottage, (herein called Cottage), is one-half miles from the junction of Chappaquid-

dick and Dyke Roads and approximately three
miles from the ferry slip.

(GREEN LIGHT)

Inspector Darby:

"FACT 14. Kennedy spent fifteen to twenty minutes in escape
and exhausting rescue effort; then he emerged from
the water channel onto the bank nearest the Malm
house at about 11:40.

"FACT 15. Kennedy rested on the shore for fifteen to twenty
minutes; then he started walking to the cottage
sometime between 11:55 and 12:05.

"FACT 16. Kennedy estimates that the mile-and-two-tenths
walk took fifteen minutes, placing him back at the
cottage at 12:10 to 12:20. He saw no lights in
houses along the way.

"FACT 17. Kennedy spoke with LaRosa, then, with Gargan and
Markham, drove back to the bridge, arriving there,
according to the clock in the Valiant, at 12:20.

"FACT 18. All three men estimate forty to forty-five minutes
spent in the second rescue attempt. This would
place them at the bridge until 1:00 or 1:05.

"FACT 19. LaRosa's skin-diving experience was unknown to
Kennedy, even though they had been friends for
eight or nine years.

"Again quoting from Judge Boyle's report: 'As previously
stated, there are inconsistencies and contradictions in the testimony, which a comparison of individual testimony will show. It
is not feasible to indicate each one.' We have reached a point
now where the testimony points up two situations that, if not inconsistent or contradictory, are most certainly mystifying.

"The first is Mr. Kennedy's failure to notice Miss Malm's

128

lighted window while he was resting on the channel bank only a short distance away. How could he fail to see this beacon of light in darkness so extreme he had to follow tree silhouettes against the night sky in keeping to the path of the road? The land from the channel bank to the house is flat, with only scrub vegetation. For fifteen to twenty minutes the rectangle of light was there, offering immediate human access, including a telephone, only steps away from his position.

"The second mystery concerns a large automobile that apparently vanished in thin air. During the time that Kennedy, Gargan, and Markham were attempting to rescue Miss Kopechne, from 12:20 to 1:00, Deputy Look saw a sedan car driving at a good pace down Dyke Road in the direction of Dyke Bridge. Almost in a matter of seconds after it left Look's position at the intersection, this vehicle would have arrived at the bridge. It did not belong to the two residents, nor did they have visitors. Yet, nowhere in the Kennedy, Gargan, or Markham testimony is there mention of a car or even car lights approaching the bridge. What became of the phantom automobile?

"Could it be a question of errors in the time notations and estimates by Mr. Kennedy? We will return now to the party group and look more closely at the circumstances surrounding the Kennedy-Kopechne departure from the cottage."

RECALL
EDWARD M. KENNEDY

Q. When you left at 11:15 with Miss Kopechne, had you had any prior conversation with her?

A. Yes, I had. I was talking with Miss Kopechne some minutes before 11:15. I noticed the time, desired to leave and return to the Shiretown Inn and indicated to her that I was leaving and returning to town. She indicated to me that she was desirous of leaving, if I would be kind enough to drop her back at her hotel. I said, well, I'm leaving immediately: spoke with Mr. Crimmins, requested the keys for the car and left at that time.

Q. Does Mr. Crimmins usually drive your car or drive you?

A. On practically every occasion.

Q. Was there anything in particular that changed those circumstances at this particular time?

A. Only to the extent that Mr. Crimmins, as well as some of the other fellows that were attending the cookout, were concluding their meal, enjoying the fellowship, and it didn't appear to me to be necessary to require him to bring me back to Edgartown.

RECALL
JOHN CRIMMINS

Q. Could you tell us the circumstances of when Mr. Kennedy left? What did he say to you?

A. He told me that he was tired and that he wanted to go home and go to sleep.

Q. Did he say anything else?

A. Yes. He told me he was going to take Miss Kopechne back; that she wasn't feeling well. The sun. She was bothered by the sun on the beach that day. I was in the cottage and he called me outside and asked me for the keys.

Q. You didn't offer to drive him back to Edgartown or the ferry?

A. No.

CALL
SUSAN TANNENBAUM (Sworn)

Q. Did you see Mary Jo Kopechne leave the cottage that night?

A. Yes.

Q. Do you recall the time?

A. I remember looking at my watch at twenty-five of twelve and Mary Jo had been gone a short time.

130

Q. Did Mary Jo have any conversation with you as to why she was leaving. Did she complain about not feeling well?

A. No.

RECALL
JOSEPH GARGAN

Q. Do you know what time Senator Kennedy left the cottage that evening?

A. I would say that it was approximately 11:25 or 11:30. I saw him go out the door with Mary Jo Kopechne. Where he went from there, I don't know.

RECALL
ANN LYONS

Q. Did you have any conversations with Miss Kopechne at the party? Did she ever comment on the condition of her health?

A. I don't think I recall any direct conversation. I recall a conversation that was related to me by someone else. My sister, Maryellen, told me she had spoken to Mary Jo and Mary Jo indicated she was having a very nice time. To my knowledge she never expressed the fact that she was tired or ill or uncomfortable at the party.

Q. Did there come a time when you were aware that either Mr. Kennedy or Miss Kopechne were not at the party?

A. Yes, sir. I saw the Senator and Miss Kopechne leave. I was sitting on the couch in the living room and I saw them walk out the door.

Q. And did you take note of the time?

A. No, sir. I don't have a watch.

CALL
ESTHER NEWBURGH (Sworn)

Q. Did you become aware that Mr. Kennedy left at a certain time?

A. Yes. 11:30. I have a rather large watch that I wear all the time and I looked at it.

Q. Where were you when you saw him leave?

A. In the living room. He was at the door. The screen door was open. I saw him walk out. Miss Kopechne was directly behind him.

Q. Who else was with you in the living room just prior to his leaving?

A. Mr. Crimmins, Mr. Gargan, as far as I can remember, all the other girls, Mr. Markham, Mr. Tretter and Mr. LaRosa.

Q. Had Mary Jo told you that she didn't feel well?

A. No.

Q. Between 8:30 and 11:30, the party activity, was it confined mostly in the cottage or outside the cottage?

A. Inside the cottage. I was helping Mr. Gargan outside for a while but it was a very hot night so it was inside the cottage where it was cooler.

THE COURT. Excuse me. Did she say that she knew Mary Jo left at 11:30 because she looked at a watch?

D.A. Yes, at a large watch she was wearing.

THE COURT. Why didn't you go back at the same time as her since you were rooming with her and were close friends?

A. Well, Mr. Fernandes asked me what time I saw them walk out of the cottage, but I didn't know where they were going.

CALL
ROSEMARY KEOUGH (Sworn)

Q. Now, sometime later in the evening did you notice Mary Jo Kopechne leave the house? And do you know the time?

A. Yes. I saw her leave at approximately 11:20. She was

132

followed by Senator Kennedy. She did not tell me where she was going.

(GREEN LIGHT)

Inspector Darby:

"FACT 20. Kennedy and Kopechne were engaged in conversation some minutes before leaving the cottage.

"FACT 21. Kennedy told Crimmins that Kopechne wanted to return to the motel because she was not feeling well; but Kopechne told no one else of illness.

"FACT 22. No other testifying member of the party group witnessed the request for nor the exchange of car keys between Kennedy and Crimmins.

"FACT 23. Crimmins gave the keys to Kennedy in the front yard and saw the car pull away; he could not identify the driver because of the extreme darkness.

"FACT 24. Witnesses other than Kennedy and Crimmins indicate an actual departure time later than 11:15, nearer 11:30.

"My only comment at this time concerns the obvious difference in the time of departure: 11:30 as opposed to 11:15. This might explain Kennedy's failure to see the lighted window. But I should point out that if we work backward from Kennedy's notation of the Valiant clock at 12:20, and allow the actual test walking time from the bridge to the cottage of twenty-three minutes, and five minutes to summon Gargan and Markham and drive back to the bridge, Kennedy would have had to leave his position on the pond bank and pass by the cottage several minutes before midnight.

"The time added would not affect the mystery of the phantom automobile. The three rescuers would still be about their work as the unidentified car drove toward the bridge.

"I believe it is important now to consider the general circumstances surrounding the departure of Kennedy and Kopechne, in particular, the question of alcoholic beverages and their consumption."

RECALL
EDWARD M. KENNEDY

Q. What transpired at the cottage after your arrival at 7:30?

A. After my arrival I took a bath in the tub that was available at the cottage, and not available at Shiretown Inn, and soaked my back; I was later joined by Mr. Markham who arrived some time about 8 o'clock, and engaged in conversation with him until 8:30 or shortly thereafter when the rest of the group arrived. During this period of time Mr. Crimmins made me a drink of rum and Coca-Cola.

Q. Were there drinks served and did anyone in particular tend bar or have charge of this particular responsibility?

A. There were drinks served. I tried initially to respond to any of the requests of the guests when they arrived and then I think most of the individuals made their drinks after that, whatever they wanted.

Q. Did you have more than one rum and Coca-Cola?

A. Yes, I had two.

THE COURT. What time was this?

A. The first was about 8 o'clock.

THE COURT. I would like to go back before that. I think you said you visited some friends at the Shiretown Inn. Did you do some drinking then?

A. I had about a third of a beer at that time.

Q. And when did you have this second rum and coke?

A. Some time later on in the evening, I think before dinner, about 9:15. It would be difficult for me to say.

Q. Who poured those drinks?

A. Mr. Crimmins poured the first one. I poured the second.

Q. What amount of rum did you put in, by ounces?

A. It would be difficult, your Honor, to estimate. I suppose two ounces.

THE COURT. I mean some people pour heavy drinks, some pour light drinks. When did you take the last one?

A. I would think about 9 o'clock. I ate about 10:00 and it was some time before that.

THE COURT. You had nothing alcoholic to drink after eating?

A. No, I didn't.

THE COURT. Was there a sustained amount of drinking by the group? Or by any particular person?

A. There wasn't that I noticed, prior to the time I left.

THE COURT. Mr. Hanify, you have advised your client of his constitutional rights?

MR. HANIFY [Edward D. Hanify, attorney in behalf of Edward Kennedy]. Yes, I have, your Honor.

THE COURT. Were you at any time that evening under the influence of alcohol?

A. Absolutely not.

THE COURT. Did you imbibe in any narcotic drugs that evening?

A. Absolutely not.

THE COURT. Did anyone at the party to your knowledge?

A. No, absolutely not.

THE COURT. In your opinion would you be sober at the time that you operated the motor vehicle to the Dyke Bridge?

A. Absolutely sober.

RECALL
JOSEPH GARGAN

Q. Prior to his leaving did you observe the Senator drinking cocktails?

A. I did not observe him drinking, as you put it, cocktails.

THE COURT. Any alcoholic beverages?

A. I would put it this way, your Honor, quite frankly, I saw the Senator earlier in the evening with a glass with ice in it, a tall glass with a dark fluid in it which I would presume was either Pepsi-Cola or Coca-Cola. Since I bought the material, I would say it was Coca-Cola. Whether there was anything in the glass besides Coca-Cola, I cannot honestly testify to, but I would say frankly that the Senator does consume rum and coke and I would assume he was drinking rum and coke at the time.

THE COURT. Was he drinking all the time that you were there?

A. Well, I saw him—oh, I would say, I noticed him on a couple of occasions with, as I say, this glass in his hand with, again as I described, a dark fluid in the early part of the evening, I will say 8:30–9:00, talking to the girls, talking to the fellows, and had this at that time. I did not notice, to tell you the truth, and to be quite honest with you, Mr. Dinis, I can't say frankly what anybody had basically to drink. For instance, Mr. LaRosa—my experience with Mr. LaRosa is that Mr. LaRosa never drinks, never has on any occasion that I know of, and yet I can't tell you whether he had a drink that night or not.

RECALL
PAUL MARKHAM

Q. Was there anything to eat or drink when you first arrived at the cottage?

A. Yes, there was some rum and coke and some either gin or vodka, and tonic. I recall I had a vodka and tonic at the time.

Q. Do you recall whether Mr. Kennedy had anything to drink?

A. Yes, he had a rum and coke at this point.

136

Q. How did you know he did?

A. Because he said to Jack Crimmins, "Who has been drinking all the rum, there is hardly any rum left." Mr. Crimmins was back and forth, and when we first arrived, Jack, I think, was in the bedroom changing, and he came out and said to Mr. Crimmins, "Gee, you didn't leave me any rum" or "you didn't get any rum for me."

RECALL
JOHN CRIMMINS

Q. Can you tell me how much drinking went on at the party?

A. Very little.

Q. What drinks were purchased to be served at the party?

A. Three half-gallons of vodka, four fifths of scotch, two bottles of rum and a couple of cases of canned beer.

Q. Did you purchase that locally, Mr. Crimmins?

A. I brought it down from Boston.

THE COURT. Is there some reason you would rather cart it all the way down rather than buying it in Hyannisport when you got there?

A. I got a price, sir.

THE COURT. What was consumed? What was the difference between what you brought and what you took back?

A. About three-quarters of a half-gallon of vodka, very little scotch, about one and a half bottles of rum, half a case of beer.

THE COURT. Did you see anyone under the influence of liquor?

A. I did not, sir.

THE COURT. Would you have any idea how much alcohol Mary Jo Kopechne consumed that night?

A. I have no idea what anybody drank but myself. Nobody tended bar, it was a self-setup on a little thing when you came in the door and you did what you wanted to.

RECALL
RAY LaROSA

Q. Did you have anything to drink during the evening?

A. I had one drink of scotch.

Q. Where were you when Senator left the cottage the first time? Did you notice his departure?

A. I believe I was in the living room sector and most everybody was standing, and I think I was over near the fireplace.

Q. Did you make any observation of Senator Kennedy's condition with regard to sobriety at the time he left.

A. I didn't notice anything unusual about his behavior.

RECALL
ANN LYONS

Q. With reference to your observations of Mr. Kennedy when he left the party, did you form any opinion as to his sobriety?

A. He was sober.

Q. I will ask you for the same opinion of Miss Kopechne.

A. Oh, absolutely.

RECALL
SUSAN TANNENBAUM

Q. Now with regards to their condition when they left, do you have an opinion as to the Senator's sobriety?

A. He certainly seemed sober.

Q. And Mary Jo Kopechne?

A. Quite definitely sober; never have I seen Mary Jo otherwise.

138

RECALL
MARYELLEN LYONS

Q. Do you have any memory about the condition of Mary Jo at the party with regard to sobriety?

A. Well, she seemed very average at the time to me. She wasn't really a drinker. She was a moderate drinker and I didn't notice any difference from the norm.

Q. And did you note anything about the Senator's behavior as to drinking?

A. No, I did not, sir.

(GREEN LIGHT)

Inspector Darby:

"FACT 25. Alcoholic beverages, consisting of rum, Scotch, vodka, and beer, were available on a self-service bar in the kitchen area.

"FACT 26. No witness admitted to more than two drinks during the party hours. No one saw Kopechne have more than one drink. No one saw Kennedy have more than two.

"FACT 27. Kopechne drank vodka, and there were three half-gallons available. Kennedy drank rum, and he complained of a shortage of rum upon his arrival at the cottage.

"FACT 28. Kennedy testified to absolute sobriety at the time he operated his car to the bridge. No witness contradicts this sobriety claim during his stay at the party.

"FACT 29. Kopechne was known by her friends to be a light drinker. No witness testified that she was other than sober at the time of her departure with Kennedy.

"FACT 30. Crimmins estimated the total quantity of liquor consumed at the cottage to be one and a half quarts of

139

vodka, one and a half bottles of rum, very little Scotch, and half a case of beer.

"Now—you will note in the foregoing testimony that there is no evidence, no evidence whatsoever, that either Kopechne or Kennedy had more than one or two drinks during their attendance at the party. This is in keeping with the small total quantity of party liquor consumed, according to Crimmins.

"Crimmins drank rum alone Wednesday night. There was some drinking Thursday night when Crimmins, LaRosa, Tretter, Gargan, Markahm, a Mr. Driscoll, Newburgh, Keough, Kopechne, and Tannenbaum were present at the cottage. On Friday night there was drinking by the same group, with the addition of Kennedy and the Lyons sisters. Mr. Driscoll was not present. LaRosa and Keough drank Scotch, Crimmins and Kennedy had rum, Markham and the young women preferred vodka. The preference of Gargan and Tretter is unknown, although testimony indicates they drank some liquor. The total quantity consumed over the three-day period was only twenty-four ounces of vodka, slightly less rum, less than half a fifth of Scotch, and a few cans of beer. Remarkably light drinking for a weekend house-party group of the size, judging from my experience in your country and mine.

"It is exactly this circumstance of light drinking that points up a major contradiction to be considered in the following—"

JUDGE BOYLE'S REPORT

State Police Chemist McHugh, who analyzed the blood sample taken from the body of Kopechne, testified the alcoholic content was .09 percent, the equivalent of three and one-half to five ounces of eighty to ninety proof liquor consumed by a person, weighing about one hundred ten pounds, within an hour prior to death, or a larger amount if consumed within a longer period.

RECALL
ESTHER NEWBURGH

THE COURT. Now, did you see Mary Jo at the time she left the party?

A. Yes, I did.

THE COURT. In a place as small as this was you must have seen her frequently during the course of the evening?

A. Yes, and I talked with her occasionally.

THE COURT. Did you see her drink any intoxicating liquor?

A. Yes. I can't recall that I saw her drink more than one.

THE COURT. What was her condition as to sobriety at any time that night?

A. Completely sober, if you can use me as an expert.

THE COURT. Nothing that would indicate to you in the slightest degree that she was influenced in any way by having taken alcoholic beverages? Not unusually jovial?

A. No. We were all very happy, but not unusually jovial because of liquor.

THE COURT. Do you know about a blood test for alcoholic content? Do you know that samples of blood are taken for the purpose of obtaining how much alcohol they contain?

A. Yes.

THE COURT. If I tell you the testimony has indicated that Mary Jo's blood had a content of .09 percentage of alcohol, which by expert testimony indicates five to six ounces of whiskey, would this change your testimony in any respect?

A. No. I wouldn't understand the five or six ounces anyway. Would that be X number of drinks?

THE COURT. Well, if you put an ounce of whiskey—what was she drinking?

A. I don't know. There was no bartender and people were pouring——

THE COURT. Does she have any particular favorite type of drink, such as scotch and soda or bourbon and water?

A. No. Notoriously among all our friends Mary Jo and I hardly drink at all.

THE COURT. That isn't what I asked you. You don't know if she has a favorite drink?

A. No, because she is not a drinker, so she wouldn't have a favorite drink.

THE COURT. Well, the alcoholic content indicates that if an ounce of whiskey or rum or scotch of 80 to 90 proof was used in each drink, that there would be somewhere between five and six drinks to reach an alcoholic content of .09.

A. Yes. I had assumed that the inquest format was relatively informal. If you would like to know, Mary Jo was not a drinker. Five or six drinks would have been completely out of order for the way she lived. And if a girl who didn't drink had that much to drink you would certainly be able to tell if she was more jovial than normal, and she was not.

THE COURT. I am only telling you what a chemical analysis shows and the chemical analysis is practically irrefutable.

A. Then I am the wrong person to be asked, because as far as I was concerned she was completely sober.

THE COURT. And you saw her the time she left?

A. Exactly the time she left.

(GREEN LIGHT)

Inspector Darby:

"FACT 31. According to chemical analysis, called by the Court 'practically irrefutable,' Kopechne consumed within

142

one hour of her death, three and one-half to five ounces of 80 to 90 proof liquor, the equivalent of at least three or four vodka and tonic highballs.

"Conforming to the Kennedy timetable, his car was driven off the bridge between 11:20 and 11:25. Assuming Mary Jo Kopechne died within ten minutes thereafter, this attestation asserts that she drank several, at least three and perhaps more, drinks containing alcohol between 10:30 and 11:15, just prior to her departure from the cottage. Newburgh, her close friend and roommate at the motel, testified that this type of drinking would be completely out of character for Kopechne, that it would have noticeably affected Kopechne, that she saw Kopechne at the exact time she left the cottage, and that Kopechne appeared to be normal and absolutely sober.

"In spite of the appearance of sobriety, was the Kopechne illness mentioned in the testimony by Crimmins, but not by Kennedy, actually a case of overdrinking during or just after a meal? Was lack of sobriety the reason she left her handbag in the cottage and failed to ask Newburgh for the room key or mention returning to the hotel to any of her friends? Why would Kopechne, by reputation a light drinker, a very light drinker, suddenly take to drink in this manner, and at a time when she appeared perfectly normal and happy?

"Perhaps there is a logical answer for all this . . . as we shall see. For the time being, however, let us again follow Mr. Kennedy and Miss Kopechne from the cottage to the bridge through the medium of his testimony—"

RECALL
EDWARD M. KENNEDY

Q. In your conversation with Miss Kopechne prior to your leaving at 11:15, did she indicate to you any necessity for returning to Martha's Vineyard or to Edgartown?

A. No.

Q. Well, when she left with you, where was she going?

A. Back to her hotel.

Q. What was your destination?

A. The ferry slip, the Katama Shores, Shiretown.

Q. Do you recall how fast you were driving when you made the right hand turn on to Dyke Road?

A. I would say approximately seven or eight miles an hour.

Q. And what were the lighting conditions and weather conditions that evening?

A. There are no lights on that road. The road was dry. There was a reasonable amount of humidity. The night was clear, extremely dark.

Q. How fast were you driving on Dyke Road?

A. Approximately twenty miles an hour.

Q. Were you aware you were driving on a dirt road when you turned onto Dyke Road?

A. I don't remember any specific time when I knew I was driving on an unpaved road. I was generally aware sometime going down the road that it was unpaved, like many of the other roads here in Martha's Vineyard and Nantucket and Cape Cod.

Q. Had you been over the road from the ferry slip to the cottage more than once that day?

A. Yes, I had, twice.

THE COURT. During your two trips, did you become aware the road from the ferry to the cottage was paved?

A. Well, I would just say that it was not of particular notice to me whether it was paved or unpaved.

THE COURT. Were you driving the car either one of these times?

A. I was not.

THE COURT. At any time after you got on the unpaved road did you realize you were on the wrong road?

144

A. No.

D.A. Q. While you were driving down Dyke Road and you noticed it was a dirt road, what happened then, Mr. Kennedy?

A. I went off Dyke Bridge into the water.

Q. Did you apply the brakes prior to going off into the water?

A. Perhaps a fraction of a second before.

Q. What happened after that, Senator?

A. Well, I remember the vehicle itself just beginning to go off the bridge and the next thing I recall is the movement of Mary Jo next to me, the struggling, perhaps hitting or kicking me and I opened my eyes and realized I was up-side-down, that water was crashing in on me, that it was pitch black. I was able to get half a gulp of air before I became completely immersed in the water. I realized that Mary Jo and I had to get out of the car.

I can remember reaching down to try and get the door handle of the car and lifting the door handle and pressing against the door and it not moving. I can remember reaching what I thought was down, which was really up, to where I thought the window was and feeling along the side to see if the window was open and the window was closed. And I can remember the last sensation of being completely out of air and inhaling what must have been a half a lung full of water and assuming that I was going to drown and the full realization that no one was going to be looking for us until the next morning and that I wasn't going to get out of that car alive and then some-how I can remember coming up to the last energy, of just pushing, pressing, and coming up to the surface.

Q. Were you aware that the windows on the passenger's side had been blown out, were you aware there was water rushing in on that side?

A. There was complete blackness. Water seemed to rush in

145

from every point, from the windshield, from underneath me, above me. It almost seemed like you couldn't hold the water back even with your hands. What I was conscious of was the rushing of the water, the blackness, the fact that it was impossible to even hold it back.

Q. And you say you had a thought to the effect that you may not be found until morning?

A. I was sure I was going to drown.

Q. Did you make any observations of the condition of Miss Kopechne at that time?

A. Well, at the moment I was thrashing around I was trying to find a way that we both could get out of the car, and some time after I tried the door and the window I became convinced I was never going to get out.

Q. Was the window closed on the driver's side?

A. The window was open.

Q. And did you go through the window to get out of the car?

A. I have no idea in the world how I got out of that car.

THE COURT. Did you see the bridge before you actually reached it?

A. The split second before I was on it.

THE COURT. Did you see that it was at an angle to the road?

A. Just before going on it I saw that.

THE COURT. Did you make any attempt to turn your wheels to follow that angle?

A. I believe I did, your Honor. I would assume that I did try to go on the bridge. It appeared to me at that time that the road went straight.

THE COURT. Were you looking ahead at the time, your attention was not diverted by anything?

A. No, it wasn't.

146

D.A. Q. Senator Kennedy, what did you do immediately following your release from the automobile?

A. I was swept away by the tide flowing at an extraordinary rate through that narrow cut there. I called Mary Jo's name until I was able to make my way to what would be the east side of the cut, waded up to about my waist and started back to the car gasping, belching and coughing.

The headlights of the car were still on and I was able to get to what I thought was the front of the car.

Q. How far were you swept along by the current?

A. Approximately 30–40 feet.

Q. Did you pass under the bridge?

A. The vehicle went over the bridge on the south side and I rested on the south side, and that was the direction the current was flowing, and I was swept I would think to the eastern shore.

Q. Now in order to get back to the car was it necessary for you to swim?

A. I couldn't swim because of the current. I swam to where I could wade and then waded along the shore to where I could go to the front of the car and start diving in an attempt to rescue Mary Jo.

Q. And you were fully aware at that time of what was transpiring?

A. Well, I was fully aware that I was trying to get the girl out of that car and I was aware that my head was throbbing and my neck was aching and I was breathless. And the last time I was hopelessly exhausted.

Q. You were not confused at that time?

A. Well, I knew there was a girl in that car and I had to get her out.

Q. And you took steps to get her out? There was no confusion in your mind about the fact that there was a person

147

in the car and that you were doing the best you could to get her out?

A. I was doing the very best I could to get her out.

AFFIDAVIT OF DOCTOR ROBERT D. WATT (read by the D.A.)

On July 19, 1969, I was called to see Edward M. Kennedy at his home. His chief complaints were headache, neck pain, generalized stiffness and soreness.

The history of the present illness was as follows: He stated that he had been in an automobile accident last night on Martha's Vineyard. The car went off a bridge. There is a lapse in his memory between hitting the bridge and coming to under water and struggling to get out. There was a loss of orientation—at the last moment he grabbed the side of an open window and pulled himself out. He was not clear on the events following but he remembered diving repeatedly to check for a passenger—without success. He went for help and returned. Again, effort to rescue passenger was without success. He was driven to the ferry slip and swam to the main body of land. He went to his hotel where he slept fitfully until 7 A.M.

Diagnosis: Concussion, contusions and abrasions of the scalp, acute cervical strain. . . . The diagnosis of concussion was predicated upon the foregoing objective evidence of injury and the history of the temporary loss of consciousness and retrograde amnesia. Impairment of judgment and confused behavior are symptoms consistent with an injury of the character sustained by the patient.

EXHIBIT B (read by the D.A.)

July 22, 1969   KENNEDY, Senator Edward

This patient was given a neurological examination in the presence of Dr. Robert Watt as a result of injuries which he sustained in an automobile accident which occurred on July

18, 1969. In describing his recollection of the events occurring at this time, he states that he can recall driving down a road and onto a bridge, and has some recollection of the car starting off the bridge which he thinks was a realization that the car struck a beam along the side of the bridge; however, he remembers nothing immediately following this; has no recollection of the car turning over or of any impact of the car against water or any solid object. There is a gap in his memory of indeterminable length, but presumably brief and his next recollection is of being in the front seat of his car which was filling with water. He somehow escaped from the car, but does not know how he did this. He states further that he can recall making repeated efforts to get back to the car by diving. Subsequent events are recalled in a somewhat fragmentary fashion with an impaired recall of their exact time relationships.

Diagnosis: Cerebral concussion. Contusions and Abrasion of Scalp. Acute Cervical Strain.

Comment: This patient gives a history of loss of consciousness and retrograde amnesia sustained at the time of his accident, and the occurrence of the head injury is corroborated by the contusions of the scalp over the vertex and in the right mastoid area. . . .

Milton F. Brougham, M.D.

(GREEN LIGHT)

Inspector Darby:

"FACT 32. Kennedy testified that Kopechne requested a ride back to her hotel with him but did not tell him of any necessity for returning, such as the sun illness Crimmins said Kennedy mentioned.

"FACT 33. Kennedy suffered a complete lapse of memory concerning the actual fall of the car from the bridge to the water, according to the recollections made before doctors on July 19 and 22, 1969, and to the Court on January 5, 1970.

"FACT 34. Kennedy's first memory of the accident was of physical contact with a struggling Mary Jo in the car after it submerged.

"FACT 35. Kennedy told Dr. Watt on July 19 that he escaped by grabbing the side of an open window and pulling himself out; but he told the Court he had no idea in the world how he got out of the car.

"FACT 36. Kennedy indicates that a very strong tide was running into the Pond at the time of the accident.

"FACT 37. Kennedy did not admit to nor complain of any mental confusion at the time he was trying to rescue Kopechne.

"FACT 38. Kennedy was aware of driving on a dirt road prior to reaching the bridge, but said he had given no particular notice to the fact that the main road was paved during two earlier trips to and from the cottage.

"FACT 39. Kennedy said he did not realize he was on the *wrong* road at any time prior to driving off the bridge.

"For the sake of brevity, I have not included the remarkably detailed and descriptive testimony Senator Kennedy gave covering various personal efforts he made to rescue Miss Kopechne. Almost every move he made in seven or eight attempts is recalled. However, he could *not* recall any of the sensations resulting from the car overturning and crashing on the bridge and into the water. The medical people called this temporary loss of consciousness and retrograde amnesia. We might also label it 'pinpoint' amnesia, as the period of time could not possibly cover more than five seconds.

"Then there is the puzzling aspect of the wrong turn onto

150

the wrong road. It does seem strange that a man as acutely observant as a United States senator must be could remain completely unaware that he was on the road to the same beach he had visited in the afternoon or that he was not on the paved road he had traveled on once in returning to the ferry and twice in going to the cottage. How could his sense of direction be so at fault when he had spent much of his life handling a sailboat in leisure hours? In sailing, a sense of direction is important, and supposedly well developed with practice.

"Perhaps even more puzzling is the indicated lack of comment or cautioning by Miss Kopechne after the turn onto the beach road. She had been back and forth on the road from the ferry slip to the cottage three times, and back and forth from cottage to beach once. No questions were asked of Kennedy about her reaction to the turn, and he volunteered nothing, so we have to assume that Mary Jo remained absolutely silent, not questioning the wrong turn off the pavement nor the trip down to the bridge. Whatever became of the storied woman backseat driver? Is she a thing of the past?"

That drew smiles, and the Inspector gave me our prearranged signal for a break.

"Ladies and gentlemen," I followed up, "we will take a ten-minute break now. Please return to your seats when I ring the bell. Thank you."

Pim and Nadia were ready with tea, coffee, and soda drinks in the dining area. It was a surprisingly quiet break. I can remember a remark by Noland Hammond that seemed to fit the mood exactly: "The Inspector casts quite a spell, Truly."

At the end of ten minutes I rang the bell, and we reassembled.

Inspector Darby:

"In our next testimonies we will find contradictions that may seem trivial; but I assure you, they do have relevancy. We are seeking to establish a credible explanation of events. Certain contradictions, while admittedly possible because of faulty recall, are just as possible because of fictional effort. In other words, memory as opposed to imagination. The sorting of these two mental powers is basic in detective work, as any devotee of mystery novels will agree. If you happen to be such a devotee, you might enjoy listening carefully now and making your own observations of conflicting points before I make my next comment.

"You will recall from earlier testimony of Mr. Kennedy that he left the bridge area sometime around midnight and returned to the cottage. To begin, we will repeat a short portion of a previous exchange—"

RECALL
EDWARD M. KENNEDY

Q. And when you arrived at the cottage, what did you do?

A. Well, I came up to the cottage, there was a white car parked there, and as I came up to the back of it, I saw Ray LaRosa at the door and I said, Ray, get me Joe Gargan; and he mentioned something like, right away, and as he was going in to get Joe, I got in the back of the car.

Q. And now did Joe come to you and did you have a conversation with him?

A. Yes, he did, and I said, better get Paul, too.

Q. What happened after that?

A. Well, Paul came out, got in the car, I said, there has been a terrible accident, we have got to go, and we took off down the road, the Main Road there.

Q. Before you drove down the road, did you make any further explanations to Mr. Gargan or Mr. Markham?

A. No sir, I said, there has been a terrible accident, and we took off.

THE COURT. Excuse me a moment. Did you go inside the cottage?

A. No, I didn't go inside.

D.A. Q. When you arrived at the cottage you asked Mr. LaRosa to tell Mr. Markham you were outdoors, outside of the house?

A. No, that is not correct. I asked Joe Gargan when he entered the vehicle to call for Markham.

Q. Did you at that time ask anyone to take you directly back to Edgartown?

A. No. I asked Mr. Gargan to go to the scene of the accident. I asked them to take me to Edgartown after their diving.

RECALL
RAYMOND S. LaROSA

Q. Did Senator Kennedy have any conversation with you around 12:15 that night?

A. I'm not sure about the time, but I was sitting out in front of the cottage alone and I heard a voice which I recognized as Senator Kennedy's call my name out twice and I only vaguely saw a form and it was extremely dark and I was looking into a light as I recall that is out in front of the cottage.

Q. Did you see the Senator?

A. Vaguely. Not so that I could recognize him, but I recognized his voice.

Q. Did he speak with you?

A. Yes, sir, he asked me to get Mr. Markham and Mr. Gargan.

Q. And where were Mr. Markham and Mr. Gargan when you found them?

A. Inside the cottage.

Q. And did they leave with Mr. Kennedy?

153

A. I don't know that for sure. They left the cottage. I didn't see them leave. I didn't see them drive away.

Q. I take it then you were inside the cottage when they left?

A. Yes, sir.

RECALL
JOSEPH GARGAN

Q. Now, prior to leaving the house, what attracted your attention to the fact that Senator Kennedy was in the back seat of the car?

A. Ray LaRosa had come into the house. I was in the kitchen area. Ray LaRosa said, the Senator is outside. He wants to see you.

Q. Did Ray LaRosa then follow you out to the car?

A. Not really. I went immediately out to the car and was about to get in when the Senator said to me, get Paul Markham. Ray was then standing in sort of what you would call the front walk of the house. I said to Ray, get Paul Markham. Ray went back into the house; Paul Markham then came out. Paul Markham and I then went into the car.

RECALL
PAUL MARKHAM

Q. Will you describe the circumstances under which you saw Mr. Kennedy again?

A. I was inside the cottage. Mr. LaRosa came in and said, "Paul, the Senator wants to see you."

Q. Can you stop there for a second? Mr. LaRosa came and asked for you?

A. He didn't ask for me. He was at the door. He said, "The Senator wants to see you."

Q. Were there others present when Mr. LaRosa made this statement?

A. Yes, sir.

Q. What did you do on hearing this?

A. I went out the front door and he said, "He is over there" and he was pointing to a car. I went over to the car. Mr. Gargan was seated in the front seat on the driver's side, and the Senator was in the back seat.

RECALL
RAYMOND LaROSA

Q. Now, when you saw the Senator out under the light when he called to you——

A. The Senator was standing out near the street, beyond the light. I was seated on the ground near the light and looking into it. I saw him standing out by a fence, a shadow, a form. I recognized the voice more than I recognized the object I saw.

Q. You did not go near him at all? Was there anything about his voice that attracted your attention when he called to you?

A. No sir, I did not go near him. He simply said, "Ray," and I looked around. I didn't know where it came from. He repeated it again and I stood up and he asked me to get Paul Markham and Joe Gargan, which I did.

Q. Did you see the Senator's car at the time when he called to you?

A. No, sir.

RECALL
ESTHER NEWBURGH

Q. At 12 o'clock what was your activity as best you remember it? Who was there at 12 o'clock that you can remember?

A. Everyone in the party except Senator Kennedy and Mary Jo.

Q. And between 12:00 and 12:30 was there any conversation or concern about getting back to Edgartown that evening?

155

A. Yes, the conversation was, "Have we missed the ferry?"

Q. And what was the conclusion?

A. I don't recall a specific conclusion. The men were talking and eventually, later than 12:30, we realized there was no chance of getting on the ferry.

Q. Were you aware that Mr. Kennedy returned to the cottage?

A. No.

Q. Between 12:00 and 12:30 do you recall Mr. Markham, Mr. Gargan, Mr. Crimmins, and Mr. LaRosa being present?

A. Yes, they were all there.

Q. Did there come a time when anyone of them left?

A. Mr. LaRosa walked outside for a few minutes.

Q. Do you recall what time that was?

A. I'm not sure exactly but I will say after 12:15.

Q. Did you see Mr. LaRosa return?

A. Yes.

Q. What did he say?

A. I didn't see him say anything. I saw him motion to Mr. Gargan and Mr. Markham.

Q. What did he do? Show the judge.

A. He did essentially what you did. Just waved his arm and asked them to come out.

Q. Mr. Markham and Mr. Gargan went out together as you remember?

A. They walked out the door. I don't know if it was side by side, but the same time.

Q. Well, either together or not together, which was it?

A. Together.

Q. Did Mr. LaRosa return to the cottage immediately after they had gone outside?

A. Yes.

RECALL
ROSEMARY KEOUGH

Q. And sometime afterwards did you learn that Senator Kennedy was outside in the car?

A. No.

Q. Were you aware that Mr. Markham and Mr. Gargan left the house later?

A. I was not there when they left later.

Q. Where were you?

A. I was walking with Mr. Tretter to the right of the cottage along the road.

Q. And at what time?

A. I didn't have a watch, but the last time I remember, it was twenty of twelve when I looked at Miss Tannenbaum's watch and went to the front of the cottage outside about fifteen minutes after that. I was in front of the cottage about fifteen minutes so I wouldn't have left the cottage for the walk until between 12:15 and 12:30.

Q. Do you know if Mr. Markham or Mr. Gargan were still there?

A. When I left, they were still there.

RECALL
ANN LYONS

Q. Could you tell us when you became aware of the fact that Mr. Kennedy had returned to the cottage?

A. I would say it was about an hour after the Senator and Miss Kopechne had left, Mr. LaRosa came in. He had been outside the cottage and he asked Mr. Markham and Mr. Gargan to go outside, the Senator had asked for them.

Q. What exactly did Mr. LaRosa say and to whom?

A. He just came in and said in a loud voice because people were talking, that Mr. Gargan and Mr. Markham, Senator Kennedy would like to see you.

Q. Mr. Gargan and Mr. Markham left the cottage approximately an hour after Mr. Kennedy left?

A. Yes.

RECALL
MARYELLEN LYONS

Q. Now, did you see Mr. Markham or Mr. Gargan leave at any time?

A. After the Senator and Miss Kopechne were gone, sometime after that, Mr. LaRosa came into the cottage where I was and called for Mr. Markham and Mr. Gargan, just asked them to come outside and after that I didn't see them again.

Q. And this was before the time you were on the road with your sister and Mr. LaRosa and saw the automobile that slowed down?

A. Oh, yes, it was before that. I hadn't gone for any walk at that time. I hadn't been out of the cottage.

Q. Did Mr. LaRosa tell you that Senator Kennedy had returned and asked for Mr. Gargan or Mr. Markham?

A. Yes, he told me that, I believe on the second walk I took.

Q. Did he describe the Senator in any way?

A. No, as I remember it, he said he didn't see him.

(GREEN LIGHT)

Inspector Darby:

"FACT 40. Kennedy completed his jog from the bridge to the vicinity of the party house sometime between 12:15 and 12:30, and on arrival noticed LaRosa standing outside the cottage.

"FACT 41. According to Kennedy, LaRosa was asked to go inside the cottage and get Gargan; then when Gargan

158

came out and got in the Valiant, Gargan was asked to get Markham.

"FACT 42. Gargan substantiates this and said he saw LaRosa, still standing outside the cottage, and asked him to go inside the cottage a second time and get Markham. The testimony of Markham agreed.

"FACT 43. Based on the testimony of these three men, Gargan and Markham received the Kennedy message separately and left the cottage separately.

"FACT 44. LaRosa testified that Kennedy asked him to get both Gargan and Markham in the original exchange. Newburgh, Ann Lyons, and Maryellen Lyons said what LaRosa implies, that LaRosa gave the message to Gargan and Markham jointly inside the cottage.

"FACT 45. Newburgh testified that she definitely saw Gargan and Markham walk out the door together.

"FACT 46. Based on Facts 44 and 45, Gargan and Markham received the message simultaneously and left the house together.

"FACT 47. Gargan and Markham left the cottage area sometime between 12:30 and 12:45, *before* LaRosa and the Lyons sisters began their walk toward the Curve. No one saw them drive away, with or without Kennedy, because all other party members were inside the house when they departed.

"We have now a direct contradiction between the Kennedy, Gargan, and Markham testimony and that of LaRosa and others concerning the relay of the Kennedy message and the departure of Gargan and Markham from the cottage. Notice, too, a third conflict in the position of LaRosa during the exchange. Gargan says LaRosa came into the kitchen area and gave him the Kennedy message, then returned to the walk outside the front door.

Here Gargan told LaRosa to get Markham. Now LaRosa goes back inside the door and informs Markham, then steps outside a third time and points out the car to Markham. None of this appears in the testimony of LaRosa or anyone else. LaRosa merely walked into the cottage after speaking with Kennedy, motioned or spoke to Gargan and Markham, then remained inside the house until they drove away in the white Valiant. Note, too, the Gargan statement that they entered the car together, while Markham says Gargan was seated in the car when he reached it.

"We might also consider the circumstances under which Kennedy, Gargan, and Markham made the drive to the beach, Truly—"

RECALL
JOSEPH GARGAN

Q. Now, at the time the Senator was in the car when Mr. Markham joined you, could we have what the Senator said again?

A. He said to me that the car has gone off the bridge down by the beach and Mary Jo is in the car.

Q. Did he say to you that he had gone off with the car?

A. No, he did not.

Q. Did he tell you any more than that about the accident?

A. No, that is all he said.

Q. How did he appear to you at the time?

A. I didn't look at him at the time.

Q. You didn't look at him?

A. No.

Q. Was he wet?

A. I didn't notice at the time.

Q. Did you have a reason for not looking at him?

A. Yes, the thing I was interested in was getting to that bridge.

THE COURT. Where was he seated?

A. In the back seat. I never looked around. He told me what the problem was and I simply drove the car towards the bridge.

RECALL
PAUL MARKHAM

Q. Was he (Mr. Kennedy) sitting or lying?

A. He was sitting. I opened the door on the passenger's side in the front seat.

Q. When you opened the door did the light go on inside?

A. I don't recall.

Q. Do you recall looking at the Senator?

A. Yes. I got in the car and put my arm on the back of the seat in this manner (indicating), and I said, "What do you want?" He said, "There has been an accident. Mary Jo was with me down at the bridge," and let's go.

Q. That is the only thing Mr. Kennedy said?

A. "There has been an accident on the bridge and Mary Jo was with me."

Q. What observations did you make of him?

A. Just that he seemed upset at this point.

Q. Was he wet?

A. I couldn't determine whether he was or not. I couldn't see him. It was very dark.

Q. Did you talk to him on the way down? Was there no conversation about anybody?

A. I don't think there was anything said from the time that he said that he was in an accident until we got there. We went there at a rather high rate of speed, very high rate of speed.

Q. Did Mr. Kennedy say he was driving at the time of the accident?

A. I don't recall him saying it at that point, but he told us at some later point that he was.

Q. Did he say he made a wrong turn on Dyke Road between the cottage and the bridge?

A. No.

Q. Did he say he made an attempt to find Mary Jo?

A. He didn't say anything that I can recall other than he had been in an accident at the bridge.

Q. Do you recall whether or not you can see the bridge as you approached it?

A. Yes, I could see the bridge as we approached it after we got down there.

(GREEN LIGHT)

Inspector Darby:

"FACT 48. The drive to the bridge was made with Kennedy making no explanatory comment and giving no details about the accident.

"The only comment here involves my curiosity about two things: how Kennedy could remain so silent about the course of events after he submerged with the car, and why the assistance of the other three men was not sought, LaRosa in particular. That a terribly distraught man, after a harrowing escape himself and a heartrending, futile effort to rescue his companion, could remain so calmly uncommunicative is incomprehensible to me—especially when we note his loquacious state during the later ride to the ferry slip with Gargan and Markham. Secondly, a thoroughly exhausted man jogs and trots over a mile because of an extreme urgency to obtain help, then stands quietly in a darkened street and asks one man to fetch another, then, almost as an afterthought, asks that man to fetch a third man. All done seemingly with no sense of urgency whatever. A remarkable example of self-discipline and composure? But why? I have heard it spoken of, the American trait of self-reliance, yet I cannot understand why Mr. Kennedy did not fully realize the immediate need for professional help. Having experienced the extreme difficulty in entering the car, why not send someone to the caretaker's house, only a stone's throw away, to telephone for help? Then go with Markham and Gargan to the bridge. There was no reason for secrecy. A driver on a strange road makes a wrong turn and has an unavoidable accident.

"I believe there are reasonable answers to all these perplexing questions, but for the present, we will return to the bridge and follow the actions of Kennedy, Gargan, and Markham in a second rescue attempt. Mr. Kennedy has already told us that Mr. Gargan and Mr. Markham removed their clothes and dove into the water. We will pick up testimony at that point—"

RECALL
EDWARD M. KENNEDY

Q. Now, how long did Mr. Gargan and Mr. Markham remain there with you?

A. I would think about forty-five minutes.

Q. And they were unsuccessful in entering the car?

A. Well, Mr. Gargan got half-way into the car. When he came out he was scraped all the way from his elbow, underneath his arm was all bruised and bloodied. This is the one time he was able to gain entrance I believe into the car itself.

Q. And did he talk to you about his experience in trying to get into the car?

A. Well, I was unable to, being exhausted, to get into the water, but I could see exactly what was happening and made some suggestions.

Q. So that you were participating in the rescue efforts? You were fully aware of what was transpiring at the time?

A. Well, to that extent. I was fully aware that Joe Gargan

and Paul Markham were trying to get in that car and rescue that girl, I certainly would say that.

Q. Did you have any idea how long Mary Jo had been in the water?

A. Well, I knew that some time had passed. I didn't add up the time and calculate it.

Q. Was it fair to say she was in the water about an hour?

A. Yes, it is.

Q. Was there any effort made to call for assistance?

A. No, other than the assistance of Mr. Gargan and Mr. Markham.

Q. I know, but they failed in their efforts to recover Miss Kopechne.

A. That is correct.

RECALL
JOSEPH GARGAN

Q. Now, you have got your car turned around at the Dyke bridge and you have your lights shining in the water?

A. They were not shining in the water, because of the position they were in, they were shining across the water in the direction of the Dyke House. I have never seen the Dyke House. I didn't notice it during the daylight or at night, but I understand it is there.

Q. What did you do then?

A. Well, I looked down and I saw this car. The car was completely underwater. I took my clothes off, including my underwear. I was stark naked. Paul Markham took his clothes off. He went into the water first. I went after him and we swam out to the car.

Q. How far did you have to swim to get to the car?

A. I would say about twenty feet.

Q. And what did you do then?

A. Well, at first we grabbed ahold of the car, because the current was tremendous and I was surprised by that at first. Paul came over and we were both holding onto this sort of long rod and holding our heads above water like this (indicating) in order to breathe.

Q. What was the Senator doing at this time?

A. I didn't notice the Senator. He was in the vicinity of the car on the bridge area. He was not in the water at the time.

Q. What did Mr. Markham do?

A. Well Mr. Markham and I were both holding onto the car. Then we made some attempts to get into the car . . . but what we found, Mr. Dinis, in doing this, the current kept dragging you away. So, I suggested to Mr. Markham that he get onto the rear of the car, that he stay there and hold on and that I would continue the attempts at diving and when I came up to reach out and grab him. The current was so terrific it would just force your eyes closed and you had to operate by feel alone. So I was doing it by feel. I reached an opening which I am sure was a window and I got myself in. I went in sideways like this (indicating) and I began to feel around, feeling around, feeling around. I then began to lose my breath and I tried to get out. I couldn't get out, I was stuck. I was stuck because I was sideways, which is stupid, and I finally realized what the problem was and I turned myself this way (indicating) and pushed myself out and came to the top of the water. After not being able to get in through the window, I spent a period of time trying to open the doors of the car and I was unsuccessful.

Q. Did you sustain any injuries?

A. My chest, my arm and my back was badly scraped.

Q. And then what happened?

A. Well, we finally determined that we just couldn't get in

the car and we got out of the water, went up onto the shore and I began to dress at the side of the car.

Q. Was there any conversation with the Senator at that time?

A. Not that I recall, Mr. Dinis. He was standing at the front of the car, Mr. Markham was also putting his clothes on, and I noticed the Senator's hair was wet and matted and very curly which it tends to be when he goes swimming. I noticed particularly his pants. They were wet and clinging. He had on yellow or light-colored pants and a black shirt that was also clinging to his body.

Q. Where did you go from there?

A. After I got dressed, I got into the driver's seat, Mr. Markham got into the front passenger's seat, and the Senator got into the back of the car. I backed up the car and almost in a daze I went over the bridge again and we started up the dirt road in the direction of the ferry.

RECALL
PAUL MARKHAM

Q. How long did you say you and Mr. Gargan were in the water trying to get into the car?

A. I will say 40 to 45 minutes.

Q. And obviously you were not successful.

A. We were singularly unsuccessful in trying to get in the car.

Q. Do you recall what Mr. Kennedy was doing while you were making your effort to retrieve her body?

A. No. The only thing I remember about that was the current was very strong. I could feel some opening and I was able to get my legs partially in. I tried to dive down several times to get in. I couldn't do it. At one point Mr. Gargan was trying to do it. Joe would attempt to get into the car and as he came up I would grab him in the cur-

166

rent. At one point he went by me and I left the car and went after him and I said, "You know, we just can't get into that car."

Q. Did you finally decide, and did Mr. Gargan concur, that the efforts were fruitless?

A. We couldn't do it.

Q. Now you came out of the water. Did you have a conversation with Mr. Kennedy at that time?

A. The Senator asked us if there was any way we could get in the car and we said we couldn't. We asked him how did it happen and he was very upset, very emotional. He said, "I just can't believe this happened." I said, "It happened. How did it happen?" He said he was going down the road. Before he knew it he was on the bridge and the car went over. He described the feeling that he had. He said, "I thought for sure that I was going to die." He said he somehow got out of the car. He tried to go back into the water again to see if he could get Miss Kopechne or try to open the door or do something. He said he couldn't. He said the only thing he could think of was to come back to get us to see if we could help, and there was nothing we could do. The girl was apparently gone. We had to get help and we had to report that.

Q. Who said that?

A. Joe and myself.

Q. So I understand it, you and Mr. Gargan suggested that you get help and report it?

A. That is correct. Report the accident.

Q. Was the suggestion about assistance, getting help, followed through in any way in the sense that someone said, "Let's get to a telephone, let's get the police"?

A. At this time we were back in the car and Mr. Gargan was driving down the dirt road.

Q. Did you notice any lights or houses?

167

A. I did not, no, sir.

Q. What conversation was going on? Where were you going to?

A. I don't know. We were just driving back to the main road. The Senator again became very emotional. He was sobbing and almost on the verge of actually breaking down crying. He said, "What am I going to do, what can I do?" I said, "There is nothing you can do," and there was some suggestion between Joe and the Senator about calling a Mr. Burke Marshall and also letting the family know. After this, he said, "Okay, take me back to the ferry," and we got back to the ferry landing. By this time there were no ferries.

Q. Were you aware that the ferry could be summonsed by using the telephone?

A. I don't know if I was aware of it or not.

Q. No one mentioned the fact that the ferry could be summonsed?

A. No.

Q. Were you aware that there was a telephone on the Chappaquiddick side of the ferry where you were?

A. No, I was not.

(GREEN LIGHT)

Inspector Darby:

"FACT 49. Kennedy did not go into the water with Gargan and Markham at the time of the second rescue attempt.

"FACT 50. Gargan noted, after his joint rescue effort with Markham, that Kennedy's hair was wet and matted and his clothes were wet and clinging to his body.

"FACT 51. The current was very strong, and the tide was rising, flowing into the Pond. The car was completely underwater.

168

"FACT 52. Gargan's chest, arm, and back were badly scraped, bruised, and bloodied, particularly one arm up to the elbow, according to Kennedy.

"FACT 53. Gargan got about halfway into the car, but failed to touch Miss Kopechne's body. Markham made no entry into the car.

"FACT 54. Gargan and Markham told Kennedy that they had to report the accident and get help, but no effort was made to call for any form of assistance.

"You will note that neither Gargan nor Markham could make any physical contact with the body of Miss Kopechne, yet Gargan was halfway into the car and stretched out his hands in various directions. All three men took it for granted the young woman was still in the car and therefore drowned. After hearing of such Herculean effort to save Miss Kopechne's life, one might well wonder why the extreme urgency with which they began their efforts was so quickly dissipated. There was no proof whatever that Mary Jo was not still alive, in or out of the car.

"Note, too, that Markham states that he did not know of an available telephone at the Chappaquiddick landing, nor did anyone suggest making a call to the police from the landing. Listen, however, to more of Mr. Gargan's testimony and then to Mr. Markham's testimony relating to actions taken around 9:00 Saturday morning—"

RECALL
JOSEPH GARGAN

Q. Did you make any effort to obtain additional assistance?

A. No, we did not.

Q. Was there a particular reason?

A. Not a particular reason, no. I mean, I dove into the water. I felt—at that moment when I went down, there was only one thing to do and that was to get into the car and as quickly as possible, because I knew if I did not there just wasn't a chance in the world of saving Mary Jo.

You must realize that Mary Jo was a very good friend of mine, a person that I hold in great esteem, great affection, and I had lost a friend. She was in the water in the car and I thought the only thing to do was to get in and get her as quickly as possible. When we failed in that, Mr. Dinis, I didn't think there was anything more that could be done.

Q. Did you have any thought as to how her body was to be removed from that car?

A. Yes, we discussed that.

Q. And was there any conversation about seeking additional assistance?

A. There was not.

Q. There was none?

A. Seeking additional assistance? You mean towards getting the car out of the water or something like that?

Q. Yes.

A. Well, after the Senator described to me what had happened he started to go into this thing about, ''I don't believe this, I don't believe this could happen to me, I don't know how this could have happened, I don't understand it,'' and I don't remember the conversation directly word for word, question and answer, but I do recall the thrust of it was that this accident, I was the one who said it, that we have got to report this accident, have got to make a report of this accident immediately. We were in the car driving in the direction of the ferry. To tell you the truth, Mr. Dinis, I don't remember this drive at all. I remember the conversation but driving the car or where we went or how we went is a blank to me.

Q. What time was this, was it somewhere around 1:00 A.M.?

170

A. I will say it would be closer to 1:30, sometime between 1:15 and 1:30.

Q. Was Mr. Markham present when you said this must be reported to the police?

A. He was.

Q. And did the Senator hear you say this?

A. No question about it.

Q. Now, you proceeded to the ferry landing on Chappaquiddick?

A. Yes, and when we arrived there we continued this conversation about the fact that he should report the accident, that he should call Dave Burke and Burke Marshall. I insisted upon that again. This conversation went around and around. This was the gist of it. ''You have got to report this thing immediately and you've got to call these two people.''

By the time we reached the ferry slip we had talked about it and I decided after the Senator was gone that he would call Dave Burke and Burke Marshall, and I also knew Jack Driscoll, who was a lawyer, was on the other side and he would probably talk at the police station with Jack. Since I was the only one who knew the girls I thought that maybe I should go back to the party as I was the best one not to alarm them and to keep them calm.

RECALL
PAUL MARKHAM

[Testimony covering conversations at the Shiretown Inn early Saturday morning]

Q. Let me ask you, did the Senator say where he was going?

A. Well, we were—what do you mean where he was going?

Q. Where he was going when the accident happened?

A. He said he was going back to Edgartown. He said he

took the wrong turn and he couldn't turn around. He said before he knew it he was at the bridge.

Q. All right. Now after the conversation between Mr. Gargan and Mr. Kennedy about notifying Mr. Burke and Mr. Marshall when you found out he had not reported the accident, what happened?

A. The Senator wanted to know where he could call. He said, I don't want to use that phone at the motel. He wanted some degree of privacy and there were going to be people around. So, Joe told him that he thought he should use . . . there was a telephone on the Chappaquiddick side that he could use and there would be some privacy.

Q. And so you went with him to the ferry and crossed to Chappaquiddick? What happened there?

A. He called Dave Burke.

(GREEN LIGHT)

Inspector Darby:

"FACT 55. At the Shiretown Inn about 8:30 Saturday morning, Gargan was aware of the telephone at the Chappaquiddick ferry landing and suggested that Kennedy use that particular phone to insure privacy in calling his administrative assistant and his lawyer.

"If Gargan knew there was a telephone at the ferry landing, why was it not used to call the police after the rescue attempts by Kennedy, Gargan, and Markham had failed. As I have just pointed out, there was no concrete evidence that Miss Kopechne was not alive. Let us suppose for a moment that a call for help had been made to the police department. What *would* have happened? We move now to the testimony of the man who actually found the body of Mary Jo Kopechne in the submerged car Saturday morning—"

CALL

JOHN N. FARRAR (Sworn)

Q. Would you please tell the Court your full name?

A. John N. Farrar.

Q. What is your occupation, sir?

A. Manager of the Turf and Tackle Shop here in Edgartown. And I am the captain of the Edgartown Fire Department Search and Rescue Division, Scuba Search and Rescue Division.

Q. And how long have you been involved in scuba diving?

A. Since I was 15 years old.

Q. And how old are you now?

A. Thirty-three.

Q. I direct your attention to July 19th, in your capacity as captain were you summoned to Dyke Road and Dyke Bridge?

A. Yes, I was. At approximately 8:25 A.M. on July 19th.

Q. How?

A. I received a message on the fire department radio that a car was upside down at the Dyke Bridge and to proceed there with scuba gear. I immediately left for the fire department to pick up the scuba gear and was joined by another fireman to go to the ferry. We missed the ferry by one trip thereby losing five minutes in transit. On the crossing over I put on my wet suit and made the tank ready to go. Chief Antone Silvia was waiting on the other side and we sped to the scene.

Q. How long did it take you to get there?

A. We arrived at the bridge at 8:45 having been in transit for 20 minutes.

Q. Were you informed that the owner of the car was Mr. Kennedy?

A. I was informed by Chief Arena who was sitting on the rear of the car in the middle of the stream that it was

173

registered to Ted Kennedy and that he thought somebody may be inside.

Q. What did you do?

A. The Chief was in a bathing suit and had attempted to
dive to the car but stated he could not make it because
the current was too swift. The tide was going out and the
water depth was about six or seven feet. The car was upside down. I went into the water and checked the car on
the driver's side. I looked through the open window and
found nothing in the front seat. I then walked around to
the back of the car and saw two feet together in the top
of the right side of the rear window.

Q. You were looking now through the rear window of the
car?

A. That is correct. And a pair of feet were clearly visible
because the light reflected off the bottom of the pond
and lighted them. I proceeded around to the right side.
On entering the open right window and looking up I
found the victim's head cocked back, face pressed into
the foot well, hand holding onto the front edge of the
back seat. By holding herself in a position such as she
could avail herself of the last remaining air in the car.

Q. Now, Mr. Farrar, having observed the body in that position, what did you do?

A. Since both right front and back windows were blown out
the removal was accomplished through the right rear
window. I had not come up at any time to tell Chief
Arena what I found. I was working under what I considered emergency conditions. I could observe a body there
by the feet, but I could not come to any conclusion as to
whether she was alive or dead.

Q. So you went into the car from the driver's side?

A. No, sir, from the right rear window. Poucha Pond had
been recently dredged and the car was resting near, very

174

near the right-hand-bank where the dredge had cut away. It was difficult for me actually to look into the left-hand (driver's) front window. I started from the driver's window, walked around the back gained access through the right rear window.

Q. Which was open?

A. Which was blown out. Fragments of glass were still in evidence around the periphery of the window frame.

Q. What did you do then?

A. I observed her position first, then carefully reached up with my hand inside taking hold of her right thigh. I turned her within the car. At this point I was aware that the girl was dead since she was hard and rigor mortis had set in. I reached her head and secured my safety line around her neck in the event I was unable swimming with her to stem the tide. For my own safety I could let her go and lose the body. I was able to stem the strong tide and I swam up to the outer rear of the car where Chief Arena waited for me. It was approximately 8:55 A.M. The recovery took ten minutes.

As soon as Chief Arena saw the body he directed the county coroner, the Medical Examiner, and the Registry of Motor Vehicles be called, and issued a pick-up order for Ted Kennedy.

(GREEN LIGHT)

Inspector Darby:

"FACT 56. Thirty minutes after the call for help Miss Kopechne's body was removed from the submerged car.

"The possibility or probability of a successful rescue if a call for help had been made just after the accident can only be based on speculative reasoning. Here is the only testimony we have access to that may be termed relevant—"

175

RECALL
JOHN FARRAR

Q. Did you go back into the water and make any other search?

A. I returned to the wreck and removed a purse resting on the roof headliner inside the car. At the time I removed her body I observed a gold chain belt around her waist that became unlinked and fell to the bottom. I picked that up when I picked up the purse. Since it was still thought that another person could be in the car we conducted another up-tide search and found no other body.

Q. Were you present when the motor vehicle was righted?

A. Yes. I swam down-tide of the vehicle in the event anything else was dislodged. I was partially on the surface and partially under water, and at the time it was righted and being towed out I observed large air bubbles emanating from the vehicle.

Q. With respect to windows and doors did you make any observations?

A. The two windows on the front and rear doors were blown out with most of the glass shattered and spread throughout the car as if from impact. The driver's window was rolled down to within an inch of the bottom. The driver's door was locked. The snap button was pressed down. The only window intact was the left rear window. I didn't have occasion to observe the two right-hand doors other than to notice there was extensive damage to both doors and the entire right side and top.

Q. Did you see whether the ignition was on?

A. Yes, sir. I found the ignition and the headlight switch in the ON position. The gear was in DRIVE and the brake off. At a later date we examined the trunk which we found remarkably dry.

Q. Mr. Farrar, did you make an observation as to how this body was clothed, dressed?

A. She had on a white blouse with a gold chain belt, dark blue slacks, and sandals on her feet. In other words, dressed as if she had just come from a party.

Q. Did you make any other observations at the scene with regard to the automobile or the body which you have not yet told us?

A. I spoke with Dr. Mills at the scene as he was making his examination of the body. Would you like me to go into that briefly or is that necessary?

Q. No, Dr. Mills has testified.

A. I spoke with Mr. Frieh at the scene. We went through the car extensively after it was drawn out . . . the inside, the back seat, the trunk, and the trunk was remarkably dry.

CALL
EUGENE FRIEH (Sworn)

Q. What is your occupation, sir?

A. Mortician.

Q. And in that capacity were you called to Dyke Bridge in Chappaquiddick?

A. Yes. Possibly between 9:00 and 9:15 A.M. There was a drowning.

Q. Now, did you have occasion to observe the body at the scene and did you observe Dr. Mills' examination?

A. I did so.

Q. And what did you observe when Dr. Mills performed his examination?

A. Well, the usual procedure of general examination of a body so found. Dr. Mills loosened up the front of the blouse, took his stethoscope and applied it to various sections of the thoracic region and the abdominal region. He also manipulated the thoracic region with his hands.

Q. Did this produce a flow of water?

177

A. It produced some water flow, water and foam, mostly foam.

Q. After you left the scene you took the body to your funeral home? And you waited until you heard from Dr. Mills?

A. I was so instructed by Dr. Mills at the dock. He called about 12:30 that noon. He said if I was perfectly satisfied with my diagnosis that no further examination such as an autopsy would be necessary and just to go ahead and make arrangements.

Q. He also told you he wanted a blood sample?

A. Yes. We produced a blood sample from the axillary region.

Q. In your preparation of the body, did you notice any external signs or marks or bruises or what did you observe?

A. Well, I assisted my own assistant in cleansing the body, soaping the body down with a germicidal soap and taking a spray and washing the body and I personally took charge of cleansing the hair which was impregnated with much salt water and a little seaweedage and in so doing I thoroughly examined the scalp and manipulated it in my fingers to see if there were any fractures, feeling in my own mind going over a bridge and crashing there might be some fractures but I didn't find any fractures.

Q. When did the body leave your funeral home?

A. At 12:30 Sunday noontime.

CALL
DONALD R. MILLS (Sworn)

Q. You are a physician and you have a special occupation with reference to your profession?

A. I am a physician and I am Associate Medical Examiner for the County.

Q. And how long have you been so occupied, Doctor?

A. In excess of twenty years.

Q. In your capacity you were summonsed to Dyke Bridge, what did you do on arriving at the scene?

A. I asked them to take the body in the litter out of the police cruiser so I might examine it. I made a thorough examination of the body of a girl.

Q. Now your duty as a Medical Examiner is what, Doctor?

A. To determine the cause of death.

Q. Any death?

A. Well, death in several categories of cases, unexplained deaths, deaths that have been unattended by a physician.

Q. You made an examination of this body at the scene, tell us exactly what you did.

A. I pulled back the blankets and saw the body of a fully dressed attractive woman. I would say in her twenties, blonde, hair swept back, wearing some bracelets on her right wrist and arm. I believe there was a ring.

Q. Could you tell us how were her arms, down in a fixed position?

A. Her arms were raised. Her hands in a sort of semi-claw position. Her head was tipped back a little to one side. She was completely stiff; that is, in complete rigor mortis.

Q. Could you tell from your examination, Doctor, approximately how long this body had been dead?

A. My estimate was six or more hours.

Q. You formed an opinion as to what was the cause of death?

A. I formed my opinion by the fact that this girl was completely filled with water; that is, her bronchial tubes were full, her mouth was full of water. There was water in her nose. This was clearly demonstrated by making just a light pressure on the chest wall in which case water would simply pour out of the nose and mouth.

179

There was some foam about the nose and mouth which is characteristic of drowning.

Q. Did you find any external marks, incised wounds or bruises?

A. No.

Q. How long were you at the scene with this body?

A. From ten to fifteen minutes.

THE COURT. Expert evidence already introduced has indicated that the white blouse was subjected to chemical analysis and shows evidence of blood. Now, assuming the white blouse was the one worn by the decedent at the time you examined her, are you able to express a medical opinion with reasonable certainty whether the presence of that blood is consistent with your diagnosis of death by drowning?

A. Yes. When a person drowns there is what we call an exacerbation of blood from the lungs in the violent attempts to gain air. And blood may be evidenced in the mouth and nose. Such blood might, in the physical efforts to avoid drowning, spread almost anywhere to the person's clothing.

(GREEN LIGHT)

Inspector Darby:

"FACT 57. The medical examiner gave the cause of death as drowning, and no other medical evidence refutes this. There were no external marks of any consequence and no skull fracture. The blood found on the blouse was consistent with death by drowning. There is some conflict in the testimony of Mills, the examiner, and Frieh, the mortician; Mills indicating a large flow of water from the nose and mouth under thoracic pressure; Frieh indicating that the flow was mostly foam.

"FACT 58. Because of the variables, the time of death could only be approximated at six or more hours prior to 9:30 A.M.

"FACT 59. There were indications of trapped air in the car even though it had been submerged for ten to twelve hours.

"FACT 60. The tide was flowing *out* with four-knot speed at 8:55 A.M., with *low* or slack tide estimated at 11:30 A.M.

"FACT 61. A purse or handbag, later identified as belonging to Rosemary Keough, was found inside the Kennedy car.

"FACT 62. The vehicle's ignition was ON, the gear in DRIVE, the headlights on FULL BRIGHT, and the driver's door locked with the window down.

"Mary Jo could have died within minutes or she could have survived for two to three hours. There were too many variables for even an approximated exact estimation by the medical examiner. His estimate of six or more hours at 9:30 A.M. meant that she could have been alive up to 3:30 A.M. While it might be adjudged possible that she died of asphyxiation instead of drowning, there is no real evidence to substantiate such reasoning. And there is no evidence whatever of violence resulting in injurious harm prior to the accident.

"The tide flow as described by Kennedy, Gargan, and Markham was *in* to the Pond; and this is correct based on Farrar's information. *Low* tide on the night of July 18 can be estimated to have been at 11:04 P.M.

"A handbag found in the car and belonging to Rosemary Keough was apparently left in the car when she and Charles Tretter drove the Kennedy car into Edgartown about 9:00 Friday night to obtain equipment to provide music. Their testimony on this was conclusive.

"The vehicle was unquestionably *driven* off the bridge, but there is no way of determining the exact circumstances, such as speed. There was some testimony based on skid marks, et cetera, indicating that Mr. Kennedy's estimate of twenty miles per hour *could* be correct. There is a puzzling element in Fact 62: Why would the driver's door be locked, with the window down? You might want to keep that in mind.

"The next testimony describes events occurring immediately after Kennedy, Gargan, and Markham leave the scene of the accident. In particular, Senator Kennedy's swim across the Edgartown-Chappaquiddick channel—"

RECALL
EDWARD M. KENNEDY

Q. And now may I ask you, Mr. Kennedy, was there any reason why no additional assistance was asked for?

A. Was there any reason?

Q. Yes, was there any particular reason why you did not call either the police or the fire department?

A. Well, I intended to report it to the police.

THE COURT. That is not quite responsive to the question.

A. I intended to call for assistance and to report the accident to the police within a few short moments after going back into the car.

Q. I see, and did something transpire to prevent this?

A. Yes.

Q. What was that?

A. With the Court's indulgence, to prevent this, if the Court would permit me I would like to be able to relate to the Court the immediate period following the time that Mr. Gargan, Mr. Markham and I got back in the car.

THE COURT. I have no objection.

MR. DINIS. I have no objection.

A. After Gargan and Markham dove they likewise became exhausted and no further diving efforts appeared to be of any avail and they so indicated to me and I agreed. So they came out of the water and to the car and said to me at different times as we drove down the road to the ferry that it was necessary to report this accident. A lot of different thoughts came into my mind at that time about how I was going to really be able to call Mrs. Kopechne in the middle of the night to tell her that her daughter was drowned, to be able to call my own mother and my own father, relate to them, my wife, and even though I knew that Mary Jo Kopechne was dead and believed firmly that she was in the back of that car I willed that she remained alive.

As we drove down that road I was almost looking out the front window trying to see her walking down that road. I related this to Gargan and Markham and they said they understood this feeling, but it was necessary to report it. And about this time we came to the ferry crossing and I got out of the car and we talked there just a few minutes. I just wondered how all of this could possibly have happened. I also had sort of a thought and the wish and desire and the hope that suddenly this whole accident would disappear, and they reiterated that this has to be reported and I understood at the time that I left that ferry boat slip that it had to be reported and I had full intention of reporting it, and I mentioned to Gargan and Markham something like, "You take care of the girls, I will take care of the accident,"—that is what I said and I dove into the water.

Now, I started to swim out into that tide and the tide suddenly became, felt an extraordinary shove almost pulling me down again and suddenly I realized even as I failed to realize before I dove into the water that I was in a weakened condition, although as I had looked over that distance between the ferry slip and the other side, it seemed to me an inconsequential swim; but the water got colder, the tide began to draw me out and for the second time that evening I knew I was going to drown and the strength continued to leave me. By this time I was probably 50 yards off the shore and I remembered being swept down toward the Edgartown Light and well out into the darkness, and I tried to swim at a slower pace to be able to regain whatever kind of strength that was left in me.

Sometime after, about the middle of the channel, the tide was much calmer and I began to make some progress, and finally was able to reach the other shore and all the nightmares and all the tragedy and all the loss of Mary Jo's death was right before me again. I pulled myself on the beach and attempted to gain some strength. After that I walked up one of the streets in the direction of the Shiretown Inn. I walked into a parking lot that was adjacent to the Inn and I can remember almost having no further strength to continue, and leaning against a tree for a length of time, trying to really gather some kind of idea as to what happened and feeling that I just had to go to my room at the time, which I did by walking through the front entrance of the Shiretown Inn up the stairs.

RECALL
JOSEPH GARGAN

Q. What happened when you arrived at the ferry landing?

A. . . . With that the Senator got out of the back seat of the car, took about three steps and dove into the water and started to swim across the cut. I then jumped out of the car. Paul Markham jumped out of the car, and we watched, and he started to swim across and I watched him until he was about half-way or three-quarters of the way across.

Q. Did you see him reach the other side?

A. I did not.

Q. Weren't you concerned about his ability to make it?

A. No. Not at all. The Senator can swim that five or six times both ways. That may seem unusual, Mr. Dinis, except I have been with the Senator 30 years swimming and sailing and I don't know if you know the breakwater off Hyannisport, but we used to swim around that and it is the only thing the Senator has done since his back injury, besides skiing. The real form of exercise now is swimming. I assume he had his back brace on that night. I was not concerned about his ability to make it to the other side.

RECALL
PAUL MARKHAM

Q. Can you tell us where he went into the waters in this ferry area?

A. I think it was just to the right of where the ferry is. We pulled down at the right-hand side of the road and I am quite sure he went in right at that point.

Q. Did he have his clothing on?

A. I don't know whether he had shoes on. He had his shirt and pants on.

Q. Did you watch him swim?

A. Yes. For as far as we could see. Probably half-way across.

Q. In time, Mr. Markham, how long did you observe him in the water?

A. Three or four minutes or so.

Q. Were you concerned whether or not he would arrive safely on the other side?

A. No, I wasn't.

185

CALL

JARED GRANT (Sworn)

Q. Your occupation, sir?

A. Owner of the Chappaquiddick ferry.

Q. And were you operating the ferry sometime on the 18th and 19th of July, 1969?

A. Yes, I operated on the night of July 18th.

Q. What time did you close up?

A. At about a quarter of 1:00.

Q. And what time did you leave the area?

A. About 20 after 1:00. It was a beautiful night, very calm, the water was like glass. That is the reason I stayed there because it was a humid night and it was too hot to sleep.

Q. Was there a moon that night?

A. I can't remember for sure. There were a lot of people. It was Regatta night. There were people on the dock; there were people fishing off the dock on the Edgartown side. There were boats running back and forth in the Harbor.

Q. Were you available for calls if someone wanted the ferry that night?

A. I was. Year round we are on call 24 hours a day.

Q. When do you normally close down, and if someone wanted you after closing where would they call?

A. Usually we close at 12:00 midnight. The number to call is posted on either side of the ferry. It is the number for my house.

Q. And did you receive any calls that night?

A. No.

(GREEN LIGHT)

Inspector Darby:

"Before proceeding, may I read from the affidavit of Mr. Donald L. Sullivan, an engineer providing information for the Kennedy legal staff.

186

During the night of July 18, 1969, we have assumed that the weather was clear and we have been unable to find anyone who can tell us whether or not there was a ground fog or haze in the vicinity of the bridge on this particular night. There was a Crescent moon. A calculation of moonset for the latitude and longitude of Chappaquiddick based on data from the nautical almanac shows that the moon was below the horizon at 10:22 P.M. that evening.

"FACT 63. Kennedy swam across the Edgartown-Chappaquiddick channel, departing from the ferry slip and arriving at a point on the opposite shore diagonally to the right. The diagonal direction was caused by the inflowing tide. Gargan and Markham could visually follow Kennedy's progress up to midchannel, but did not see him arrive on the Edgartown side.

"FACT 64. Neither Gargan nor Markham showed any real concern for Kennedy's safety in making the swim, although they must have been aware of the tide effect described by Kennedy.

"I must say I am impressed by the confidence shown by Mr. Gargan and Mr. Markham in Mr. Kennedy's ability to swim across to Edgartown and to cope all alone with a most trying situation. Only once in their testimony is there even a slight mention of anxiety about the physical and mental condition of a man who had caused a fatal automobile crash; escaped death from drowning by mere seconds; spent himself to the point of sheer exhaustion in a single-handed rescue effort; walked, jogged, trotted, and stumbled well over a mile in an urgent and desperate call for help; broken down in almost hysterical sobbing from the emotional trauma; and who, finally, could be seen being swept toward the open sea in the darkness of the moonless sky. Here is that testimony—"

RECALL
JOSEPH GARGAN

Q. What happened when you arrived there?

A. . . . We then got in the car, drove down the road to the cottage. At that time I said to Mr. Markham that maybe we better go back to the ferry slip and I will swim across, so we went past the cottage, turned the car around. We bypassed the cottage and went back to the ferry slip. By the time we reached the slip we talked about it and I decided since the Senator had gone he was going to report the accident. I felt he would call Dave Burke, Burke Marshall and I also knew Jack Driscoll, a lawyer, was on the other side and would probably talk at the police station with Ted, that since I was the only one who knew the girls that maybe I should go back to the party because I was probably the best one not to alarm them and to keep them calm at the time.

RECALL
PAUL MARKHAM

Q. You were not concerned about Mr. Kennedy's safety. All right. What did you do after you had lost sight of him half-way across?

A. Mr. Gargan and I got back into the car. We started to go back to the cottage.

Q. What time were you on this landing area, approximately?

A. I would say sometime about 20 past, half past 1:00.

Q. You left to return to the cottage?

A. Yes, sir. Not directly. We drove back to the cottage. We had some discussion about maybe one of us or we [both] should be with him so we turned around. I think it was just before we came to the cottage when we said we better do that. So we circled around, came back to the landing. I said, "I can't swim across, my leg is throbbing," at this point. I didn't know the girls. This was the first

188

time I had met them and we thought we better do as he
suggested, go back and keep them calm.

Q. At the ferry area at any time did Mr. Gargan make an attempt to go into the water.

A. I don't recall that he did, no.

(GREEN LIGHT)

Inspector Darby:

"FACT 65. Before a final return to the cottage, Gargan and
Markham made one complete trip to the party-house
area and back because of a thought that at least one
of them should cross over and join Kennedy. The
extreme need to keep Mary Jo's friends calm took
precedence over the desire to be helpful to Mr. Kennedy.

"We might conclude from the foregoing that there was *some*
concern for Mr. Kennedy's welfare. Perhaps enough for a
phone call and an offer of assistance. Why not a suggestion that
Markham wait at the ferry landing for the arrival of the police
and accompany them to the accident scene? After all, Mr. Kennedy would not have to be awakened; on the contrary, he would
be quite busy with all he was expected to accomplish. But how
could Mr. Gargan make a telephone call?

"We have heard Mr. Markham testify that Mr. Gargan suggested the ferry-landing telephone for privacy later that morning. At 1:30 in the morning can we assume that Gargan was
aware of a telephone not more than a few feet away? Here is
Mr. Gargan's own testimony on the subject—"

RECALL
JOSEPH GARGAN

Q. Now did the Senator leave with you when you left the
Shiretown Inn at 8:30 or 9:00 o'clock?

189

A. He did.

Q. And where did you go?

A. We went to Chappaquiddick to that little thing that looks like an MTA station with a phone in it.

Q. Was there any particular purpose in crossing over on the ferry at that time in the morning?

A. So he could make a phone call.

Q. And that was the only purpose you had in mind at that time?

A. That is correct. You have to remember that I have been coming here and racing for thirty years and one thing you can't get in an Edgartown weekend, Mr. Dinis, is a telephone. I know all the telephones on this island well and where they are and you just can't get them.

(GREEN LIGHT)

Inspector Darby:

"FACT 66. Gargan knew there was a telephone at the ferry landing when he, Kennedy, and Markham arrived there at 1:30 in the morning after leaving the scene of the accident.

"There can be little doubt that the availability of a telephone at the ferry landing was known to at least one of the three men. Then why wasn't a call for assistance made at that point? We have heard the names Dave Burke, Burke Marshall, and Jack Driscoll, the lawyers, and those names are repeated many times in the testimony relating to the moments just after the Gargan-Markham rescue attempt, but what about the *victim* of the accident? There was absolutely no proof that she was dead. Where is the immediacy of concern for Miss Kopechne?

"There was a close and friendly relationship between the young woman and Mr. Gargan and Mr. Kennedy. And there was great concern over the reactions of her own close friends.

We have heard Mr. Gargan's testimony about his friendship with Mary Jo; what about the relationship with Mr. Kennedy? Let the senator describe in his own words the relationship and his desire to protect the emotional feelings of her friends—''

RECALL
EDWARD M. KENNEDY

Q. Had you known Miss Kopechne prior to July the 18th?

A. Well, I have known her—my family has known her for a number of years. She has visited my house, my wife. She has visited Mrs. Robert Kennedy's house. She worked in the Robert Kennedy Presidential campaign, and I would say that we have known her for a number of years.

Q. Now, directing your——

A. If the question is, have I ever been out with Mary Jo——

Q. No. This is not the question. The question was whether you just knew her socially prior to this event.

A. Well, could I give you a fuller explanation of my knowledge of Mary Jo, your Honor?

MR. DINIS. I have no objection.

THE COURT. Go ahead.

A. I have never in my life, as I have stated in my television broadcast, had any personal relationship whatsoever with Mary Jo Kopechne. I never in my life have been either out with Mary Jo Kopechne nor have I ever been with her prior to that occasion where we were not in a general assemblage of friends, associates, or members of our family.

THE COURT. I think we can put in the record this question. Why did you not seek further assistance after Mr. Gargan and Mr. Markham had exhausted their efforts in attempting to reach Mary Jo?

A. It is because I was completely convinced at that time that no further help and assistance would do Mary Jo any more good. I realized that she must be drowned and still in the car, and it appeared the question in my mind was, what should be done about the accident.

MR. DINIS. Your Honor, may I introduce this statement made by Senator Kennedy in a televised broadcast?

THE COURT. You may. Exhibit #3.

Q. Now, Senator, in that televised broadcast, you said and I quote, ''I instructed Gargan and Markham not to alarm Mary Jo's friends that night,'' is that correct?

A. That is correct.

Q. Can you tell the Court what prompted you to give this instruction to Markham and Gargan?

A. I felt strongly that if those girls were notified that an accident had taken place and that Mary Jo had in fact drowned, which I became convinced of by the time that Markham and Gargan and I left the scene of the accident, that it would only be a matter of seconds before all of those girls who were dear friends of Mary Jo's to go to the scene of the accident and dive themselves and enter the water and with, I felt, a good chance that some serious mishap might have occurred to any one of them. It was for that reason that I refrained—asked Mr. Gargan and Mr. Markham not to alarm the girls.

RECALL
JOSEPH GARGAN

Q. What happened when you arrived at the ferry landing?

A. —at that time or at the end of this conversation the Senator said to me, said to both of us basically, ''All right, all right, I will take care of it, you go back, don't upset the girls, don't get them involved; I will take care of it.''

192

RECALL
PAUL MARKHAM

Q. What happened when you got to the ferry area?

A. We got there and the Senator said, "I will take care of it, you people go back, don't alarm them back at the cottage, I am going to go across," and with that, I don't know whether we were out of the car or in the car, but he got out of the car and swam across.

(GREEN LIGHT)

Inspector Darby:

"FACT 67. Gargan and Markham were given definite instructions to return to the cottage and keep the other young women in a calm state. This was their prime duty as they saw it, and the taking of any other action was precluded.

"Very well, now we have Senator Kennedy on his own, on his way to the police station with proper legal advice; and Mr. Gargan and Mr. Markham on the way to calm, and cause to remain calm, the five young women friends of Mary Jo. These friends, unaware for the time being of her death, would most certainly learn of it in a relatively short time when the police were notified and came to Chappaquiddick and Dyke Bridge—and to the cottage, of course, as a matter of procedure. As we have heard from previous testimony, the search and rescue division of the Edgartown fire department and the police department were well organized for fast, efficient response to calls for assistance in situations where a life may be at stake. And Mr. Gargan and Mr. Markham would naturally want to be of every assistance to the rescuing force, as well as to attend to the normal emotional response of Mary Jo's friends when they learned of her tragic passing.

"We will return now to the party cottage and see how and at what time these two gentlemen went about their appointed task. First, I suggest that we look once more at the vital element of time in our thought deliberations—"

RECALL
JOSEPH GARGAN

Q. Do you know what time it was when you arrived back at the cottage?

A. I would guess it would be around 2:15.

RECALL
PAUL F. MARKHAM

Q. Now you are returning to the cottage. Do you know what time you got back there?

A. No, I don't.

Q. I think you said you thought you were at the landing approximately 1:30 the first time. And you traveled back and forth, would 2 o'clock be a safe approximation?

A. Yes. As I say I don't know the exact time.

RECALL
MARYELLEN LYONS

Q. Do you know what time Mr. Gargan and Mr. Markham returned after you speculated about their being missing?

A. I would say it was approximately 2:15, 2:30, in that vicinity.

RECALL
ANN LYONS

Q. After the walk, what did you do upon arriving at the cottage?

A. I asked the time and someone told me it was approaching 2:00.

Q. Sometime thereafter did Mr. Markham and Mr. Gargan arrive?

A. I went to bed at that point in the bedroom. But I heard them return.

Q. Could you tell about how long after you returned they arrived?

A. I would say a half hour, 45 minutes.

Q. So, it is safe to say approximately 2:30 or thereabouts?

A. Yes, sir, but again I can only estimate. I didn't have a watch.

RECALL
ESTHER NEWBURGH

Q. Did you see Mr. Gargan and Mr. Markham return?

A. Later that evening I did, yes, after 2 o'clock.

RECALL
ROSEMARY KEOUGH

Q. And what time did you return to the cottage, do you know?

A. I believe about 2 o'clock.

Q. Did you find anybody at the cottage at that time?

A. Yes, sir, everyone had returned to the cottage except Mr. Kennedy and Mary Jo.

CALL
CHARLES TRETTER (Sworn)

Q. Do you know what time you returned to the cottage?

A. I think it was around 2 o'clock.

Q. And you tell the Court when you returned after the second walk Mr. Gargan, Mr. Markham, Mr. LaRosa and various other people were present?

A. Yes. When I came into the cottage, people were starting to settle down. Mr. Crimmins and Mr. Gargan were talking.

Q. Could you tell us where these people were when you came in?

A. As best I can recall, Mr. Crimmins and Mr. Gargan were standing in the kitchen area on the right-hand side. The cottage was dark. People were settling down to sleep. I believe Mr. Markham was either lying on the floor or on a pulled out couch.

THE COURT. When you returned and found all the group there with the exception of Mr. Kennedy and Miss Kopechne, everybody else was suddenly there and had not been there when you left?

A. With the possible exception of Mr. Crimmins.

THE COURT. Did you inquire as to what had happened, where they had gone, why they had gone leaving you two all alone?

A. I may have, but my impression is of my coming into the cottage and Mr. Gargan saying, "Jack, it is late, let's get some sleep," and I could hear the two Lyons sisters who I know very well, saying, "It is late, let's get some sleep."

THE COURT. Was there any unusual excitement when you got back to the cottage and found them all there?

A. No. I think it was just aggravation.

THE COURT. No indication and nothing said about anything unusual happening?

A. No.

RECALL
JOSEPH GARGAN

Q. You went back to the cottage about 2:15 and you remained silent about the accident?

A. That is correct.

RECALL
PAUL MARKHAM

Q. Could you tell us who was present when you arrived back at the cottage?

A. There were present, Mr. LaRosa who I think was in bed in one of the bedrooms, Mr. Crimmins who was still up. There were two of the young women there, Miss Tannenbaum and Miss Newburgh, one was laying down on the couch, the other was seated on the couch. The two Lyons sisters were in the other bedroom.

Q. Did you have a conversation with any of these people?

A. This is the only conversation I had at that point. I came into the house, I was very tired and I sat down on the edge of the couch and kind of slumped back (indicating) like that, and I apparently hurt her leg or something. The girls were not in a very good mood at this point, I might add. She said something to me about watch out you are laying on my legs, and I said I'm sorry, I'm tired and exhausted, and I said something about you are not going to believe what happened. She then got up and I slumped down on the couch for half an hour or forty-five minutes, put my leg up on the couch, then got up, walked outside, came back in, sat down on a chair, and went back out again and sat in the front seat of the car for an hour or so. It was dawn by this time and I came back in.

THE COURT. Let me just stop there one minute. I understood previously when you talked about the incident of leaning back against the girl's leg and she remonstrated in some way that you said you won't believe what happened?

A. Yes, sir.

THE COURT. Then you were stopped. Well, there must have been more to it than that. You were making the beginning of a statement, weren't you? You won't believe what happened. You didn't just stop there?

A. No. I said I am tired, exhausted. You won't believe what happened or what we are doing, or words to that effect.

THE COURT. And you said no more?

A. No more. She got up and left and there was nobody to talk to at that point.

D.A. Q. Did anyone say to you, well, what do you mean?

A. No.

Q. Was this about the same time Mr. Gargan had said that you are taking the Senator to the ferry when he swam across; that all took place at the same time?

A. At about the same time we came into the cottage.

RECALL
SUSAN TANNENBAUM

Q. Now, when Mr. Gargan returned did you have any conversation with him as to the whereabouts of Mary Jo or the Senator?

A. No.

Q. Did you hear Mr. Gargan tell some of the girls what had happened?

A. No.

Q. Did you have any conversation with Mr. Markham?

A. No, but I overheard him say he was very tired. I think he said this to Miss Newburgh and to me.

Q. Did he give you any reason why he was tired? What was his appearance? Was he excited?

A. No, he just seemed tired.

Q. And what about Mr. Gargan's appearance, did you make any note about that?

A. No.

RECALL
ESTHER NEWBURGH

Q. Did you observe their [Gargan and Markham] appearance when they returned?

A. Definitely.

Q. Was there any difference?

A. When they came back, Miss Tannenbaum and I were in the living room on the couch. Mr. Gargan came in and collapsed. He walked to the couch with Mr. Markham, and he almost fell at the bottom of my ankles. He said to me, ''please get up,'' and he said something to the effect, ''I'm exhausted, if you knew what I have been through you would let me lie there.'' He was red in the face and looked tired and exhausted.

Q. How about Mr. Markham?

A. I was concerned mostly in trying to get some sleep and I wasn't looking at them specifically.

Q. Was there any discussion by anybody other than what Mr. Gargan had said?

A. Yes, we asked where Mary Jo was.

Q. You asked who? Who is we?

A. The two Lyons sisters and I were asking each other the question. We didn't ask any of the men. And we determined in our minds that she must be back at the motel and she was lucky, she was asleep.

Q. Didn't you ask Mr. Gargan what he meant when he said, ''I am exhausted''?

A. At some point later on I heard him saying something to the effect that the Senator swam across and perhaps my own mind then assumed that Mary Jo was back at the motel.

Q. How did you conclude that?

A. Well, she had taken the car. I don't know. It is very confusing now.

RECALL
MARYELLEN LYONS

Q. Mr. Gargan and Mr. Markham returned to the cottage sometime later?

A. Yes. When they arrived, we asked them where they had

been; what had happened? And it was, oh, don't even ask us, we have been looking for boats. It was confused.

Q. They said they had been looking for boats?

A. That was one of the things they said, and somebody said Miss Kopechne was back at Katama Shores and the Senator was back in Edgartown.

Q. Now, who said that Miss Kopechne was back at Katama Shores?

A. I believe that it was Mr. Gargan.

Q. Did he say how she got there?

A. I assumed that—I can't remember whether he said it, that she made the last ferry.

Q. And they told you that the Senator jumped into the water and swam across the channel. Did you ask why the Senator decided to swim across the channel?

A. No, I didn't.

Q. Wasn't there any one conversation about that behavior?

A. Well, no one was concerned really about anything. When they got back, we thought they had been stuck in the sand, and where have you been, and that was about the size of it. It was confusing.

Q. Did anyone ask where the Senator's car was?

A. As I remember, Mr. Gargan told me Mary Jo had taken the car on the last ferry.

Q. Was there any further questions about these particular events? Did you find them unusual?

A. At the time? No, I didn't. As I say, it was a very confused thing. It wasn't that somebody came back and everybody was waiting for a story. Some of the people had gone to bed. We just said, what's going on and it wasn't in any chronological order. It was just that everything was just fine and they had been swimming and this and that and so forth.

RECALL
ROSEMARY KEOUGH

Q. Had you heard any conversation concerning the whereabouts of Mary Jo or Senator Kennedy?

A. I did ask Mr. Gargan.

Q. And what did he tell you?

A. He said not to worry about it, that Mary Jo and the Senator had probably taken the ferry.

Q. Did anyone else hear Mr. Gargan tell you that?

A. I don't believe so. I was talking directly to Mr. Gargan.

Q. And what happened then?

A. Everyone tried to find some place to go to sleep.

RECALL
ANN LYONS

Q. Did anyone ask where Miss Kopechne was that morning of the nineteenth?

A. Well, after I went to bed and Mr. Gargan and Mr. Markham had returned, Miss Newburgh and my sister came into the bedroom and later Mr. Gargan knocked on the door and he came in and was talking. I don't recall the conversation, but I can recall what I said. The first was, it is late and you have to sail in the morning, let's get some sleep; and then I asked Mr. Gargan where Miss Kopechne was. He told me she was at Katama Shores.

Q. Did you ask where Mr. Kennedy was?

A. He said he also had returned to his hotel.

Q. Was there any other conversation?

A. I asked where they had been.

Q. And what was said?

A. I am trying to recall. I think that they had gone with the Senator to the ferry and the ferry wasn't there and the Senator had swam across.

Q. Did anyone say, where is the car?

A. Yes, but I don't recall if it was myself or my sister.

Q. And what was the response?

A. That Miss Kopechne had taken the car to the Katama Shores.

(GREEN LIGHT)

Inspector Darby:

"FACT 68. The best estimate of the time of arrival at the cottage by Gargan and Markham is sometime between 2:15 and 2:30 A.M.

"FACT 69. Gargan and Markham did not tell anyone about the accident and the death of Mary Jo Kopechne.

"FACT 70. Gargan told two or more persons that Mary Jo had taken Senator Kennedy's car and returned to her motel on the last ferry and that the senator had swam across the channel and went to his hotel.

"FACT 71. There was no apparent evidence of or mention of the severe injuries to Gargan's chest, back, and arm described in earlier testimony. There is no evidence provided by testimony that these wounds were ever treated in any manner.

"Before I make further comment on the preceding testimony, permit me to wonder if you were impressed by the seeming lack of alarm or disturbance caused by the unannounced departure of four members of the party group in the middle of the night. Judge Boyle appeared somewhat nonplussed by the attitude of the young women in this respect. Note his questioning of Miss Esther Newburgh. But there was a general assumption and a viable explanation offered by Gargan, as we notice in the testimony of Miss Ann Lyons—"

202

RECALL
ESTHER NEWBURGH

THE COURT. And it is your understanding there is going to be an evening cookout?

A. Yes.

THE COURT. And you will return to your motel?

A. That is right.

THE COURT. Now, suddenly the one closest to you, the one staying in the room in which you are staying leaves. You see her leave with Mr. Kennedy.

A. Yes.

THE COURT. Now, so far as you know nothing is said by her to you, her roommate, or to anyone else, as to where she is going?

A. I assumed several things, that either she was going into the front yard and later I had the assumption that it was a long day watching that race, she was exhausted, and the Senator was probably driving her back to the motel so that she could get some rest.

THE COURT. Without her saying a single word to you or to anyone else at that party?

A. That is right.

THE COURT. Now, suddenly later two of the men leave?

A. Yes.

THE COURT. Under unusual circumstances?

A. They weren't particularly unusual to me. Why would they have been?

THE COURT. Why not?

A. Well, I didn't hear anything unusual said.

THE COURT. When somebody comes in and nods and suddenly two men leave?

A. Not an unusual nod, just a motion.

THE COURT. Nothing is said, some signal of some kind is given?

A. Nothing is said that I heard.

THE COURT. And two men leave the party?

A. Yes.

THE COURT. You know the ferry leaves at 12 o'clock. There has been some talk about there can be a later ferry for an extra payment of money, so at that time you are expecting, you and the other girls, expecting to go back to your motel?

A. That is right.

THE COURT. Now, did you suddenly discover also there are no more vehicles in the yard? Didn't somebody walk out and see two motor vehicles gone, no more transportation?

A. This was much later that there weren't any cars left after we knew we had missed the ferry.

THE COURT. At some time you knew that there was no more transportation?

A. Yes.

THE COURT. Now, certainly at that point somebody must have said something, there must certainly have been some discussion. You are quite intelligent girls, are you not?

A. We think so.

THE COURT. You expect to get back to your motel that night?

A. Not after we knew we missed the ferry, Judge Boyle.

THE COURT. Well, you told me that there was talk about the ferry to be used for extra compensation.

A. That is correct, but after approximately 1 o'clock we realized that we weren't going to go back that night and something was said, "We have got to make the best of a bad situation and attempt to sleep."

204

THE COURT. This was before any of these three men had returned?

A. This was after Mr. Gargan and Mr. Markham had left.

THE COURT. Yes, and Mr. Kennedy.

A. That is right.

THE COURT. The three men had gone.

A. And Mary Jo Kopechne.

THE COURT. Yet none of you had any discussion between yourselves about, ''Are we left here on our own, are we going to get back to the motel; What are we going to do, what is happening, where are the motor vehicles, where is our transportation,'' no questions of any kind are discussed among you?

A. We wondered where Mr. Gargan and Mr. Markham had gone. We wondered where Miss Kopechne was. We wondered where everyone was, but we made assumptions. In retrospect we were wrong. She was not back at the motel. We assumed that she was. We assumed the Senator was at the Shiretown.

THE COURT. You could think of no reason why the two men should leave you and take the last transportation available without saying a single word to you, not even a by-your-leave, didn't excite you at all, didn't seem to be at all unusual?

A. (No response.)

THE COURT. Your title is Administrative Assistant?

A. That is correct.

THE COURT. I have no further questions.

RECALL
ANN LYONS

Q. Was there any discussion in your presence concerning the car getting stuck in the sand?

A. Yes, earlier in the evening when Mr. Gargan and Mr. Markham didn't return immediately after they left we assumed that the Senator's car had been stuck in the sand, that they went to help them, and they, too, had gotten stuck in the sand. A conversation describing a similar incident was pursued during the evening. So, we assumed that was what happened to the people who had left.

Q. Did you ask them anything about getting the car out of the sand?

A. No sir. We asked where they had been.

Q. And what did they say?

A. I think they stated that they had gone with the Senator to the ferry and the ferry wasn't there and the Senator swam across.

Q. Was there any discussion about getting a boat to cross?

A. After Mr. Crimmins remarked that the last ferry was at midnight, no one seemed particularly concerned because someone else suggested that boats were accessible and that we could go back at any time.

Q. Did Mr. Markham or Mr. Gargan indicate why Mr. Kennedy decided to swim when boats were available?

A. They had been looking for a boat, couldn't find one and the Senator dove in and swam.

Q. So, Mr. Kennedy did search for a boat?

A. I would assume, knowing the Senator and the relationship, that he asked Mr. Gargan and Mr. Markham to try and locate a boat and he probably waited at the ferry.

(GREEN LIGHT)

Inspector Darby:

"I think we can safely say that Mr. Gargan and Mr. Markham successfully performed their task of providing an air of calm in the cottage—if not solid comfort for sleeping purposes. I cannot give them a very high grade in sensitive foresight, however, in not preparing their friends in some manner for the impending arrival of the police with the grievous news of Mary

Jo's death. I might also add that the two gentlemen exhibited a remarkably casual attitude about the general atmosphere and environment awaiting the arrival of those same officials. One might almost be tempted to explain away their attitude by saying that the police were not expected to pay a call.''

The Inspector turned to me and questioned with raised eyebrows. I nodded agreement and spoke: "Ladies and gentlemen, we will have another recess now. Pim has something especially prepared at the bar for those of a mind to give up tea and coffee for their harmful effects. Please return to your seats when the bell rings.''

Since the sun would be sinking below the yardarm, I had told Pim to serve from the bar at the second break while Nadia served in the dining area. It was a smart move; my beverage business was split about fifty-fifty between hard and soft drinks. You have to be aware of customer wants if you expect to succeed in the roadside-inn business. Mint juleps in frosted mugs were on the agenda for the cocktail hour; so I had instructed Pim to offer, at this early hour, a libation invented by my Georgia-born friend: a Magnolia Blossom—fresh peaches steeped in crème de cassis, squashed and partially strained, mixed with pink gin and soda water, served over crushed ice in a large old-fashioned glass, two thirds ringed with mint sprigs. The house limit is the same as for the mint juleps—two to a customer in any twenty-four-hour period, to avoid any necessity for a bouncer.

Tommy Highsmith offered to bring drinks from the bar for Charles, Priscilla, and the innkeeper. We placed our orders and stretched our legs in a walk out onto the deck.

"Mr. D.A., is your voice giving out? Your last few questions were a little squeaky.'' It was Priscilla, with more amusement than real concern on her face.

Charles and I laughed, and Charles joined the put-down: "The committee has foreseen the possibilities, Truly, and they have a substitute available in the final session. Why don't you relax and mingle with the audience?" There was a peculiar inflection on the word *mingle*.

"But no necking in the balcony with the redhead!" Priscilla broke in. "You like her, don't you?"

"Am I supposed to *dislike* your friends, Priscilla?"

"No, but you are not supposed to nibble at their ears with your eyes thirty feet away either!"

This was too much for Charles. His English restraint gave way to a good horse laugh as Tommy arrived with three Magnolia Blossoms and a gin and tonic for the Inspector.

"What's funny? Did I miss a dirty joke?"

"No, Tommy," I replied, "it's just two of my former friends having fun at my expense, accusing me of ear nibbling at ten paces!"

"Oh! You mean you and the redhead. Hell, man, you're darting glances at her like a Jesuit priest peeping at a porno centerfold—oblique, quick, and often!"

"Thank you, Tommy," Priscilla clinked her glass with his, "that is the perfect description."

I gave them my smile of condescension and spoke with a lofty air of disdain: "I understand you have an assistant D.A. ready to take over in the final act. May I be favored with the name of your selection?"

"Ray Angelo," replied Priscilla. "He's a lawyer and will be perfect as the assistant D.A."

"He is more suited as a public defender, my dear, but I will accept him. He knows the Trulex operation; has he been coached on our routine?" He is also a teetotaler, I reminded myself, and would not be blossoming as I was at the moment.

"Thoroughly coached," she sounded rather proud of herself. "We were never too sure to begin with that you would take the D.A. spot."

208

"Why not? I have often pictured myself as another Tom Dewey attacking the forces of evil!"

"There's a stronger resemblance to Don Quixote tilting with windmills." It was a typical Tommy Highsmith quip—impertinent. I turned to a much amused bystander, Charles Darby, and suggested a resumption of the business at hand, after apologizing to him for the loss of my services. My three loyal friends left to seek out the neophyte Angelo, and I noticed Syrus Boynten moving toward me from the opposite end of the deck.

"Truly, my compliments to all of you on a most remarkable piece of analytical discourse."

"Thanks, Sy. Please express that to Priscilla and the Inspector; they are mainly responsible."

"Indeed I shall. And now, if I have it correctly, you have been given Darby's theory and you believe it to be logical, is that right?"

"Yes, much more so than what has been offered before. His theory is just one of dozens, of course, but I prefer it to any other I have been exposed to."

"And you want my reaction to its credibility?"

"Yes, you know my respect for your opinions, Sy. Let me ask you a question I haven't had an opportunity to ask you before—do you believe the Kennedy story?"

"Not entirely, no. I go along with Judge Boyle that he never intended to take the ferry and that the turn onto the bridge road was intentional. From that point on, I don't know what to believe. But I would like to believe something. Kennedy is just too important a man to have something of this nature left in a miasmal limbo."

"Exactly my own feelings, Sy!"

The assembly bell was ringing. We walked inside, and I took a seat high in the terrace section. For several reasons I felt relief at being deposed from my position of Mr. District Attorney: one in particular—I would no longer have to face an audience aware of my proclivity for ear nibbling at ten paces.

The questioning was resumed after an announcement by "Judge" Walters that Assistant District Attorney Angelo would take over at the request of Mr. Trulimann. At *my* request—how about that!

RECALL
EDWARD M. KENNEDY

Q. Do you have any idea what time you arrived at the Shiretown Inn?

A. I would say some time before 2:00.

Q. When you arrived, did you talk to anyone at that time?

A. I went to my room and I was shaking with chill. I took off all my clothes and collapsed on the bed, I was very conscious of a throbbing headache, of pains in my neck, of strain on my back, but what I was even more conscious of is the tragedy and loss of a very devoted friend.

Q. Now, did you change your clothing?

A. I was unable really to determine, detect the amount of lapse of time, and I could hear noise that was taking place. It seemed around me, on top of me, almost in the room, and after a period of time I wasn't sure whether it was morning or afternoon or nighttime, and I put on—and I wanted to find out and I put on some dry clothes that were there, a pants and shirt, and I opened the door and I saw what I believed to be a tourist or someone standing under the light off the balcony and asked what time it was. He mentioned to me it was, I think, 2:30, and [I] went back into the room.

CALL
RUSSELL E. PEACHEY (Sworn)

Q. Are you the innkeeper at the Shiretown Inn? And were you so occupied on July 18–19, 1969?

A. Yes, sir.

Q. Did you have occasion to see Mr. Kennedy sometime in the early morning hours of July 19th?

A. Yes. I just happened to be standing in front of the office after having walked back and forth from the end of the property out to North Water Street and I heard footsteps coming across the deck. There were no lights up there, so I just thought I would wait to see who it might be, whether the person had any business being up there or not; and the individual came down the steps and as he touched the ground, he turned around the steps and I asked if I could help him.

Q. Did you recognize him?

A. It wasn't until I spoke to him that I realized who it was.

Q. There are no lights on the deck of the Mayberry House?

A. There is a light up there, but it seemed to me someone had switched it off. I'm not sure, I can't really say whether that light was on or not.

Q. So what did this person say?

A. I asked if I could help him. He said no.

Q. Did you initiate the conversation?

A. I did. He said he had been awakened by a noise coming from a party next door. He went to look for his watch, he couldn't find it, and wondered what time it was. I turned and looked in the office window at the clock in the office and I told him it was 2:25.

Q. And what did this person do?

A. Thanked me, turned and went back up the stairs.

Q. He complained about the noise in the party?

A. He really didn't, and didn't ask me to do anything about it either.

(GREEN LIGHT)

Inspector Darby:

"FACT 72. Kennedy was observed by the innkeeper of the Shiretown Inn at 2:25 A.M. Apparently he was dressed in fresh, dry clothes.

"Mr. Peachey testified that he observed Mr. Kennedy from a distance estimated at 40 feet, and in the semidarkness Mr. K. appeared to be wearing a jacket and slacks. There was no indication of the traumatic experience he had just endured; he appeared perfectly normal in dress and manner, made no request to stop any noise, just turned away and went back up the balcony stairs.

"I find I cannot agree with Mr. Peachey. I believe he misread the office clock by at least one hour. If we work backward from the witnessed arrival of Mr. Gargan and Mr. Markham at the cottage about 2:15 or later, Mr. K. would have begun his swim across the channel no earlier than 2:00. You have heard Mr. K. in his own words describe everything he did after he left the ferry landing and after he arrived in his room. All of this in twenty-five minutes? Quite, quite improbable! More like an hour and twenty-five minutes!"

There was an implication here that startled me, as I am sure it startled everyone else.

The Inspector continued: "I must confess a certain amount of bewilderment, too, at Mr. Peachey's apparent unconcern about noise from a neighboring hostelry that was so great, in Mr. Kennedy's words, quote, it seemed around me, on top of me, almost in the room, unquote. Why had Mr. Peachey made no move to protect his own guests in a situation like that, at such an early hour? And why were there no other complaints?

"We will return to the cottage now and observe the events as the stranded party guests begin a new day—"

RECALL
JOSEPH GARGAN

Q. Now you say you went back to the Chappaquiddick cottage at 2:15. Did you remain there the entire morning from 2:15 until 9:00 A.M.?

A. I did not remain there from 2:15 until 9:00 A.M. I left the cottage, to the best of my recollection, and took the ferry across to Edgartown in the vicinity of 8 o'clock. In the morning when I woke up I wanted to get over to the Martha's Vineyard side of the Island as quickly as I could. I went to the Shiretown Inn.

Q. With whom?

A. Charles Tretter, Suzie Tannenbaum, Cricket Keough and Paul Markham.

Q. What did you do at the Inn?

A. I came into the yard and I saw the Senator standing on the porch. I went immediately to the upstairs porch and spoke to the Senator.

Q. And what time was this?

A. I would say it was around 8 or 8:30.

Q. Did you go back to the house at Chappaquiddick after that?

A. Yes, I did, around 9:00 or 9:30. It may have been as late as 9:30.

RECALL
PAUL MARKHAM

THE COURT. Did you inform anybody at the cottage that night and prior to your leaving in the morning what actually happened?

A. No, your Honor.

Q. What time did you leave the cottage and with whom?

A. I would think about 8:30. I really don't know. I left with

213

Mr. Gargan, Mr. Tretter, Miss Keough and Miss Tannenbaum.

Q. And where did you go?

A. I went to the Shiretown. I went up the back stairs to the porch which was outside of the Senator's room. The Senator was seated on the porch at a table.

Q. What did you do on arriving there, what did you say?

A. I didn't say anything. It was obvious to me at that time that nothing had been done. There was no commotion. He was just seated there at a table.

Q. Alone?

A. No. I remember Mr. Richards being in the immediate vicinity and also another gentleman, Mr. Stan Moore.

Q. And did you have a conversation at that time?

A. At that point no. I went directly to the door of his room. It was locked. He told Joe Gargan he had left the key inside and closed the door and Joe went down and got another key. The three of us went in and closed the door and I said, what happened? He said, I didn't report it.

Q. Did he say why?

A. We asked him why? I just couldn't believe that he didn't report it. I said, what happened to you? He said he swam across that night, went up to the hotel room. He remembers sitting down on the bed. He got up, went out of the room, he recalled seeing somebody. He said, it was just a nightmare, I was not even sure it happened. And I said, well, it happened, and you have got to report this thing and you have got to do it now.

Q. So, what was done next?

A. I think he described the accident again.

Q. What did he say? Did he say how the car rolled over or how it fell into the water?

A. He said he just went off the bridge. You could feel it tip over.

Q. He said he could feel it tip over. Did he say what part of his body struck anything?

A. He said he remembers trying to get out one side and being unsuccessful and giving one final lunge. He said he had the feeling his lungs were filling up with water and he said he thought he was gone.

Q. Did he say how fast he was traveling? Did anyone ask?

A. No.

Q. What did you do after this conversation?

A. He and Mr. Gargan talked about getting ahold of Dave Burke and Burke Marshall and you have got to let the family know. This thing is, you know, it is worse now than it was before. You didn't report the thing and we have got to do something.

Q. Let me ask you, did the Senator say where he was going?

A. He said he was going back to Edgartown. He said he took the wrong turn and he couldn't turn around. He said before he knew it he was at the bridge.

RECALL
JOHN CRIMMINS

Q. Were you present in the kitchen with Mr. LaRosa, Mr. Tretter, Mr. Gargan and Mr. Markham at approximately 2 o'clock in the morning?

A. I got up to go to the bathroom.

Q. That is not what I asked you.

A. I remember getting up and saying something and going right back to bed.

Q. What did you say?

A. I don't know.

Q. Do you remember anything being told to you?

A. Nothing was told to me.

Q. What time did you get up?

A. 8:00 or 8:30. I was the last to rise.

Q. Who was left at the cottage when you got up?

A. The two Lyons sisters, Esther Newburgh, and Ray LaRosa.

Q. What did you do?

A. We sat around awhile and discussed what we were going to do. We all started to walk down the road.

Q. Was there any discussion at this time that Mr. Kennedy had returned the night before?

A. Knew nothing about it. We walked down towards the ferry and met Mr. Gargan coming back. We got in the car and returned to the cottage. Mr. Gargan said the Senator has had an accident and we can't find Mary Jo.

Q. Did Mr. Gargan say anything about the fact that he had gone to the scene that night?

A. He did not. He took the girls to the ferry and Ray LaRosa and I picked up the cottage.

THE COURT. Let me ask you a few more questions, if you will. How old are you, Mr. Crimmins?

A. Sixty-three.

THE COURT. Exactly what is your relationship with Mr. Kennedy?

A. I am a part-time chauffeur. I am a weekend and evening chauffeur when he comes into this state.

THE COURT. And have been for how long a period of time?

A. Nine years.

RECALL
RAYMOND LaROSA

Q. When did you learn that Mary Jo Kopechne had been drowned?

A. I learned that when I arrived back at Edgartown somewhere around 11 o'clock on Saturday morning.

Q. When you left the cottage, did you leave in a group?

A. Well, I left on two occasions. The first somewhere after 9:00, maybe 9:20 or 9:30. We were waiting for a ride and decided to walk. A car driven by Mr. Gargan stopped and we got in and he said there has been an accident, and when we asked what kind of an accident, we really got no reply until we got back to the cottage and went inside and he said, "Sit down, there has been an accident" and that Miss Kopechne was missing.

Q. Now had you seen Mr. Gargan and Mr. Markham earlier in the morning about 7:00?

A. Yes, sir, at the cottage.

Q. And neither one told you anything about the accident?

A. That is correct.

Q. Was there any further discussion about the disappearance of Mary Jo Kopechne?

A. There were a lot of hurried questions.

Q. Was there a reply to those questions?

A. No, just that there had been an accident and there was no explanation really. Mr. Gargan left the cottage with the young ladies that were remaining. Later Mr. Crimmins and I began walking and a woman and a child offered us a ride. We rode back to Edgartown with them.

RECALL
CHARLES TRETTER

Q. Did there come a time whenever anyone left the cottage?

A. Yes. I got up around 7:00, it would be after 7:30, Mr. Gargan, Mr. Markham, Miss Keough and Miss Tannenbaum drove to the ferry. I went with them.

Q. Was there any conversation either at that time or previous to your retiring that evening about the whereabouts of Miss Kopechne?

A. I can't recall any such conversation.

RECALL
ROSEMARY KEOUGH

Q. What time did you get up in the morning?

A. I woke up about 5:30 or 6:00. I was awake pretty much all night.

Q. Did you miss your purse sometime during the day?

A. I missed my purse after I left it in Senator Kennedy's car. I knew it was there.

Q. What time did you do that?

A. Approximately 9:30 Friday night. We left the party to go to the Shiretown Inn to get a radio.

Q. What time did you learn that Mary Jo had this accident?

A. When I returned to Katama between 11:00 and 11:15. I learned of it from Maryellen, Nance and Esther. Mr. Gargan had told them there was an accident, that Senator Kennedy had driven off a bridge; that we didn't know where Mary Jo was.

Q. Was there a reason why you returned separately?

A. Because I left earlier. I traveled with Mr. Markham and Mr. Gargan from the cottage to the Shiretown Inn, then later to the Katama.

Q. Did they tell you what happened the night before? Did you ask them anything? What did they talk about?

A. I didn't speak with them. We arrived at the Inn and the two of them left and went up to Senator Kennedy's room. We didn't discuss it.

RECALL
SUSAN TANNENBAUM

Q. What time did you arise in the morning?

A. About 8:00 . . . 7:30.

Q. When did you know that Mary Jo had died?

A. Mid-morning, about 11:00 at the Katama Shores. Correction. I only learned that Mary Jo was missing at first.

Q. You heard she was missing then later Mr. Gargan told you she had died. Who was present with you?

A. The four girls.

RECALL
ESTHER NEWBURGH

Q. How was it that you found out about what happened to Mary Jo?

A. I found out about 9:20 or 9:30. The group that was left at the cottage walked towards the ferry because there weren't any cars left and a car came up the road and Mr. Gargan was driving and he told us to get in. He said something had happened and my first reaction was the Senator, and we drove back to the cottage and he wouldn't say anything until we got inside. Then he told us Mary Jo was missing and that was all.

Q. What exactly did Mr. Gargan say happened, the circumstances under which she was missing?

A. He said there had been an accident and Mary Jo was missing.

Q. Did he say who was driving or describe the accident?

A. He said the Senator was with her. He told us to stay calm and that he would phone us later that morning at the motel.

RECALL
MARYELLEN LYONS

Q. When did you learn that Mary Jo was dead?

A. The next morning. When I got up in the morning, some of the people were gone and we waited around. We thought Mary Jo would come back and get us with a car. About 9:30 we walked towards the ferry. Mr. Gargan came along and told us to get into the car that he had something to tell us. We went back to the cottage and I believe he said, ''There has been an accident and Mary Jo is missing.'' Then we started asking what happened, what is the story, and I don't think we really found out until we were back at the Katama Shores motel.

Q. When Mr. Gargan was asked about what happened, what did he say?

A. He just said that he didn't know, that there was an accident and Mary Jo was missing.

RECALL
ANN LYONS

Q. Everything settled down at the cottage and you slept and you got up at what time?

A. About a quarter of eight in the morning.

Q. And you say at that time some of the people were leaving?

A. They evidently had gotten up earlier than we had and they were leaving without us. There was only one car and we were upset.

Q. Was there any discussion about bringing you another car?

A. No. I think Maryellen made the statement that if they didn't come back Mary Jo would come back for us.

Q. Did you see Mr. Gargan in the morning?

A. When he returned to take us to Martha's Vineyard.

Q. Did you make any observations with reference to injuries?

A. No, sir. But it was fairly obvious when he came to pick us up in the morning that something had transpired by the expression on his face.

Q. When he returned from trying to get a boat, did you make any observations about him?

A. No, sir. In retrospect I could compare the two and say it appeared when he returned then that he had no knowledge of what had actually transpired.

Q. Did anyone clean the cottage?

A. Yes, sir. I did the dishes and I swept the living room.

Q. And with reference to anything that had been left over at the party did you throw that out?

A. We had one of those large plastic bags and I just put everything in there and stored it in the corner.

Q. Did that include empty bottles?

A. Yes, sir. Coke, tonic and vodka bottles, I believe.

Q. How many empty bottles of liquor were there?

A. Two empties and one half bottle of scotch, I believe, and an empty bottle, I don't know what it was.

Q. When you saw Mr. Gargan on the road, what was the conversation at that time, as best as you can remember it?

A. Well, I can only relate my reaction at the time looking at Mr. Gargan's face I knew that something was wrong and I said, "Is something wrong?" and he said "Yes, get in the car" he just said there had been an accident. When we arrived at the cottage we were all pressing him and he said there had been an accident and Mary Jo was missing.

Q. What were the answers?

A. Mr. Gargan kept repeating that he had no details.

(GREEN LIGHT)

Inspector Darby:

"FACT 73. Gargan and Markham arrived at the Shiretown Inn about 8:10 A.M. and found that Kennedy had not reported the accident to the police.

"FACT 74. Gargan told Crimmins, LaRosa, Newburgh, and the Lyons sisters about 9:30 A.M. that there had been an accident and Mary Jo was missing. He gave no further details, stating that he had no detailed knowledge of the circumstances.

"FACT 75. Tretter, Keough, and Tannenbaum were told nothing of the accident on an early-morning trip into Edgartown and the Shiretown Inn around 8:00.

"FACT 76. The cottage was cleaned up in the morning by Crimmins and LaRosa prior to their departure around 11:00. Miss Ann Lyons cleaned up the dishes and swept the living room at some point not definitely stated.

"An interesting point emerges from this testimony—the fact that nothing was said by Gargan or Markham about the accident until approximately 9:30 in the morning, and even then the death of Mary Jo was not disclosed, nor did Gargan admit to knowledge of the details. Why was he unable or unwilling to tell a straightforward story at this time? Mr. Kennedy has given us his reason for instructing Gargan and Markham not to inform the young women at 2:00 in the morning—his fear that they would, quote, within a matter of seconds, unquote, go to the scene of the accident and themselves dive, with a chance of serious injury to any one of them. A question arises: Did Gargan know at 9:30 that the Kennedy car had been found? And if he did, why wasn't the Kennedy version of the details given at that time? We will now trace the actions of Mr. Gargan and others from the time Mr. Gargan and Mr. Markham arrive at the Shiretown until Mr. Gargan returns to the cottage—"

RECALL
EDWARD M. KENNEDY

Q. Directing your attention to the 19th, what time did you get up that morning?

A. I never really went to bed that night.

Q. After that noise at 2:30 in the morning, when did you first meet anyone, what time?

A. It was sometime after 8:00. I met the woman that was behind the counter at the Inn and I met Mr. Richards and

Mr. Moore, very briefly Mrs. Richards, and Mr. Gargan and Mr. Markham, and I saw Mr. Tretter, but to be specifically responsive as to who I met in my room, it was Mr. Markham and Mr. Gargan.

Q. What time was this?

A. I think it was close to 8:30.

Q. Did you have any conversation with Mr. Moore, or Mr. Richards, or Mrs. Richards?

A. It is my impression that they did the talking. Mr. Moore was relating about how some members of his crew were having difficulty with their housing arrangements.

Q. What time did Mr. Markham and Mr. Gargan arrive, and did you have a conversation with them?

A. I would think about 8:30. They asked, had I reported the accident, and why I hadn't reported it; and I told them about my own thoughts and feelings as I swam across that channel and how I was always willed that Mary Jo still lived; how I was hopeful even as that night went on and as I tossed and turned, paced that room and walked around that room that night that somehow when they arrived in the morning that they were going to say that Mary Jo was still alive. I told them how I somehow believed that when the sun came up and it was a new morning that what had happened the night before would not have happened, and did not happen, and how I just couldn't gain the strength within me, the moral strength to call Mrs. Kopechne at 2:00 in the morning and tell her that her daughter was dead.

Q. Now at some time you actually did call Mrs. Kopechne?

A. Yes, I did.

Q. And prior to calling Mrs. Kopechne, did you cross over on the ferry to Chappaquiddick Island?

A. Yes, I did.

Q. And was Mr. Markham and Mr. Gargan with you?

A. Yes, they were.

Q. Now, did you then return to Edgartown after some period of time?

A. Yes, I did.

Q. Did anything prompt or cause you to return to Edgartown once you were on Chappaquiddick Island that morning?

A. What do you mean by prompt?

Q. Well, did anything cause you to return?

A. Other than the intention of reporting the accident, the intention of which had been made earlier that morning.

Q. But you didn't go directly from your room to the police department?

A. No, I did not.

Q. What was the particular reason for going to Chappaquiddick first?

A. It was to make a phone call to one of the oldest and dearest friends that I have, Mr. Burke Marshall. I didn't feel I could use the phone that was available outside of the dining room at the Shiretown, it was my thought that once I went to the police station I would be involved in a myriad of details and I wanted to talk to this friend before I undertook that responsibility.

Q. You did not reach him?

A. No, I did not.

Q. And then I believe the evidence is that you left Chappaquiddick Island, crossed over on the ferry and went to the local police department at approximately 10:00 A.M.?

A. I think it was sometime before 10:00.

RECALL
PAUL MARKHAM

Q. After the conversation between Mr. Gargan and Mr.

224

Kennedy about notifying Mr. Burke and Mr. Marshall, what happened?

A. The Senator wanted to know where he could call.

Q. And so you went with him to the ferry and crossed to Chappaquiddick? What happened there?

A. He called Dave Burke. I don't think he called Mr. Marshall. He only called Mr. Burke and asked Mr. Burke to try and get ahold of Mr. Marshall, he wanted to talk with him and just to stand by. The place was going to be flooded with calls pretty soon and to get down to the office. Then he concluded the telephone conversation. I said, do you want me to go to the police station with you? He said, yes. He said, Joe, you had better go tell the others what happened.

RECALL
JOSEPH GARGAN

Q. Did you have any conversation with the Senator and Mr. Markham on the Chappaquiddick landing that morning?

A. No, not to any great degree. The Senator did all the talking and that was on the phone. After he finished I think it was I that suggested that Paul go with him to the police station; that I would go to the cottage, tell the girls what happened and take them back to Katama.

RECALL
CHARLES TRETTER

Q. Do you know what time you arrived at the Senator's room?

A. Sometime between 8:00 and 8:30, I guess.

Q. And Mr. Gargan and Mr. Markham and the Senator were there?

A. Yes. I knocked on the door, looked in the window, and the Senator was sitting in such a position I thought he motioned me in. I walked into the room and closed the door behind me and there was no conversation between

225

the three and the Senator looked at me and said something to the effect of, this is going to be a private thing. Do you mind?

Q. How did he appear to you?

A. Well, I thought there was something bothering him because I was a little angry myself, having worked for him long enough, I thought I recognized the sign to come into the room and then when I got into the room, I was instantaneously told to get out in so many words and I thought there was something wrong, but I didn't know whether it was at me for interfering with the conversation or what.

Q. Where did you go after that?

A. I went downstairs and had some juice and coffee.

CALL
ROSS W. RICHARDS (Sworn)

Q. Did you have occasion to see Senator Kennedy at approximately 7:30 on Saturday morning the 19th?

A. Yes, sir. I was entering from Water Street, taking a left into the cottage at Shiretown and he was walking in a westerly direction towards me and I was walking in an easterly direction. We said good morning and he turned and walked back to the Shiretown and our rooms.

Q. And did you have a conversation with him?

A. Yes, I did. It was about the race the day before. I happened to win the race and he congratulated me and we discussed that back and forth for maybe ten or fifteen minutes.

Q. How long would you say you were in his company all told?

A. It was until 8:00 o'clock, half an hour.

Q. Was there any discussion about Chappaquiddick Island?

A. There wasn't a word mentioned of Chappaquiddick.

Q. Were you joined by anyone during this conversation?

A. Stan Moore followed behind us and he was sitting on the porch with us. My wife came out around 7:50 from our room. She sat for five or ten minutes.

Q. Were you ever joined by Mr. Markham and Mr. Gargan?

A. I remember the bell at 8:00 o'clock. We asked the Senator if he would like to have breakfast with us and he said no, but he may join us later. And at that time Mr. Markham and Mr. Gargan——

Q. May I stop you. You said the Senator discussed the possibility of joining you at breakfast, then Mr. Gargan and Mr. Markham came on the porch?

A. Yes, sir.

Q. What happened when they came up on the deck?

A. They went directly to the Senator's room and he went with them.

Q. Now what observations did you make of the Senator at this time as to injuries, appearance or attitude?

A. I noticed nothing out of the ordinary in his speech or appearance.

CALL
RICHARD P. HEWITT (Sworn)

Q. Your occupation, sir?

A. Ferry operator.

Q. On the morning of the 19th, what time did you have occasion to see Mr. Kennedy, as best you remember?

A. It was approximately 9:00 o'clock. He walked on the ferry, Edgartown side, with two others. From pictures I have seen, I recognize one as Mr. Markham.

Q. Could you tell us where they went on Chappaquiddick?

A. They didn't go very far. They stood around the point over there. They appeared to be just milling around waiting for something or someone.

Q. How long were you in their vicinity?

A. I would say approximately 20 minutes or so. I made two or three trips in between the time I took them over and the time I took them back.

Q. Did you see anyone use the telephone?

A. No, but they were within fifty feet of the telephone.

Q. Did you have a conversation with Mr. Bettencourt?

A. Yes. He told me that the car that went off the bridge had been identified as Mr. Kennedy's.

Q. And did you relay that information to Mr. Kennedy?

A. I did, not to Mr. Kennedy but to Mr. Markham.

Q. What did you tell Mr. Markham?

A. I asked him if he was aware of the accident and he said yes, we just heard about it.

Q. Those were his exact words?

A. We just heard about it.

Q. And after that what did you do?

A. I had passengers on the ferry. I went back to Edgartown within a couple of minutes. They went back with me.

(GREEN LIGHT)

Inspector Darby:

"FACT 77. Kennedy was incapable of mental adjustment to the tragedy of Mary Jo's death and gave this as his reason for not going to the police station on his return to Edgartown.

"FACT 78. Counter to Fact 77 is Kennedy's apparent calmness and naturalness in conversations with Mr. and Mrs. Richards and Mr. Moore early Saturday morning, and his appearance before Mr. Peachey at 2:30 A.M.

"FACT 79. Kennedy, Gargan, and Markham all gave need for telephone privacy as the reason for crossing to the Chappaquiddick landing area about 9:00 A.M.

"FACT 80. The ferry operator was informed by a Mr. Bettencourt that the submerged car had been identified as Mr. Kennedy's, and he gave this information to Markham. Markham and Kennedy left on the next ferry for Edgartown, and Kennedy went directly to the police station with Markham just before 10:00 A.M.

"We have already noted the exceptionally gifted performance of Mr. Gargan and Mr. Markham in a pretense of normality under extremely trying conditions. Now we must compliment Mr. Kennedy. Until he reached the police station Saturday morning and made his statement admitting to knowledge of and personal responsibility for the accident, there is virtually no indication from witness testimony, excluding Gargan and Markham, that the senator was deeply affected in any way. Why *his* pretense, if it was pretense?

"Why would a man, suffering the long night of mental torture described to Gargan and Markham, follow with casual, conversational sociableness of his own making? Could he not foresee the possible sensibility shock of his companions upon learning that he would engage in such commonplace intercourse while the body of a young woman reposed unrecovered in a watery entombment of his own doing? Applaud his performance, if you will, but question his motive.

"From the conversation in Mr. Kennedy's room came the decision to cross to the Chappaquiddick landing for telephone privacy. We should remember at this point that Mr. Kennedy was faced with two dilemmas, one involving morality and humaneness, and one involving his legal position. He was in dire need of top-level thinking and advice, just as his brother had been for the Bay of Pigs and the Russo-Cuban missile crises. Yet the testimony shows only one call made from Chappaquiddick, and that call went to his administrative assistant in Washington. We should ask ourselves then, Was there another reason for the trip to Chappaquiddick, and how did the unexpected accident discovery relate to that purpose? Shortly after the three gentlemen arrived at the Chappaquiddick landing area, it is reported that a Mr. Bettencourt, sent to the ferry slip from the bridge by Chief Arena to pick up the medical examiner, recognized Mr. Kennedy and told him about the car and the girl's body. Ferryman Hewitt, also informed of the car by Mr. Bettencourt, spoke to Mr. Markham some twenty minutes later.

"It would appear, then, that for almost the entire period of their stay on Chappaquiddick they were aware of the car's discovery and the fact of Mary Jo's death. Why then the delay in going to the authorities? Was a change in plans involved? Was some precipitate decision made that left Mr. Gargan with no details, with a confused picture of exactly what was in the mind of Mr. Kennedy when he left for the police station? We might well make this conclusion from the immediately preceding testimony.

"The Kennedy decision to leave the landing area is understandable. A procession consisting of a hearse bearing Mary Jo's body, a wrecker towing his car, a fire-department rescue team, police cars, and assorted citizenry is not precisely the class of parade an American senator normally reviews in the pursuit of his duties.

"Let us follow now in the senator's footsteps and observe the actions taken at the police station moments later—"

RECALL
EDWARD M. KENNEDY

Q. You arrived at the police station and you made a statement in writing, is that correct?

A. That is correct.

Q. Did the chief reduce this to a typewritten statement, do you know?

A. No, he did not.

Q. Now, I have in my hand what purports to be the statement you made to Chief Arena at that time, and I would like to give you a copy. Would you read it, Senator?

A. Yes. That is correct.

Q. With regard to the statement, Senator, you wind up by saying, "When I fully realized what had happened this morning I immediately contacted the police." Now, is that in fact what you did?

THE COURT. Mr. Dinis, are you going to ask the statement be put in the record?

MR. DINIS. Yes, your Honor.

THE COURT. Mr. Kennedy already said this was a copy of the statement he made. He already testified to all his movements. Now, won't you let the record speak for itself?

MR. DINIS. All right, your Honor.

RECALL
PAUL MARKHAM

Q. You went to the police station and you were present with Mr. Kennedy when he made his statement and an accident report was prepared?

A. Yes, sir.

Q. Can you tell us how long you were in the police station?

A. I would say at least two hours.

Q. Could you tell the Court who prepared the report?

A. I think I did the actual writing. The Senator described the accident again and I wrote it out. I gave it to Chief Arena.

Q. Did you tell him that you had attempted to rescue?

A. No, sir.

Q. Did he ask what had happened?

A. No, the Senator told him what had happened.

Q. Did he tell him anything else than what is in that report that you remember?

A. Yes, we did tell the Chief that Mr. Gargan and I drove the Senator to the ferry and that the Senator swam across.

Q. There was no mention of the rescue attempts or the position of the car or anything else?

A. No. The Senator that morning, when we were at the telephone booth or sometime before we went to the station, told us, look, I don't want you people put in the middle on this thing. I'm not going to involve you. As far as you know, you didn't know anything about the accident that night. I'm quite sure it was when he made the phone call, because Mr. Gargan was present when that was said on the Chappaquiddick side.

Q. So nothing was said to the police in light of this conversation you had with Mr. Kennedy earlier?

A. No. Chief Arena asked if he had a statement and the Senator dictated the statement that I wrote that was filed with the police.

Q. Now, as I understood your testimony, Mr. Markham, the reason that you or Mr. Gargan did not seek assistance or notify the police was that you assumed that Mr. Kennedy was going to do so when he arrived in Edgartown after the swim?

A. That is what he told us.

THE COURT. Let me ask a question. Seeking assistance and reporting the accident are two different things. Do you mean you didn't seek assistance in recovering the body because Senator Kennedy was going to do it?

A. He was going to report the accident.

THE COURT. This isn't what I asked you. The reason you didn't seek assistance in recovering the body was because you thought Senator Kennedy was going to do it?

A. Yes, your Honor.

RECALL
JOSEPH GARGAN

Q. Did you assist Senator Kennedy in the preparation of the statement that he left for the police department?

A. I did not. I didn't know what was in it. I did see the sheet of paper that the Senator was working on, but I did not read it.

Q. Did you tell the police that you went to the scene?

A. Never spoke to the police, not about that or anything else.

RECALL
DOMINICK J. ARENA

A. After John Farrar left the water, John Ahlbum, the owner of the Depot Corner Service Station arrived at the scene and as I was walking by him on the bridge I said it was Senator Kennedy's car and he said to me, "I just saw him down by the ferry landing." So I proceeded to Mrs. Malm's house and called my desk officer to send somebody down to the landing to see if they could find Senator Kennedy.

Q. What time is this about?

A. I would say after 9 o'clock, but I don't really know. When I called Mrs. Albocter she said, "The Senator is here." He wanted to talk to me so he got on the phone and I said, "I am sorry, I have some bad news, your car was in an accident over here and the young lady is dead." He said, "I know."

I said, "Can you tell me was there anybody else in the car?"

He said, "Yes."

I said, "Are they in the water?"

He said, "No."

I said, "Can I talk to you?"

He said, "Yes."

I said, "Would you like to talk to me here?"

He said, "I prefer for you to come over here."

I walked into my office and Paul Markham was on my right and Senator Kennedy was on the telephone. The Senator hung up, came over, said hello, shook my hand, I said something to the effect I am sorry about what happened.

He said, "Yes, I know, I was the driver," so I don't think I said anything for a minute.

He said, "What would you like for me to do, we must do what is right or we will both be criticized for it."

I said, "The first thing we will have to do is have a statement from you about what happened."

He asked me if it would be all right if he wrote it, I said, "Yes, it would be."

Q. What time were you at the station?

A. I think it is close to 10 o'clock.

Q. What did you do after having requested the report?

A. Even at this early time the reporters were beginning to crop up in the station and I said, "If you would like to have a little privacy to write this statement, I will let you in the Selectmen's office." I took him to the office down the hall then drove back to the bridge where they were in the process of towing the car out. After it appeared to me that the car was well in hand I designated one of my men to stay with the Registry men and I returned to the station. George Kennedy, one of the Registry men, went back with me.

Q. What time was this?

A. Close to 11 o'clock. When I arrived Mr. Gargan was in the corridor. I went to the Selectmen's office and Mr. Markham was writing what he said the Senator had dictated. I said, "I'm not sure I can read your writing, do you mind if I type it?" I made two copies, one for the Senator, one for myself. I went back into the room and while the Senator read his copy I read mine. He didn't make any comment, just said, "Okay." Then he said, "We are trying to get ahold of Burke Marshall."

234

Q. Do you have the original handwritten statement?

A. I am sorry to say that after I copied it I threw it away. I didn't think there would be any need to keep it.

Q. Did they sign any of these statements?

A. No.

Q. Did you ask the Senator any more questions?

A. No, I don't think I did.

Q. In your observation of Mr. Kennedy, did you make note of any injuries or bruises?

A. No injuries. He just appeared to be very depressed mentally.

Q. At what time did you prepare a citation?

A. I was in the midst of preparing one and he left close to noontime, saying he wanted to contact his family attorney and would be back to me. I was asked to hold the statement until they contacted the family attorney.

Q. By whom?

A. Mr. Markham. He asked if I would hold it until they were able to talk with Burke Marshall. As I recall, close to 3 o'clock, because of the constant pressure in my office, people were clamoring for information, I felt I could no longer hold back and I released the statement.

Q. You subsequently issued a citation charging leaving the scene of an accident?

A. Yes, sir.

Q. Did you ask Mr. Kennedy any questions as to why he had not reported the accident soon after it happened?

A. No, sir, I didn't.

Q. Were you able to speak with anyone who attended the party that you subsequently discovered?

A. I didn't know about the party when I called her, but I called Rosemary Keough around noon or 1 o'clock at the Dunes. I had this key number. I advised her that we had her pocketbook and asked if she could spell Mary

Jo's name. Nobody could spell it and I wanted to have it right so we would not make any errors for the press. Sometime later Charles Tretter picked up her pocketbook.

Q. Did you speak to anyone else who attended the party?

A. I didn't know at the time that there was a party and when I discovered that, all of those people had left the island.

Q. Did you have any further conversations with Mr. Kennedy, or Mr. Gargan or Mr. Markham?

A. Mr. Gargan called close to three to say they had not reached Mr. Marshall and they wanted to know if I could hold up the statement a little longer and I said it was too late, I had already issued it. I called late that evening to inform Mr. Markham that I was issuing a citation to the Senator by mail. After that, I had no further conversations with any of that group.

CALL
GEORGE W. KENNEDY (Sworn)

Q. Your occupation?

A. I am supervisor of the Registry of Motor Vehicles in Oak Bluffs.

Q. And so there is no question, are you related to Mr. Edward M. Kennedy?

A. None whatsoever.

Q. Now, in your capacity as an inspector for the Registry were you summonsed to Dyke Road and Dyke Bridge on July 19th?

A. Yes, I was. When I arrived at the scene I observed a car in the water on the right side of the bridge. I had noticed skid marks on the wooden bridge starting at the edge of the bridge at the gravel road and continuing straight to the right and over. I found a large gouge along the right

236

side of the rub rail between the two skid marks of the tires.

Q. Would you also describe Dyke Road as in the vicinity of the bridge.

A. It is a wide gravel road with dirt shoulders on the right side. On the left side there is a large area that people have been using for parking while fishing.

Q. From the skid marks can you give us an estimate of the speed of the car?

A. Approximately 20 to 22 miles per hour.

Q. After leaving the scene, where did you go?

A. Back to the Edgartown Police Station with Chief Arena about a quarter of 12:00. Senator Kennedy, Mr. Markham and Mr. Gargan were there when we arrived.

I asked Senator Kennedy what happened, and he said, "I intend to make a statement and I would just as soon have Mr. Markham and Mr. Gargan in my presence." Then he got up from the police office and walked out to the other room where Mr. Markham and Mr. Gargan were and said, "They want a statement, let's sit down and get one," and when I got there, "I would rather talk it over with my attorneys." He asked us to leave and then he made out a statement. I read it and then I asked him this: "I would like to know about something." He said, "I have no comment."

Q. He said Mr. Markham and Mr. Gargan were his attorneys. Did you ask them anything?

A. They said he would make a further statement later and he would answer more questions.

Q. Did you receive a further statement later from him?

A. Only the accident report which was essentially the same as the typewritten statement.

Q. You saw Mr. Markham and Mr. Gargan at the police station. Were you in close proximity to Mr. Gargan?

237

A. I was.

Q. Would you tell us what he was wearing as you best remember?

A. He was wearing a chino pair of pants and a short T-shirt.

Q. Did you have occasion to see his arms?

A. I did.

Q. Did you observe any marks?

A. I did not.

Q. Did you make any observations as to limping or any sign of injury to anyone?

A. No limping on anybody.

Q. You say you left the police station at quarter of three, where did you go?

A. Inspector Molla and I transported Mr. Gargan, Mr. Markham and Mr. Kennedy to the Martha's Vineyard airport.

Q. And during that time was there any conversation about the accident by anyone?

A. The Senator was in the front seat and he kept mumbling, oh my God what has happened. What's happened. There was no direct conversation about the accident whatsoever.

(GREEN LIGHT)

Inspector Darby:

"FACT 81. Sometime between 11:00 and 12:00 noon Saturday, Kennedy gave Chief Arena a statement on the accident. The statement was dictated to Markham, who wrote it out in longhand, and Arena later typed it for Kennedy's approval. It was approved, but never signed.

"FACT 82. Kennedy spoke of Gargan and Markham as his attorneys in conversing with Inspector Kennedy of the

Registry. He also refused to answer questions about the accident from the inspector.

"FACT 83. Gargan and Markham made no mention of their rescue efforts. Kennedy told them he did not want them involved, to plead ignorance about the accident.

"FACT 84. Arena knew nothing about a party-cottage group on Chappaquiddick until late Saturday when all had left Martha's Vineyard and his jurisdiction. Other than Kennedy, no party person was questioned about the accident itself.

"FACT 85. Again testimony is given in which there is no indication whatever of Gargan having a badly scraped arm, or injuries to Kennedy or Markham.

"FACT 86. Kennedy and Markham left Martha's Vineyard Airport by plane about 3:00 P.M. Saturday. Apparently, just before they left, Gargan called Arena and asked that the statement not be released until further notice; but Arena had already released it to the press around that same time.

"FACT 87. On the immediate approach to Dyke Bridge there is a parking area to the left and a narrow shoulder on the right. Skid marks on the wooden surface of the bridge indicated braking just as the car reached the bridge surface.

"Ladies and gentlemen, I am a guest in your country, and it would be bad manners for me to impugn the machinery or the implementation of the machinery of justice in the American juridical system. Disraeli reminded the British that 'it is much easier to be critical than correct.' Please keep this in mind now when I draw your attention to one point in particular: the very limited knowledge that would be available for our consideration if there had been no inquest into the death of Mary Jo Ko-

239

pechne, and the somewhat circumscribed knowledge available because of the limitations of the inquest itself, a rare and unusual legal proceeding in the Commonwealth of Massachusetts.

"Mr. Kennedy gave a brief explanation of the Chappaquiddick incident in the form of an unsigned statement in another man's handwriting, which was later discarded by an official in favor of a typed copy, also unsigned. The officially required report to the Registry of Motor Vehicles was essentially the same as the original statement, and it would have to bear signature; so, in effect, the original statement may be considered authoritative. Now here is that statement:

> On July 18, 1969, at approximately 11:15 P.M., on Chappaquiddick Island, Martha's Vineyard, I was driving my car on Main Street on my way to get the ferry back to Edgartown. I was unfamiliar with the road and turned onto Dyke Road instead of bearing left on Main Street. After proceeding for approximately a half mile on Dyke Road I descended a hill and came upon a narrow bridge. The car went off the side of the bridge. There was one passenger in the car with me, Miss ——, a former secretary of my brother Robert Kennedy. The car turned over and sank into the water and landed with the roof resting on the bottom. I attempted to open the door and window of the car but have no recollection of how I got out of the car. I came to the surface and then repeatedly dove down to the car in an attempt to see if the passenger was still in the car. I was unsuccessful in the attempt.

> I was exhausted and in a state of shock. I recall walking back to where my friends were eating. There was a car parked in front of the cottage and I climbed into the back seat. I then asked for someone to bring me back to Edgartown. I remember walking around for a period of time and then going back to my hotel room. When I fully realized what happened this morning, I immediately contacted the police.

"Voluntarily, Mr. Kennedy added the following information in his television speech:

Instead of looking directly for a telephone after lying exhausted in the grass for an undetermined time, I walked back to the cottage where the party was being held and requested the help of two friends, my cousin Joseph Gargan and Paul Markham, and directed them to return immediately to the scene with me—this was some time after midnight—in order to undertake a new effort to dive down and locate Miss Kopechne. Their strenuous efforts, undertaken at some risks to their own lives, also proved futile.

Instructing Gargan and Markham not to alarm Mary Jo's friends that night, I had them take me to the ferry crossing. The ferry having closed down for the night, I suddenly jumped into the water and impulsively swam across, nearly drowning once again in the effort, and returned to my hotel about 2 A.M. and collapsed in my room. I remember going out at one point and saying something to the room clerk.

"In brief, the Gargan-Markham rescue efforts, instructions not to tell anyone at the cottage about the accident, the swim across to Edgartown, and the talk with Mr. Peachey at Shiretown provide some additional information. The request for an autopsy was denied. One other possible source of relevant testimony was also denied. It was deemed not feasible because the end result would not be helpful and would not alter the findings of the Court. I would like for you to hear the following exchange between the Court, the district attorney, and the assistant district attorney; and then the final outcome of this exchange—"

THE COURT. Mr. Dinis, did you make any investigation through the Registry of Motor Vehicles to determine how many cars in Massachusetts are registered with the L7 hm, hm, hm, 7?

MR. DINIS. No, your Honor, we did not.

THE COURT. I think it is so important that I will even postpone this inquest. Now, I don't know, it may turn out that there is no other car that has an L7 and a 7 ending, or it could be a white car.

MR. DINIS. We could have that in an hour, I think.

MR. FERNANDES. Your Honor, we will start it right away. I will get on it with the Lieutenant.

MR. DINIS. First, we will have to find it.

MR. FERNANDES. We will have the information.

THE COURT. Well, you will have all day tomorrow, because I would suspect we would have all day tomorrow to go with those girls. I consider it could be very important.

MR. DINIS. What is the combination, your Honor?

THE COURT. The first letter L, the first number 7, and the last number 7, — — — 7. We don't know how many numbers in the middle.

MR. DINIS. Well, there are only six numbers on plates.

THE COURT. I figure it would have to be three or four possible combinations.

MR. FERNANDES. I don't know how many will be on Chappaquiddick at that time.

THE COURT. I don't know. Number one, maybe no other car happens to have that combination or the other car is a Volkswagen.

MR. FERNANDES. Precisely.

THE COURT. Or the other car is a white car. I mean, I don't know, but I can see where it might be important.

JUDGE BOYLE'S REPORT

During the inquest, a preliminary investigation was initiated through the Registry of Motor Vehicles to determine whether a tracking of the location on July 18 and 19, 1969, of all dark colored cars bearing Massachusetts plates with any and all combinations of numbers beginning with L7 and ending in 7, would be practicable. The attempt disclosed that it would not be feasible to do this since there would be no assurance that the end result would be helpful and, in any event, the elimination of all other cars within that registration group (although it would seriously affect the credibility of some of the witnesses) would not alter the findings in this report.

(GREEN LIGHT)

Inspector Darby:

"You may feel differently than Judge Boyle about completing the tracking down of that license plate. You are not mainly concerned with search for proof of an unlawful act or information that would seriously affect the credibility of some of the witnesses, and neither am I. We are seeking a credible explanation of the events surrounding the death of Mary Jo; and information confirming or denying the possibility of an encounter with the Kennedy car by Deputy Look is of importance in *our* deliberations. Tonight we will delve deeper into this matter, I assure you.

"Consider now the failure of Chief Arena to interpret the Kennedy statement itself as worthy of immediate, on-the-spot investigation. Arena states that he knew nothing about a party. Yet, the Kennedy statement informs him of both the party and the presence of an available witness to Mr. Kennedy's actions. I quote: 'I recall walking back to where my friends were eating. There was a car parked in front of the cottage and I climbed into the back seat. I then asked for someone to bring me back to Edgartown.'

"Failure to pursue an immediate investigation, I suppose, might well be attributed to Arena's perspective from three viewpoints: one, the prestige and influential image of Kennedy; two, the reluctance of higher officials to become involved at the time; and three, the pressure and clamor for information by the press.

243

"However, we must ask: What would have been the result if Arena had asked Kennedy what cottage he returned to, who drove him to Edgartown, and at what time? Were these the questions in part that Registry Inspector George Kennedy wanted to ask when Edward Kennedy refused further comment?

"We must ask: what would have been the line of questioning at the inquest if the Court had insisted upon a thorough check of the license plate and found it impossible for any car other than the Kennedy car to have appeared at that intersection at 12:45 A.M., July 19th? Here was a piece of evidence so vital that it could, conceivably, refute the entire statement and testimony of a person readily admitting responsibility for a fatality by pleading guilty and receiving a suspended sentence on a relatively minor charge.

"This leaves me to confess perplexity on the true purpose of the inquest itself. The principal findings are: that Miss Kopechne died of drowning, that there is probable cause to believe that Edward M. Kennedy operated his vehicle negligently, and that such operation contributed to the drowning. If the license plate had refuted the Kennedy statement and certain testimony, then a whole *new* set of facts would have had to be established *before* the Court could come to any conclusion, thus leading, perhaps, to a whole new set of findings. At the point in the inquest where the preceding exchange was recorded, nineteen persons had testified, including Kennedy, Gargan, and Markham. The Court recognized the possible impairment of credibility and said so.

"We must ask then: What was more important, the truth at all costs, or assurance that the end result of any form of investigatory effort would be helpful and alter the findings before it was undertaken? As a former investigator for Scotland Yard, I can visualize the astonishment of my colleagues and myself if higher authority had suggested that we forgo any and all effort that would not guarantee a helpful end result. I venture to say that a very, very large percentage of our endeavors would have been eliminated, and further, that a great majority of our solvable problems would not have been solved, and still further, that most of our creditable achievements would have rested solely on the perspicacity and generosity of Sir Arthur Conan Doyle, Miss Agatha Christie, and the like.

"We come now to the concluding portion of the testimony—"

RECALL
CHARLES TRETTER

Q. After crossing on the ferry Saturday morning, where did you go first, the Katama?

A. No, we got off the ferry with Mr. Markham and Mr. Gargan, then Miss Tannenbaum, Miss Keough and I walked to the Shiretown. I asked the girls if they wanted a ride back to the Dunes at Katama, they said, yes, I said, well, let me find the keys to Mr. LaRosa's car. It was somewhere around the Shiretown, but I didn't know for sure where the keys were. I said, why don't you use my room if you want. They said they would like to lie down, we are tired. Mr. Markham and Mr. Gargan went off to the Senator's room. I took a shower, shaved, left the girls in the room and went up to Senator Kennedy's room.

Q. We understand why you left his room. When was the next time you conferred with either Mr. Gargan, Mr. Markham or Mr. Kennedy?

A. Mr. Gargan came downstairs not too long after and said, why don't you take the girls back to the Dunes. Why don't you get them some breakfast? I asked the girls if they wanted any breakfast and they said no, they wanted to sleep awhile, so I went back and had some more coffee. I saw a couple of people I recognized from the day before and we just chatted a bit.

Q. Now, sometime you went to the Dunes?

A. Yes, I returned with Miss Keough and Miss Tannenbaum.

Q. And at that time, did Mr. Gargan present himself, was he there?

A. No, when we got there, we went to the three rooms that the girls had side by side. One of the girls that was already there came out of a room and said there has been an accident, something's happened to Mary Jo.

Q. Did anyone say she had drowned?

A. No, just that there was an accident.

Q. There came a time when you learned she died?

A. Yes, at the Dunes. I don't know exactly what he said, but Mr. Gargan was explaining to the girls that there had been an accident. The Senator's car had gone off a bridge; that the Senator had made an effort to find Miss Kopechne or save her and that apparently she was dead at this time.

When he said that apparently Mary Jo was dead, the Senator tried, had gone into the water and so forth; there was a tremendous emotional breakdown of all these girls around me. For five or ten minutes there was nothing but crying, not of an hysterical nature, but they were just all going off by themselves. Then they asked him, what happened, what happened, and he explained that the Senator had called him and Mr. Markham out of the cottage, had told them what had happened, and asked to be driven to the ferry. He said the Senator was distraught, that neither one of them talked to him. He just kept saying, get me to Edgartown, get me to Edgartown; so they drove him to the ferry, the Senator dove off the slip and swam across and that they went into the water after him.

Q. They went after him?

A. After him, gave up, turned around, came back to the slip, got in the car and went back to the cottage. Mr. Gargan then asked me to stay there and take care of the girls. I left Martha's Vineyard on the 6:00 ferry with Mr. LaRosa, Mr. Crimmins and Mr. Gargan.

RECALL
ROSEMARY KEOUGH

Q. Now, what time did you learn that Mary Jo had this accident?

A. When I returned to Katama between 10:45 and 11:15. I learned of it from Maryellen, Nance and Esther. They said there has been an accident, the car had gone off the bridge and we didn't know where Mary Jo was. The Senator had driven off the bridge. Mr. Gargan had told them this.

RECALL
ANN LYONS

Q. After you arrived in Edgartown, you returned to your hotel room?

A. We took a cab from the ferry to Katama Shores, Miss Lyons, Miss Newburgh and myself. We got there fully expecting to find Miss Kopechne there but she wasn't and we sat and waited. Mr. Gargan had said he would call as soon as he had any details.

Q. You had heard the evening before that she had returned to Katama and now you heard she was missing?

A. Yes, sir. We arrived at the motel around 10:00. Mr. Tretter arrived with Miss Tannenbaum and Miss Keough about 11:15. They were not aware that anything had happened. At one point Mr. Gargan called and I took the call and asked if the car had been recovered and he said yes and Mary Jo had been in the car. We kept questioning him and he kept telling us he had no details. I think at Katama he told us the senator had been driving the car and had already reported it to the police.

Q. Can you tell us what time you left the Island?

A. I think we got the 3:00 or 4:00 o'clock ferry to Woods Hole.

Q. In your observations of Mr. Gargan and Mr. Markham that day did you notice any injuries?

A. No, sir.

RECALL
MARYELLEN LYONS

Q. Now when did you learn that Mary Jo was dead?

A. I don't think I really knew it or felt it until we learned that the skin-diver had been down. I think this was on the phone from Mr. Gargan or somebody.

Q. Did Mr. Gargan tell you anything about how she died?

A. No.

Q. You left on the steamship about 4:00 for Woods Hole, do you remember any conversation on the boat about what happened?

A. We were just stunned. I don't remember any conversation.

RECALL
ESTHER NEWBURGH

Q. And did Mr. Gargan phone you at the Katama.

A. Several times and then he came over. He finally told us she had drowned, something to the effect that the car went into the water, the Senator was driving, and Mr. Gargan said the Senator dove repeatedly to try to save her and he kept repeating, I want you all to know that I believe it and I want you to know that every single effort possible was made to save her.

Q. Was anything else said?

A. And then you had five girls who just lost a friend who can't remember very much at that point.

(GREEN LIGHT)

248

Inspector Darby:

"FACT 88. Between 8:30 and 9:00 Saturday morning, prior to leaving for the Chappaquiddick ferry landing with Kennedy and Markham, Gargan told Tretter to take Keough and Tannenbaum back to the motel at Katama.

"FACT 89. Keough and Tannenbaum preferred napping and did not arrive at Katama until about 11:15. On arrival, they were informed of the accident by Newburgh and the Lyons sisters, who only knew that an accident had occurred and that Mary Jo was missing.

"FACT 90. Sometime after 11:15, Gargan phoned and talked with Ann Lyons, informing her that the skin diver had found Mary Jo's body. When pressed for details, he had none, except that Kennedy had been the driver.

"FACT 91. Gargan emphatically assured the girls that everything possible had been done to save Mary Jo's life, but he made no mention of the rescue attempt by Markham and himself.

"FACT 92. The Lyons sisters, Keough, Newburgh, and Tannenbaum left the island of Martha's Vineyard by steamer ferry at 4:00 P.M.

"Two more interesting points for you to ponder, if you wish. First, why did Gargan, in several conversations, make such a big to-do about Kennedy being the driver of the car? And second, given the circumstance of a car lying undiscovered in Poucha Pond, and the arrival of Tretter, Keough, and Tannenbaum at Katama around 9:00 A.M., what sequence of events might have occurred?

"Thank you again, ladies and gentlemen. I wish you all a

pleasant cocktail hour and a hearty dinner; and then we will all gather in the parlor, so to speak!''

There was a sudden, spontaneous outburst of applause that surprised me. Why I was surprised, I don't know; I was just as spontaneous as everyone else. It was a commonly felt human reflex action to show respect and admiration for a truly singular personality—Inspector Charles Darby.

Ten: Women Who Weave

Prissy and I walked out to the car with the Inspector. Pim was waiting to take him to his home for a rest and dinner with his niece and nephew. The long afternoon session had been tiring for Charles, and it was showing in his face. However, the rejuvenating effect of an enthusiastic hug and a smacking kiss on the cheek from a beautiful blonde works wonders.

"Charles," the blonde said, "you were wonderful!"

"Charles," I said, "don't let that go to your head. Go home and sleep it off!"

"Truly," Charles said, "mind your own business!"

As the car drove off, we walked inside, and the blonde said wistfully: "He is the dearest human being in the world. I wish he would adopt me. I never had a grandfather; they both died before I was born."

"Adoption would make him your father, not grandfather. You need a middle man. I will adopt you, then he can adopt me, and you are in business."

"If you adopt me and keep me on the payroll, you will be accused of nepotism."

"Better nepotism than Lolitaism."

"Truly! That's not funny!"

We rejoined the group lingering in the terrace room just as Pat Johnson announced a choice of tennis, badminton, croquet, or swimming, with a promise of recuperative cocktails to follow at 6:30. Since it was a very warm afternoon, the ladies chose a dip in the pool. The gentlemen chose likewise. As Noland Hammond expressed it: "There is no lifeguard; we owe it to the ladies." Seventy-five years ago, in the days of bloomer-and-skirt bathing suits, this remark would have been normal, chivalrous. In the times of the teeny bikini, a more honest man would have said: "We owe it to ourselves." There is so little frankness and honesty from men today about sex; there is so much from women that little is left over for our use.

As Pat began making arrangements for dressing rooms, Mia asked: "Truly, could I have a guided tour of Chaumière Canot by the master of the house? Your home is absolutely fascinating, and I want to see it all, if I may?"

"You may, but what about the pool? Do you want to change first?" I asked, hopefully.

"Fifteen minutes of touring, then I will change."

This was an excellent incentive for me to be concise. In twelve minutes we had passed through the bedroom and game-room levels and now stood alongside *Vitellus,* my power cruiser, in the docking area.

"It's magnificent, simply magnificent!"

"It's a she—*she* is magnificent," I corrected. "Designed to my specifications with umpteen-hundred-horse and bye-bye speed."

"And that funny-looking canoe?"

"Now that's an 'it'! Only one in the world, completely sexless, far as I know. You may call it 'it.' "

"Prissy says it propels itself because bugs eat water."

"Prissy is not of scientific bent. It has dozens of electrodes specially coated with bacteria. When the electrodes are lowered into saltwater, the bacteria feed on the organic matter in the seawater. When the bacteria feed, they create electricity. The electricity turns dozens of little propellers on the bottom of the canoe. When the propellers turn, the canoe moves forward at four-knot speed. I sit in the stern and steer; you sit in the bow with a parasol and look demure and frightened at the tremendous speed.''

"Can I substitute a bikini for a parasol?"

"Why not? The lighter the weight, the greater the speed. Are you a daredevil?"

"Wait till you see the bikini!"

I could hardly wait. Fabric texture, print design, and haute couture always stir me. I felt the devil within me would be dared.

"My bag is in Prissy's room."

There was a most peculiar inflection on the last two words. I must compliment the female of the species on the use of a change in pitch or tone of voice to convey meaning. There really is very little need for them to expand vocabularies after a fourth-grade education. This is why tone-deaf men get along with women so much better than do men with pitch-sensitive ears. There is less jolt and subtle agitation in relationships.

We were passing through a corridor leading from the boat-house dock to the elevator when she noticed a small door sign. "Dare I ask what is behind this Forbidden Area warning?" She made the remark a challenge.

"That's our experimental laboratory. Top secret and off limits even on master-of-the-house tours. May I offer a substitute after the canoe trip, my sanctum sanctimonium, a pleasant spot and something you might enjoy?"

"With soft music, champagne, etchings, that sort of thing?"

"Exactly!"

"I'll think it over. Where do I meet you for the canoe ride?"

"Knock on my bedroom door when you have changed. We'll go back as we came, to avoid complications."

"What complications?"

"The canoe only holds two."

"I'm glad!" A squeeze of my arm and she disappeared in the direction of "Prissy's room." I stripped and changed into dungaree slacks and deck shoes, then sat staring at the door like a dirty old man in a burlesque front row waiting for the curtain to rise. And all to no avail: Mia returned covered from head to toe in a long flower-print caftan.

The electric canoe is completely silent; it gives one the feeling of drifting downstream on a lazy river. Fifty yards out into Oyster Bay we were spotted from the pool deck and had to turn deaf ears to the many ribald remarks shouted at us when Mia removed the caftan. What a figure—like Chinese brush calligraphy—aesthetic yet purposeful. I think we both felt a little guilty about the Indian stealth of our departure, so with mutual accord we turned to serious comment about the afternoon's presentation by the Inspector. Mia said she was tremendously impressed by the manner of presenting the testimony so that all could uderstand Charles Darby's point-by-point analysis. I told her of the contributions made by Priscilla, Tommy, and Pat Johnson in organizing the details.

"I can hardly wait," Mia said. "I'm just itching with curiosity about what he will tell us tonight."

"You couldn't guess from the trend of what you heard this afternoon?"

"Not even an inkling!"

"Then Prissy is much the better detective of the two of you."

I don't know why I said it, unless subconsciously I had been comparing Mia and Priscilla, and reached a conclusion based on an obviously silly premise.

Mia gave me a long appraising look. Then our conversation took a sudden turn. "Truly, do you think Prissy is in love with you?"

"No."

254

Her question was so unexpected and I answered so matter-of-factly, this had to be an honest opinion. But Mia was not satisfied. She did not want to be cut off with one-syllable words; that was obvious from the impatient patience in her eyes. And it was beginning to dawn on me, to coin a phrase, that Mia had a modus operandi for getting straight answers.

"If she was, would you want to marry her?"

This time I was more prepared, and I responded with my enigmatic smile, a facial expression I have practiced many times before a mirror. I begin by crimping the muscles of my cheeks just enough to uptilt my lips in the outer regions; then I lift the left eyebrow slightly higher than the right and lower my right eyelid about halfway, leaving the left eye wide open. I find this quite effective with myself. It is virtually impossible for me to read my true thoughts when I see my face so arranged in a mirror.

Mia's reaction was rather strange. She began laughing, turned away, looked back over her shoulder, and almost fell out of the canoe. All the while she was emitting a series of repressed titters and giggles. It was difficult for me to understand her attitude, but I maintained my enigmatic smile a moment longer, then abandoned it in favor of a stern expression and said: "What is so funny about me wanting to marry Priscilla? If I did want to?"

"Nothing, Truly, nothing!"

She was returning to normalcy, so I relaxed my stern expression before continuing: "I am very, very fond of Prissy, and I——"

"Now don't start talking like an old man denying interest in a young girl. It doesn't become you."

"Mia, I'm not——"

"Truly, I'm not being fair. And Priscilla would push my head under this water and hold it if she knew I had asked you such a question."

"It's been asked many times, by many persons, I suppose, in the past few months. But sotto voce, never in the way it should be asked—openly—if someone has both our interests at heart."

She let her fingers trail in the water and remained silent. To change the subject, I mentioned Teddy Roosevelt's attempt to end the Russo-Japanese War with negotiations begun on board his yacht, the *Mayflower,* anchored in Oyster Bay. My childhood imagination had been greatly stirred by my father's stories about this event and the visits of many great warships of the past to the waters we were passing over. As a consequence, this particular section of Long Island's north shore became the site of many great battles fought under the inspired leadership of ten-year-old Faulkner Trulimann.

I had launched into the details of one of these battles, when Mia broke her silence in a thoroughly exasperated tone of voice: "Truly, what do you have against the joining of two consenting adults in marriage?"

"Nothing, nothing at all! Why do you ask?" I was all innocence.

"You have never been married?"

"No. But I think it is a splendid institution."

That long appraising look again. I had to make certain navigational changes and prepare for a landing as we neared the dock. I waved at the reception committee of four men watching my masterful approach maneuvers, but the response was lackluster, generating within me the feeling that my removal of Mia from the swimming-pool scene had not increased my popularity.

The lady herself was studying me with such intensity I felt like an insect pinned down for inspection by a curious and not too compassionate child. Which arm or leg would come off first? or would it be my head? I opened my mouth to speak. She quickly turned away and gave the reception committee a dazzling smile.

Something of apprehension must have shown on my face. Priscilla was hanging over the pool-area railing, holding out for my approval a tall, frosted mint-julep mug, my favorite drink. And she called down, with a satanic grin on her face: "Shall I add another jigger? You look a little green around the gills."

I tried to catch Mia's eye for a moment of reassurance and found both of her eyes busy trying to arrange a meeting point for her two hands with four pairs of hands outstretched to assist her from the canoe. Tommy, Gabby, Paul, and Batchey arm-lifted my passenger and immediately began a shepherding operation toward the ramp leading to the pool deck. I was left to fend for myself. It was a deliberate and indelicate joint attempt at revenge. Friendship is of so little consequence when the male animal prowls. I looked up at a still-grinning Priscilla and gave her the "right on" signal. A double-jiggered julep seemed the best way to restore my faith in humanity.

Back in the pool area, I made one more effort to catch the redhead's eye, but she looked by, through, over, and around me as though I, a practicing nudist, had wandered into a Buckingham Palace family dinner.

Later, fully dressed, I joined Pidg Paley, Ray Angelo, and Sy and Sue Boynten at a table on the deck and remained there throughout the dinner period. Nadia had my second julep waiting, but Priscilla's overload was quite effective, and I consumed the follow-up as a starving man eats shoe leather—very slowly.

Inspector Darby's inquest-testimony analysis was the subject of conversation when I sat down, and everyone agreed: It was a masterful presentation, stimulating to the intellect, but, as Pidg expressed it: "We have all been playing guessing games while you and that gorgeous redhead did your Sitting Bull and Hiawatha act in a canoe, but we have the feeling he's left us playing solitaire with a fifty-one-card deck, and the missing card is up his sleeve. Do you know the answer, Truly?"

"I thought I did, but he threw me some curves this afternoon, too. Now I'm not so sure."

I did not want to anticipate Charles. It was his show. If I started answering questions, I could go too far and spoil the impact of his opinion. Even worse, I might involuntarily and unknowingly say something to destroy its credibility. I had warned Priscilla of this, so I alerted myself as well and attempted to steer the conversation into other areas. But my companions were too involved.

"One point that the Inspector seemed to ignore," said Ray Angelo, "has struck me as significant in a way. In his testimony about escaping from the car, Kennedy laid such stress on how totally dark it was in the car after it submerged. He mentioned the 'blackness' underwater several times, but then he said that after escaping, he could locate the car because the headlights were still on. It seems to me the diffusion from these lights would have eliminated any *total* blackness if he had had his eyes open. And that's another thing, how could he keep his eyes open in that current as he claimed? Gargan testified the current forced his eyes shut underwater and he had to operate by feel alone."

"Are you questioning whether he was actually in the car?" I asked.

"That's the general idea."

"That's an interesting point," Sy Boynten interjected. "Let me make another one about other testimony that seemed to be in conflict, but Inspector Darby passed it by. Miss Keough testified that she and Mr. Tretter went walking on the road 'to the right of the cottage,' that is, between the cottage and the Curve intersection leading to the bridge, at the exact same time Mr. Kennedy said he was jogging along the road on his way back to the cottage. Yet, they did not see each other. How could that happen, Truly?"

"A very good point, Sy. I remember that bit of testimony,

258

and it puzzled me too. The only suggestion I have is simply that Charles does not deem these things evidential enough to have any real bearing on his conclusions, or he may have actually overlooked both of your points.''

As Nadia began serving the dessert, I noticed Priscilla beckoning from the game-room doorway. Excusing myself, I joined her inside by the bar.

"Tommy and I are picking up the Inspector at nine forty-five. Everything is arranged for him to begin about ten o'clock.''

"Okay, C-o-S, you're doing great!'' I brushed a kiss across the cheek of the chief-of-staff as an additional plaudit, then as she went stumbling away from the electrical effect of my lips, I walked to the back of the game room, where Mia and Batchey were playing pocket billiards.

Paul, Gabby, and Rita Angelo were perched on the spectator chairs, watching, with open-mouthed astonishment, a very businesslike Mrs. Joycelyn run seventeen straight balls without a miss. Batchey is our house champion and, physically, somewhat roly-poly. With a nod to the great Minnesota Fats, Batchey is called Baby Fats whenever he picks up a cue stick at Chaumière Canot, much to his annoyance.

After Mia's miss of a rather simple shot, Baby Fats ran out the fifty-ball game, but it was close, very close: 50–46. He was impressed, and so was I. As the game ended, I salaamed a salute in the lady's direction, and she pointed to the bar: "Deserving of a crème-de-menthe frappe?'' she asked.

"Deserving of a crème-de-menthe frappe on a silver platter, Madame. Where did you learn to do that?''

"My father. He was a good teacher.''

Timothy Batchelor III was standing by, and after I poured Mia's frappe, he picked up the glass, made an elaborate bow, raised the glass toast-fashion, took a sip, kissed the back of her right hand, closed her fingers over the glass stem, and walked silently away. Batchey is a retired alcoholic turned teetotaler. I think we both had the same sneaky thought: Mia had purposely "thrown" the game by that simple miss.

It is interesting how males react to females who invade their presumptive domain of superiority with talented performances, be it pocket billiards, tennis, poker, or whatever. Ruffling the feathers of a preening-cock ego in this manner is, I suspect, one of woman's most enjoyable pastimes.

Mia's eyes followed Batchey as he wandered outside and joined a group on the pool deck. Then, turning back to me, she said: "So much for Women's Lib. You were going to take me to the sanctum sanctorum, do we have time?"

I looked at my watch. "It's eight fifty. Over an hour before the Inspector goes on. Yes, we have time."

My sanctum is in the same general area as the experimental laboratory and workshop in the rear of the landing dock. It is one large room forty-eight feet long, thirty feet wide, and fourteen feet high. Opening off one wall is a small bar, a lavatory, and a vault for family records and possessions of a very personal nature. Carved wood paneling from a fifth-century monastery, oriental rugs, deep leather seatings, and a log-burning fireplace lend a pleasant feeling of warmth and comfort. Very few persons are invited here. Not that the few are deemed worthy and others unworthy, only that the room is exactly what I call it—a sanctum sanctorum—a place of great privacy.

The room is also a repository of what one might call the material trappings of wealth—fourteen and a half million dollars worth of artwork, at the last appraisal, the products of human inspiration and workmanship given great value by other humans lacking in comparable creativity, but not lacking for cash. The range in the variety of these trappings is quite remarkable, stemming as it does from two such divergent sources: the accumulations of many generations of the von Trulimann tree and acquisitions made with Peg Leg Faulkner's Texas money.

The room contains, too, a collection of memorabilia of no value to anyone but myself. It is a place where I can reach out and touch, stand and admire, or just sit and be surrounded by, the tangible and intangible things I respond to in a very personal way. In their silent company I find replenishment through meditation, direction and purpose through contemplation, and the courage and reassurance I can sometimes find only through the faith that comes with prayer.

Mia was greatly amused by the method of gaining entrance to the chamber. We descended in the elevator to the proper level, then entered a paneled corridor with no windows, no doors. I spoke a seven-word Sanskritic phrase, an exaggerated open sesame. Five seconds later, paneling moved out from the wall behind us, sealing off the elevator entrance; and paneling on our left swung inward, revealing the room fully lighted. I explained that my voice pattern in the spoken phrase had been compared electronically with a prerecording of my voice speaking the same phrase. Only if the two patterns match will the door open. The phrase itself is incidental; it is the tonal quality and inflection that operate the mechanisms.

Mrs. Joycelyn stood for a moment just inside the door, her eyes studying detail. "Truly, this must be one of the most beautiful rooms in the world."

"And you must be one of the most beautiful women in the world!" I was standing just behind her, intensely aware of the exciting splendor of natural reddish gold hair. A slight lean forward and I was even more intensely aware of the subtle superfeminine fragrance that was Mia. She turned to face me, and I knew I had never spoken truer words. To me, at that moment, she was exquisitely dissimilar to any woman I had ever known. This, I suppose, is what is meant by "beauty lies in the eyes of the beholder." It is the sum and total of dissimilarity, but a sum and total of that which attracts, excites, and appeals to you, the beholder. I had often felt the same way about Priscilla. A blue-eyed blonde, and now—a blue-green-eyed redhead. Mia read my thoughts:

"I'll bet you say that to all the girls," she said pseudodemurely, fluttering her eyelashes.

"Not a very original comment, Mrs. Joycelyn," I replied, "but one good cliché deserves another: I say it to all the girls, but I don't seal it with a kiss like this!" I made a move to pull her straight forward, but she developed a defect in her neck. Her head turned and tilted downward. My lips arrived at a spot midway of an eyebrow and an ear.

"Lord Cornball! You have to do better than that!"

Lord Cornball! Prissy! Little Miss Bigmouth! Mia moved quickly to a place of refuge behind a high-backed wing chair, excellent protection from a wolf with a fluffy white tail and a bright yellow streak down his back.

"Why don't you make us a drink while I make a tour of this sex trap you so respectfully refer to as a sanctum sanctorum?"

I felt like a bucket dropped into ice-cold well water by a virtuous country maiden.

While I tended bar, Mia oohed and aahed around the room, making surprisingly relevant comments about the paintings, sculpture, sketches, and so forth. I delivered the fresh frappe and answered questions about photos, citations, souvenirs, and the like as we wandered through the room. I tried diligently, with serious demeanor and emphasis on the true nature of the room, to dispel the sex-trap appraisal. We finally settled on a sofa near the fireplace. I flipped a switch, and Mantovani came in over the background-music and communication system.

"Are you going to invite me in here again, Mr. Trulimann?"

I wasn't sure whether the "Mr. Trulimann" was a conciliatory gesture after the "Lord Cornball" or a formality well designed to enclose my passionate nature in concrete.

"Of course, why?"

"Because I would rather not spend any more time talking about the contents of this room. Some other time, yes. I am inspired and consoled just being here. Everyone needs that, Truly, and I am actually proud of myself for being invited. Priscilla has told me of the rarity of such invitations."

"Do you speak Sanskrit?"

"No, why?"

"Just thought I might give you a key all your own."

"You fool!" she said delightedly, eyes sparkling like emeralds.

"What do you want to talk about?"

"You . . . your life . . . Priscilla. Mostly about what makes you tick."

I got up and turned on the espresso coffee machine. She sat quietly until I returned, then: "In the canoe, you said she is not in love with you."

"In love with me—no. Loves me—yes. But there is a difference."

"I spent two days and two nights with Prissy in New York. You were all she talked about. Truly this, Truly that. I remember some writer declaring that women are always looking for that 'safe harbor,' knowingly or unknowingly, hoping to find that one unbreakable thread they can weave into a snug little cocoon all their own. I think you have become Priscilla's 'thread.' " She hesitated, waiting for my reaction. When I said nothing, she went on: "And you can argue all you wish about the semantics of *in love* versus just *love*. Once the weaving starts, very few can, or even want to, define and know the difference."

I could not help staring in fascination at Mia Joycelyn's feminine loveliness and wondering what was her safe harbor? who was her thread? where was her little cocoon . . . now? That morning Priscilla had said that there was none. Two years separated, six months divorced, the loss of an only child, and they were—the harbor, the thread, the cocoon—memories.

"Mia—" As she turned to face me, there was no mistaking the glistening, remote look in her eyes. Had I tuned in to her exact thoughts? "Just how much has Priscilla told you about 'us'?"

"Most everything, I think. But don't worry. I suspect she has gone to great pains to protect your honor." That was nice; my mother would be pleased.

"Even the Lord Cornball bit?" I said, trying not to be bitter.

"Oh, especially the evening you 'rediscovered' each other, and the earlier days of Devious Dapper Dan, the Mechanical Genius." She started to laugh, and her eyes sparkled. "Quite a fascinating story, with one chapter you never got to read."

"What was that?"

"Off the record?"

"Off the record."

"Priscilla decided that night she had been in love with you since the tree-climbing days and should marry you."

"You are kidding!"

"No, I'm not! Girl Scout's honor, cross my heart, hope to die! That's the way the female mind works." She was wearing that awful look women have when they say something disturbing and hope it will be devastating.

"Well, why didn't she——"

"If you ask why she didn't propose to you, I'll pour the rest of this frappe over your pointed head!"

There were only a few drops remaining, but they would not have improved the appearance of my pointed head. I needed time to think. I took the glass out of her hand, moved to the bar, and started to make a refill.

"Very light Scotch and soda, please, Truly. I'm back on my no-sweets diet."

I made the switch and sat down beside a grinning Cheshire

cat. The cat spoke first: "I'll tell you something else. There were times when she might have proposed to you, except, as she saw it, one should not propose an incestuous marriage."

"Incestuous! That's crazy!"

"No, it isn't. Priscilla feels you have never stopped viewing her as the baby sister."

"Now that is really crazy!"

"Oh, there have been moments that were not very brotherly and sisterly. I'm not naive. But the overall attitude is 'Big Brother watches over all.' And adoring little sister is just busting her britches trying to please Big Brother."

"And that's bad?"

"It's not good. If you two are trying to build something solid, stop tapping toothpicks and start pounding nails, or I warn you, Dapper Dan, Priscilla is just too much woman to go on playing patty-cake forever. You can lose her, and it will hurt like hell if you do!"

"And just what role are *you* playing in this 'Courtship of Lord Cornball'? I remember another Priscilla who——"

"Now, now, Truly, don't be devious. I'm no female John Alden, and I don't like debate beyond a certain point. You said if I was concerned, I could ask questions."

"Well, ask questions. And stop trying to put me on a spot with foot-high letters reading: 'Why don't you ask Priscilla to marry you?' " I could not help feeling vexed and showing it.

She remained silent for an instant, obviously weighing a decision to advance or retreat. She advanced: "Well—why don't you?"

"I guess it's because I don't allow myself to think that way. I haven't got the guts to face rejection. I never have had. I've been an out-and-out coward about this sort of thing all my life. As Batchey puts it, I clock fast in early-morning workouts, but comes time to run for the roses, I'm back in the stable or prancing around in the paddock."

265

A quick laugh, lowered eyelids, and a slight turn away from me as she rose from the sofa. Then, in a very soft voice: "But why, Truly? What you are really saying is that by refusing to believe a woman can be in love with you, you find ample reason for not offering love yourself. That's not as cowardly as it is selfish. Love is what it is all about; please don't fear to give it or receive it. Does the age difference with Priscilla bother you?" That modus operandi for getting straight answers was at work again.

"Yes. When she came into my life again last year, I realized I was twice her age: twenty-three and forty-six, old enough to be her own father."

"But you can never be twice her age again, and from now on you age evenly, year for year."

It was a simple remark, but I found it both exciting and encouraging. The statistics and female logic were correct. I would have to age two years to her one to remain twice her age, and with proper exercise and diet this should be impossible. From here on, we *were* even. A very happy thought.

"Feeling better, Truly?"

"What do you mean?"

"You look like a man who has just seen the Messiah. You really are in love with Prissy, aren't you?"

"Well, I suppose if——"

Abruptly the music stopped, and Priscilla's voice came over the communication speaker: "Calling Dr. Trulimann. Calling Dr. Trulimann. Please join Dr. Darby in the operating room at once," (there was a slight pause) "and stop flirting with that redheaded nurse with the corn-fed bundle of goodies, you philanderer!"

Mia burst out laughing. "If that isn't a jealous woman speaking," she said, "I never heard one. And jealousy seeking cause is hypochondria of the worst kind, Dr. Trulimann."

I picked up the communication-system mike and started to

respond with an indignant denial of Prissy's slur on my character. However, some of my best friends are philanderers, and I did not want to appear bigoted. Instead, I said: "Prissy is not the jealous type, Mia."

"There's no such woman, if she cares enough and is provoked enough."

"I've given her no reason to be provoked."

"And vice versa! Scorpio and Pisces—water people—floating serenely, like lily pads on a stagnant pond."

"Now Mia!" She took the mike out of my hand, fumbled with it for a moment, then flipped the ON switch and said: "Calling Dr. Darby. Calling Dr. Darby. Will Dr. Darby and Nurse Rogers report immediately to the Level Three emergency room? We have a situation here requiring immediate open-heart surgery." Priscilla's voice was quick in response: "On the way—with a very sharp knife!"

"Now what the hell is that all about?" I asked rather testily. I started to lead the way out, and she moved directly in front of me. With the devil's own light in her eyes, her hands came to rest on my shoulders, and I placed mine gingerly on her hips. I was terribly confused. "Shall we dance?" I asked. "One rebuff per hour is my limit, doctor's orders—*my* doctor!"

She laughed, relaxed, and swayed forward, her head tilted upward and at a slight angle. A time-honored invitation begun with Eve. I never did believe that apple story. She kissed me lightly, briefly, and with carefully closed lips, then still in my arms, said: "Truly, I admit I'm tempted, but with us it would just be game playing. You and Prissy have something I myself am hoping to find, and I know how rare it is. For your sake and hers, don't screw it up!"

We could hear the elevator descending, and Mia gave me one more light kiss before moving away toward the sound. As Priscilla and Charles came into the room, Mia spoke matter-of-factly to both: "Dr. Darby, the emergency is now well in hand,

and I hate riding in elevators alone." She practically shoved the Inspector back inside the lift and pressed the gate button as she said to Priscilla: "Prissy, Truly has something he wants to say to you." The door closed, and a thoroughly baffled blue-eyed blonde turned toward me with a simple and direct question: "Well—?"

I thought for a moment, then said the first, second, and third thing that came to mind: "Prissy, will you marry me?"

She walked slowly across the room, brought her face close to mine, let her eyes wander all over my face, placed one hand on my temple, let it slide down my cheek, and said in a hoarse little whisper: "Yes." Then she kissed me, and I knew the yielding difference of the woman in love, the difference that gives a woman's lips such soft succulence in a moment of true surrender, the difference that man cannot buy, force, or reason for.

When I was reminded quite a few minutes later that a number of good friends were awaiting our return to the terrace room, I excused myself, entered the vault, opened a special small safe, and removed from it a very small gold box. Rejoining Priscilla, I said: "My mother must have known this would happen. Just three days ago she telephoned from Bavaria and said she wanted you to have the Klippsburg sapphire. I hope it fits the correct finger."

The Klippsburg is one of the world's most renowned star sapphires and has been in the von Trulimann lineage for centuries. It has a cluster of diamonds and rubies surrounding the sapphire. The ring was a perfect fit. Priscilla was speechless and practically breathless, but I managed to get her into the elevator without too much difficulty. When we stepped out onto the terrace-room level, there seemed to be a forest of upraised arms holding champagne glasses, and Inspector Darby was calling for a toast: "Ladies and gentlemen, to Miss Priscilla Ann Rogers, the future Mrs. Parnell Faulkner Trulimann, and to her future happiness.''

Mia had purposely left the mike switch on when she left the sanctum, and some twenty persons had heard my carefully thought-out and remarkably well-phrased proposal. Mia had then instructed Pim to shut off the entire system until further notice. A kind and thoughtful gesture for which I was grateful.

When the round of congratulations and well-wishing had run its course, we ''gathered in the parlor'' to hear the Inspector's opinion.

Eleven: The Inspector's Opinion

"Ladies and gentlemen," the Inspector began with a smile and a twinkle in the eye, "I am sure you are all familiar with the theatre-world expression *a scene stealer,* and you know the type of person it describes. I just want to point out to Mr. Parnell Faulkner Trulimann that that kind of thing can be overdone and ask that he be a little more contained in his future joint efforts with me."

I nodded my understanding and agreement as Charles continued: "However, the show must go on, so I ask you now to recall with me the lines of Lord Byron:

> As soon
> Seek roses in December, ice in June;
> Hope constancy in wind, or corn in chaff;
> Believe a woman or an epitaph,
> Or any other thing that's false, before
> You trust in critics.

Recall with me also the lines of Daniel Webster, who defines a critic as one who expresses a reasoned opinion on any matter, involving its values, truth, or righteousness. I suppose my expression here tonight of a reasoned opinion defines me as a critic, but I recall for my own sake Sir Henry Wotton's simile: 'Critics are like brushers of noblemen's clothes.' From this, perhaps, is derived the descriptive term *a nit-picker*. And so I must be careful, for I am certain that a 'nit-picking' commentary on the Chappaquiddick bridge incident is not what you desire to hear this evening.

"Rather, you want what we might call an all-gather-in-the-parlor chapter of the mystery novel—the surprising, startling, stupefying unravelment and disclosure that the butler isn't the culprit after all, it is the recently returned and unrecognized long-lost stepbrother, who is guilty of bloodcurdling murderous desire for revenge!"

The Inspector's ominous tone and roll-out of the last phrase drew a good laugh. It is easy to understand his appeal to the world of the lecture tour.

"So I will strike a bargain with you," he went on. "This presently unemployed old sleuth will give you his final-chapter solution, and you will accept what he has to say as opinion without judgment—of values, of veracity, of righteousness.

"I remind you of my remark this afternoon when we began our study of the testimony. To wit, I said that an expanded set of facts, viewed in the light of, quote, the commonly accepted experiences of mankind and the inferences which reasonable men would draw from experiences, unquote, might enable us to gain a wholly new perspective. And with new perspective and additional facts, I would attempt to construct, quote, a *natural* explanation, unquote, of what occurred on Chappaquiddick Island and in Edgartown on July 18th to 19th, 1969.

"Well, here we are, and here we go! I will begin with my reason for casting aside almost the entire Kennedy story. It is *not* a *natural* explanation. There are too many story elements inconsistent with the laws of nature—and normal, reasonably expected human behavior.

"I will give you five key elements in which I find conflict.

Several more will be pointed out later but not in detail. We will begin with Mr. Kennedy's statement that he drove the car off the bridge sometime between 11:15 and 11:30. If this timing is true, we must consider the statement of Miss Sylvia Malm, quote, I read in bed underneath an open window which faces east (toward the bridge) from 11:00 to 12:00 midnight, looking at the clock just before I turned my light out. Between 11:15 and 11:45 I heard a car going fairly fast on the Dyke Road. I didn't look out the window, so I am uncertain of the direction, but thought at the time it was heading towards the Dyke. I heard nothing further that night. Unquote. This window is only 200 to 250 feet away from the bridge. The land is flat shorefront terrain, lightly vegetated.

"Notice, please, this photo taken from a spot in front of the window looking toward the bridge. It shows the relationship between Miss Malm's window and the scene of the accident."

Inspector Darby had requested facilities for exhibiting pictures and diagrams. The movie screen had been dropped into position before he started, and the Inspector had been instructed in the control methods, with Priscilla as his assistant.

"Now, it was a very dark night, the moon having set at 10:22. It was a clear and windless night. Under such conditions even the slight sound of a splashing fish can be heard over long distances in all directions. Miss Malm distinctly heard the car passing by on the way to the bridge—and nothing more. Why did she not hear the skid sounds of the braking tires on the wooden bridge surface, the undercarriage of the car striking and gouging the timber curb railing, the smashing sound of the car as it crashed into the water, and Mr. Kennedy shouting Mary Jo's name several times shortly thereafter? To hear nothing was *not* natural.

"The next picture is a newspaper aerial photo: a panorama of the Malm house, the approach to the bridge, and the bridge proper.

"Consider the situation about fifteen minutes after Mr. Kennedy's car goes off the bridge. According to his testimony, he came out of the water onto the west bank, here marked with a cross. He rested there for fifteen to twenty minutes in full view of the window, then began his walk back to the cottage, all before 12:00 midnight. By his own time estimate, this window, fully lighted until midnight, would appear as a beacon in the almost total darkness described by Mr. Kennedy during his walk back to the cottage. In his own words, quote, never saw a cottage with a light on it, unquote, he denies seeing this lighted window.

"So here is our situation: A man innocently makes a wrong turn driving on an unfamiliar road, drives off a hazardous bridge, makes a harrowing escape from death, tries valiantly to save the life of a friend, the passenger, recovers his breath and strength enough to hasten well over a mile for assistance—and does not notice this lighted window beckoning with hope for the immediate help he needs so desperately. Failure to see the light was *not* natural.

"Next, Mr. Kennedy is, quoting from his testimony, 'walking, trotting, jogging, stumbling as fast as I could' back to the cottage. His mission: to get help for a second rescue attempt for Mary Jo, who has now been under water for thirty to forty minutes. Time is of the essence, so he hurries. And when he arrives at the cottage, he remains in the darkened street and asks Mr. LaRosa to fetch Mr. Gargan, and then, according to Mr. Kennedy, almost as an afterthought, he asks Mr. Gargan to fetch Mr. Markham. Mr. LaRosa stated that he never actually saw a recognizable Mr. Kennedy, only a form and a familiar voice, with no unusual quality that would lead Mr. LaRosa to suspect anything wrong. Under the extreme urgency of the circumstances, this calm, almost casual approach to the organization of a rescue attempt is *not,* in my eyes, normal, reasonably expected human behavior.

273

"Picture next, if you will, the United States senator climbing onto the Edgartown shore and walking, dripping wet, through the Regatta-night streets to the police station to report the accident and request assistance. Visualize, if you please, the senator returning to the bridge with the police and rescue forces, accompanied by a band of curious citizenry drawn by the late-hour commotion at the ferry dock. The dock is adjacent to the town pier, the center of nighttime activities in Edgartown. Now, carry your thoughts along to the recovery of Miss Kopechne's body and the subsequent questioning of the senator. This would lead, quite naturally, to a party-cottage visit by Chief Arena and, possibly, Inspector George Kennedy, if for no other reason than to give the accident victim a name. You will recall that Mr. Kennedy did not include her name in his Saturday-morning police statement, because he could not spell it.

"Picture the scene now as this group arrives at the cottage. We know from the testimony that Mr. Gargan, Miss Keough, and Mr. Tretter slept on the floor just inside the front door, one or two girls on the sofa, Mr. Markham on a chair, two or three girls in one bedroom, two men in the other. We know there was at the time a considerable assortment of liquor adorning the bar and a generally very untidy cottage interior. Now, the senator and the two officers of the law enter and pick their way carefully around the sleeping bodies, finally returning to the bar near the front door. Chief Arena surveys the room quietly, then turns to Senator Kennedy and says, half apologetically: 'Senator—I hate to wake up your friends at this late hour. Why don't we three just have one for the road; then I'll run you down to the station in my car and you make a personal statement? You write it out, and I'll type it—you don't have to sign it. Then we'll give you a quick sobriety test and call it a night, what do you say?' "

This got such a laugh Charles had to hold up his hand to quiet us. Then he said with a smile: "I am not being facetious; I am trying to make a point. You must remember that Kennedy, Gargan, and Markham emphatically stated they were in complete agreement with Mr. Kennedy when he swam to Edgartown—he would report the accident and get immediate assistance. Both Gargan and Markham testified over and over that they expected this of Mr. Kennedy. Yet these two gentlemen made no effort whatever to prepare for the arrival of the authorities. Would they not, being lawyers with criminal-background experience, draw an obvious conclusion that the cottage would be visited and questions asked? I view their failure to act on such a likelihood as contrary to reasonably expected human behavior and—unforgivable. The consequences could have been most harmful to Senator Kennedy's reputation.''

This drew some rather repressed laughs. It was apparent that the Inspector's audience was slightly fearful of accepting any statement of his as humorous, unless he gave some kind of a tip-off that humor was intended. Unseemly levity is not a part of his nature. The average person, however, facing intelligent discourse by high authority in any field, appears to seek and welcome wit and humor as apportioned relief.

Inspector Darby continued: ''One more situation in detail, ladies and gentlemen. I could give you more, but that might approach the nit-picking I said I am anxious to avoid, for your sake. In my profession, we become accustomed to looking for the nits—one of them might very well be the big brass key that opens the door.

''Consider, finally, the Case of the Phantom Automobile with license plates remarkably similar to the Kennedy car plates, with body and color closely related, with male driver and female passenger, last seen disappearing in a cloud of dust down Dyke Road at 12:45 A.M. With less than a minute to travel before it arrives at Dyke Bridge, this automobile literally vanishes into thin air. At least, according to their testimony, it never arrived in the vicinity of the bridge where Mr. Gargan and

Mr. Markham were engaged in their rescue effort under the watchful eye of Senator Kennedy.

"With apologies to the spirit of Harry Houdini, I call this the SUPER-*natural!*"

There was no mistaking his intention this time. Everyone had a good laugh at the picture he painted.

Charles paused for a moment, then continued: "And so, with a further apology to Mr. Kennedy, I must state that there should be a more *natural* explanation of the events of that night. An explanation that takes into account every known and acceptable detail, that allows for the physical laws of nature, that denotes reasonably expected behavior response, that presents us with a more lucid and credible story.

"I believe it was Albert Einstein who likened any particular moment in time to a single grain of sand on a beach. And there are learned men who will say: There is no such thing as time—only existence. It is true that there are on this planet today whole peoples who know nothing of time in a definitive sense—no calendars, no clocks with hours and minutes, no time methodology whatever—only existence. It is civilized man who, by one means or another, generates and methodizes time, separating it into measurable portions of past, present, and future.

"In His omniscience, perhaps, knowing that time itself is nonexistent or irrelevant, the Almighty has deliberately failed to include the development of a ticking clock in our senses, so that we could automatically identify time with thought and action, as we identify a rose by its fragrance, a tinkling bell by its sound. And so it is that a detective seeking truth is often faced with the dilemma of a confusion in time as expressed by opinion or witness.

"The detective's answer to this is—logical sequence. For sequence does exist, and sequence does allow for logical, definitive progression of events.

"Seldom in my experience have I found a situation in which

276

the element of time could be so treated and distorted that pure fabrication became impenetrable, given the means of evolving a logical sequence. Once a logical sequence is at hand, it may be used to apportion time in accordance with acceptable, known facts. If the sequence and the facts are completely, and I mean completely, in compatible form, it is more than likely that we will find the truth of a particular situation.

"This is what I offer now as my opinion of the Chappaquiddick incident: a sequence of events and the relationship of all major facts and details as derived from the inquest testimony.

"I might add that never in my entire career have I felt so strongly the presence of predestined human actions focusing on a few moments in time and place. The progression of events at one point involves such exquisite detail in coordinated timing that the element of pure chance and coincidence seems incapable of producing the inevitable result. Evidence of the handiwork of a master of fateful plotting appears a second time, when a succession of events appears deliberately designed to frustrate one course of action and initiate another."

Charles halted for a moment or two as though filling his lungs for a diver's plunge, then:

"I said this afternoon we had a tentative beginning for our time structure when Mr. Kennedy asks Mr. Crimmins for the car keys at 11:15 P.M. I also pointed out the doubts we should harbor about Miss Kopechne consuming some four vodka and tonic highballs within forty-five minutes or less prior to 11:15. Irrefutable laboratory analysis showing the degree of alcoholic content in her blood sample would demand this, if she died shortly after 11:15 or 11:30.

"In my opinion, Miss Kopechne consumed most of this alcohol *after* she and Mr. Kennedy left the cottage around 11:25.

"I suggest that Miss K. and Mr. K., as I shall call them now for brevity's sake, became involved in a pleasant and stimulating conversation during and just after the dinner period

277

beginning between 10:00 and 10:30; and that Mr. K. proposed that they drive down to the beach after dinner, and that Miss K. accepted. Mr. K. then took glasses, liquor, mixings, and ice in a container out to his car *before* he asked Mr. Crimmins for the keys. There was no intention of returning to the hotel; consequently, Miss K. did not take her bag or mention returning to Katama in the presence of her roommate or anyone else.

"Mr. Crimmins stated that Mr. K. spoke of Miss K.'s desire to return because of an overdose of sun during the day, but Mr. K. testified that she gave no reason. Could it be possible that Mr. Crimmins saw Mr. K. take the container of ice out to the car and just assumed it would be used to cool and soothe an oversunned brow?

"About 11:25, Miss K. and Mr. K. leave the cottage and drive to the beach; and on this drive it happened so that Mr. K. was mostly correct when he said, quote, I passed no other vehicle and I saw no other person and I did not stop the car at any time between the time I left the cottage and went off the bridge, unquote. His error is simply that he did not drive off the bridge at that time. He crossed the bridge and parked in the turn-around parking area adjacent to the beach, then prepared drinks for himself and Miss K. There were no crashing accident sounds for Miss Malm to hear before midnight. There was no accident.

"Now—we have heard testimony that Miss K. was not a steady or heavy drinker, but no evidence that she was a non-drinker. The same thing appears to be true of Mr. K.'s drinking habits. However, on occasion, when the mood is right, light drinkers have been known to drink more liquor in less time than the more experienced drinker, who, by custom, paces himself or herself in more leisurely fashion. We might assume that something like this happened: Miss K., a close and devoted former employee of Mr. K.'s brother, Robert, found cause to overcelebrate, shall we say, an opportunity to recall and relive for a few

278

moments the excitement and fulfillment she had felt in association with the Kennedy political magic. Her feelings find a response in Mr. K., as they are wont to do in any man tied to heavy responsibility who unexpectedly finds himself in the company of an attractive woman stimulated by his presence and offering even a momentary surcease of care and tension with her wit and charm. One drink leads to another, and three are consumed in about forty-five minutes. Then a precautionary note enters the conversation when one of them looks at the clock in the car. In response to a question from the district attorney concerning the time of arrival at the bridge with Mr. Gargan and Mr. Markham, Mr. K. responded, quote, I think it was 12:20, Mr. Dinis, I believe that I looked at the Valiant's clock and believe it was 12:20, unquote. Perhaps the clock was actually in the Oldsmobile, and the late hour brought up a question in Mr. K.'s mind: How do we return to Edgartown if the ferry closes down at midnight? The subject had been discussed earlier by Mr. Gargan and Mr. Crimmins in the presence of Senator Kennedy, according to the testimony of Mr. Gargan. We might assume now that the senator, recalling that no decision had been made for arranging late ferry transportation, became a bit apprehensive and decided to return to the cottage to be certain the proper arrangements were made. We know that he was in the vicinity of the cottage around 12:30 when he spoke to Mr. LaRosa.

"So Mr. K. and Miss K. leave the beach area and drive by the Dyke House *after* Miss Malm has turned out her light and gone to sleep. Mr. K. does not see this shining beacon offering help, because no help was needed, and there is no jogging, trotting, walking trip back to the cottage.

"Nearing the cottage, Mr. K., for reasons of his own, decides to park his car in a strip of woodland near the cottage instead of in the cleared parking area immediately fronting it. He leaves Miss K. in the car and walks up to the rail fence separating the parking area and the front lawn. This photo will help you visualize the situation. Mr. LaRosa has just come out of the house and is sitting alone near the front door. Notice the lamppost between the front stoop and the rail fence. Mr. LaRosa must look past this light and is partially blinded by its glare effect. Since Mr. K. has remained in the darkness of the road and parking area, he can only be identified by his voice. Mr. LaRosa is asked to summon Mr. Gargan and Markham. There is no urgency in the voice or manner of Mr. K. There is no reason for either; Miss K. is unharmed and sitting in the Kennedy car just out of sight of the cottage across the road. After making his request of Mr. LaRosa, Mr. K. turns and walks back to his car to chat with Miss K.

"The photo on the screen now is taken from a spot directly in front of the cottage, facing the door stoop. The camera now turns about forty-five degrees to the right to photograph a spot one hundred and fifty feet beyond the cottage, coming from the Curve intersection. Notice the automobile parked just in the woodland off the road. This is where the Kennedy car was parked, without lights, on a dirt roadway leading to an unoccupied cottage. In the extreme darkness it would not be noticed when Mr. Gargan and Mr. Markham leave the cottage and walk out to the parking area where the Valiant is standing. They make an assumption that for some reason Mr. K. has driven away. Now suppose Mr. Crimmins did observe Mr. K. taking a bottle of liquor from the bar earlier in the evening and has mentioned this to Mr. Gargan. The cousin is slightly apprehensive when he sees no sign of Mr. K. He and Mr. Markham enter the Valiant and drive off in search of the senator.

"Mr. K. is aware of this from his car in the woodland, but does nothing to stop the twosome—the Irish sense of humor? Perhaps he and Miss K. have a laugh about it. They decide to sit and wait and enjoy their drink. The time now is 12:35, and Mr. LaRosa and the Lyons sisters go for a walk in the direction of the Curve intersection. Because of the darkness, they also fail to notice the Kennedy car parked nearby.

"Mr. Gargan and Mr. Markham drive down to the bridge area at the beach and find no trace of Mr. Kennedy or his car. They conclude that he has gone to the ferry landing. The time is now about 12:40. They leave the beach area for the ferry landing, where Deputy Sheriff Look has just arrived and started to drive along Main Street on the way to his home. The two cars pass each other about midway between the Curve intersection and the ferry landing.

"At 12:43 Mr. K. decides to follow his two friends, Gargan and Markham, and he leaves the woodland parking place. It is Mr. K.'s car that passes Mr. LaRosa and the Lyons sisters and meets with Deputy Look's car at the intersection. We heard testimony this afternoon by Mr. LaRosa describing the passage of a single car going in the direction of the Curve. Remember, he said he stood with arms outstretched to protect the sisters when the car passed. This has to be the dark sedan Look describes. The distance is short, and neither Look nor LaRosa and the sisters mention any other car coming from the direction of the cottage.

"After passing the threesome on the road without giving any recognition signal, Mr. K. is nearing the Curve intersection when he notices another car approaching the Curve from Main Street on his left, and it begins to slow down. Deputy Look has testified that he almost came to a complete stop as a safety measure as he started into the Curve. Mr. K. notices that the car is slowing down instead of proceeding normally around the curve, but the terrain of the field on his left does not allow him to readily recognize the car. He is somewhat blinded, too, by the headlight glare. However, he makes an assumption based on the almost total lack of traffic on a road traversing a remote and sparsely settled countryside: The car on his left must be the Valiant carrying Mr. Gargan and Mr. Markham. He drives straight ahead into Cemetery Road and stops, with his wheels just off the macadam Curve; he is awaiting and expects recognition from the other car's occupants, after it rounds the Curve and stops. Mr. K. slowly backs out of Cemetery Road, and then, in the illumination provided by his reverse lights, he sees a uniformed police officer approaching his car.

"While Deputy Look is only bent on offering assistance to a befuddled driver unfamiliar with the road, Mr. K. would most certainly not expect a representative of that helpful American institution, Traveler's Aid, to appear at that moment in that spot. He sees only an officer of the law intent on questioning an errant driver. Assuming that Mr. Gargan and Mr. Markham will be in the vicinity of the beach bridge, and feeling that immediate company will provide less misery if there is questioning, he turns onto Dyke Road and drives away.

"Deputy Look decides not to follow, continues on his way, has the encounter with the happy threesome from the cottage, and arrives at his home a mile beyond the cottage at 12:55 A.M.

"To make it easier for you to grasp, I will project three pictures here. This is an aerial view showing the intersection in fair detail. When Deputy Look slowed his car at about the point of the upper left arrow, Mr. K. would be at the lower left arrow. The dark sedan came to a stop very near the spot where the white-roofed van is parked. The Deputy testified that the car on his right passed directly in front of his car, heading into the single-lane road above the van. His car's headlights, therefore, swept across the dark sedan, enabling Deputy Look to see the occupants and receive an impression of the body style and color of the vehicle. The officer stated that he then continued around the Curve, looked into his rearview mirror, and noticed the other car starting to back up. Thinking the driver might want directions to the ferry or someone's house, he stopped his car just around the Curve, got out, and started walking back, approaching to within twenty-five or thirty feet. This is about as far as

282

from where I am standing to the pianos. His position and the sedan's position at the closest point would be about where I have placed the red circle and the red oblong.

"The next picture is taken from a spot between the Curve and the cottage, where Mr. LaRosa may have stretched out his arms to protect the Lyons sisters as a car passed coming from the cottage direction. The telephone pole in the center of the photograph marks the intersection. Deputy Look's encounter with Mr. LaRosa and the Lyons sisters would also be near this spot. Note the curving-arrow warning sign on the right, indicating to a driver that the road turns sharply to the left. Next is a photo from the other end of the Curve. Here we have the Curve as Deputy Look would see it while making his approach and slowing down. Dyke Road lies straight ahead."

Pim was standing near the Inspector with a tray holding a glass of ice water and a brandy and soda highball. Charles turned and transferred the glasses to the projector control table, then turned back to his audience and said: "I should ask you to join me. Instead, I ask you to indulge me while I add liquid for the boilers. Once I get up steam for something of this nature, I prefer to keep going." He took a swallow or two of the highball. There were smiles from everyone, but not a word was spoken. Plainly, a spell had been cast by the Inspector's sequential descriptions, and no one wanted to chance breaking it. Charles switched off the projector, then he continued:

"Going back now, we pick up Mr. K. driving down Dyke Road after spotting the uniformed officer behind his car. He watches in the rearview mirror to see if he is going to be followed and is reassured when no car lights appear on the road behind him. Reaching the bridge area, he is surprised to find no Valiant with Gargan and Markham. Still apprehensive about the patrolling police car, as he thinks of it, he parks short of the bridge on the left-hand side of the road, leaving the car lights on and the motor running. Miss K. is aware of the situation, and it is discussed briefly but in a serious vein. Both realize that the circumstances, innocent though they might be, could appear otherwise to a questioning night-patrol officer of the law. Identification and recognition of the senator was a foregone conclusion; uncomfortable embarrassment was almost as certain without some plausible excuse.

"In my opinion, it is at this time that the thought of a 'wrong turn' explanation first came up; and it was seized upon the following morning as the best possible answer to Mr. K.'s dilemma. However, what appeared perfectly logical in the situation the night before became equally illogical under other circumstances.

"Now, I don't want to burden you with an 'overthinking' of the various possibilities. There really was very, very little time for precise planning; there may well have been no planning at all, only immediate and spontaneous reactions.

"Let us go back to Mr. Gargan and Mr. Markham, driving around in search of Mr. K. Arriving at the ferry landing about 12:45, they find no Kennedy car and the ferry closed down. Mr. Hewitt, the ferry operator, stated that he closed down the ferry at about a quarter of one, meaning that he tied up the ferryboat for the night on the Edgartown side of the channel just before the two gentlemen arrived. Knowing of the midnight-closing custom and finding the ferry shut down, they would assume that Mr. K. had not crossed over to Edgartown. Therefore, he was still on Chappaquiddick with Miss K. They drive back to the cottage, hoping to find the Kennedy car parked there. Recall, please, that Mr. Gargan and Mr. Markham testified that they made a return trip to the cottage area from the ferry landing, that they circled around without stopping and bypassed the cottage, going again in the direction of the Dyke Road intersection.

"I submit that this was done in a continuing search for Mr. K. and that a second trip to the beach and bridge area was made after a swing by the cottage. The Valiant turns now onto Dyke

Road at about one o'clock in the morning. I want you to see another aerial photo here. Notice the intersection at number two and the long, straight stretch of roadway after the slight curve to the right just beyond number three. From that curve to the bridge at number four, approaching auto headlights on a very dark night would be immediately noticeable to anyone in the bridge area, even though the vehicle might be still several, twenty or thirty, seconds away.

"This picture will show Dyke Road as it stretches out in a long open approach to the bridge; and this one shows the roadway immediately in front of the bridge. The gouge mark directly below the black arrow indicates the spot where the car left the bridge in its fall. Notice the wheel-tread marks leading onto the bridge in the foreground. There is actually very little angle here if the approach is from the center of the main path of the road.

"The angle, however, is much sharper if the car begins its approach from the left-hand parking area at about the spot of the white station wagon in the next photo. A vehicle driven onto the bridge from this position is much more likely to go off the bridge at the gouge-mark point. One more picture, an aerial view, also illustrates the decided increase in angle if a car starts from the parking area. And a car parked here, facing the bridge, would be difficult to turn around; the right-hand shoulder of the road is very narrow and drops off sharply into the marshland shore of the pond. Across the bridge, just beyond a short causeway, is a more sizable parking area and a better place for turning a car around. This is where beach-goers park, and from the testimony of Mr. Crimmins we can assume that this is the place where the party group parked earlier in the day when they went swimming. A short walk down this sandy path and bathers reach this rather deserted beach.

"Very well. Now that you have all of this pictured in your minds, I will continue with our sequence."

Charles paused for a sip of water. His audience appeared to be transfixed by the succession of photos he had thrown on the screen.

"When the headlight beams of the car driven by Mr. Gargan flash across the sky behind their car, they are noticed by Mr. K. and Miss K.; and mistakenly, they think POLICE! The night patrol officer is now only a few moments away, and Mr. K. makes a quick decision to take an action he has discussed briefly with Miss K. He slides out from under the wheel, tosses the glasses and bottles out into the pond, and moves hurriedly away toward the heavily foliaged bush growth fronting the banks of the pond.

"Miss K. is to drive back to the cottage alone, while Mr. K. remains out of sight until the patrol officer's curiosity is satisfied. Mary Jo moves over into the driver's seat and presses down the door-lock button, an instinctive custom quite prevalent among female drivers, especially at night. She starts for the familiar turn-around area across the bridge.

"The driving arrangements of the car are strange to Miss K., but the motor is running, the lights on. She sets the automatic drive and, feeling motion, accelerates with the petrol pedal, and the car lurches forward. It is far more powerful and responsive than the Volkswagen she is accustomed to driving; the seat is adjusted back for the taller Kennedy, and she has difficulty reaching the brake pedal. The narrow bridge is only a short distance away. The car reaches it almost instantly and demands skillful handling, because the bridge angles away to her left. In her haste and excitement, Miss K. miscalculates; too late the brakes are applied; the car strikes the guard rail, flips over, and plunges into the water.

"Mr. Kennedy, sensing Mary Jo's struggle with the lurching car, stops short of the bush and recognizes the Valiant when Gargan and Markham arrive. The entire scene is brilliantly lighted by the headlights of their car, and all three men witness the tragic accident happening to the young woman. Mr. Kennedy runs onto the bridge in time to see the overturned car sink in the channel about twenty feet from the bridge. Gargan and Markham join him, then Kennedy rushes to the beach end of the bridge and tries desperately to get to the car. Perhaps 'frenzy' is the best word to describe his reaction, an uncontrolled outburst of emotion and desire to help Miss Kopechne. I am sure no one would question his heartfelt sympathy for her nor deny that he did everything humanly possible to remove her from the car and save her life. Nor would anyone deny that Mr. Gargan and Mr. Markham might eventually unite in this effort and make exhausting attempts at a rescue. But the car is completely submerged, and the current is far too strong. You will recall that Chief Arena stated that he found it impossible to make any real attempt to enter the car, even in broad daylight. Arena, a strong swimmer in excellent condition, found his struggle with the current more a fight for survival than a means of rescue. Even Mr. Farrar, a highly skilled diver fully equipped, experienced great difficulty in combatting the tidal current.

"I believe Mr. Kennedy made a desperate, almost suicidal try to get to the car, as described in his testimony. And in my opinion, this effort was witnessed by Mr. Gargan and Mr. Markham. One of them, Paul Markham, is quoted as saying to a friend the next morning: 'He almost drowned himself,' agitatedly repeating it over and over, 'he almost drowned himself.' Experience suggests that his extreme agitation stemmed from something he witnessed and vividly recalled. He cannot be referring to actions taken by Kennedy when he and Gargan purportedly returned with him from the cottage for a second rescue attempt. All three men testified that Mr. K. never entered the water at that time. And Markham's testimony expresses no concern whatever about the Kennedy ability to swim across the channel to Edgartown. Only the actual sight of a frenzied man deliberately endangering himself would evoke such a recall response. For this and other reasons, I propose that Mr. Markham witnessed the car going off the bridge and Mr. K.'s rescue attempt immediately thereafter, a frightening and deeply disturbing experience.

"Naturally, Mr. Gargan and Mr. Markham would have to give immediate thought to dissuading Mr. Kennedy from harming himself. I recall from wartime London many incidents where survivors of bombed and burning buildings had to be physically restrained from rushing to almost certain death in the flames in the hope of saving a friend or loved one. In such situations a certain amount of madness can assert itself. Once Mr. K.'s desperation was cooled by sheer exhaustion, and *his* safety assured, I can readily imagine Mr. Gargan and Mr. Markham undertaking a more temperate and reasoned rescue attempt, as described by their testimony. But all to no avail; simply put, they were not equal to the task."

There was a long pause—for brandy and soda, without apology. I knew Charles had much farther to go in giving us his complete opinion; for a moment I felt reluctant to let him continue without another short rest period, but he forestalled an interruption.

"Ladies and gentlemen, before continuing in sequential fashion, I would like to comment on my presumption that Miss K. drove the car off the bridge. To begin with, we heard Mr. K. testifying to a complete failure of memory on two specific points—and only two points—the fall of the car into the water and the manner in which he escaped. Certainly there is some indication here that he may not have been in the car when it left the bridge. Then we have the locked driver's door, a most peculiar thing for a driver to do, especially with the window down, unless it was motivated by the reflex thoughts and action of a person accustomed to driving at night under conditions where inside locks are wise at all times. Mr. K. seldom drove a car; he was chauffeured on most occasions. It seems much more likely that Miss K. would think of and use the lock.

"Next, a photo of the Kennedy car just after it was pulled out of the channel water. An auto-crash expert would probably tell us that the car struck the water with the passenger side full on, or parallel with the surface of the pond. Notice that both passenger-side doors are crushed inward and the passenger-side window glass obliterated, blown out of the frames by the impact. The vehicle dropped about eight feet from the bridge to the water. The roof was crumpled and the windshield shattered, but the major impact damage is to the side of the car. Under such conditions, it seems reasonable that Mr. K., in the driver's seat, would have been catapulted to the right and downward against Miss K., pressing her toward the window and subjecting her to multiple cuts and lacerations by the window glass when it shattered and was blown into the car at impact. Still, she suffered not a single scratch. Did this happen because Miss K. herself was in or near the driver's seat at the moment of impact, thus allowing seawater to cushion the effect of the shattering glass before it reached her face and body from the passenger side? I believe it likely.

"Evidence substantiating the theory that Mr. K. was driving and in the car when it left the bridge centers primarily on medical affidavits indicating the following (in my own language, by the way, not the terminology of the esteemed gentlemen of medicine, which is understandable only to their colleagues): a sore spot about half an inch in diameter on the top of the senator's head; a sore spot with a half-inch abrasion on the mastoid area near the right ear; a painful stiff neck; a strange, difficult-to-describe sensation in both ears; a headache; a temporary loss of consciousness and inability to remember the car striking the water or the method of escape from the sunken car. X-rays of the skull were negative for serious injury; an encephalogram was within normal limits. Considering the strenuous actions taken by Mr. K. in seven or eight attempts to enter the car and the dangerously difficult swim later across the Edgartown channel, I see nothing in such evidence that could not have been a direct result of these efforts rather than of the car accident.

"We have to remember what happened to Mr. Gargan as given in his testimony, quote, my chest, my arm and my back was badly scraped, unquote. This is confirmed by Mr. K., quote, Mr. Gargan got halfway into the car. When he came out he was scraped all the way from his elbow, underneath his arm was all bruised and bloodied, unquote.

"However, my principal reason for presuming Miss K. as the driver springs from the postaccident remarks, behavior, and actions taken by Mr. Kennedy, Mr. Gargan, and Mr. Markham, as you will see. We join these three gentlemen now in the Valiant car, driving away from the bridge area.

"Mr. K. and Mr. Markham testified that they drove directly to the ferry landing, talked there for a few moments, whereupon Mr. K. swam across to Edgartown. Concerning this drive, however, it was Mr. Gargan's turn to suffer retrograde amnesia. He testified, quote, I don't remember this drive at all, Mr. Dinis. I remember the conversation in the car but driving the car or where we went or how we went is a blank to me, unquote.

"In my opinion, there was much more to it than a brief drive to the ferry landing and a brief discussion before Mr. K.'s crossing to Edgartown. By their own testimony, these three men left the bridge area convinced that Mary Jo Kopechne was dead of drowning, that she could not have remained alive in that tidal current. This, in spite of the fact that there was no evidence of her actual demise or that she was still in the car. The thought of an air pocket in the car sustaining her or of an unexplainable, miraculous escape similar to that of Mr. K. either did not occur to them or did not seem possible. Did they reason, then, that since nothing more could be done to save Miss K., immediate thought should be given to Kennedy the man and Kennedy the name and reputation? No law had been broken, no crime committed, no great moral precept abandoned. But the truth, the simple unadorned truth, might be disastrous to Senator Kennedy. Remember Coleridge: 'But whispering tongues can poison truth'? These three men, in a state of shock and confusion bordering on consternation, had to present a plausible story with reasonably favorable circumstances, not only to the authorities but to the world. I don't envy them their predicament.

"You will note that I said the three men had to present a plausible story. I did not say they had to tell the truth. By my statement it may seem that I condone the corruptive influence of man's quest to save himself no matter what the fate of others may be, no matter the dissolution of personal integrity; of man's succumbing to the law of survival, of self-preservation rather than to the laws of righteousness and humanity. No, I do not condone this. I just conclude that Mr. Kennedy, Mr. Gargan, and Mr. Markham came to an agreement to protect Senator Kennedy. And having done so, they conspired to present a story offering reasonably favorable circumstances for his protection, as well as that of Mr. Gargan and Mr. Markham. And I say they did this not out of full conscience, but simply because they thought they could get away with it. Frankly, because of the very limited time available, I can see no great amount of soul-searching going on before a decision was made. You and I can debate the moral issues for hours and still not come to know what really went on in their respective minds. What we do know are the actions taken and the actions not taken.

"Let me give you just one interesting angle. Immediately following the Chappaquiddick incident, some of the angriest questions came from the local residents and were addressed not to Mr. Kennedy but to Mr. Gargan and Mr. Markham. Why did *they* not call for help? Why did *they* leave the young woman's body in the car all night? You have heard the testimony. They did not do anything because Mr. K. was going to report the accident on his return to Edgartown. You have heard how Mr. Gargan reassured the other young women that everything possible was done to save Mary Jo.

"I show you a photograph taken from a spot immediately in front of the party cottage, looking down the paved road leading to the Curve intersection. Notice the Chappaquiddick Volunteer Fire Station not more than five hundred feet down and across the road. Clearly visible from the road and burning all night every night is a very large red light. Just inside the unlocked door is a siren alarm button. Just across the road and within a stone's throw of the Lawrence cottage lives Foster Silva, captain of the volunteers, who has stated that his volunteer group, all residents of Chappaquiddick, could have reached the bridge area within three to fifteen minutes. Mr. Gargan and Mr. Markham passed the fire station several times in both day and night hours. They would have to be incredibly unobserving not to recognize the red light as a signal of available assistance. So much has been said about Mr. K.'s failure to see lighted houses on Dyke Road. *If* he had made that long walk back from the bridge, how could he have failed to see the station light indicating either a telephone or alarm or both? Granting that dazed confusion may have blotted out the significance for him, this certainly would not be true of Mr. Gargan or Mr. Markham. Why did they not turn in an alarm? These gentlemen are not heartless idiots."

He hesitated for a moment, then, in ever rising tones of inflection, he charged: "Mr. Gargan and Mr. Markham did not sound an alarm or call for assistance because to do so would invalidate a decision made with the full knowledge and approval of Senator Kennedy. A decision to present to the world the false face of astonishment, ignorance, and grievous affliction. Astonishment at the disappearance of Mary Jo Kopechne, ignorance of her whereabouts, and grievous affliction on the discovery by others of her tragic demise. Truth now is abandoned,

292

humaneness forsaken, righteousness rejected. Conspiracy, subterfuge, and fabrication begin. Casting aside every consideration except protection of the Kennedy name and reputation, these men choose a path that eventually led to the pitfall so aptly described by the lines of the bonnie Scot: 'The best laid schemes of mice and men gang aft agley.' '' He halted, as though surprised at his own touch of vehemence. Then: "At this point, ladies and gentlemen, I will ask for a brief respite. The remainder of the story as I see it will bind together in more intelligent fashion if we begin and end without interruption, and these old underpinnings of mine could do with a short rest."

The Inspector had insisted on standing as he gave his opinion, a matter of some concern to me, as I knew of a leg and hip injury suffered in a hunting accident many years past. Recent demands put upon him by his popularity on the lecture circuits had caused some weakening and pain. I resolved upon some changes before we reassembled for the concluding portion of his opinion. Priscilla and Jenny had Charles in tow, heading for the outside deck area. I turned and signaled to Tommy and Ray to join me.

"Before he begins again, let's rearrange the seating in a circle on one level so he can sit down and talk," I suggested. "Get Pim and Johnny Balken to help you, okay?"

"What about pictures?"

"There are no more that I know of. Look on the projector stand. If he wants more, Priscilla can manage them. Move some of the furniture from the firebowl section over here to the center of the room. There are plenty of extra chairs in the storage room for the men. Give the ladies the soft stuff, and give the Inspector that big leather chair near the window; he likes it."

"Will do, Truly," Tommy replied and Johnny nodded. "Give us ten minutes or so?"

"You have it." I glanced at my watch and then at the two groups above me. Sy, Sue, Pidg, Rita, Pat, and Batchey were gathered in the center of the terraces; Paul, Mia, Noland, Natalie, David, and Pete were near the bar. All were involved in serious, intense discussion. I was reminded of my last stint as a member of the county grand jury and the inevitable private debates that followed provocative testimony. Well, I thought, now you have it—the Inspector's theory, at least in part—but hang on, there's more to come, and it was the postaccident reasoning that had clinched it for me.

I walked out onto the deck and joined two young ladies bent forward in their chairs in earnest, purposeful discourse of some kind, obviously. I sat down nearby without a word. Jenny was speaking to Inspector Darby, who was, just as obviously, enchanted.

"—you have spent your life solving crimes. Doesn't it make you feel people are pretty terrible, the things they do to other people, I mean?"

"Not at all, Jenny. I decided a long, long time ago I would try not to think of any act as a criminal act in itself or of any human being as something outside the bounds of human decency. Judgment and punishment, I decided, would lie with the courts, the individual conscience, and most of all, the Almighty. My job was merely to seek the truth about a set of circumstances and conditions so that lawful authority appointed by the society of man for its own preservation could render justice to both perpetrator and society. This is done best when the full truth is known. I have never deliberately set out to hang a man, nor thought of him as despicable if he hung."

"It sounds so beautiful, to spend a life seeking truth!"

Charles's eyebrows peaked a bit on that one. I am certain he has never quite managed to view his life and vocation as a thing of beauty and a joy forever. But he *had* led with his chin in his previous statement. I waited to see how he would reply.

"To *seek* truth in all things, young lady, is the spiritual substance of our life, the trunk of our tree. The *living* of truth, with its hundreds of branches and its thousands of leaves, can be very difficult. There are many, many truths. At your age, the most sought after is probably: *Who* am I? where am I going *in* life? At my age, it is more likely to be: *What* am I? where do I go *after* life? Because you are given complete freedom of will on earth, the answer to your question is very much in *your* hands. The answer to my question may depend very much on what I have done with your question."

Priscilla asked: "Do you agree with Sartre: We make ourselves what we are and who we are by the choices we make from moment to moment?"

"Oh, yes! How could it be otherwise? But Priscilla, it isn't choice alone, it is choice followed by action, decisive actions rather than inner, latent dispositions; conscious, deliberate actions carried out, rather than purpose and motive reasoned; I believe that's the way Sartre's philosophy is expressed. 'To be, or not to be' is an inspired summation of the opportunity of life, especially if we think of it as 'To *do,* or not to be.' "

I thought it time for me to join the intellectuals. "Someone once said," I offered, "that the only difference between a rut and a grave are the dimensions." There was absolutely no response, one way or the other, but I had tried. Charles held back with the patience and manner of a man waiting for hot soup to cool, then continued.

"Returning to the Soliloquy . . . Kierkegaard, Nietzsche, Heidegger, Jaspers, and Sartre just might all agree that the next lines are plainly put, appropriate phrasing touching on existentialism: 'Whether 'tis nobler in the mind to suffer the slings and arrows of outrageous fortune, or to take arms against a sea of troubles and by opposing end them.' "

Four beautiful eyes had swung back to Charles with his first words. Wiliy the Bard had won again, and I was alone, all alone. In need of companionship, I welcomed a beckoning gesture from Pidg Paley standing in the doorway.

"Are you taking *Vitellus* to the Vineyard for the Regatta?"

"Yes, leaving Thursday."

"Are you taking Charles? Please say no. I want him as my guest on *Réjouir*."

"I was going to ask him tonight, but I defer to your great beauty and charm. He will be happy to accept, I know. He thinks you have great possibilities."

"I've had those for a long, long time, as you well know, dammit. Thank you, Truly. I've just simply fallen in love with everything about your friend the Inspector."

"You and Priscilla and Jenny and——"

"Jealousy doesn't become you, lover boy! Who are your weekend guests?"

"Prissy, Mia, Penny, Pete, and Dave Dallas, maybe more."

"Will you bring them aboard for buffet Saturday night?"

"Delighted, Madame!"

The rearrangement of furniture was well done. Two semicircular rows were aimed across the room toward the leather wingback chair, giving everyone a good view of the Inspector. A turn of the head and the screen was comfortably visible. I thanked Tommy and Johnny, then asked Tommy to round up the barflies and get them seated. Pidg took care of her group, so I walked onto the deck and rudely interrupted the guru and his pupils. Never before had I seen a guru smoking a meerschaum pipe, but rapt pupils were familiar.

"Shall we have another go?" he asked.

"Whenever the Maharishi is ready."

"The *What?*"

I thought I'd better drop it, so I made a sweeping gesture toward the door and a humble bow. His back had been turned on the furniture movers while sitting on the deck; a surprised expression and a smile lit up his face as we crossed the threshold. He was pleased and relieved. I knew it from the tone of his voice and the pat on my shoulder.

"Thank you, Faulkner, thank you very, very much."

Prissy, Penny, and I took our seats. The Inspector remained standing, with one hand on a wing of his chair. The other, pipe-filled hand swung around to include the new seating arrangement.

"Now we have a real all-together-in-the-parlor, and I feel I should warn the culprit not to try to escape when I point him out. The Yard has every exit covered!"

"Not the chim-ny, Guv-ner! Blimey! You forgot the bloody chim-ny!" It was Tommy Highsmith with a high-pitched, Cockney voice imitation, and it got a big laugh. When the laughter subsided, Charles began—still standing. Oh well, I thought, when he wants the chair, it's there.

"When we began this evening, I pointed out five key elements in conflict, and I have now given you what I think is a natural-and-normal-behavior explanation of why these conflicts were present. Why Miss Malm heard the passing car around 11:30 but no sounds of the accident; why Mr. Kennedy passed up lighted houses on his return to the cottage about 12:30; why the mystifyingly calm and detached manner of recruiting a rescue force and failure to enlist Mr. LaRosa's experienced services; and why the Phantom Automobile never appeared during a second rescue attempt at the bridge. Hopefully, I have also been able to explain for you the high alcoholic content in Miss Kopechne's blood sample. And may I say at this point that I have no quarrel with the possibility of intent to return to the Edgartown hotels when Miss K. and Mr. K. departed from the cottage. The trip to the beach could very well have been a capricious act; but I will suggest it was caprice with a portable bar.

"We come now to the fifth key element in conflict: the failure of Mr. Gargan and Mr. Markham to prepare for the arrival

297

of the authorities after Mr. Kennedy reported the accident and requested assistance. In my opinion, their behavior and conversation on returning to the cottage around 2:15, coupled with the behavior of Mr. K. in the presence of Mr. and Mrs. Richards Saturday morning, is the real key to our entire mystery.

"When Faulkner first asked for my opinion on the Chappaquiddick incident in the summer of 1969, I was aware of nothing more than what I had seen on the telly and read in the papers immediately after the accident. Frankly, I was inclined to accept the explanation of a man so manifestly trapped by horrendous circumstance and confused by traumatic physical and mental experience. Then our friend Faulkner needled me quite deftly by denoting that a plea of guilty to leaving the scene of an accident after causing personal injury without making himself known was tantamount to an admission that all actions taken by Mr. K. were taken while he was in full control of his faculties. The concluding line in the original statement, quote, when I fully realized what happened this morning, I immediately contacted the police, unquote, not only implied but actually laid claim to actions taken while not in a sound mind. The plea of guilty was a legal denial of any such claim.

"I did not hear or even read the contents of Mr. Kennedy's television speech at the time. I was deeply engrossed in writing my memoirs for a somewhat impatient publisher. Looking back now, I can see exactly where I became a victim of Faulker Trulimann's curiosity and my own vanity: when Faulkner indicated the implications of the guilty plea and when he gave me a copy of the speech by Mr. Kennedy in which I read that he had called upon the help of two friends in making a second rescue attempt instead of looking directly for a telephone. Those were his words, I believe, something very close to his exact words. And when I realized that all these desperate secondary efforts were made after the young woman had been underwater for nearly one hour and were followed by a ten-hour wait in reporting the accident by not one but *three* men, the whole thing made no sense at all, just no sense at all.

"*Unless* . . . unless the long wait was deliberate and had purpose, part of a plan, a plan that must have gone awry, because, in the long run, the long wait still made no sense."

Charles had been gesturing at times with the stem of a cold pipe. He sat down, refilled the pipe from his tobacco pouch, and began lighting up. There was a slight smile on his face as he took several deep puffs to get it going to his satisfaction. His audience sat like wax dummies at a picnic waiting for the baskets to be opened, and the Inspector was enjoying every moment of it.

"I realize at this stage that I am about to involve you in considerable cerebral gymnastics; but there really is no way of avoiding this if I am to achieve a complete explanation. Let me give you an analogy. A juggler performs by keeping two or more balls moving continuously from hand to air to hand. Think of the Kennedy police and television statement as the first ball, the accounting I have just given you of the accident as the second ball, and the plan of action adopted by the three gentlemen immediately after the accident as the third ball. If any one of you has a strong desire to fully appreciate their individual and collective predicament in the hours and days just after the bridge incident and during the inquest testifying procedure, try your hand at juggling three tennis balls simultaneously. It may help you in understanding the utter confusion that can result."

The Inspector made his point amid smiles and light laughter; then he continued in a more serious vein.

"There was a plan, in some ways a very sensible one. But let's not forget our sequential progress; we will come back to the plan itself in a moment. We left the three gentlemen driving away from the bridge about 1:30 in the morning. Mr. K. has explained why he was out of the car, and this brings to mind a police officer on patrol in the vicinity, likely to make an appearance at any time. Their presence at the bridge and the condition of Mr. K.'s clothes would be big question marks. Where to go talk in quiet and seclusion? Not the ferry landing—the police officer again. And certainly not the cottage. But why not near the cottage in the wooded area where Mr. K. had parked and remained unnoticed? I will say they spent at least a half hour here, and I will try to reason as they might have reasoned toward protecting Senator Kennedy yet accounting for the accident.

"Now we know that Senator Kennedy was greatly disturbed, mentally and emotionally, perhaps incapable of asserting his normal degree of leadership in reasoning and decision making. Still, some kind of a decision was made on a plan of action in a relatively short time, within half an hour to forty-five minutes, based on departure from the bridge area at about 1:30 and return to the cottage between 2:15 and 2:30. And there are strong indications that a decision was made *not* to report the accident; instead, to pretend personal ignorance and noninvolvement with the accident.

"Just to refresh the memory I have jotted down a few lines from the testimony. The first by Mr. Gargan:

Q. You went back to the cottage about 2:15 and you remained silent about the accident?

A. That is correct.

"Then there is the testimony of Miss Maryellen Lyons.

Q. Mr. Gargan and Mr. Markham returned to the cottage sometime later?

A. Yes. When they arrived, we asked them where they had been; what had happened? And it was just, oh, don't even ask us, we have been looking for boats. It was confused.

Q. They said they had been looking for boats?

A. That was one of the things they said, and somebody said

300

Miss Kopechne was back at Katama Shores and the Senator was back in Edgartown.

Q. And what else did they say?

A. . . . they had been down to the ferry landing . . . the Senator dove in the water because there was no boat available for him and he wanted to get back to the other side . . . and they dove in after him. I believe they said because of his back they sort of instinctively dove in after him . . . they were concerned.

Q. Now when you were told this, were there others present or was it a private conversation with you?

A. No, it was general, it was in the main room of the cottage.

Q. What time did you retire that morning?

A. I would say it was shortly after they came back around 2:30—quarter of 3:00. After they came back I went right to bed.

Q. And they told you that the Senator jumped into the water and swam across the channel. Did you ask why the Senator decided to swim across the channel?

A. Well, no one was concerned really about anything. When they got back, we thought they had been stuck in the sand, and where have you been, and that was about the size of it. It was confusing.

Q. Did anyone ask where the Senator's car was?

A. As I remember, Mr. Gargan told me Mary Jo had taken the car on the last ferry.

"And finally, we have Miss Ann Lyons:

Q. Did anyone ask where Miss Kopechne was that morning of the nineteenth?

A. Well, after I went to bed, Miss Newburgh and my sister came into the bedroom and later Mr. Gargan knocked on the door and he came in and was talking. I don't recall the conversation, but I can recall what I said . . . I asked Mr. Gargan where Miss Kopechne was. He told me she was at Katama Shores . . . that she had taken the car to the Katama Shores . . . Mr. Kennedy also had returned to his hotel.

"Both of the Lyons sisters distinctly recalled Mr. Gargan's statement on his return to the cottage to the unqualified effect that Mary Jo had taken the Kennedy car and crossed to Edgartown, *by herself,* on the ferry, on her way to the Katama Shores Motel. The 'third ball' story, therefore, was obviously based on Miss Kopechne's separating from Mr. Kennedy *before* 12:00 midnight. With this premise as a starting point, a rather simple explanation could be made, an explanation that provided all three with noninvolvement and that was actually *substantiated* in large measure by other witnesses. Three legally trained minds would readily appreciate the importance of witnessed actions and conversations, and I believe the following points were taken into consideration: One, Mr. K. appeared at the cottage at least twenty to thirty minutes *after* 12:00 and spoke to Mr. LaRosa; two, his request to summon Mr. Gargan and Mr. Markham from the cottage had been made in a calm, unperturbed manner, indicating no cause for alarm; three, Mr. LaRosa had not seen the Kennedy car or Mary Jo; and finally, Mr. LaRosa's summons within the cottage had been witnessed by several other members of the party group. Incidentally, the later encounter with Deputy Look must have been regarded as inconsequential because he could make no positive identification.

"The gist of their story, then, would be like this: Mr. K. and Miss K. decide to catch the ferry before closing time at midnight, and Mr. K. expects to make arrangements to have the ferry stay open until a later hour so that the party will not have to break up. Prior to their departure, they have been engaged in a serious conversation, mostly about Senator Kennedy's brother Bobby, and after obtaining the car keys, they sit and talk awhile in the car in front of the cottage. Suddenly realizing that the

302

twelve-o'clock hour is nearing they hasten toward the ferry; then Mr. K. realizes he forgot to tell Mr. Gargan and the others he would arrange for a later ferry. He stops the car and tells Mary Jo to go on to the ferry, cross over to Edgartown before the ferry closes, and request that the ferry operator remain available a while longer until someone from the cottage group arrives to arrange for transportation at a later hour. Mary Jo drives off hurriedly, and Mr. Kennedy walks about a mile or so back to the cottage, arriving about 12:20 or 12:25 and calling out to Mr. LaRosa from the roadway. When Mr. Gargan and Mr. Markham come out, all three men get in the Valiant and drive to the ferry landing. When they see no sign of Mary Jo or the Kennedy car, it is assumed that she has crossed to Edgartown and gone on to Katama. Since there is also no sign of the ferry operator, it is also assumed that he could not wait, and they begin searching for an available boat to transport the party group. Finally, finding no boat available, Mr. K. decides to swim across, and Mr. Gargan and Mr. Markham return to the cottage. Mr. Gargan engages the Lyons sisters in conversation and makes his statements that will set the stage for ignorance and noninvolvement with the accident.

"I will add here that every other action witnessed and conversation recalled in testimony by members of the party group, Mr. Peachey, Mr. Richards, and others, bears out the fact that Mr. K., Mr. Gargan, and Mr. Markham pretended no knowledge of the accident until it was reported to them by Mr. Bettencourt on Chappaquiddick shortly after 9:00 Saturday morning.

"Even on the trip into Edgartown that morning with Mr. Tretter, Miss Keough, and Miss Tannenbaum, there was not the slightest hint by Mr. Gargan or Mr. Markham that Miss Kopechne would not be found at the Katama Shores Motel. Why? If Mr. K. was expected to report the accident some six hours earlier, as Gargan and Markham testified, news of Mary Jo's drowning would be awaiting the two young women at the Katama Shores. Reticence about the accident on this ride into Edgartown could have no element of solicitous consideration. Just the opposite, solicitude would demand that Mr. Gargan prepare them for the tragic truth. But he said nothing about Mary Jo or the accident.

"Looking further, we see Mr. Kennedy's calm, properly dressed appearance before Mr. Peachey, and his unperturbed, casually conducted conversation with Mr. and Mrs. Richards at 8:00 A.M., even a partially accepted invitation to breakfast."

The Inspector laid his pipe on the table beside him, drank from the fresh highball Pim had provided, then rose and walked behind the wingchair. Leaning forward with his elbows on the chair back, hands clasped, he continued: "So much for the prologue, now for the play. Their scenario calls for the discovery of Mary Jo's disappearance, a request for police assistance, a search, and the finding of her body in the sunken car. The assumption could then be made that Miss K. missed the last ferry, set out to return to the cottage, but missed the sharp turn onto School Road and mistakenly drove down Dyke Road. Coming suddenly upon the bridge, she miscalculated the turn necessary to negotiate the angle of the bridge and drove off the side.

"Let us proceed now with the first act of their carefully plotted story. After a lengthy discussion in the seclusion of Mr. K.'s room, from which Mr. Tretter was somewhat unceremoniously ejected, the wheels are set in motion. Mr. Gargan seeks out Mr. Tretter and suggests he take Miss Keough and Miss Tannenbaum back to the Katama Shores. Shortly thereafter, Mr. K., Mr. Gargan, and Mr. Markham cross on the ferry to the Chappaquiddick landing. This is a puzzling move. Why cross to this ferry landing just for telephone privacy? There were telephone booths all around the Shiretown Inn area. And at that hour of the morning, Edgartown was not exactly bustling with telephone callers. I have strong doubts that privacy was the sole reason for the Chappaquiddick visit. In reality, it appears that very little use was made of the phone. Mr. K. mentioned a single unsuccessful call to Mr. Marshall, and telephone records show no completed calls while they were there, if I correctly interpret the company representative's testimony. I believe there was a far more compelling reason for this trip to Chappaquiddick, a reason arising from an afterthought of disturbing proportions. When the search begins, the night ferry operator will be questioned, and his response will indicate that Miss Kopechne never left Chappaquiddick Island. The beach area, then, would become one of the logical search points. So far, so good.

"But now put yourself in their shoes. You will recall that the Kennedy car was completely submerged when the three gentlemen performed their valorous rescue effort the night before. Suppose the sunken car is unnoticeable from the bridge even in the daylight? Because of water glare, this could be possible if the water is deep enough. Or suppose the strong tidal currents have swept the car farther out into the deeper waters of Poucha Pond? If the car is not discovered, and rather quickly, Senator Kennedy finds himself in an untenable position. He is the last person to see and be with Miss K. It is one thing to feign ignorance of the fate of a friend involved in a fatal accident after borrowing your car and driving away alone in it and quite another to face a questioning world when a friend borrows your car and disappears from the face of the earth.

"Resolved circumstance versus unresolved mystery. Reputation protected versus reputation in suspense. Before any further actions are taken, someone must drive out to the bridge and determine the visibility of the submerged car. And I have little doubt that the gnawing bite of conscience was taking its toll of Mr. K. in those early-morning hours. The human soul is strongly endowed with the humane, and it is not forever denied. Mr. K. was probably finding the role of innocent bystander more and more difficult, the necessity to simply sit and wait upon events ever more impossible and, most assuredly, the thought of Mary Jo's body left abandoned in the sunken vehicle more and more horrifying.''

Another draft from the highball and he returned to his chair. I trust I am not giving the impression that Inspector Darby is a prodigious drinker. He is not. He is Churchillian in his fondness for fine brandy; but his drinking is always in moderation, and always in the manner of the picture-book English gentleman. As Dr. Wickstrum has said, a septuagenarian is entitled to prime the pressure pump if he so desires, and *when* he so desires, if he is in good health.

"Permit me to digress now for a moment," he continued. "Earlier this evening I spoke of the causal coincidence that so pervades the Chappaquiddick occurrence and my suspicion that a master of fateful plotting was somewhere behind the scenes. The episodic sequence surrounding Deputy Look's encounter with the dark sedan at the Curve was one example. We come now to another. While Mr. Gargan and Mr. Markham are conferring with Mr. K. in his room at the Shiretown, two young fishermen discover the sunken car, and the police are notified. Miss K.'s body is found and the medical examiner summoned. Chief Arena dispatches Mr. Bettencourt to the ferry landing to meet and transport the examiner back to the bridge. Just before Mr. Bettencourt sets forth from the bridge area, Mr. Kennedy is identified as the owner of the sunken automobile. Mr. Bettencourt arrives at the landing just after Mr. K. arrives; he recognizes Mr. K. and tells him about the recovery of his car and Mary Jo's body.

"This most peculiar coincidence is perhaps the crucial turning point, an unexpected development that leaves Mr. K. and his companions tumbling in indecision as dice tumble in a bird cage. But why, you may well ask? Was not discovery without Kennedy involvement and direction what was wanted and planned? Yes—but under different circumstances. Senator Kennedy is suddenly put into the negative position of having to explain Mary Jo's death to the police, instead of the positive position of going to the police and requesting their help in solving the problem of her disappearance. Of course, he could have adhered rigidly to the completely fabricated noninvolved story, but he did not. We can only surmise for one thing that impulsively he recognized the need to tell, if not the whole truth, at least partial truth, to bend truth in his favor but not to discard it entirely. To abide by an out-and-out lie told under circumstances not of his own choosing, with the likelihood that every member of the party group would be questioned under unfavorable conditions, was both precarious and hazardous. A shift in strategy was indicated and adopted. And whatever the full intent of the new approach, it is apparent now that it successfully shut off immediate investigation. By assuming the entire burden on his own shoulders with a definitive statement for Chief Arena, by appointing Mr. Gargan and Mr. Markham his attorneys, by evacuation of the party group from Martha's Vineyard at the earliest possible hour, there is no question that thorough investigation was circumvented."

There was a short break as Charles loaded his pipe and lighted up, then went on: "According to the testimony of Mr. Hewitt, the ferry operator, at least twenty more minutes are spent in conference before Mr. K. and Mr. Markham rush off to the police station and Mr. Gargan departs to inform Mary Jo's friends at the cottage. Some decision on a story for the authorities has been made, but it is a story almost totally devoid of particulars. This is apparent from Mr. Gargan's remarks to the group in the cottage. When he left the landing, he was plainly given no clear idea of what Mr. Kennedy intended to tell the authorities. He announced that Mary Jo was *missing,* not drowned but missing, probably a mental hangover from the earlier planning; then he repeated over and over that he had no details.

"This was around 9:30 in the morning at the cottage, and he

was still without details to give on several phone calls made to the Katama Shores Motel before noon. When he finally went there and told of Miss Kopechne's drowning, there were only some sketchy particulars, such as Mr. Kennedy's being the driver. There was no acknowledgment whatever that he and Mr. Markham attempted a rescue of Miss K. Why this deliberate evasion if he was so anxious, as he said, to reassure the young women about the maximum effort to save her life?

"Apparently he was bound by a decision made at the ferry landing. May I remind you of Mr. Markham's testimony, quote, the Senator . . . when we were at the telephone booth . . . before we went to the station . . . told us 'I don't want you people put in the middle on this thing. I'm not going to involve you. As far as you know, you didn't know anything about the accident,' unquote. Senator Kennedy realized that their acknowledgment of an awareness of the accident the previous night made their position indefensible without some plausible excuse. And at the time they could think of no excuse. Consequently, when Mr. K. abided by his not-to-involve commitment, we can assume Mr. Gargan followed instructions and remained silent.

"We can also assume, my friends, that Mr. Kennedy demonstrated a willingness to distort and evade the facts."

Sy Boynten was sitting directly opposite me, and he caught my eye as the Inspector paused. Sy winked and nodded agreement; Charles had made a telling point with him.

"But the astonishing thing is," the Inspector was saying, "that Mr. Kennedy, after making this commitment to refrain from putting Mr. Gargan and Mr. Markham 'in the middle,' as he phrased it, openly admitted on the very same day that he had received help in trying to rescue Miss Kopechne. This occurred only hours after he purposely omitted mention of the Gargan and Markham effort in making his statement to the police in Edgartown. Once again I quote from the affidavit of Dr. Robert

D. Watt, who was called to the home of Senator Kennedy on his return to Hyannis Port late Saturday afternoon or evening. Quote, On July 19, 1969, I was called to see Edward M. Kennedy. . . . His chief complaints were headache, neck pain, generalized stiffness and soreness. . . . He stated that he had been in an automobile accident *last night*. . . . The car went off a bridge. There is a lapse in his memory between hitting the bridge and coming to under water and struggling to get out. . . . at the last moment he grabbed the side of an open window and pulled himself out. He was not clear on the events following but he remembered diving repeatedly to check for a passenger—without success. *He went for help and returned. Again, effort to rescue passenger was without success.* He was driven to the ferry slip and swam to the main body of land. He went to his hotel where he slept fitfully until 7:00 A.M. . . . Physical examination revealed his vital signs and neurological examination to be within normal limits. Unquote.

"This case history, written Saturday, July 19, also gives a clear-cut explanation of how Mr. Kennedy extricated himself from the sunken car, something he could not recall in his police statement and inquest testimony. The swim to Edgartown is included here, but not in the statement. It just may well be that the senator, in deciding to step away from a truthful presentation of the circumstances surrounding the death of Miss Kopechne, found what so many other evaders in my experience have found: that fictionalizing requires carefully structured detail if it is to replace truth in a believable fashion. The statement to Dr. Watt is just one example of how hurried abandonment of the 'I know nothing about it' story and sudden, last-minute adoption of the 'wrong turn' story left all three men victims of shallow, imprecise, confused thinking.

"The wrong-turn theme provided an irreproachable reason for the Kennedy car and its occupants to be in the vicinity of the bridge, the unfamiliar road gave cause for the accident, and personal shock and injury covered the failure to report the accident.

But it left Mr. Gargan in the embarrassing position of having to explain the unexplainable; it left Mr. Kennedy and Mr. Markham trying to piece together a statement for the authorities, and it left everyone else thoroughly baffled as to the truth.

"In the police statement we see a highly curtailed accounting, with a bare minimum of detail; we also see an attempt late in the afternoon to hold up even this story until Mr. K. could confer with advisers. He badly needed high-level, Cuban Missile Crisis thinking; Mr. Gargan and Mr. Markham were not strategists, policy makers, or writers of the neatly turned phrase. Unfortunately, Chief Arena succumbed to the pressure of the press for information, and the die was cast.

"In the television speech six days later we see the result of stratagem and phrase-making. First, a way satisfactory to all is found to include the Gargan-Markham effort, killing three birds with one stone by augmenting the minuscule rescue effort, accounting for the hour and a half absence of Gargan and Markham from the cottage, and providing some degree of eyewitness substantiation of the wrong-turn story. Second, a friendly 'time' witness is added, Mr. Russell Peachey. I have already given you my opinion of this situation.

"Now this is mighty skimpy building up of structure and detail, but anyone who has ever played Pick-Up-Sticks in his childhood will recognize the problem."

This drew such a round of laughs I had to ask Priscilla for an explanation. Evidently, my childhood had been blighted by an oversight: I had never played Pick-Up-Sticks.

The laughter seemed to be a relief for Charles. There was a sudden change in his expression. He glanced over at Tommy Highsmith and spoke with mock sternness: "I presume *all* exits are now covered, including the chim-ny!"

Tommy picked him up in the Cockney voice: "All tight, Guv-ner! All tight and all manacles at the ready!"

There was a gentleness in his voice when he continued speaking. There was the tone of an understanding heart, of a person who has "been there," of one who has no desire for anything other than fairness in an expression of his own opinion. The northeaster winds of the Yard Inspector on-duty-bent had blown over; the air of the country squire had returned. Charles let his eyes roam across the intent faces before him.

"There is little more to be said now about the death of a fine young woman. I have tried to give you an accounting of the tragic Chappaquiddick incident as I believe it occurred. And in concluding, I find I have no culprit to 'hand over' in the traditional manner.

"A culprit is defined as one 'guilty of a crime or a fault.' Senator Kennedy pled guilty to the charge of leaving the scene of an accident after causing personal injury without making himself known. As I have just explained, I do not consider him guilty of this charge, because he did not cause the injury, he did not drive the car off the bridge. Judge Boyle concludes that there is probable cause to believe Mr. Kennedy operated his vehicle negligently, thus contributing to the death of Miss Kopechne. Again—not guilty: He was not operating the vehicle at the time of the accident.

"I cannot, therefore, point out guilt on the basis of a crime committed, of a law of the land broken. And it is not for me to weigh and presume final judgment of fault in others.

"Mr. Kennedy might well ask, as he did on that calamitous night, according to the testimony of Mr. Gargan and Mr. Markham: How could this happen to me—I can't believe it!

"How could it indeed? had he not suffered enough? had his family not suffered enough?"

He rose and stood silently, as if searching for last words, an artist scanning a canvas before placing a final brushstroke. A decision made, he glanced first at me and then at Priscilla, inviting, it seemed, our special understanding.

"No, this was not a case of criminality—this was tragedy. The end of life for a young woman for whom I have come to have the deepest sympathy and the most sincere admiration. In the course of my considerations, I came across a magazine article relating an interview with her parents. Seldom will a parent find more to be proud of in a daughter. Mary Jo was a 'child of happiness' from the day she was born, called by her mother the most thoroughly and continuously happy person she had ever known. Miss Kopechne was kind, thoughtful, and generous far beyond the average. Charitable to an extreme, devout, and very much in love with a young foreign-service officer, planning marriage. And like so many young people of today, Mary Jo Kopechne had a dream of helping her country through participation in the political processes of democracy, a dream turned into reality by dedicated hard work, talent, and devotion to the great causes of political personalities of her time. She was highly respected by her friends, her fellow workers, prominent political figures, and by members of the Kennedy family.

"The Chappaquiddick incident is really Mary Jo's story, the perfect example, sorrowful as it may be, of a human being caught up in the infinite unpredictability of that sometimes monstrous little preposition—*if*. The same little monster that time and again serves as a needle-sharp pivot point in the turning of events for individuals and mankind alike.

"Mary Jo had not really planned on going to Edgartown because of a previous conflicting job commitment. Because another young woman agreed to take her assignment at the very last moment, she changed her plans and journeyed to Martha's Vineyard for the reunion weekend."

Another pause—the artist again, seeking a place for signature?

"Perhaps *our* question is: How could it have happened to Mary Jo? If we knew the answer to that, we might know the answer to much more, to the question of God's will in the course of human events, of fate's ascendancy over free will—an answer for all of us.

"Thank you, ladies and gentlemen, for your very kind and courteous attention."

312